"Monteleone has a dark imagination, a wicked pen, and rare ability to convey an evil chill with his words."
—Dean Koontz

"Tom Monteleone is an expert storyteller. Period"
—F. Paul Wilson, author of *The Keep*

"Monteleone grabs the reader with his first paragraph and never relaxes the tension."
—the *New York Times*

"An original vision of evil, with all the energy and power of Stephen King's best."
—*Omni* magazine

"Monteleone is pure storyteller. This one will grab you and not let go."
—David Morrell, author of *Creepers*

"Monteleone writes with emotional power. His characters are real, his themes universal."
—*Fantasy Review*

"A lush, sensual tale by horror's best prose stylist."
—*The True Review*

also by Thomas F. Monteleone:

NOVELS
SEEDS OF CHANGE [1975]
THE TIME CONNECTION [1976]
THE TIME-SWEPT CITY [1977]
THE SECRET SEA [1979]
GUARDIAN [1980]
NIGHT THINGS [1980]
OZYMANDIAS [1981]
DAY OF THE DRAGONSTAR (WITH DAVID F. BISCHOFF) [1983]
NIGHT TRAIN [1984]
NIGHT OF THE DRAGONSTAR (WITH DAVID F. BISCHOFF) [1985]
TERMINAL ROAD [1986]
CROOKED HOUSE (WITH JOHN DECHANCIE) [1987]
LYRICA [1987]
THE MAGNIFICENT GALLERY [1987]
FANTASMA [1989]
DRAGONSTAR DESTINY (WITH DAVID F. BISCHOFF) [1990]
THE BLOOD OF THE LAMB [1992]
THE RESURRECTIONIST [1995]
NIGHT OF BROKEN SOULS [1998]
THE RECKONING [1999]
THE EYES OF THE VIRGIN [2002]
SERPENTINE

SHORT STORY COLLECTIONS
DARK STARS AND OTHER ILLUMINATIONS [1981]
ROUGH BEASTS AND OTHER MUTATIONS [2003]
FEARFUL SYMMETRIES [2004]
THE LITTLE BROWN BOOK OF BIZARRE STORIES [2004]

ANTHOLOGIES
THE ARTS AND BEYOND [1977]
MICROWORLDS [1984]
BORDERLANDS [1990]
BORDERLANDS 2 [1991]
BORDERLANDS 3 [1992]
BORDERLANDS 4 (WITH ELIZABETH E. MONTELEONE)[1994]
BORDERLANDS 5 (WITH ELIZABETH E. MONTELEONE)[2003]

NON-FICTION & ESSAYS
THE MOTHERS AND FATHERS ITALIAN ASSOCIATION [2003
THE COMPLETE IDIOT'S GUIDE TO WRING A NOVEL [2005]]

Serpentine

Thomas F. Monteleone

Borderlands Press
Baltimore, MD ❑ 2007

Serpentine Copyright © 2007 by Thomas F. Monteleone

ISBN# 978-1-880325-76-6

Typesetting and page design by E. Estela Monteleone
cover by Mario Martin, Jr.

Printed in the United States of America

Borderlands Press
POB 660
Fallston, MD 21047

800-528-3310

www.borderlandspress.com

this one is for
Paul and Mary Wilson

Prologue

Scarpino, Sicily

Enrico Corbi shambled through the narrow streets of the village with an indifferent intimacy. The old man walked slowly, navigating the cuts and turns through the silent streets without thinking. He had walked these streets, this same route, for more than seventy summers, and the pathways were forever etched into his memory.

His village—a place believed to hold a terrible secret.

The sky above the low rooftops was smeared with pinks and orange, but the white stucco buildings still lay in the long shadows of dawn. He passed the old village church and started to tip his cap in a time-honored show of reverence and respect for the Lord, then caught himself. The tiny stone building was now empty; its contents—including the altar, which had been transferred yesterday to the new church Eucharist—at the other end of Scarpino. The old place, its stained glass windows taken by laborers and grafted into the *new* church, seemed so tiny, so dead now. The population of Scarpino had finally grown too large for its twenty pews and, by order of the Palermo archdiocese, a new church had been built. Corbi had attended the first Mass yesterday morning, but he still thought of the small stone structure as his church.

His slow gait took him to the edge of the village, where the hilly contours of the land were harsher. He turned down a stone path worn smooth by centuries of human traffic-a path to the cemetery where Corbi worked as its caretaker.

It was in this small village, west of Palermo, where something had happened.

Corbi had no idea what it had been, but when he was a young man he had heard stories about the village priest of long ago, Father Mazzetti, who faced and defeated a terrible evil. It was something he tried not to think about, something he did not wish to know. He was a simple man, and he only wished to do what was expected of him: to live out his remaining years in peace before meeting his God.

And yet, as he passed beyond the crumbling wall which marked the borders of the villa—built in a past century when bandits still roamed the surrounding hills—he felt a tightening in his chest, a dryness in his throat. He licked his lips, feeling a sudden desire for a swallow of red wine. He did not want to go into the cemetery on this bright, clear morning, but he knew he must.

The previous night, as he sat by the banked coals of his fire, lost in the memories that old men keep, there had been a knock at his door. The rapping had been so light, as though by the wind, or perhaps the Angel of Death, that he had been reluctant to unlatch the door. But the sound repeated itself persistently, and Corbi had no choice.

Opening the door, he felt the chill of the night air smack his cheeks as he stared into the face of an old woman. It was a face many years older than his own, a face known to everyone in the village of Scarpino—that of Teresa DiCaponitti. It seemed that she had always been old, as timeless as the legends, which still thrived in the mountain villages. The children in the village called Teresa La Strega, and Corbi was not so certain that they were mistaken.

"Let me in," she said, pushing him back from the threshold.

"I'm sorry. I was expecting no one."

Teresa laughed and brushed her brittle gray hair away from her face, letting it fall upon her thick black shawl. Her eyes of green silver seemed to penetrate him like a sword. He did not like to hear Teresa laugh.

"No one ever expects Teresa," she said. "But don't worry, I won't be staying long. It is a message I have brought you."

"A message? From who?" Corbi moved back toward the hearth and sat uneasily in his chair.

"The dogs. They are howling tonight, yet there is no moon. Have you not heard them?"

Corbi shook his head, uncomfortable hearing this kind of talk.

"No, you heard nothing," said Teresa. "Old age gives us that privilege, does it not? We hear only what we desire to hear." She chuckled softly. It was a disconcerting sound to Corbi. "But you know why they howl, Enrico. You know the dogs hear sounds that we cannot . . . and tonight they hear the sound of stone grinding upon stone."

"No!" he cried, holding his hands over his ears like a child being taunted in a schoolyard.

Teresa smiled and nodded her head. "In the morning, I think it would be wise to look in upon your charges. Better that you take care of things quickly and quietly . . . unless you want more outsiders nosing into our affairs. Surely you have not forgotten the last time? That writer from Rome, remember him and the silly book he was writing?"

Corbi nodded once, then looked away from her to stare into the fire. "All right, old woman . . . I have listened to your message. I . . . I will check on things . . . in the morning. Now please leave me."

But even as he spoke, Teresa had turned toward the door, her dark clothes billowing away from her scarecrow's body. She paused at the threshold and stared into his eyes. "Do not fear, Enrico. As always, you will take care of things."

She disappeared into the night, leaving him to stare into the darkness that had devoured her.

The previous night already seemed years in the past, so long a restless night had Corbi spent. As he walked up the stone path to the cemetery, he felt his breathing become labored and his pulse rate increase—not from the effort of the climb as much as the anticipation of what lay in wait for him. How long since the last time? Not in his lifetime, of that he was certain. There had been stories that his grandfather had told, but they spoke of a time long ago . . . .

But here it was . . . one more time, at least.

That is, if he were to believe the words of *La Strega*. And on such matters, the old woman was usually correct. Corbi began to wonder what secrets she carried, but stopped himself. Such thoughts were better left alone.

He had reached the entrance to the cemetery. It lay embraced by a wall of cut stone, and could be entered only by a single wrought-iron gate. A classic arch curved over the gate, and a long-dead mason had carved a poetic couplet there:

Un tempo fummo come voi,
Presto sarete come noi.

Corbi knew the lines by heart, but he always read them before entering the graveyard: "Once we were as you. Soon you will be as we."

How true, thought Corbi. But not yet. There is still work to be done.

The cemetery of Scarpino lay on upward-sloping ground that led into the foothills above the village. Grass grew grudgingly here, and appeared only in tough little patches above the older graves. Stone slabs and crosses littered the place at odd angles, their simple lines broken only by the monolithic shapes of family mausoleums. In a village as poor as Scarpino, however, there were very few of these structures. Mausoleums were reserved for the remains of the wealthy or powerful, such as landowners, politicians, or clergymen.

Passing under the prophetic arch, Enrico Corbi paused to make the Sign of the Cross, then walked carefully up the gentle slope. He ignored the grassy mounds and weathered stones; his gaze was held by the black marble building farther up the hill—the mausoleum of the Mazzetti family.

It was a darkly foreboding structure. There were no fluted columns, no carved angels along the frieze, no frills of any kind. Twin wrought-iron gates guarded a foot-deep threshold, held fast by a heavy lock at eye level. When he reached the tomb, Corbi stopped to stare at the lock, drew a deep breath, and reached into his pocket for his rosary beads. He kissed the crucifix, and placed the string of beads around his neck. After unhitching a ring of keys from his belt, he selected the proper key and slipped it cleanly into the lock. But it had been many years since anyone had entered this place, and the key would not turn. It was possible that the internal tumblers had finally frozen in a final grip of rust.

Straining against the resistant metal, Corbi forced the key to turn, and with a gritty sound, the lock disengaged. He swung open one of the gates and stepped into the threshold to face a single marble door. Selecting another key, he forced it into the door's keyhole, and the lock yielded.

Gripping the carved handle, he pulled the massive stone slab outward, surprised that it moved so easily on its hinges. There was a delicate balance in the door, an ageless display of superior craftsmanship that was lost on the simple peasant caretaker. His heart was beating very fast now; he was not interested in the lost art of stone-cutting. He peered into the black shadows of the crypt.

The Mazzetti mausoleum was sunk halfway into the earth, and a small case of stairs led into the main chamber—a flat stone floor lined by walls of shelved alcoves. Ordinarily, in a mausoleum such as this, coffins would line each shelf of each alcove. But on this particular morning in this particular tomb, things were different.

Corbi gasped a single breath as he stared at the desecration before him. Not one of the coffins rested on a shelf. They lay instead in a confused heap across the floor of the mausoleum, as though someone of incredible strength had thrown them about like matchsticks.

Several of the coffins had split open like ruptured pieces of fruit, spilling their dusty contents upon the cold stone. Corbi made the Sign of the Cross again as he descended into the chamber. There was a closeness in the air of the tomb, a stale dry smell of things long dead. He did not want to breathe for fear of taking death into his lungs—an irrational thought, but it was very real to him.

He walked to the nearest coffin, which was little more than a trough cut from a block of sandstone with a lid that slid across the top. This one had tilted at an odd angle when it had tumbled from its niche in the alcove, and the lid had fallen away to reveal the skeletal contents. The plaque on the end of the coffin identified the resident as Arnascento Mazzetti, who had been the Mayor of Scarpino more than a century past.

Corbi stood over the open casket, peering down at the desiccated bones. The skull stared up at him, its hollow sockets as deep and dark as night itself. He noticed that the jaw was open wide as though the skull was locked in an eternal scream, as though it was still enduring its final agony of death and passage into the next world. Corbi wondered what horrors those dead eyes now saw. And surely they must be horrors, because there was an aura of evil about this place—it permeated the atmosphere like the stench of a rotting corpse.

In the back corner of the small open space, there was another casket ripped out of its shelved alcove, lying open at an odd angle. The plaque at the end of the long stone box was tarnished, but the raised letters could still be read: *Reverend Father Francesco Mazzetti, 1821-1899.* The lid was also off this coffin, and Corbi peered inside with a great reluctance. What he saw made his flesh ripple, his testicles draw up against his body. The remains of the Reverend Father had been savaged; there was no other word for what he saw. The burial robes had been ripped away; the fragile husk of desiccated skin and brittle bones were smashed into white fragments.

A shiny object lay at the bottom of the casket, in the broken hollow of a battered rib cage. Trembling, Corbi eyed it carefully, not recognizing it. He forced his hand to move into the coffin, careful not to brush against the shattered bones. His fingers touched the cool metallic surface and he gingerly picked it up, drawing it up from the place of death. Upon inspection, holding it close to his old eyes, he saw it was a gold crucifix that had been warped and twisted into an almost unrecognizable shape.

He could not help thinking of what kind of evil force had invaded the crypt, had disrupted the dead in their final rest, committed such sacrilege. And for what purpose? What did it all mean?

Corbi did not know; was not sure he even wanted to know.

But it was obvious that an evil presence had passed through this place, like a cruel wind through dead leaves, disturbing the dead as though in revenge.

The old man shook his head. He made the Sign of the Cross and prayed to his God. Whatever had been here was now surely gone, he thought as he went to work.

He did not want to think of where it might go next . . . .

Chapter 1

Palermo, Sicily

Her name was Sophia.

It was several hours before dawn and the lights of stars still burned with awesome magic. There was no moon, yet she could see her way along the simple mountain path. Below, and miles distant, there was the sparkle of a great village, a city, actually, which must be Palermo. Yellow ribbons of brilliance sliced through the city's center from all directions; lighted towers soared into the night, and the ground glowed like jewels flung upon black velvet.

A cool wind twisted through the wild olive trees on the slope, and although she was not affected by the low temperatures, she was suddenly aware of her total nudity. A young naked woman, walking through the foothills after dawn would surely attract undue attention. Later Sophia would accept the lusty stares of both men and women, but she would need time. Time to adjust. To acclimate.

Softly, like a thief in the night, she circled the outer edge of Scarpino while the tiny village slept. She searched for an isolated cottage away from the worn paths and cobbled streets. Several stone houses with tiled roofs were scattered along the edge of the hills, where some of the more prosperous villagers tilled small orchards and crops. She picked a house farthest from the path, farthest from the village itself, and walked silently in the moonless night to a shuttered door.

She slipped inside the small home, making no sounds. The stark interior was cloaked in deep shadows, the furniture taking on the shapes of creatures and monsters, but she paid them no attention. Moving rapidly with the instinct of darkness, she sought the bedroom.

The sounds of human sleep—labored breathing, turns upon a noisy mattress, dreamless whisperings—called out to her, and she followed these night noises to their source. Entering the bedroom, she saw two humped figures in a brass bed. Wrapped in blankets and quilts, they were oblivious as she moved to the chiffonier in the opposite corner of the room.

Silently, Sophia opened the doors to the dressing cabinet. In the dim illumination from the window, she could see an assortment of drab peasantry—muslin blouses, cotton skirts, denim workpants, chambray shirts. The clothes of those who lived and worked close with the land, there was even an earthy smell about them. Quickly she selected a wrap-around dress of light-colored cotton. She dropped it over her arm, then padded barefoot from the room to the door.

Unlatching the lock, she slipped into the night, a smile forming at the corners of her perfect mouth.

Picking her way carefully down the slope, she headed toward one of the ribbons of light that snaked through the foothills. It was apparently a trail or a highway, and even from this distance she could see carriages moving along its path. They seemed to be moving so fast, it did not seem possible. How much time has passed, she wondered idly . . . .

The first traces of dawn were tightening the sky when she reached the edge of the highway. From a small copse of willow trees that edged the road, she studied the scene with fascination. The highway was hard and solid, like some kind of black stone. White stripes raced along its length, and silver towers washed it with harsh yellow light.

Staying within the cover of the trees, she heard a ratcheting sound, like the rumble in an animal's throat, only louder. Looking up the highway, she saw one of the carriages approaching. No horses pulled it, and it rolled along at great speed on four thick wheels, roaring like a beast as it passed. But there had been two men seated near the front of it, their faces staring straight ahead through a pane of clear glass.

Above the highway, the lights in the towers winked out, their harsh yellows having been washed away by the sunlight. She wondered if someone had turned out the lamps deliberately and if they were nearby. Perhaps she had been seen?

Time passed as Sophia waited in the trees' shadows, but no one came by, and she seemed to be alone. Smoothing the peasant's dress over her body, she was proud of the way her flesh seemed to swell against the flimsy fabric. With its waist-cinching cords, the clothing could be adjusted to be as provocative as she wished. But first she must reach Palermo. There would be plenty of time for encounters, she thought calmly.

She moved out to the road and began walking toward the city as the sun rose higher above the hills. Birds sang in the nearby trees, butterflies danced above the meadows, and there was a strong smell of lemon blossoms in the air. Some things never changed.

A bright yellow speeding carriage approached her from the direction of Palermo. It was not as large as the first one she had seen, but it was moving faster, if that was possible. Two men were seated behind the glass window and the carriage slowed down as it passed her. One of the men yelled something unintelligible at her, smiling and waving his hands wildly. She returned the smile, knowing what had attracted them, and continued walking.

Before the sound of the passing carriage had faded, another noise warned her of another advancing from the opposite direction. Tossing her hair over her shoulder, she looked back to see a small vehicle bearing down on her. It was bright red and had no roof on its cab. A sheet of glass shielded a single woman, whose medium-length hair was whipped by the windstream. Sophia smiled as the carriage approached, slowed down appreciably, then swerved off the highway, coasting along the shoulder. As it drew closer, she was surprised to see that the occupant was not a woman after all, but a young man with longish brown hair.

"Hello," he said in Italian that was flavored with an island dialect. "Can I give you a lift?"

She looked at him and his strange carriage. He had a wide, confident smile and large brown eyes, which were taking her in with a great thirst. He wore an open white shirt with a long, pointed collar, and a gold necklace gleamed in the sun upon his hairy chest.

"A lift?" she said, unsure as to what he was talking about.

"Sure. You going all the way to Palermo?"

Sophia nodded coyly, averted her eyes for an instant, then looked back at him with a penetrating gaze, feeling him come under her sway. "Yes, I am. . . ."

Leaning over, he threw a lever and part of the carriage parted, swinging open to reveal shining, smooth seats. "Okay, then! Hop in!"

Carefully, Sophia entered the vehicle, mindful not to stare too conspicuously at the array of strange little windows with numbers and moving needles like clock faces. The man was holding on to a small wheel with one hand, his other on a stick that rose between the two seats.

As she pulled the door shut, he moved his feet, which were resting on small treadles. The carriage made a roaring sound, and it's wheels spun briefly on the gravel before leaping back to the highway. Within seconds she was being carried along at an incredible speed. She gasped for her breath as she watched the countryside tear past the vehicle while fingers of the wind ran through her long hair.

During all this, she could feel the young man's gaze occasionally touch her, racing quickly up and down her ripe body. And even though she was distracted by the wild ride and the sheer speed of their journey, she was also aware of his desires, his pet fetishes and needs, coming to the surface. Unconsciously she responded to his libidinal thoughts.

By his deft handling of the wheel, the vehicle snugged itself to the road and seemed to leap around the tight turns like a mountain cat. As they crested a ridge, she could see the city of Palermo baking in the morning sun.

"So where are you going?" asked the young man, his eyes constantly darting between her and the road.

She paused for a moment, stuck for an answer. "The market," she said finally.

He laughed. "The market! Which market? There are only hundreds in Palermo!" He laughed again, looking at her more longingly. "Besides, where is your basket? You don't even have a purse or a pair of shoes!"

Now her mind was completely on the task at hand. The situation called for quick thinking, and she began speaking smoothly, confidently. "My uncle is a vendor in the Piazza Caraciollo. I do not go there to buy, but to work for him, selling fruits and vegetables."

This reply seemed to satisfy him, for he nodded and smiled.

"Why don't you stay on the farms? Surely there must be plenty of work out here in the country?"

"I come from a large family. There is plenty of help. Besides, I am tired of the country. I want to be a city girl. "

The young man chuckled as he took the carriage into a hairpin turn, then straightened it out. "I don't blame you. There is so much to do in the cities. If you had the time, I could show you some wonderful things."

I'm sure you could, thought Sophia, and the first would be that weapon between your legs. She smiled and looked at him, feeling the lust blow off of him like steam from a boiler. He would be easy . . .

"By the way, my name is Paolo. What's yours?" She told him and he considered it as one might sample a strange new wine. "Never heard of a name like that. It's very different. "

"Yes, I suppose it is . . ."

"I'm a salesman of fine clothing. I work for Tommaso di Calderone. " He said the name with a certain reverence, a touch of respect, as one might say "I am with the court of Louis XIV," and she assumed that the house of Calderone was a prestigious one. He continued talking about his position with this clothing firm, trying to impress her with his importance, his knowledge, and his responsibilities.

She smiled as he talked on, thinking of how most men were so very much the same. How they were so taken with themselves, so full of self-blown importance, so forgetful of how the world will usually roll on without them, never missing a beat.

It was only the unusual man, the special man with personal energy and vision, who left a void in the world at his passing. It was these men whom Sophia sought, and surely not a dress salesman from Florence. But, she thought calmly, there would be time for all such things.

First things first . . . .

By the time they reached the teeming streets of Palermo, her driver was considering them to be close friends. Sophia was surprised to see the streets filled with carriages like his own—"cars" he had called them—and the skill with which people whipped them about the streets.

She studied the architecture of the city, seeing that it was a chock-a-block blend of old and new. Tall buildings of shining metal and glass soared above the narrow avenues and crowded shop fronts. The morning sun created curious shadows and strange perspectives, imparting an almost unreal quality to the cramped side streets. As Paolo turned onto a wide boulevard, the Via Ruggero Settimo, the surroundings suddenly became more cosmopolitan. Sidewalks were lined with boutiques and brightly adorned shops, restaurants, and alfresco cafés. Everything swarmed with pedestrian traffic, tourists and olive-skinned natives alike, moving with a vitality that excited her.

Sophia watched as they entered the Vucciria—a gigantic outdoor marketplace where the crowds flowed and bubbled like lava. She could feel the air crackling with the rush of voices and laughter, and could smell the thick, roiling aromas of roasted nuts, baked onions, oregano, and marinades. She was instantly reminded of the Algerian flea markets, Turkish bazaars, Arab *suqs*.

"Where is your uncle's place?" asked her driver. "Is it anywhere near here?"

"No, but it's not that far." She paused. "I'm still early. He does not yet expect me."

Paolo picked up the implied message in her words, looking at her as he stopped the car at an intersection. As the crowds streamed past the sloping hood, her beauty was sucking him in, falling into a vortex of desire. She shifted her position in the plush seat, subtly moving to make her breasts jut outward, threatening to break free from the thin confines of the dress. She could feel his passion rising, emanating from him like a strong animal scent.

"My . . . my office is nearby," he said haltingly. There was a fire behind his eyes, a thickening in his throat, and other places. Surely he had never felt so overwhelmed by lust as at that moment. "We could stop by, if you'd like . . . I could show you some of my samples. You can appreciate fine clothes, can't you?"

Sophia smiled. "I can appreciate many things."

Paolo allowed himself a chuckle. "Does that mean yes?" He sounded as excited as an adolescent.

"Take me," she said, "to your 'office'."

Now he smiled broadly as he drove the car quickly through the intersection, past the rows of vendor stalls and tents, turning at the next large crossing street.

"You won't be disappointed," he said confidently.

Actually, Paolo was not totally correct in his prediction. As a lover he was only adequate, but he represented a source of other things, and so she used him as completely as possible. When she took him into her, he gasped as she seemed to grab him with her perfect body, massaging and squeezing him with unseen hands. And while they grappled in the ancient struggle of love, his eyes glazing over from the sweetness of the experience, she stared impassively into his soul, reaching for his essence and his energy, and found it shallow and lacking. He was a man like most men—full of flash and boast, but little substance beneath the surface.

Smiling, confident, and in total control, with her legs coiled serpentine over his back, she pulled him in as deeply as possible and took everything from him. Never would this shallow man be the same, not after experiencing her.

Afterward, as he lay atop her, recovering what strength still remained to him, she could see that the fire in his eyes was now replaced with a static dullness, a flat opacity that betrayed the emptiness beyond. In one quick moment she had destroyed him, so depthless he had been. In more normal times, she would have never preyed on him. She needed more than he could give. Much more.

He rolled away from her, still trying to regain his previous stance of posturing macho confidence, and she cared not at all. Arising from his couch in the small balconied room above the Via della Liberta, she moved into the bath facilities, enjoying the pleasure of the shower—a wonderful modern contrivance.

When she returned to the room, Paolo was still supine upon the couch, looking like—the twisted form of a mortally wounded soldier lying in a trench.

"I'm going to take some of your 'samples' now," she said in a soft, yet firm voice. She moved to a large closet with sliding doors and threw them back to unmask racks of finery, shelves of shoes and boots, millinery, and outerwear.

Pulling armfuls of dresses from the racks, she carried them down to his car, piling them in the back deck with boxes of shoes and accessories. It was a simple task, a necessity, and she did it with a calmness that was without pity or rancor—it was merely something that had to be done.

When she finished her selections, she returned to him, where he still lay like a deformed fetus. "I'm going to be taking your car, too, she said quietly. He would not be needing anything soon anyway.

He nodded but could say nothing, as though he knew his fate.

Before departing, she went through his belongings until she found what she was looking for—a small metal chest containing stacks of crisp lira notes. She cared not for the amount, and viewed the money only as another tool, but she knew that it was a wondrous substance which greased many an axle, turned many a wheel. Some things, she knew, truly never changed.

She looked at him one last time before going down to the street and his shiny red car. Already he appeared smaller, thinner, more pate and colorless.

He had hardly been worth the effort.

A week passed quickly for her as she acclimated to the subtle differences, the nuances of time and change. But she was, if anything, adaptable, and she adjusted quickly, taking in knowledge through heady experience. She gave, but she always took much more, and soon she grew tired of the provincial ways of the Sicilian city.

Learning to handle her little red sports car, a Fiat, as it was called, had been simpler than she had expected, and her journey east through Termini, Cefalu, Barcelona, and on to Messina was a joyful thing. Like the flight of a bird of paradise, she moved gracefully into the world again.

Taking the ferry to Reggio on the mainland, she drove up the southern half of Italy, not stopping until she reached Rome, anxious to see how much it had changed, how much it had remained the same. She remained in "the eternal city" long enough to obtain false documents, including a passport, from an entranced government employee. Then it was north again, across the Alps, into Switzerland, then on through Western Europe. The trains were marvelous and the array of passengers was endlessly entertaining. As her trip progressed, Sophia gained in wealth, knowledge, and experience. She sought her special prey, and although it seemed quite scarce, she found flashes of the brilliance and invention that was once the trademark of the region.

But it was not long before she learned of a strange and wonderful place—a place that had been a struggling child in the previous century, but now grown to full, bristling adulthood. It was a place of vitality and energy and the essence she so greatly needed.

She decided that she must go to this place called America.

Chapter 2

New York City

Like a giant, predatory bird, the plane approached Manhattan from the southeast. Its flight path afforded all passengers in the left-window seats a postcard picture view of the monster skyline.

Sophia peered through the window of the supersonic jetliner, to see the awesome forest of stone and glass for the first time. Despite her worldliness, she was impressed. While on the Continent, she had heard so many tales about the famous American city, that she felt almost familiar with it. But upon seeing its raw power and strength, its giant array of phallic towers, she felt a decidedly sexual quiver pass through her body. As the sleek plane circled above JFK International, she could sense the vibrant energy rising up from the city like musky waves of desire.

Already she was convinced that it had been a wise choice to come here. Europe had become so decadent, so stagnant in her absence. But the "New World" would be so very different. She could almost taste the vitality of its soul!

Lights began flashing and the voice of the airship's captain penetrated the cabin crisply. The passengers were instructed to fasten their seat belts for the landing. Still watching from her window seat, Sophia felt the ship bank sharply to the right. The long strip of Manhattan plummeted from view as the jetliner whipped into a holding pattern above JFK. Then suddenly it began dropping like a kite in a capricious wind, circling, catching itself, and then sliding downward. The plane was tilted upward as it fell; the ground rushed up with great speed.

It was the third time Sophia had flown in the jetliners and she was still fascinated with their power and speed. The world had come so far, so quickly. There was so much to learn, so much to do.

There came a brief scratching sound as the great tires kissed the runway, then an insane rush of speed as the plane taxied the length of the ship before slowing and turning toward the terminal. When the ship finally came to rest, a voice crackled in the air, telling everyone to prepare to deplane.

Walking through the terminal was tike entering the belly of a great beast—flowing lines of shaped concrete, glass and shining metal, all blended together like a living thing. Sophia carried an over-the-shoulder bag as she tried to slip through the throbbing mass of people. Even the crowds at the Crystal Palace were nothing compared to this frantic rush of human traffic.

She had no conception of where she was going, but it did not bother her. She was burning with an inner energy, suffused with a spirit of adventure, which she had not felt in many years. Pausing before a mirrored wall, she brushed her long blonde hair from her face, admiring herself for an instant. The fashionable clothes she had purchased in Paris had been perfectly tailored to her body. Her high, full breasts were almost bursting from the white satin blouse; her skirt flowed lightly about her long legs. Even from a distance her serpent-green eyes danced with their own light and heat. Sophia smiled, satisfied with herself.

Yes, she was going to do very well here, she thought as she began planning her next series of moves. It was a technique she had perfected long ago: a way of quickly becoming familiar with a new place.

As she continued walking through the terminal, scanning the crowds, she saw a young man dressed in a three-piece suit with a trench coat draped over his arm. He walked with a determined stride as he headed for the exit signs.

"Excuse me," she said, appearing at his side. "Could you tell me where I could get a taxi into the city?" Her English was rough but functional; she had not spoken it for a very long time.

He looked at her and she could instantly feel the effects of his desire building. It was a familiar sensation, and she could not help smiling. Subtle changes took place and she reveled in them.

The man was so stunned by her appearance that he seemed momentarily dumbstruck. "What did you say?" Sophia smiled again and repeated her question.

"Oh, sure! It's right out this way," he said, pointing ahead of them. "As a matter of fact, I'm going into the city myself. We could share a cab if you'd like?"

He spoke in a smooth, baritone voice. Quickly recovering from his initial awkwardness, he exuded a confidence and a touch of arrogance she always found exhilarating, if not a bit amusing. Men were so often little boys in disguise, and this one was no different than the myriad she had known.

"Yes, I would like that," she said, and gestured that he lead the way.

Once inside a yellow Checker, the kind with a backseat as big as a living room couch, he managed to sit very close to her. "I'm Rob," he said, grinning a tilted smile. "Rob Lester. I work for the Morris Agency. How about you?"

She could smell the lingering aura of his aftershave mixed with his perspiration. It had an intoxicating effect on her and she began to hunger for him. "My name is Sophia Rousseau," she said slowly, looking directly into his eyes, where an inferno raged. It was an interesting game they played with each other—an ancient mating ritual with which she was so familiar.

"You're French?"

"I have just come from Paris, yes."

Lester cleared his throat, his gaze darting away from her. "Are you here as a tourist?"

"No, I think I'm planning to stay. I have heard so much about America. I think I would like to be here for a very long time."

"What kind of work do you do?" He inched a bit closer to her as the cab slipped onto the Belt Parkway, heading west.

She was gazing out the window, pretending to not be listening, as she prepared a credible answer. The last man in Paris had suggested that she could be a magazine cover girl, and she decided to use his posthumous help. "I am a model," she said. "Mostly fashion work."

Rob Lester smiled. "Yeah, well I can believe that. You're perfect for the job."

She nodded, and returned her gaze to the passing scenery-now an endless parade of Brooklyn high-rise apartments. "Thank you," she said after a dramatic pause. Then with a sudden directness: "What is this Morris Agency you mentioned? What is your work there?"

He smiled and reached into his breast pocket, pulling out a small white card and handing it to her. "You never heard of the Morris Agency? Jeez, we're the biggest talent agency in the country! We represent all the big people—models, actors, producers, screen writers, directors—you name it, we do it."

Sophia pretended to study the card, quickly reading the proclamation that Mr. Lester was an "agent." It was beautiful piece of fortune to have met a man who could provide her with so many contacts in so many creative fields. She shifted her position on the seat so that her leg rubbed lightly against his. She was careful to keep things subtle at this point.

"I'm sorry," she said, handing the card back to him with a condescending air, "but in Paris we have our own agencies. "

Lester seemed to be deflated somewhat by the tone of her remark, but he recovered quickly. "I'm sure you do, Ms. Rousseau, but I think you will need American representation now that you are in this country."

Hearing the words she had been expecting, she verbally pounced on him. "Are you offering me such representation, Mr. Lester?"

He smiled, displaying very nice teeth. "Are you kidding? Who wouldn't? You're dynamite, honey. I can make you a fortune."

Sophia took back his card and placed it in her shoulder bag. "Shall I call at your office, then?"

Lester grinned. "I'll be in the office tomorrow, but we don't have to wait that long."

"What do you mean?"

"You never told the cab driver where you wanted to go. Is somebody expecting you, or were you going to a hotel?"

"A hotel," said Sophia, her voice cool and even. It was best to allow him to think that he was engineering the entire encounter. "Why do you ask?"

"I was just wondering if you wanted to stop by my place. I've got a great place on Riverside Drive. You can relax from the trip, have a drink, and we can . . . talk. About your career."

"That sounds like an interesting offer, Mr. Lester. Sophia smiled, and gave off a wave of heated desire. It washed over him, catching him off-guard. She could smell his excited secretions, and she knew that all was going better than she could have planned.

Her effect on men was a constant source of amusement and fascination to her. Naked, her perfect flesh gleaming with the sweat of performance, she lay back on Mr. Lester's bed and coolly regarded his sleeping face. Young, unlined, unwise, but handsome in a rugged kind of way. Sleeping, he appeared so innocent, so undefiled . . . so devoid of the energy that she craved. It would have been easy for her to destroy him, and in fact, there was a part of her that wished to do so—if only to teach him a final lesson that he was not as irresistible as he thought.

But no, she thought. I will need him for a short time. And so I will let him suck me and fuck me, let him think that he is the one who controls all the events, until that short time is at an end. Only when it is too late will Mr. Rob Lester possibly realize that she took far more from him than he from her.

She rose from the bed and entered his bathroom while he slept the sleep of the innocent. It was decorated in maroon tiles and accented with cedar planks and track lights. Like everything about the apartment, all was very chic, and tasteful to the point of boredom. Although there was an exotic element to the modem decor, Sophia also felt an essential coldness in it. She felt more comfortable in the baronial clutter of the Victorians, the lavish sensuality of the baroque period, or even the steaming earthiness of the Mediterranean.

And yet there was something uniquely American about this apartment, which reflected the spirit of this strange, young country. In her haste to catch up on her history, she was amazed at how far this nation of mongrels had progressed so quickly. It was a hotbed of originality, of vision and invention, of power and imagination. There was no other place in the world more suited to her kind.

Standing before a full-length mirror, she regarded The Body and felt pleased with its litheness. She was petite, yet voluptuous; cool, yet full of passion. She liked the way her full breasts sat up as though defying gravity; the fullness of her roseate nipples and the flatness of her stomach. Her legs were long and slender, muscled yet accented by soft highlights.

She was the perfect female of the species, and yet she often longed for the freedom to be something else. It was the single curse of her existence, something she had lived with for a very long time.

Moving from the bathroom, she passed the platform bed and entered the living room. Large plate-glass windows lay open to Hudson River. To the right, she could see a great suspension bridge in the distance, the tops of its silvery towers still glowing with the last light of the setting sun. It was a magnificent city, she thought. She was going to like it here.

A sound came from the bedroom, where Rob Lester was rustling in the sheets, calling out her name tentatively. She turned and walked back to him, wearing her nudity like a proud uniform.

He had started to speak, but the vision of her had stopped the words in his throat. She smiled as she watched him getting hard again—such was her effect on men.

"I . . . I was wondering where you'd gone. I must have drifted off to sleep. Sorry, I never do that."

Why did they always have to make amends for their natural masculine weaknesses? she wondered. "It's all right. I was just admiring the view," she said, pointing toward the living room.

Lester smiled. "Yeah, so was I."

She moved to him, crawling across the bed to straddle him. He was ready instantly, and entered her again. As she gripped him with her small muscles, slowly sliding up and down, playing with him, she considered how long he would be of use to her. As Lester gasped in exquisite ecstasy, Sophia considered her options.

Despite her own performance, she was deriving little from the union. Rob Lester proved to be like most men—a flashy exterior, a facile line of conversation, but no depth, no soul, and consequently, very little energy. It was no surprise that he had fallen into an exhausted sleep after their first coupling; he lacked the spirit, the inner resources.

It was clear she did not need his kind, and yet he would prove useful for a short time—he would connect her with the correct type of people. She would draw from him, as she drew from him now, and when he was no longer useful, she would discard the empty husk of him. Thinking of this, Sophia felt no remorse or sadness. It was imply her nature, and it need not be defended or rationalized.

Rob Lester was reaching a second climax, and she returned her attention to the situation. He was a noisy, brash lover, with little of the gentleness that she secretly craved, even though she did not require it. He was the kind of man who offered little and attempted to take everything, but Sophia would change all that.

Finally he was finished, obviously weakened by the power of their union. He looked at her with a stunned expression, but could not speak. Within a minute, he had lapsed into a deep sleep, and Sophia laughed lightly as she slipped off of him, and walked to the shower.

An hour later, she was dressed and ready to leave his plush apartment. Leaving a note, which promised she would be in touch on a professional basis, Sophia slipped out the door into the hall, heading for the elevator. Before she could begin in earnest, she must make living arrangements, establish her identity, and conduct a thorough study of her new surroundings.

Her time in Europe had been a fruitful one, and she carried many thousands of converted francs and pounds in her shoulder bag. It would be best to check into a hotel for the evening, then spend the next day hunting a proper residence.

When she reached the street, she hailed a cab, as she had seen the natives do it, then climbed in quickly. The night was growing cool, but not at all unpleasant, and the streets were full of light and motion.

"Could you suggest a fine hotel, Monsieur?" she said to the cab driver. Sophia leaned back in the seat, her legs parting her skirt just enough to afford him a tantalizing view.

"What're you, from outta town, huh?" he said turning around, whereupon he paused, his mouth hanging open for an instant as his gaze dropped to the desired place.

Sophia crossed her legs, closing them from his view. "Yes. I would like an excellent hotel. Can you recommend one?"

The cabbie swallowed, blinking his eyes. "Oh yeah, I'd figure the Waldorf's a nice joint. I never stayed there, but I hear people talkin', you know?"

Nodding, Sophia stared at him with sea-green eyes.

"Then take me there. Quickly."

The cabbie swiveled in his seat and grabbed the wheel. "Yes ma'am. No problem."

He attempted to keep the conversation going as he drove along by asking inane questions, but after she had ignored three or four of them, he gave up, muttering something about "stuck-up foreign broads."

The Waldorf-Astoria was indeed a splendid choice, even though it appeared to have some age on its furnishings, and made no attempt to make use of the more modern fixtures she had seen in the airport and Lester's apartment. There was a stately elegance about the hotel which she admired and recognized as being lifted from most of the finer European hostelries. Yes, this would be quite suitable until she had located a more permanent place.

A bellman carried her bags to a suite on the twenty-fifth floor, and while they shared the elevator, she could sense his silent appraisal of her, could feel the heat and the scent of him as he became aroused. He was an older man with wispy gray hair and a bent back, but he was not too old to sense that he was in the presence of an extremely sexual woman. When he lingered at the door, after placing the luggage in the bedroom, Sophia was at first amused that he might be conjuring up the courage to make a pass at her. Only when she realized that he was expecting a gratuity at best did she truly laugh at herself. She gave him several folds of paper money and dispatched him.

When finally alone, she stripped off her clothes and inspected the suite of rooms and the period furniture from the eighteenth century. They were probably not authentic, but handsome copies nonetheless. The bed was soft, but large, and there was a Bible in the drawer of the nightstand. Sophia laughed as she saw the book, which appeared to have never been opened. It reminded her of what a mongrel country this United States was. Mongrel in blood, but also in spirit, culture, and philosophy.

She moved to the bedroom's window, which looked down upon the intersection of 49th Street and Park Avenue. South on the great boulevard loomed a giant building which appeared to block the path of the traffic; north, more tall towers of light and the forest called Central Park. She stared out at the night-city, feeling a shiver of anticipation rush through her body. It was a beautiful city—so full of movement and energy, of passion and ideas. She would enjoy an endless banquet here; she would never leave this place.

Chapter 3

London

Matthew Cavendish was a man of extreme organization. Over the years, he had established certain schedules and rituals for himself, and at the age of fifty, he had become a slave to most of them.

He arose precisely at 7:00 every morning, showered, shaved his neck, and scissor-trimmed his beard. He usually dressed in a pair of baggy corduroy pants, an oxford shirt, and a cable-knit sweater. He had a vast assortment of corduroys, oxford shirts, and bulky sweaters—only the colors and combinations changed from day to day. He had three pairs of glasses (all the same Ben Franklin style), two of which he kept as spares. Without them, he would be unable to read, and since books were his last living passion, the thought of not reading was appalling, almost frightening.

Wasn't it Somerset Maugham who said he'd rather read a train schedule than nothing at all? How true, thought Cavendish, as he affixed his glasses behind his ears, and walked down the stairs to the kitchen.

Mrs. Whittington, his live-in cook and housekeeper was bustling about the kitchen as fast as her sixty-six years would allow. Having been employed by Matthew for more than twenty of them, she was finely attuned to his routine. Coffee perked in a old porcelain pot, a rasher of bacon lay pan-frying, and eggs heated in a poacher. Many years ago, on Matthew's first visit to the United States, he had discovered the joys of a hearty "Colonial" breakfast, and had forever disdained the morning tea and crumpets of his childhood.

"Good morning, Mrs. Whittington," he said as he passed the door to the kitchen, walking down the hall to the front door of his flat. Unlocking the latch, he swung open the oak panel to find his morning *Times* lying in wait on the doormat. He picked it up and brought it inside with a warm feeling. The weather looked typically balmy, but there was freshness in the air that was usually absent.

Returning to the kitchen, Matthew sat down and unfolded the paper before him. Although he was not particularly political, he read everything so that he remained informed. There was no excuse for ignorance when one has the weapons to combat it, he had always felt.

"Here's your coffee, sir," said Mrs. Whittington. "Bacon and eggs are on the way."

Matthew nodded but said nothing, continuing to peruse the front pages. Mrs. Whittington did not mind his silence, and it fact actually expected it. She was the ideal companion in that respect: she knew his habits and wants, and made no demands upon them. Mrs. Whittington had allowed Matthew to establish a comfortable routine and then did her best to adapt to it.

Of course, things had not always been like this . . . .

After college, Matthew had met and married Elizabeth, and had taken a job as the editor of a magazine dedicated to the popularization of archaeology. It was good work, but Cavendish had always felt restricted, suffering from a disease well known among editors throughout the world. He had the urge to write himself, having the heartfelt conceit that he was a better writer than most of those whom he published.

But Elizabeth was not a healthy woman, almost from the beginning of their marriage. She had never been able to work, had never given him a respite from the burden of being the sole provider for their family of two. Children were out of the question but that bothered Cavendish not a whit. Their marriage was a good one—based on intellectual sharing, physical expression, and emotional freedom—and both of them had been happy.

Matthew began writing in the evenings, soon after the doctors had diagnosed his wife's malaise as a crippling, and eventually terminal, disorder of the nervous system. She spent most of her time in bed, and after coming home from the office, Matthew would spend a few precious hours with her. In the late evening, after reading Elizabeth to sleep, he devoted time to his private pursuits. His interests leaned toward philosophy, ancient history, and the realm of unexplained phenomena. In college, he had been a member of the Fortean Society, and had always found the writings and findings of Charles Fort to be fascinating.

It was not surprising, then, that his earliest essays concerned themselves with strange phenomena. After several were accepted by the *Fortean Society Magazine*, Matthew Cavendish began to believe that he had discovered his literary niche.

Several events followed, one after the other, which reinforced his newfound career. The first was the untimely death of Elizabeth at the age of twenty-nine, which left him devastated for more than a year. He could no longer concentrate on his editorial obligations, and no longer felt the need to keep up the pretense of a full-time job. After leaving the magazine, he forced himself to return to his writing, and eked out a living writing articles and conducting investigations of the unexplained. Several years passed, Matthew living on the edge of subsistence until he published his first book, The Dark Path, a compendium of bizarre events and mysteries in the tradition of Charles Fort and Frank Edwards. The book became a worldwide bestseller, and Matthew Cavendish, through a series of prudent investments, became financially independent for life.

He continued to write with renewed vigor, using his money to travel the world in search of the mysterious, the odd, and the unexplained. Recently, he was becoming a well-known personality in the press and on the occasional television talk show. His long, bespectacled face, crisply trimmed beard, and mannered British accent gave him an eccentric, scholarly aspect which delighted both American and British television audiences in a way that only the *untermenschen* who watch such prattle can be delighted.

But Matthew had never let it bother him. The hell with the fools who think of me only as an amusement! What did they know of the vast mysteries, which surrounded them? Not much, apparently, but the masses definitely had an interest in such things because Cavendish's book kept selling and selling.

After breakfast, he retired to his study to continue working on his latest opus. He wrote with a pen and paper on yellow legal pads with a slow, deliberate scrawl that was decipherable only to his typist. His desk was piled high with reference volumes, photographs, and shoeboxes filled with newspaper clippings from all over the world. Each box was labeled with arcane words such as "disappearances," "lights," "sky-falls," "graves," "burnings," and "artifacts." And it was from this primitive filing system that Matthew Cavendish compiled his fascinating articles and books,

His editor at Faber and Faber had been badgering him to purchase a notebook computer so he could write , employ a lightning-quick data base, and keep track of his finances all at a single console, but Matthew would not hear of it.

It was not that he had any great fear of technology or hatred of the future, but more so that he possessed a greater respect, and a fondness for the past. In addition, Matthew was often traveling to various parts of the world to investigate odd events, and he reasoned that he could not be worried about toting a computer about like a piece of luggage, whereas paper and pen fit neatly into his valise.

He remained writing for two hours until Mrs. Whittington interrupted him.

"Excuse me, sir, but a package just arrived. I suspect it's your clipping service."

A warm note chimed in Matthew's heart. The clipping service! He employed the services of a research company, which scanned the various national and foreign newspapers, looking for items and articles, which might be of interest or use to him. He had given them a list of topics and categories, and they collected everything on a weekly basis. For an extra modest fee, the service also translated the foreign clippings. And so once a week Matthew received a veritable treasure box of intriguing occurrences from around the world. It was like getting a new gift or a new toy (and Matthew knew that men never outgrow their toys) every week of the year.

"Thank you, Mrs. Whittington. Do bring it here, won't you?"

She deposited the packet on the desk, took his empty coffee cup in exchange, and left the room. Matthew opened the end of the heavy envelope with a sharp letter opener, and dumped its contents onto the desktop. He always had a feeling of exhilaration as he sorted out the clippings and attached translations. One never knew when he would find a real gem of information, a new happening that might warrant investigation.

For the next hour, he carefully read each item, then categorized it according to its pre-assigned heading. He marked the more intriguing articles with a red felt-tipped pen so that he might further investigate the events mentioned. It was through this clipping service that he was able to compile books of the unexplained, which continually dealt with new phenomena, and were not simply stale rehashes of older more familiar events. It was the judicious use of the clipping service, which gave the books of Matthew Cavendish their special character and appeal.

There were several items which piqued his interest and which felt the touch of the red marker, but it was not until he read a piece translated from the April 12 edition of *Il Messaggero*, the morning daily in Palermo, Sicily, that he became truly intrigued.

In the nearby village of Scarpino, west of the city, workmen employed by the Conti Demolition Company were clearing the site of the old village church in Scarpino, when they encountered a strange event. While laborers dismantled the marble altar of the church, they reported seeing a bright, green serpent emerge from the sealed stone. The snake slithered off into the debris and escaped before the startled workmen could react. It is not known how the snake could have remained alive for uncounted years while sealed within the stone.

Cavendish reread the article several times, ignoring the somewhat awkward translation as he pondered the significance of the event. There were several well-documented occurrences of frogs and toads being found alive after being freed from stone and/or brick enclosures, but this was the first instance Matthew had seen which mentioned a creature as large as a snake. Of course there was always the credibility factor—the laborers could have been bored that day, merely concocting the story to see if they could get their names in the paper. They hadn't, Matthew mused ironically, but the incident itself had been considered newsworthy.

There was something about the serpent in the stone, which intrigued him, but he could not identify what further meaning the event might imply. Something he had read long ago, perhaps . . .. He attempted to dredge his memory for the item, to make an association with the present occurrence.

Matthew made a note on his pad to check out any other references to this sort of thing, then continued to read through the remainder of the clippings. Several minutes later, he encountered another clipping from *Il Messaggero*, this one dated April 14.

The ugly stain of vandalism appeared in the Scarpino Village Cemetery yesterday when Caretaker Enrico Corbi discovered the coffins of the Mazzetti family mausoleum to have been violently disturbed. Reluctantly admitting his discovery to reporters, Signore Corbi said that someone had entered the Mazzetti mausoleum and pulled many of the coffins from the alcoves. One coffin that of the Reverend Francesco Mazzetti, had been particularly singled out for desecration. According to Corbi, the coffin lid had been splintered and the priest's bones had been disturbed. Corbi admits that there was no evidence of forced entry into the mausoleum, and claims to have the only key to the structure.

Hello! Now this was something to think about!

Matthew reread the clipping, noting how singular that there could be two odd, and perhaps unexplainable events occurring within the same general location, and both within forty-eight hours of each other. Although nothing concerning either of the events suggested that they might be connected, or in any way related, Matthew felt that they were indeed. Seeing the two admittedly odd items both originating in the same small Sicilian village *had* to be more than coincidence.

Taking a piece of notepaper, Matthew jotted down a list of prominent words from both articles, separating them into two columns on the sheet. He played a mental game that he often employed when trying to make new associations or deductions from seemingly unrelated subjects. His lists looked like this:

Church	cemetery
altar	coffins
stone	remains
serpent	priest
green	keys
sealed	locked

By combining various words in one list with different words in the second list, Matthew attempted to set up new associations, to see what new connections or correlations might be suggested.

The most obvious association, springing immediately to mind was *religion*. Although religion played a very small part in, his own life, Matthew was careful not to exclude it from any equation when its presence was warranted. Snakes were often associated with evil in Christian theology. The words *sealed* and *locked* were both associated with *tombs*. Both the altar and the mausoleum could be considered tombs. The priest, and the snake had both been entombed . . . but now one was free.

He considered the various thoughts and possible connections. Were the two events a mystical or metaphorical expression of the triumph of evil over good? The serpent vanquishing the priest? What significance was the disturbing of the coffins? Why was the old church being demolished? Why were the remains of the priest singled out for particular desecration? Was it indeed true that the caretaker of the cemetery possessed the only keys to an otherwise locked mausoleum?

The more he pondered the separate events, the more possible

it seemed that they might be connected. It appeared that there existed a multitude of connections, which in turn posed an even larger number of questions. The events intrigued him, and he could not get the nagging thought from his mind that the snake sealed in stone had a special significance.

If only he could remember what it meant, or at least here he had seen or read references to such a thing.

Matthew continued to play with the word associations until he believed that he had exhausted all the combinations that might come immediately to mind. There was a fatigue factor in playing the word associations, after which was pointless to continue. Experience had shown him at when he reached the limits of associative fatigue, it as far more productive to quit the exercise, coming back it only when his mind was again fresh. And so, he laid the clippings and his notes aside, finishing his initial scan the remaining items from the clipping service.

It was close to lunch before he had finished the task, which included categorizing, labeling, marking, and filing in his various boxes. Leaning back in his chair, Matthew looked over the ordered clutter of his huge desk, noting at the most intriguing items received that day were indeed the two events in the village of Scarpino. There was only one thing he could do to assuage his curiosity.

"Mrs. Whittington!" he called in his loud voice, knowing that his housekeeper would not be out of range. As the afternoon dinner hour approached, she could usually be found hovering about the first floor, waiting for him to announce that he was hungry.

In a moment she appeared at the door to his study. "Yes, Sir?"

"Prepare me a quick lunch. Some of that herring, perhaps, and some chips will do."

"And what will you be having to drink, Sir?"

"A pint of Guinness will be fine."

"Yes, Sir," said Mrs. Whittington, turning to leave.

"And, Mrs. Whittington . . . ?"

"Yes, Sir?" She stopped in mid stride and looked back at him.

"After you finish with that, I'd like you to call Heathrow, and book me on the earliest flight to Palermo, Sicily."

"Palermo, Sir? Whatever for?"

Matthew smiled. Her tone of voice often reminded him of a mother speaking to a fanciful child.

"Isn't the reason rather obvious? My work takes me there."

Mrs. Whittington smiled. "I'd say it was the other way around, Sir."

"Yes, yes, you may be right. But nonetheless, I've got to be in Palermo as soon as possible. And I'll be needing luggage packed. Enough for a week, I'd say."

"Whatever you say, Sir. Although I must be admittin' that I can't see the sense in jumpin' all over the world for a bunch of silly stories."

This was a familiar conversation with Mrs. Whittington, a stolid Methodist, who found no use, and certainly no understanding in his habit of chasing down new information, no matter where the traveling might take him. He smiled and nodded, telling her that he was aware of her opinions, politely reminding her that he was hungry and anxious to begin his latest journey.

She disappeared into the hallway, and Matthew began gathering up the tools of his trade: a digital recorder, a digital camera with a 15x optical zoom, some notebooks, and various odds and ends. He scanned the bookcases, pulling out various reference works that might be useful, and began arranging everything neatly in his valise. He always felt a surge of excitement when he prepared for a new investigative trip. His pulse quickened and his appetite waned. It was as though he became too busy to be concerned with such mundane things.

Finished with his preparations, he returned to his chair, picking up the two newspaper clippings to study them one final time before placing them into his notebook.

Scarpino, he thought calmly. What secrets might you hold for me?

Chapter 4

*Mantua, Italy — **1583 A. D.***

James Crichton walked along the Piazza Sordello, his mind ablaze with an unquenchable lust. It had been almost a week since he had seen Beatrice, and he felt as though he were in the terminal stages of withdrawal from laudanum. In fact, he often referred to the beautiful woman as my "addiction" or "my drug" when thinking of her.

How dare she disappear without giving me notice! He thought furiously as he moved along the street with a long-legged stride. James Crichton cut a rather striking image in his wide-brimmed hat of plumage his high-collared cape, and dangling rapier. He was well known in many of the city's social circles for his cavalier, as well as his scholarly, exploits.

Although many of the passersby seemed to recognize him as a popular figure, he paid them no attention. Fuck them all, he had said many times to his barroom friends. Sycophants were only good for those whose self-images were weak and needed supporting. Men who *knew* they were great needed no one. These words had always been one of James's favored axioms, and those close to him understood that he had been referring to himself.

And yet, he needed Beatrice like a wretch needed his drug . . .

He smiled at the irony of the fact. Does every idol have feet of clay?

To his left sprawled the bed brick facade of the Reggia, a Gothic extravaganza that dominated almost the entire length of the Piazza Sordello. James often took his walk alongside the majesty of the Ducal Palace because it was one of the cleanest parts of the old city. Having been raised in the small village of Cluny, Scotland, he had been accustomed to the quaint, but hygienic ways of his fellow Scots. But when he left the land of the clans to travel across Europe, he discovered the ways of the city.

There was one aspect of cities like Mantua which James Crichton had never fathomed, never learned to love and that was the incredible filth, the overpowering smell of offal and garbage, and the legions of commoners who lined the streets to huck simple wares and beg for money and food. Aside from the wide piazzas, Mantua was a labyrinth of twisting, narrow streets, filled with tiny shops and houses. Everything seemed jammed together, as though in a smithy's vise, and there were places so crooked, so sunken that the sun's light never touched them. Everywhere, James could find alleys and lanes that passed as streets, and low arches of crumbling stone. Broken Roman columns still stood in unexpected places as a reminder of the age of the city.

James continued walking toward the end of the Sordello, marked by the massive Cathedral of Mantua, which was still under construction. On sunny days, he and Beatrice would often come down to the park behind the great building and watch the insect-like army of laborers scurry about the scaffolding. He often marveled at what a feat it was to construct such monuments to the greatness of God, to the dreams of men, but Beatrice had never seemed very interested in such things. Never had he met such a hot-blooded woman . . . .

It was better, he told himself, to keep his thoughts away from her. Too long dwelling on such things as the flesh made him mad as a dog in beat. Turning right at the end of the Sordello, James ducked into a narrow avenue and scowled at the ranks of commoners in the streets. The odors in these more enclosed spaces threatened to choke him with their foulness, and he wondered how the people could stand to live in such abject conditions.

The sound of the chimes in the Clock Tower at the Palazzo delta Ragione echoed through the narrow streets and he knew that it was the noon hour. He was now officially late for his appointment with his patron, Aldus Manutius, and he quickened his pace. The old man was a stickler for promptness, if little else.

The tavern was located on the corner of two vile streets crowded with other shops and stalls. There was the constant thrumming of vendors and hagglers, beggars and wives, filling the air with lingual aberration, and James found it charming on one hand, repulsive on the other. Such was his love-hate relationship with all the great cities of Europe.

The light inside the tavern was dim and flickering, the air smoky from ill-burning tapers and thick with the perspiring musk of customers. Aldus Manutius sat at his usual table in the far corner, where he could survey all who might enter the somber place. James approached him with an impish grin as the old man spotted him in the gloom.

"By Christ, lad! Are you never on time for an appointment?" Aldus spoke in a cultured northern Italian dialect, but in such a way that it seemed informal. He was dressed in a brocaded jacket and pantaloons, accented by a flowing, hooded cape, and looked like the royalty he often represented.

I'm sorry," said James. "I stopped to watch the work on the cathedral." Crichton spoke in the same northern dialect, which was piteously easy for him. He had mastered eleven languages by the time he was thirteen years, and the gradual addition of many dialects was less than adding sauce to an already-cooked goose.

"Ah . . ." The old man scowled. "They'll be building that place long after both of us are under stone. You can watch them any time.

"I said I was sorry. Would you have me down at bended knee?"

Aldus Manutius laughed. "That would be a rare day indeed to see the Admirable Crichton on his knee!"

James smiled. "Then I'll simply take a seat . . ."

"Please do," said the older man, signaling for the tapster or the barmaid, then looking back to his young protégé.

"Now, how goes the epic poetry?"

James sighed, leaning back in his chair. "As usual, it goes well, but slow. I'm completing the verses in Latin and English, as well as an Italian version."

"But why is it taking you so long? I've had a publisher awaiting the finished pieces for almost a year now! He was actually drooling at the prospect of bringing out a man of your stature, but you have dallied for so long I fear his interest will have waned."

James smiled. "Genius takes time. If he wants doggerel, tell him to stop by any local college!"

Aldus Manutius leaned forward, a serious expression on his wrinkled face. "Listen, lad, there's a few things we must speak of."

"Like what?"

Aldus started to speak but was interrupted by the barmaid who placed a flagon of mead before James, smiling tartly at him once before departing. He picked up the container and drank with all the panache he could muster. "It is difficult to speak of these things, but . . . but I must confess that I am worried about you."

"Worried? For me?" James chuckled. "Why ever for?"

"Because you've changed, son."

The words stung James deeply, and he sensed the concern and the possibility of an underlying fear in the patron's voice. It was as though Aldus had touched upon a secret part of him, a dark part of James's mind which also suspected that "The Admirable Crichton" had indeed changed.

"In what manner?" James asked after a short pause.

"I am not sure I know myself. But you are *different* from the boyish genius I met in Genoa." Aldus smiled in remembrance. "When I saw you ascend the dais at the Genoese Senate and heard you address them in such perfect Latin, I was so amazed! As dumbstruck as the Senators themselves. I was! And you were so . . . so *innocent* then! Maybe that's it . . . . Never had I seen a young man, not yet out of his teen years, bubbling with such brilliance, such wit and scholarship! I knew then that I had come upon the presence of true genius."

"And now you are not so certain?" James was being serious. His usual impish grin now absent.

"No. Of your genius, there can be no mistake. And yet I fear that you have become tempered in the flames of the world. You have lost your naive, wide-eyed enthusiasm, I fear.

"Now, Aldus, please. I fear you are becoming too dramatic in your later years."

"Perhaps, but hear me out," said the old man. "When I took you to Venice with me, and agreed to be your patron, you were as gracious and mannered as any man can expect an artist to be. Your energy was boundless, and your output of essays and poetry were of the highest order. All of Venice believed your talent was un-equaled on the entire continent. "

"I never realized that until you told me, until they *all* told me." James wondered where the conversation was heading. His immense training in public debate prepared him to think in such ways, to attempt to anticipate an argument a proposition, and already be preparing a rebuttal. But at this point, he felt a hollowness, an emp-tiness inside, though he were suddenly going to be stripped naked before old Manutius.

"Be that as it may I fear you've lost something vital.

"You refer to my appearance at the University of Mantua, no doubt?" James cringed at bringing up the subject. Aldus had been angered he would challenge the faculty without his consent to a public debate.

Manutius sighed, shook his head. "We've already been through all that. You know I disapproved. That is not the point. No, more importantly, I refer to the *difference* between your performance at the University of Padua few years ago, and this circus you staged within a fortnight here in Mantua."

"A circus?"

Aldus nodded. "In comparison. Think of it, lad! Recall what you had accomplished in Padua—a four-day public debate with the *entire* University! A challenge to *any* subject, using the rules of logic, mathematical demonstration, or extemporaneous Latin verse! Never had there be such a spectacle! And never had anything like your complete triumph ever been witnessed!"

James smiled as he recalled the total display of his powers, and how he had become the sensation of the Royal Court in Padua. "Yes," he said wistfully. "It was a triumph, was it not?"

"You employ the proper word—*was*. What you attempted last week was an embarrassment!"

"I know . . . I was not prepared."

"That is to what I refer!" cried the old man. "You have *changed*, James. Something is happening to you, and I have heard the rumors. You go the way of all flesh!'

"What rumors?" James felt his defenses rising up, fearing what Manutius might say next.

Aldus smiled, but it was a false smile. A mask meant to conceal his true emotions. "I understand the juices that run in a young man. Believe it or not, I was your age once. There is no fault in running with the whores of this city, but I fear you have become obsessed with it! Brilliant as you may still be, remember, lad, that you are not the discoverer of copulation!"

"That sounds suspiciously like a lecture to me." James grinned in an attempt to defuse the old man's rising temper.

"No . . . it is just that . . . I have read some of your poems to this . . . this 'Beatrice' . . . and—"

"Who *told* you to read those poems!" Anger flared from him uncontrollably as he gripped the flagon in a white-knuckled grip.

"Be still!" Aldus cried in a shrill voice, so loud that other customers turned to stare. "I am your patron, and I have every *right* to peruse what you might create! I supply you with your food and shelter and coins to squander on your whores!"

"Beatrice is no whore!"

The old man harrumphed. "That's not what I've heard."

Without thinking, James reached across the table and grabbed Manutius by the edge of his cape, pulling him roughly forward. "Who says such things?" he cried loudly, his face flushed with rage. The other customers in the tavern were staring openly now. One of the younger men took a few steps toward the corner table.

Aldus did not answer, but merely looked at him with eyes that eddied with sadness.

In that moment, James realized what he was doing, and released the old man, ashamed. "I am . . . I am sorry, Aldus . . . I lost control of myself."

"No," said Manutius. "You have been losing control for quite some time now. This display is merely the culmination."

"Aldus, I am sorry. I truly am. Forgive me." James fell back in his seat, his heart pounding wildly. His mind a conflux of emotions. He had actually felt hate for the old man when he disparaged his lady.

"If I forgive you," said Aldus Manutius, "I fear it is a different man I forgive ."

"What are you saying?" James looked at him with a new apprehension.

Manutius sighed dramatically. "You are not the young man I championed. You have changed."

"You will not forgive me?"

"Oh, I will forgive you, son. But I am afraid that I can no longer support you."

The words were like a burning acid as they penetrated the confusion in James's mind. "You cannot mean that."

"But I do. I must. My publisher cannot be made fool of any longer. You continue to make a spectacle of yourself. All your wit and charm and scholarship have become a thing of artifice, not art! You have assumed an *identity*, and have ceased to become a person, James. This kind of behavior I can no longer support." Manutius's speech completed, he could only stare blankly at James.

"No!" he cried as he slammed the table with his open palm, spilling his flagon of mead. "You will not embarrass me like this! I will not allow it!"

"Sit down, ere you make yet another spectacle." Aldus tried to ignore the outburst.

All the anger and the rejection and the pain welled up in James as he stood up from the table, glaring at his former patron. If the old bastard wanted spectacle, he would soon get it!

Suddenly, a third voice intruded on the little scene.

"All right, I think you had better take control of yourself, Sir."

James felt a hand upon his shoulder, and he spun quickly to see a well-dressed man staring coldly at him. "Take your leave,". James said through clenched teeth. "This business is none of yours."

"I am sure that it is," said the man. "I think it would wise if you left this public place."

James looked at the man, who rested his hand on his hip, deliberately pushing back his cape to reveal a rapier. It was an unspoken challenge. "I think it would be wiser still for you to stay away from me," said James.

The man smiled. "Do you not know who I am, boy?"

"No, and I do not *care*, either. I advise you, Sir, do not show your sword to me . . . unless you intend to use it."

A small crowd had gathered on the fringe of the confrontation and now a murmur surged through them.

Aldus Manutius reached out to touch his sleeve. "James, please, I beg you—"

"Leave me be!" he cried. "I have business to attend."

"Are you challenging me to a duel, boy?" asked the smiling man.

"No one intrudes on my affairs," James said, placing his hand on his weapon.

"So be it," said the man as he drew his rapier.

The tapster of the pub cried out for them to stop, but they had already crossed swords. His training as a fencer had been rarely tested, and now he plunged what could be a fight to the death. *Why am I doing this?* he thought for an instant. But before he could address the question, his opponent made his initial thrust. Space in the tavern among the tables was limited, and he was not able to use his quick feet and excellent balance to full advantage. The older man was also exceptionally quick and his attacks were nimble and well planned. James parried the blows and countered with several ripostes, which were equally blocked then countered. It was an even match.

They danced about the confines of the dim room while the crowd looked on in silence. Only an occasional, half-hearted plea from old Manutius broke the stillness, accented by the ringing of steel, the sliding song of blade against blade. His opponent smiled openly as he played an advantage, backing James against a wall. His blade a whirring blur, catching the candlelight of the pub in flashing trailers. It had been months since James had been in such a match and his wrist began to weaken, his hand feeling the first effects of fatigue. The man was a master of the rapier and he attacked with an unflinching confidence, a powerful thrust and parry combination that was wearing him down.

Although James continued to at least keep the blade at bay, he was tiring. His attempt to keep a disaffected grin on his face was failing, and his opponent seemed to notice that the scales of advantage were tipping in his direction.

"Had enough, young pup?" said the man in a moment of pause when their cupolas had locked. "Say the word and you'll have your life, if not your honor . . ."

James broke free and danced to the left, spinning in an instant of unexpected motion, he lashed out with his blade and nicked the man's fighting arm above the elbow. Although little more than a touch, and certainly not a wound, he served notice that there would be no surrender.

The touch seemed to infuriate his adversary, and the man attacked with a renewed fury. The thrusts and attacks came in a blur of motion, and James felt fortunate to hold them off as he retreated to a better position, slipping between two tables. The man would have to squeeze past both heavy oak slabs in order to continue his attack—and that was what James hoped for. He outlined the moves that would be necessary to begin the counterattack and watched the man's feet for a moment.

The swordsman advanced, trying to pass between the tables as nimbly as James had, but he was a bigger man, his thighs and hips were pinched by the edges of the heavy fixtures. For an instant he was held, as though in a vise, and his forward motion, the thrust of his attack, was contained. As he realized this and prepared to back up, James countered with a flurry of moves that pushed his weakening wrist and hand to the limit. The man's sword rose up at the wrong angle, admitting James's blade to the interior area of the chest. With a quick, outward flick, James penetrated his flailing defense, and leaped forward with a powerful thrust.

The blade punctured the man's jerkin with a pop, slid off his ribs and easily through his chest. There was a gasp and then a soft sigh as James ran the blade home close to the hilt, then pulled it back with a savage, twisting motion. The man staggered back, his sword arm dropping limply. He tried to speak, but only a bubbly-pink froth issued from his lips. This was followed by a stream of blood as he collapsed to the floor.

The crowd buzzed and moved forward slowly, looking from the mortally wounded man to James. He looked at them with uncertainty, the shock of his deed only now making sense in his mind.

"He killed him! " someone cried. "The boy killed him!"

"Go to him, quick. He might not be done in said some one else.

The tapster appeared and looked at him grimly. "That man was the duke's champion, lad. You've faced a terrible opponent today."

"Is he dead?" asked James dumbly. His mind was a blank slate, the traces of the tapster's words dimly fading from it.

"If he ain't, he will be. I best be sending for the Duke's men."

"Am I in trouble?" James moved back. He looked at the blood on his blade, not knowing how to remove the stains before replacing it to his sash.

The tapster laughed, as he bent down to the stilled form of he swordsman. "That would be up to the duke, now would it not?"

Aldus Manutius moved to his side, touched his sleeve.

"You have embarrassed me, James. You have scandalized yourself. But nothing can compare with this."

"Aldus, help me. Let me go with you."

"I am sorry, lad. But I am finished with you. You are no longer welcome in my home. Take leave of your belongings as soon as you can see to it." Manutius turned to leave.

"But wait!" cried James. He felt small and weak and lost. "Where will I go?"

His old former patron smiled tightly as he stopped at the door and looked back. "Try your lady Beatrice. Perhaps she can give more than a pair of long legs around your hips.

Backlit by the stars and the moonglow reflected off the Mincio River, she stood in front of her room's window, the dim light dancing upon her naked silhouette like magic aura. James lay in the bed, watching her move toward him as though gliding on ice.

"You were splendid, my James. And I shall reward you for your exploits."

"Beatrice . . ." was all he could say.

Moving to him, she swept her soft hands over his clothing, the buttons and fastening dropping away as though by a spell. In an instant he was as naked as she, feeling the silky slide of her flesh along his. She felt cool and yet flushed with an inner fire that radiated into him, setting him ablaze. Whenever she made love to him, it never seemed to be the same, an endless variation on a perfect theme.

He had come to her that evening, after the news of his killing the duke's champion had spread throughout Mantua. He felt as though he had run a marathon race when reached her luxurious home on the Piazza delle Erbe. She had told him she had inherited a great wealth from her father, an adviser in the court of Ludovico il Moro. The expanse of her fortune was certainly reflected in her living quarters: original paintings by Guilio Romano, sculptures by d'Este and even Pedrocchi, floors covered by Byzantine carpets, and halls lighted by gilded sconces.

James had been so tired when he arrived—lately he been feeling weak and spent with increasing frequency. It seemed that his usual vigor and strength were slow waning, and he secretly feared he had contracted some kind of consumptive disease. What with the general filth of the city, he would not actually be surprised. Still, it had not been long ago that he could have conducted seven or eight sessions of swordplay without pause. And now he labored under the threat of total exhaustion—the duel with the duke's champion swordsman had almost killed him.

But Beatrice was as loving and full of understanding as one could ask. She had bathed him and fed him and was now taking him to her bed. Despite his fatigue she inspired him to new heights of achievement and they lay in the humid darkness for more than two hours of frantic coupling. It was like an alchemy of the flesh, James had often thought, and had written about their nights in one of his poems to Beatrice.

Afterward, as they lay in her great bed, James attempted to speak with her. Although his body felt taxed to its limits, his mind was a beehive of thoughts.

"Beatrice, I must talk . . ."

"At such a time?" She giggled and the sound was like music in the darkness. "Speak to me with your tongue, if you must . . . but speak no words!" She giggled again.

Just the sound of her laughter, the not-very-subtle suggestion of more sexual activity, caused a conflict of feelings in him. He was drawn to her like a moth to flame, but the thought of another bout seemed impossible. She seemed to draw his very life from him when she took him inside as though an unseen pair of hands were holding him, squeezing his vital energies away.

"Please, Beatrice . . ." he whispered. "I must have words."

Her hand snaked through the darkness, found his own sweaty palm, touched it with her cool heat. "Speak, my James . . ."

"Now that I have lost my patron," he began, "I am afraid I will fail."

"There are other patrons. Other cities full of foolish old men with no talents of their own, but the coins to own another's." She stroked his thigh with long fingernails.

"I fear I lack the folly and energy of youth to go through the pain of finding another like Manutius. . . .Perhaps he was correct when he said I have changed? I feel it also—I don't have the impetus, the *soul* for my pursuits as I once possessed."

Beatrice laughed, her voice pealing like a wind chime in the humid night air. "Do not be so silly, my James! You are the shining star of Mantua, of Italy, and all of Europe!"

As though he did not hear her, his mind cast about for solutions that seemed beyond his grasp. "And what of my duel? Can you not realize what I have done? It is not every day that one kills the duke's personal champion! I fear Ludovico will have my head for this."

"James, if you have bested the duke's best, does that make you the best? The new champion?"

He sighed and rolled away from her touch, staring at the sculptured ceiling where smoky shadows danced. "It could . . . but that depends upon the duke and his whims. One must apply to the court for such a title . . . ."

"And . . ." she giggled again, moving closer to him under the silk coverlet.

"And I fear the gaze of Ludovico."

"Would you rather his foot soldiers come for you in the middle of the night?"

James felt confused, frightened, punctuated by bursts of his old swagger, his boldness, which upon reflection seemed so hollow. There was a twinge of panic in his heart. "I . . . do not know, Beatrice! I . . . do not know *what* I want, or what is happening to me!"

"Perhaps I might be of help. . ."   she touched his belly with her silky fingertips.

Trying to ignore her touch, and the passion it suggested, he spoke again. "How could you possibly help me in this?"

Her hand moved lower to the edge of his pubic hair. "I have had dealings with the ducal court. Perhaps I might make an intercession with Ludovico . . . ?"

"You know the duke?"

Beatrice giggled. "Of course. My father's connection with the court did not end with his death. There are always favors to be called in among the royalty. Besides, the duke fancies me."

James chortled. "I should think so! He *is* a man, is he not?"

"And so are you, my James . . ." Her hand moved lower still, performing her special magic upon his flesh.

Two fortnights' passage had seen great changes in the life of James Crichton. The beautiful Beatrice interceded for him at the Court of Mantua, and James enjoyed an audience with Ludovico il Moro. Surprisingly, the duke had been very cordial and warm, effusive even. The man had been familiar with the exploits and triumphs of "The admirable Crichton," and claimed it was an honor to meet him.

"It is rare, indeed, young Crichton, that we see a man skilled in the mental arts," il Moro had said. "And still that the selfsame man could be such an excellent swordsman. If any one ever deserved the title of Ducal Champion, it must be James Crichton!"

James was of course stunned by the public pronouncement, even though the warm flood of applause had become a natural thing in his life. He received an illuminated parchment from the Duke, a writ of decree, which named him Ducal Champion.

But there was more.

It seemed that the duke's eldest son, a brash youth named Vincenzo, was growing up to be a callous, incorrigible man, and the Duke sought a companion for his son. The ideal companion would be someone who might teach the boy a more cultured view of the world, while at the same time, school him in the ways of being a man.

The ideal companion, the Duke decided, would be James Crichton.

He was not certain how much influence Beatrice had exerted in gaining his position in the court, and he was not certain how grateful he should be for it. The appointment was a double-edged sword. There was plenty of money and courtly accoutrements, but there was also the company of Vincenzo—a young, coarse-featured, rough-voiced thug. Vincenzo's idea of entertainment was to carouse with a pack of rowdy friends till the taverns closed, then patrol the narrow, dirty streets in search of an unfortunate drunk who could be teased and played with as a cat might taunt a cornered mouse.

It was clear that James would teach the boy little of the ways of the world. He was too dense, too dull, and he possessed a vicious mien.

So while James's nights were filled with Vincenzo and his vile associates, his days were passed in growing frustration as he struggled to create the essays and epic poems commissioned by his new patron, Ludovico il Moro. He feared that Aldus Manutius had been correct.

Sitting in his suite at the Reggia, James waited for the words to appear on his crisp sheets of vellum, to trail from the end of his quill in dark, magic swirls. In the past, his work had flowed as effortlessly as the ink, and now the words simply would not come to him. He feared what all artists fear—the rueful day when he will be used up, his energies spent, his ideas expressed, his special vision faded like morning mist.

His Beatrice offered little in the way of encouragements other than her usual wanton readiness to take him to her bed. After struggling through pointless, artless days and drink-filled nights, he would drag himself to her door upon demand to be sucked into her silk sheets and cool fire. His days became so barren and empty, it seemed in a very short time, Beatrice became the only element of his life, which could inflame him to his old passion, his old enthusiasm. Locked in amorous combat, they would shake the oaken bed stand with their fury, and then she would leave him spent and so terribly tired.

To complicate all matters, James's fear of contracting a terrible disease increased. There were definite signs that he was indeed ill. His usual florid color was waning, and he had taken on a pale, wan aspect. His gait, once powerful and full of swagger, had been reduced to a slow, aimless shamble. And the light behind his eyes now seemed a dull flickering. He visited a surgeon who proscribed leeches to draw off some of the bad humors in his blood. Although it was a common medical practice, James had never wholly believed in the treatment. But he submitted this time because he had reached that point of despair that will accept anything that offers even the dimmest hope of relief.

A fortnight passed in endless repetition, and James found none of the relief he so desperately sought. Vincenzo grew more surly, unaffected by James' influence, and began to resent his presence during his escapades. The boy called him his father's watchdog, and the description was closer than James cared to admit. The duke grew impatient with his lack of output and began to question the brilliant reputation that had preceded his new champion. The crowds no longer followed him along the streets, and the university students stopped seeking his tutelage and scholarly advice. Every day became a labor, a burden requiring the greatest effort to simply endure.

But perhaps the cruelest blow was his rejection by Beatrice. He came to her in the middle of the night, his body drunken with sack, his mind numbed by its passage. She took him to her bed and for the first time he lacked the energy to respond. He felt as hollow as a rotten tree, as empty as the wind.

"I am sorry, my love. . ." he whispered weakly as she drew away from him.

"Do not be sorry," she said firmly. "It is not your fault."

There was a chilly edge to her voice and James suddenly felt cold as he lay by her. "I fear my life becomes unseamed . . . ."

Ignoring his plea for understanding, Beatrice glided from bed and stood by the window overlooking the Mincio River. Pale yellow moonbeams danced upon its currents. Turning, she faced him in glowing silhouette. "I must leave Mantua," she said softly, yet firmly.

"What?" James gasped, shocked by the declaration. "Why?"

"My family business is spread throughout Europe. My uncle in Paris has sent me a message by courier—he needs me there."

"Then I shall go with you!"

She laughed easily. It was a simple, innocent sound, yet was touched by the hint of condescension, as one may smile at the antics of a child. "No. That would be impossible. I must travel alone."

James sat up in the bed. The very moment was an effort and the weariness he felt seemed to center in the marrow of his bones. "Then, when will I see you again?"

Beatrice approached the bed, took his drawn face into her hands, and caressed his checks gently. She looked at him, her green eyes glowing in the darkness, their gaze penetrating him like a blade. "Ah, James, you are so young . . . so foolish and yet you were so wise . . . . Old Aldus was correct: you were different from most. And you remain so."

James felt nothing but confusion. What was she trying to tell him? "Beatrice, when will I see you again?"

She kissed him, parted his lips with her tongue and snaked into his mouth. For an instant there was a rush of passion in him, but she drew away and looked deeply into his eyes. "After tonight, never."

He felt as though he had been stabbed. The pain in his chest was so real, so terribly bright and edged with the ache of dread. "No!" he heard himself cry, sounding like a child. "What are you saying?"

"Only the truth, my James. I can tell you nothing else. I must leave this city, and I fear that I will not be returning."

"But I love you, Beatrice! I need you!" he almost shouted the words as he forced himself to stand, walking to her in his nakedness.

"Forget about me . . . . Our time together is almost passed round. Let us not end it this way."

She spoke with such finality, with such strength in the wake of his pitiful mewlings, that he knew his words were in vain. There was a weakness in him that even he detected, that he knew never had been there before. He felt that he must sound pathetic to her, and he wished to change this image. "No," he said, vowing to alter his attitude, his total posture. He grabbed her thin wrist and applied considerable pressure, pulling her close to him. "I will not let you leave!" He spoke through clenched teeth, summoning up all the anger and strength available.

"James . . . what are you doing?"

He pulled her to him roughly. "You go nowhere without me! You are mine. . ."

Moving with grace and incredible power, she broke his grip, seized his shoulders in her thin fingers, and pushed him back. He felt as though he had been yanked about by a smithy's pincers!

"No, James, I am no one's . . . not even completely my own." She pushed him, more gently this time, back to bed. "Don't make me hurt you—any more than I must."

There was something about the way she stood, a pose of defiance and an unbelievable power, which frightened him. In the darkness of the room she seemed to be an amorphous shape, an ever-changing creature as she moved through the textured moonlight. He had the feeling he had never really known this beautiful but mysterious woman, and *that* frightened him even more.

He wanted to speak, but some force prevented it. There welling up in the core of his being, in the deepest recess of his mind which was cloaked in the black shadows night. Part of him sensed he was facing a presence and an energy far greater than his. Never had he known a woman like Beatrice, and he knew that after her, all other women would be but pale imitation.

He fell across the bed and she seemed to hover over him. Long hair fell down in an endless cascade about her, past her shoulders to touch the swell of her breasts. Her skin seemed to glisten and give off radiant heat. As she spread her thighs and moved over him, he could smell the moist, musk odor of her natural scents. He felt her cast a wizard's spell as she touched him with invisible touches and urging him to hardness.

"One last time, my James," she said sweetly. "It will be easier this way."

He could not reply for she had descended upon him, grabbing him and lifting him up in her rhythmic motion. She carried him along on her journey of passion, staring into his eyes as he watched helplessly. Her eyes grew wide and shimmered with green iridescence. As he her, she seemed lost in her own ecstasies, oblivious to him beneath her. She was like an animal in heat, a maddened wheel turning in upon itself. He felt as though he could be devoured by her, so savage were her thrusts and moves.

And yet she did not utter a sound. Not a whimper, not a single cry of delight or pleasure. As frantic a joining she orchestrated, it was also cold, detached, and completely dispassionate. So exhausted, so drained did he feel, it seemed an eternity before she brought him to the edge and then pushed him beyond, the explosion leaving him practically incoherent. As she slid away from him, she spoke, but he could not make out the words. For an instant thought that he might expire from the effort of simply rolling over to his side.

" . . . and that will be the last of it," he finally heard her say. She moved to the dressing closet, pulled on a gown, then returned to him. "Did you hear me, James?"

'What?"

"I must now prepare for my journey. I leave at dawn."

"So early . . ." It was an effort for him to speak.

"Yes, and you must now depart. This was our union of farewell, as I said."

Suddenly he was fully awake, and her words stung him as before. "What? You . . . you want me to leave? To simply walk away from your life . . . as though I never knew you?"

She smiled and he could see a suggestion of sadness in her eyes. "I know you could never do that, my James, but believe me when I tell you that I must leave . . . and therefore, you also." She turned back to the dressing closet, pulled out racks of clothing, and began throwing them upon the bed.

"Get dressed," she said calmly as James continued to stare at her in disbelief.

The words were spoken like a queen's command, and without thinking, he found himself standing up, drawing on his stockings and britches, and buttoning his blouse about his sunken chest. He did not remember finishing the task, but he was finally dressed, staring at her. She touched his shoulder and urged him toward the door to the stairs, which led down to the street.

"You were sweet, James. As sweet as the buds of youth can only be. And you will always be in my thoughts, wherever I go," She kissed him once, without passion. "Good-bye . . ."

He stepped back and the door was sliding toward him. It touched the sill softly, followed by the click of the latch holding fast. He felt so exhausted that every step was an effort, and his progress down the Piazza delle Erbe was slow and aimless. Surely he was very ill. The leeching had not helped his condition, of that he was certain. But it was too late to care about such things. His Beatrice was leaving him. The rest of his life was in broken pieces, and he finally knew the meaning of desperation. He had nowhere to go, no one to see.

The Piazza was deserted as he moved down its wide paving. The city was quiet as a tomb, and dawn would be touching the dark places within the hour. Along its concourse, perpendicular streets and alleys cut off into deep shadows, twisting out of sight. He stepped into one of them without thinking, and continued to move without purpose or thought. He felt nothing other than a heavy sense of dread, of futility and uselessness.

Suddenly there came the sound of voices. In the distance, the raucous banter of young men came snaking up narrow, dirty passages. Some were singing, while others cursed boldly. James rounded a bend in the street, passing under an ancient archway, to see the small band of revelers. They moved as one, huddled together as a pack of predators in the night.

One of them spied him in the foreground and pointed his way. The others laughed and jeered, and they all scuttled after him like insects. James drew his hooded cape up his head, veiling himself in shadow.

"It's late to be walking these dark streets," said one of rascals.

The crowd laughed drunkenly.

Perhaps we should show you what can happen to people out by themselves . . . on a dark night . . . on a dark street."

James said nothing, but stood in the shadows, realizing that there was a familiar sound to one of the voices in the pack: Vincenzo, the duke's profligate son.

Finally, he thought, Fate had given him the answer.

Without saying a word, he drew his rapier. The pack drew back in one quick motion. He heard the sound of garments rustling, of weapons being drawn.

'Fool!" cried one of them. "You dare face us all?"

"I face your best first," said James in a hoarse whisper. The effort to draw and raise his sword had been staggering. "Each of you will have the chance to taste my steel."

There was a chorus of laughter from the band of rowdies, and, as James expected, Vincenzo stepped forward, a malevolent drunken grin upon his homely face.

"Your first will be your last, stranger!" cried the duke's son, and thrust forward.

James parried the blow reflexively, such was his training, but he sensed that he had not the strength nor the determination to counter. Under other circumstances, he could have dispatched Vincenzo in an instant. But this moment was different . . . .

The youth withdrew and twisted inward, bringing up his blade in a basic move. The handle and hilt seemed an impossible weight in James' hand, and he could not parry the attack. There was a ring of metal against metal, and a brief resistance, then the rapier was whipped from his weak grip. It clattered to the cobblestones amid the cheers of the pack.

Falling back against the wall of a shop, James looked calmly into the wild eyes of Vincenzo, who was glowing with the thrill of his small triumph.

"I submit," said James, "to your mercy."

Vincenzo laughed, "Fool! For those who would attack me, I have no mercy!" And with that he stepped forward, driving his steel into James's chest.

He felt a cold puncture, which slid off a rib to enter his heart. There was a galvanic spasm that radiated up his neck and down his arms as his lifeblood gushed from the wound before the blade had even been fully withdrawn. He slid down the face of the wall, summoning the last of strength to speak a final phrase: "Your lack of mercy . . . is all I hoped for."

The last thing he saw was the confused expression on Vincenzo's face.

Chapter 5

New York City

I Love New York!

Sophia had seen the phrase all over the city, symbolized by the black and white lettering and the red heart. At first she was confused by the cryptogram, but when she learned its simple meaning, she made it her motto.

She *did* love Manhattan, convinced that there was no other modern city, which offered more adventure or opportunity. Standing at the window of her suite in the Waldorf-Astoria, she looked down Park Avenue, where the morning sun burned across the edges of the powerful skyline. She would do very well here, she thought. There was a knock at the door and she turned to answer it. Wearing only a flimsy coral peignoir she had purchased in Paris, she unlocked the door and pulled it open.

A young man in a white waistcoat and black, silk tie stood transfixed by the vision that greeted him. He stood hunched over a chromium cart decked with silver service, his mouth slightly agape for an instant.

"Uh . . . you called for room service?"

Sophia smiled. "Of course. Bring it in, please." She whirled away from him with a dancer's move, feeling his gaze burning on her back as he followed her into the room.

The young man carefully brought up several folding leaves from the edges of the cart, transforming it into a miniature table. He rearranged the setting, unveiling a breakfast of steak and eggs, buttered croissants, a sliced grapefruit, and a pot of tea. There was a single yellow rose in a silver vase to accent the entire display, and Sophia found it to be very beautiful.

She moved to her dressing table and removed a ten-dollar bill from the cash compartment of her shoulder bag, then glided back to the waiter and handed it to him. He took it reflexively, not even noticing the denomination.

"Thank you," she said, unable to repress a small giggle.

"Oh, yeah, thanks," he said, backing toward the door as though unable to stop looking at her.

If she had been feeling more playful, she might have teased him a bit and then taken him, but she had too much work to do, so she ushered him to the door, pushing it closed behind him. She was famished from her day of traveling and the encounter with Rob Lester, and she repaired to her breakfast immediately.

On the bottom of the shelf of the cart there was a copy of the *New York Times*, which she had specifically requested. There would be much to learn about her new home, and the best way to discover things such as available residences, furnishings, banks, transportation, and entertainment would be to consult the local publications. As she perused the pages, she learned much from the articles and advertisements.

There were many things going on in the city, and she was truly amazed at the amount of information to be gleaned from the pages. She ate slowly, digesting her food as well as the cyclopedic data, taking notes on a small pad. Several hours passed as she constructed a list of things to do and places to visit. The next few days were going to be very busy for her. She knew she would need a guide, a native who could maximize her time, and she knew who that person would be.

Moving to the telephone, she called Rob Lester.

"William Morris Agency," said a distracted young female voice.

"Connect me with Mr. Lester, please."

"May I tell him who's calling?"

"Sophia Rousseau."

The secretary asked her to repeat the first name, which she did. There followed a series of clicks, some kind of muted, bland music, and then another click.

"Sophia, baby! How are you?" Lester's voice was crisp and perfectly modulated.

"Hello, Rob, I was wondering if I could ask a few favors of you."

He laughed. "Hey, are you kidding? You just name it." He paused, cleared his throat. "You know, I gotta tell you, I'm a little surprised to be hearing from you."

"Really? Why is that?"

"I don't know . . . just a feeling I had. But look, what can I do for you?"

She explained to him her need to find a residence, to establish herself, then asked him if he could find the time to help her.

"Hey, are you kidding? I mean, what are friends for right?"

"Right," she said, smiling to herself.

"All right, listen where are you? I gotta take lunch with this guy, but I could meet you around two this afternoon. That sound okay?"

"Yes, that will be fine. I am staying at the Waldorf. Call for me at the desk when you arrive."

"You bet, honey. See you at two."

She replaced the receiver and stood up from the bed, stripping off her nightgown. It felt good to be naked against the suite's warm air, and she wished she could be free of the restraints of clothing more often. It was odd how the societies of men became more repressive as they became more advanced, she thought idly, and walked off to the shower.

"This is probably the best section of town," said Lester as he escorted her along Riverside Drive north of 88th Street. "If you're looking for an older place, that is. They've got some great co-ops and condominiums on the East Side near the U.N. Building."

"It *is* very pretty along here," she said. "I loved the old brownstone back there, but I also liked the models in the Trump Tower. I can't decide, Rob."

He laughed. "Jeez, everybody should have such problems. How'd you get such heavy change, lady?"

"Heavy change?"

"Sorry . . . that's an American idiom. It means money, *beaucoup* money."

She smiled. From what little she had learned of the American language, she already enjoyed the penchant for clever phrases. The English were so stolid and proper all the time, and this new variation of the language was a refreshing change. "I told you that I was very successful in Europe. Modeling and acting can pay very well. And I made some wise investments."

He shook his head. "You *must* have. I make some good bucks myself, and I'm not going to be moving into the Trump Tower any time soon."

They turned left at the next cross street and walked toward

Columbus Circle. The weather was balmy, but the sun occasionally broke through the clouds warm and bright. It was a perfect April day, and many of the alfresco restaurants had tables filled with a fashionable lunchtime crowd. Lester guided her to a table in front of a small place called Chez Shay and held her chair.

Pulling her notepad from her shoulder bag, she began checking her list methodically. "Let me see, I've taken care of my international currency, my banking, and I have to make a decision about my residence. Will it be necessary to purchase an automobile?" She looked at him with a gentle smile, being careful not to excite him. He had been taking her in with a lustful eye ever since he met her in the Waldorf lobby, and since she had serious business to attend, she had been doing her best to downplay her natural attributes.

"What?" He had been staring at her, but obviously not listening.

She repeated her question and he shook his head. "I don't know. I've got a Jag in a midtown garage, and I hardly use the damn thing. When I think of what I pay to park it and the insurance and all that kind of shit, I wonder if it's worth it."

"Really? I think so many of the autos are so . . . sensual. So beautiful."

"Yeah." He smiled. "You would, wouldn't you? I don't know, it's like I said. If you can afford it, you can get anywhere you want in the cabs. There's buses and subways, but they're full of *gonifs.*"

"Full of what?"

"Oh . . . more slang, sorry. That's Yiddish. You know, like German. Do you speak German?"

"I have been known to do so."

"Yeah, well, Yiddish is like German. The Jews speak it. My grandmother spoke it all the time.."

"You still haven't told me what you said . . ."

Lester smiled. He was, in some ways, a charming little boy. He had a lot of slickness about him, which she tried to ignore, but once in a while, his real self slipped out. "Oh, yeah, right . . . gonifs: that's *thieves*. You get the picture?"

"I think so."

A waiter appeared and handed them menus. The wind tossed Sophia's long blond hair off her face as she looked up at him, and the young man paused to appreciate her stunning appearance. "Hi," he said weakly. "My name is Billy, and I'll be at your service. Just signal me when you're ready."

Lester opened the menu and scanned it quickly.

"Think I'll get the London broil and a Beck's. What about you?"

She ordered quiche and a glass of the house white wine, disappointed that they had no Montrachet Poulligny. Then she returned to her list. She would have to give her decision to the realtor quickly. She could not operate out of the hotel indefinitely, regardless of how plush she was treated there. In the final analysis, the hotel was a temporary existence, and she preferred to be surrounded by things that suggested a more permanent state of being.

She drew in a deep breath and smiled. Oh, it was so *good* to be so free!

"What're you smiling about?" Lester had been watching her again.

"Nothing. You would not understand."

"Try me."

"I have already done that. You are adequate."

He laughed nervously. "Hey, nice put-down! Whoa! I didn't know I had that one coming."

Ignoring his attempts at humor, she spoke again. "Regardless of what you say, I may purchase an automobile."

"Whatever you say, lady. If you can afford it, go for it, that's what I say. You only go around once, right?"

She looked at him oddly. "What was that?"

"You only go around once. You only live once, and it's not for all that long, so you may as well live it up, right?"

She looked at him and pondered the philosophy of the statement. The hedonists would be proud to know their doctrines had not been eroded by time. A little more crudely phrased, perhaps, but still valid all the same. It made her think of how fragile human life actually was, and how fortunate the Three Sisters had been to her.

"Yes . . ." she said after a pause. "You only go around once."

Lester looked at her, noticing the sudden change in her mood. "What's the matter, I say something wrong?"

"No, I was just thinking."

The waiter returned with their orders and reluctantly drew away from the table.

"You know, you're a pretty strange lady sometimes, I don't mind telling you. I've never met anybody like you before."

She grinned, nodding slowly as she sipped the white wine. It was flat and harsh, lacking any real bouquet. "I have been told that before."

"Yeah, well it's true." Lester looked at her with an odd expression, and she wondered what he was thinking. When she said nothing, he shook his head and smiled sheepishly, then began eating the rare beef entrée. She sampled her quiche, and watched the pass-ersby as they dined in silence for a few moments. If everything about the people of the city could be revealed by the way they dressed, then she had already seen, within a few short minutes, representatives of every social class. Most of the blacks and Latin foreigners seemed to occupy the lower economic niches; the Asians and Europeans were more scattered across the scale; the majority of the upper-class representatives seemed to be primarily Euro-pean/Caucasians. She thought it interesting that Americans liked to call their country a wonderful democracy with a classless soci-ety, but it was obviously not true, and never had been.

"You know," said Lester, interrupting her thoughts. "I've been thinking . . ."

She looked up at him, noticing he had lost all his veneer of confidence and bubbly flair. He seemed nervous. "Yes?" she said simply.

"I've been thinking that you might be interested in getting some work . . . you know, modeling, acting, whatever."

Sophia smiled. "And you would like to help me?"

He cleared his throat. "Well, yeah. I'd like to represent you, actually. Help's not the right word here. I was wondering if you'd like to have an agent. William Morris—the biggest and the best. I get my people the best gigs."

"Gigs?"

He grinned, regaining a bit of his usual style. "Gigs, you know, jobs, assignments, work."

"Oh, yes, I see . . . More slang?"

"More like jargon, really. Specialized language of the indus-try. You don't get jobs, you get gigs, get it?"

"If you say so." She sipped her wine.

He finished off the last of his dark German beer, and wiped his lips with a napkin. "So what do you say? I represent you and handle all the contracts, all the bullshit, and I only take my ten percent."

"Your fee, I presume."

"Hey, I'm not a nonprofit organization. Something's gotta pay the garage fees for that Jaguar." He chuckled. "So, do we have a deal? I would've said that I can make you a star, but they all say that. Besides, this time I think it's true, so who needs to say any-thing—it's probably gonna happen anyway."

"I am glad that you feel that way. Ten percent is the standard fee. That is quite satisfactory." She paused to sip the inferior white wine. "What kind of . . . 'gigs' do you have in mind for me?"

Lester leaned closer across the table, taking her hand. She purposely tried to keep him from getting excited. "Listen," he said in a conspiratorial tone, "I gotta tell you straight: with a face and a body like yours, I can get you *anything*! I ain't telling you this so it gives you a swelled head, but it's the truth. You could go a long way in this business."

She looked at him with a noncommittal expression. Having Lester bring up the proposition was exactly what she had expected. Working in the field of modeling and acting would be a perfect way to meet the kind of people she needed. It was funny to hear Rob talk about her getting a 'swelled head' . . . as though she was not aware of her effect on people.

"So, what do you say?" asked Lester, who had been waiting impatiently.

Smiling, Sophia released his hand and leaned back in her chair. "I say okay."

Lester burst into nervous laughter, rubbing his hands together. "Really! Hey, that's great! Just great, honey. All right, listen. Let's go back to my office, and I'll have the contracts drawn up. If you want, I can have you working tomorrow!"

"I think that is a bit early. I still have some business to take care of, remember?"

"Yeah, right, well I can get you a gig whenever you want to start, how's that?"

"That sounds fine."

Lester signaled for the waiter and the check, pulling an American Express card from his billfold. He smiled broadly as he signed the receipt and stood up from the table. "Okay, baby, let's go. We're going to go a long way together . . . and you can go to sleep on that one, believe me!"

The escalator carried her majestically up through the initial levels of the huge Italian marble atrium. It was a daring piece of modern architectural triumph: polished chrome and brass, cantilevered banks of hanging gardens, a waterfall gently whispering down its ten-story cascade to a fountain bay in the lobby, where a string quartet played Haydn. As she transferred to each new level of the Trump Tower, Sophia casually noted the types of boutiques and shops offering their exclusive wares. I'm so glad I decided upon the Tower, she thought warmly. It symbolized everything that was new and bold and challenging about her new home.

She could have taken the elevators from the lobby level directly up to her penthouse, but she preferred using the tiers of escalators up to the level of the solarium above the shops. It was more leisurely, and certainly more aesthetic. What a beautiful place to live!

From the solarium she boarded a high-speed lift to the fiftieth floor, and walked down the heavy-carpeted hall to her door. After she had signed the papers, the Tower management had begun executing her interior design selections, and after a week the work had been finished. Her furniture had been delivered, and she was busy getting things organized. It was so difficult to start over from practically nothing, and she had been thankful to have made wise investments in the past. Gold and precious stones had saved her, as they had in other bad times.

The phone was ringing as she entered the apartment, and she moved quickly to answer it. "Hello?"

"Where've you been, baby?" It was Lester. "I've called three times this morning. Don't you ever check your machine?"

"I just this moment arrived. I have not had time to do anything. What is it?"

"I've got a jeans commercial with Touché. They need three ladies who rock, and I thought of you. It's not a big deal, but it's a good place to start. Touché runs their ads on the tube all the time. It'll be great exposure for a new face." He paused. "So what do you say? You want it?"

Sophia smiled. Her first assignment. Jaded as she could be, the thought of it excited her. "Yes! Of course I want it! That's wonderful, Rob."

He chuckled softly. "Okay, meet me at my office at two this afternoon. We'll take a ride over to the studio where they're going to shoot so you can meet the director and the crew."

"When do we 'shoot'?" she asked as she surveyed the spacious living room with approval.

"They're scheduled for Friday. That's okay with you, I assume."

"Friday will be fine."

"Okay, gotta run. See you at two." There was a click at the other end of the line, and she replaced the receiver. There was so much to do! Even though her furniture had been delivered, the apartment still had a cold, barren aspect to it. The chocolate-brown leather chairs and wrap-around couch looked lonely and abandoned as they floated in the bone-white froth of the thick carpeting. She had yet to select pictures for the walls or accessories for the shelves and tables. The rooms lacked any of the personal touches, which always marked her residences of the past.

But that would change . . . .like many other things that touched her life.

Chapter 6

Scarpino, Sicily

Low-slung clouds scudded across the moody sky as Matthew Cavendish stepped from his hotel on the Via Ruggero Settimo, frowning. Because his plane into Palermo International Airport had been delayed for several hours, he had not reached his quarters until late afternoon, which meant he would have to begin his investigation just as night was coming on, or wait until morning. Damn! It would be difficult to start poking around in a mountain village just as dusk was settling in. Peasants were a superstitious, suspicious lot when it came to dealing with strangers, and it was doubtful that they'd be too terribly cooperative in the daylight . . . much less by the light of the moon!

The bloody hell with it, he thought, as he hailed a taxi from the many blurs which careened down the wide boulevard. I can at least go up there and get my bearings. These bumpkins won't keep me from the truth!

A red Fiat snicked out of the traffic flow and wheeled toward him. Its tires squealed and the chassis strained at its suspension as the taxi jerked to a halt by the curb. Matthew climbed into the backseat as the cab ripped away from the sidewalk before he could even close the door—the act of rapid acceleration accomplished the task without him. He found himself wondering how the olive-complected driver could be in such a damnable hurry when he did not yet know his destination.

The cab lurched to a stop at the next intersection, and the driver turned to look questioningly at Matthew. "You Americans, you like-a the fast cars, yes?" he said with a smile. "Where you want me take-a you? Anywhere! You name it, Signoree!"

"I am not American, and I don't give a damn how bloody fast your car might be. What I would like is a ride to Scarpino. "

The driver chuckled. "Britannico! You are Inglese! I am sorry, Signoree. I thought you were one of those silly Americans!"

Matthew forced himself to smile and sunk back into the seat. "That's quite all right . . . now, can you take me to Scarpino?"

"Why you want-a go there? Is nothing in Scarpino."

"Please, can you take me there?"

"Sure, I take you. Gonna cost some Euros, though."

"That is quite all right. Now, please, let's be off!"

Turning back to the wheel, the driver laughed and popped the clutch, making the little car leap away like a frightened rabbit. Doing his best to ignore the man's antics, Matthew watched the city of Palermo pass by his window. It was a very cosmopolitan center, easily the largest, most modem city on the entire island of Sicily. The cab performed a complex dance, a traffic-weave down the wide boulevard, and Matthew watched as they passed endless shops and boutiques, alfresco restaurants, and cafes. As the cab headed west, the streets became more narrow, the buildings more quaint, and the evening sky more gray. He passed a gigantic outdoor market where the crowds bubbled and flowed like lava. Through the open front window, Matthew could smell the aromas of roasted meats, baked onions, and marinades, all mixed in an atmosphere that crackled with laughter and a rush of voices.

As the taxi moved through the narrowing streets, the lights and attractions became more scarce until finally Matthew was passing simple avenues of residential homes all squeezed into tight, clean little blocks. Upon reaching the outskirts of the city, he noticed the road began to get rougher, steeper. He passed hilly farms and shepherds' rocky land as the taxi strained into the foothills.

Within a half-hour, the driver stopped the car in the center of a small village. There was a fountain in the middle of the square, and a few pedestrians passed by the almost empty street. There was a cafe nearby, where several men sat outside, drinking and talking loudly.

"Scarpino, Signoree," said the driver, shaking his head. "You will want-a me to wait for you, si?"

Matthew considered the question. It would be difficult to get transportation back to Palermo from here, especially after sundown. He nodded and gave the driver a 50-Euro note, telling him to relax at the cafe while he waited. The driver smiled and promised that he would be ready whenever Matthew wished to return.

Matthew climbed from the back, of the Fiat, hefted his valise off the seat. He walked briskly across the square as the village men watched his approach with wary silence.

Here I go again, he thought wearily. The odd stranger asking lots of nosy questions about their "secrets." It was a role he had assumed in many out-of-the-way places around the world, but one to which he had never grown accustomed.

He walked up to the closest table where three older men sat hunched over wineglasses and a plate of olives, bread, and cheese. They eyed him as though he had just stepped out of a flying saucer, and no one spoke.

"*Mi scusi,*" said Matthew, his Italian not very good, his Sicilian dialect far worse. "*Mi chiamo* Cavendish. Matthew Cavendish . . . *Buona sera . . .*"

The largest of the three men, who wore a brown cap and smoked a dark cigar-ette, smiled mockingly. "*Come sta?*" he asked.

Matthew returned the smile. "*Sto bene, grazie.*" He paused and looked about the square. "*Vorrei fare la conoscenza del sacerdote?*"

The men looked at him with some surprise, an he was not certain they understood. "I would like to meet the priest of your village. *Lei parla Inglese?*"

"I speak a small English," said an older man with a silvery beard of several days growth. "What do you want?"

Matthew explained to the man that he was a writer of travel books who needed to interview Scarpino's priest about the new church they were building. It was an old scam, which usually stopped a lot of questions. Almost every peasant and small-village native lusted after the chance to bring tourist-dollars into their own pockets. The men at the table were suddenly very cooperative and all three attempted to escort him to see Father Mancusio, their pastor. He could see the church, which was readily visible down the main avenue, its white spire easily the highest structure in the village. Matthew thanked them and began walking down the street toward the church.

Father Mancusio was nothing like Matthew had expected. Blond and smooth-faced, the young Neapolitan priest had just been sent to his new parish in Scarpino. He was a modem, well-educated man, who seemed genuinely happy to meet Matthew and speak with him. They sat in the parlor of the rectory and talked in English for several hours. During that span, Matthew learned much of what he would need to conduct his investigation.

"Scarpino is growing," said Father Mancusio. "That is why they built a new church. But in some ways, it remains a very small village. News travels quickly in a place like this, and even the best-kept secrets are soon known to everyone."

Matthew nodded and smiled. "How else would I have ever heard of your strange happenings here!"

The priest nodded but did not smile. Matthew supposed that the cleric did not approve of the kind of books Matthew wrote—books that sensationalized that which God-fearing folk would call miracles of the Creator. And the books of Matthew Cavendish never mentioned any creator, or god, or anything that smacked of the divine. That would have been too easy, and would rob so much of the mystery—and, therefore, the appeal—from Cavendish's best-selling volumes. Matthew fingered his notepad and pencil anxiously. The conversation was starting to collapse under its own weight, and there were still a few items that he felt he must mention. The pastor looked at him with clerical patience, but appeared to be tired of Matthew's questions.

"Tell me," said Matthew, with a laconic grin, "What do you know about the history of this village? Of this Father Mazzetti in particular."

"What do you mean?"

"I mean, doesn't it strike you that perhaps someone was out for revenge on the poor chap? Rattling about his bones, and all that? Seems rather nasty to me . . ."

Father Mancusio nodded with a measure of solemnity. "Oh, yes, I see." He paused to consider the question. "Well, to be honest with you, I'm still fairly new to this parish, and I haven't had the time to catch up on its history. There is a journal kept on the history of each parish. There are several bound volumes in the library, but I have not looked at them since first taking this assignment. If you would like, I could look up the years of Father Mazzetti's tenure here. . . ."

"Yes, that would be splendid," said Matthew. "if you truly wouldn't mind, I would he very grateful." He stood up and began packing his things back into his valise, noticing a faint suggestion of relief upon the priest's face. "Well, I must be going now, Father. It's getting late, and I don't wish to keep you from your own duties."

"Really, it has been a pleasure to meet you, Mr. Cavendish."

Matthew shook his hand and smiled. "Yes, well thank you very much for all the information, and your offer to check up on the history of Father Mazzetti. Would it be all right to stop by tomorrow afternoon?"

"Certainly."

The young priest walked Matthew to the door, ushering him out into the cool air of the Sicilian night. As Matthew walked down the deserted street, its narrow confines forming huge pitch-dark shadows, where even the light of the moon and the stars could not reach, he felt as though he were being watched by many unseen eyes, as though the village were aware of a stranger in its midst.

Upon reaching the cafe, he was surprised to find it closed. His taxi driver had returned to his Fiat, where he was dozing easily behind the wheel. Matthew tapped his fist on the roof of the small car to rouse the man, who smiled and stuck out his left hand, asking for an advance on the return fare.

Matthew climbed into the backseat, produced another note from his billfold, and settled in for the harrowing ride back to his hotel. The taxi moved quickly through the small streets, down a grade, and past the village cemetery. Matthew glanced at the stones glowing in the pale moonlight, and wondered what rough beast might have stalked these grounds.

"And could you possibly describe what you saw when you lifted the slab?" Matthew waited for his question to be translated into the Sicilian dialect by the Conti Demolition Company's office clerk. He had awakened early, and decided to possibly interview the laborers who had initially reported the serpent in the stone, before returning to Scarpino.

Guiseppe, the laborer who had claimed to have been the first to see the serpent, nodded and issued forth a rapid stream of excited language. The man seemed uncomfortable sitting in the brightly lit offices of his employer, and his eyes darted about with a mixture of fear and suspicion.

"He says that when he lifted the slab," said the interpreter, "there was a loud hissing sound, like air brakes on a truck. It was obvious that the old altar had been sealed tight like a vault or a tomb. Then he looked down and saw a huge green snake. It was very long and very bright green, like a green neon sign in a tavern. He says he yelled and moved back, and that's when the other workers crowded around. They all saw it, he says . . . but there was something about the way the snake looked at them, the way it just stared into all of their eyes . . . that none of them moved. They all just stood watching it, as it wriggled off into the rubble and disappeared."

Matthew nodded, and looked benignly at the Palermitan laborer. "Can you describe its eyes, the way it looked?"

After the company clerk translated his question, Guiseppe nodded and swallowed. He spoke more softly this time, as though with a reverence for what he was remembering. "He says that they were not the eyes of a snake which looked at him, but a monster, a demon, a thing of great and terrible knowledge."

"How could you know this?" asked Matthew.

After hearing the translation, the laborer looked at Matthew and smiled nervously, then spoke quickly to the clerk. "He says that if you ever see that snake, you will simply know."

Matthew studied the laborer. There was a subtle, emotional residue in the man's eyes, a remembrance of something that had instilled respect, and probably fear, in him. Matthew knew he was telling the truth. Turning off his portable tape recorder, a signal that the interview had been completed, Matthew thanked the translator and the young laborer for their cooperation. He promised them that they would be included in his next book, which pleased them immensely.

That was the last of the men who had been present when the altar of the old village church had been dismantled. Interviewing each man separately, Matthew had been able to scrutinize each story and discover any inconsistencies that might exist. To a man, each laborer told a story so similar that Cavendish was convinced it could not have been a fabrication. The attention to details, when he asked for them was exquisite and spontaneous—a sign that the story being told was true and not memorized earlier. Matthew had long ago learned not to accept prepared statements from his subjects. Too easy to lay on the bullshit, he thought with a smile.

No, these simple workmen were not making up a story, of that he was certain. They all described the snake as being a bright iridescent green, its scales sparkling with all the colors of the rainbow at different moments. And they all claimed to have been somehow captivated by the mere sight of the creature, so they were powerless to make an attempt at catching it.

Now it is up to me to decide what the hell it is and how it got there, Matthew thought, smiling to himself as he walked down the hall toward the door to the street. Well, maybe I need not decide, but merely offer a few speculations . . . . Yes, that was always the best way to handle it: in the tradition of Charles Fort himself.

Matthew left the offices of Conti Demolition and looked for a cab. Luckily, he had been able to arrange all the interviews with the laborers early in the day, and he still had plenty of time to spend back in Scarpino. A large sedan pulled up to the curb and a female cabbie leaned out and smiled at him. Things were looking up, he thought jauntily.

"What makes you think I would show you the mausoleum?" asked Enrico Corbi as he stared at Matthew. The man was short and very old, but he moved with a strength and a surety that bespoke a much younger man. Corbi's eyes were gray and cold but full of depth, and his deeply lined face was that of a survivor, a man who would do anything necessary to come out a winner.

Matthew smiled as he leaned back in the chair at Corbi's simple table. The Spartan confines of the caretaker's cottage surrounded him like a woman's shawl. He knew what the old man was angling for, and Matthew was in no mood to play games. He spoke haltingly in the slangy dialect of the island.

"I'll pay you, if that's what it will take. Now let's stop this crap! I want some information, you want some lira. Fine. Let's get going with it!"

Corbi smiled, revealing uneven, rotting teeth. "You are a smart man, Signoree. All right, I will show you what you wish to see. Come."

Matthew followed him toward the door, inwardly cursing the caretaker. When Matthew had first introduced himself to Corbi, the old man had played very dumb. It had required almost thirty minutes before Corbi would admit to even the possibility of something strange happening in his village, and then it was only by the most subtle implication. He admitted to drinking too much at the cafe one evening several weeks ago, and then observed coolly that rumors could spread like brushfire through small villages like his own. As to how the story had reached the city papers—even as a filler on a back page of the financial section—Corbi had no idea, and could care less actually.

The old man led the way out of his cottage and walked with a slow, deliberate gait through the narrow streets, a ring of keys jangling at his belt. Even in the harsh sunlight, there were comers and nooks that still lay in deep shadow. Matthew followed Corbi, taking in the details of the town, casting them in his mind's eye so that he would be able to describe them adequately when he wrote up this incident for his next book. Scarpino was a picturesque village, and he would have no trouble summoning up evocative images to capture it.

Eventually they came to the gates of the cemetery and the stone archway. Matthew read the inscription and smiled grimly. Once we were as you / soon you will be as we.

Funny how the Mediterranean countries such as Spain and Italy had such a fascination with death . . . but that wasn't quite the right word. It was not so much fascination as familiarity. Many of the peasants considered Death a member of the family, a part of life, so to speak.

Corbi gestured him into the cemetery and began walking toward the marble structure on a slight rise of ground—the mausoleum of the Mazzetti family.

"Not all of us can be buried so well, you know," said Corbi. "This was a well-to-do family, the Mazzettis . . . . My father used to speak that name with reverence."

As Matthew approached the black marble edifice, he began to let his mind free-associate. In the bright sunlight, with the smell of the lemon-tree blossoms in the air, it was difficult to think about what dark forces may have been at work here. And yet the grim, dark, aboveground crypt was a harsh, foreboding piece of work.

Approaching a heavy wrought-iron gate, Corbi pulled a key ring from his belt, and placed a key into the gate's lock. It yielded after some jimmying and pressure, swinging open to allow access into a stone threshold. A marble door faced them, and Corbi produced a key to unlock it.

"Watch your footing," said Corbi as the door swung inward into a dark abyss. "There are steps right here."

Matthew descended the seven steps into the main chamber of the mausoleum, which seemed much larger than he had thought from the outside. There were alcoves to both sides, each holding a coffin.

"Which one is the priest?" he asked.

Corbi pointed to a particular shelf.

"Can we open it?"

Corbi shrugged. "I would never say anything. But why?"

"Just a precaution. Let's have a look, all right?"

Corbi moved carefully, sliding the coffin off its shelf, tilting it down, then opening the lid.

What had been the skeletal remains of the village priest had been reduced to broken fragments and powdery residue. Dry rotted pieces of his burial raiment were stuffed down into the foot of the coffin.

"You replaced the remains?" Matthew asked Corbi.

The old man nodded. "As best I could. It was a terrible mess in here. I did not wish to linger."

Matthew scrutinized the contents of the coffin. As jumbled together as everything might be, he wanted to be certain not to over-look anything. There was nothing in particular he was searching for, not consciously at least, but he allowed his gaze to scan the interior of the coffin with a slow and studied eye.

Just as Corbi was about to speak, Matthew saw something.

" Wait!"

"What is it?"

"I don't know . . . but look, tucked into that fold of cloth, see it?"

"I see nothing," said Corbi.

Matthew took a small cellophane envelope from his briefcase and placed it by the fragments of Father Mazzetti's burial clothes. There was a semi-transparent, parchment-like membrane that Matthew eased from the folds of cloth and slipped into the envelope.

"Do you see it now?" he asked with a sardonic grin.

"Yes, but I still don't know what it is."

"That's what I'm going to find out. All right, you can close this up now."

As Corbi closed the lid, Matthew looked about the interior of the crypt, along the walls, the backs of the alcoves, the stone molding that ran along the comer of the walls, and the ceiling. On the wall opposite the entrance, he looked at the small window near the ceiling. With closely spaced bars it looked more like a vent than a window, and Matthew assumed that it served some sort of ventilating function.

The old man had sworn that the locks outside had been stiff and rusty when he entered the mausoleum—proof no one had preceded him for quite a long time. And yet the coffins had been strewn about like a deck of cards, the one of the village priest dreadfully savaged.

The only entrance, other than the locked door and gate, would be the small window. Matthew knew there were not many things that could fit through such an opening.

But he could think of one in particular.

Teresa DiCaponitti was the village termagant, the prototypical "wise old hag." And at the same time, she was just a tired, broken old woman. Her long gray hair was like bundled, brittle straw, and her face resembled a rain-runnelled field. She chuckled when Matthew introduced himself in his personal version of the regional dialect, but made no effort to be coy in answering his questions.

"Enrico sent you to me, didn't he?" She laughed, sounding

like the clichéd cackle of a hen.

Matthew nodded as he took a seat in front of her oven. She smiled as she continued to stir several small pots by the stove. Her kitchen was crammed with so many utensils and accessories that it was difficult to discern the original color or pattern of the walls.

"Did he tell you that I knew of things before he actually saw them?"

"Yes," Matthew said. "That is why I am here to see you. I write books about strange occurrences, and this incident is getting stranger by the minute. The more I hear, the odder it gets."

Teresa shrugged. "Not so strange. I hear the dogs howling and there is no moon. It is said that dogs can hear what we cannot."

Matthew shook his head and smiled. "No, Corbi said you knew. He said you told him to go to the graveyard."

Another cackle. Another shrug. "All right . . . how can I tell you? I get . . . feelings in my head, do you understand? Sometimes I just know what is happening . . . not always, but sometimes."

Matthew nodded. "It's not that uncommon, I assure you. Not surprising, really. So you knew that the grave had been disturbed . . . . All right, then, can you tell me by whom, or should I say by what?"

Teresa stirred her pots, then looked him straight in the eye. "No, of course not. I only knew that there was something wrong."

"What does it mean . . . to disturb the coffins like that?"

Teresa looked at him grimly. "Don't you know? It is the work of demons, of course!"

Matthew swallowed and nodded with as much nonchalance as he could muster. "Of course. Now, one other thing: did you know this priest, this Father Mazzetti?"

"You certainly can flatter a woman, Signoree Cavendish. I am old, but not that old. No, Father Mazzetti was dead before I was born."

"Do you have any idea why anyone might have a vendetta for a long-dead priest, or perhaps his family?"

Teresa smiled. "Vendetta is a very common word in this part of the world. There are vendettas for everything imaginable! I am sorry, Signoree, but there is no answer to such a question."

As he knocked on the door to the rectory, Matthew thought about that particular line the old woman had spoken and wondered if she could be correct.

"Si?" asked an elderly man who answered the door.

"I am here to see the pastor," said Matthew. He was ushered inside and escorted to a study off the foyer.

Father Mancusio appeared several minutes later, smiling weakly, carrying a large, deteriorating ledger. "Mr. Cavendish, Buon giorno! I have been expecting you."

"I hope I'm not stopping at an inconvenient time, but I just now finished interviewing some of the villagers, and I thought I might stop in." Matthew eyed the ledger under the priest's arm. "Found that diary you were talking about, did you?"

Mancusio's pale smile vanished. "Yes . . . yes, I did. I looked up the years of Father Mazzetti, and read them last night."

The inflection in the priest's voice conveyed a sadness, an unspoken wish that he had never peered into the dust of the old parish ledgers, thought Matthew. Funny how you could pick up on a person's feeling just by the sound of their voice—it didn't matter what language they might be speaking.

"Good reading, was it?" Matthew decided to be as glib as possible. It was a tactic that tended to disarm those who he sensed were becoming defensive.

The young priest sat down at a drawing table, set the ledger on the blotter, and avoided Matthew's gaze. "No, not really . . . . It was rather boring, actually. Made me wonder if my own entries made such tedious reading. Yes, Signoree Cavendish, it was quite boring. . . ."

Matthew smiled politely, but spoke quickly. ". . . except for the part about the snake, right?"

The expression of surprise on the young priest's florid face was all the answer Matthew needed. He had gambled and won, as the saying often went. The young man looked as if he'd been collared for shoplifting. He chuckled nervously and nodded unconsciously. "Why, yes! But, how did you know?"

"Oh, I didn't. Not for certain, anyway. But I am an investigator, Father . . . and I did have my suspicions, you know."

"I see . . . ."

"Care to tell me about it? I'm not very good at reading Italian."

Father Mancusio slumped back into his chair, his muscles losing some of their tension. "Very well, listen." The priest told the following story:

Although the entries in the old parish ledger were terse and without much description, it had been possible to piece together the essential elements of a fantastic tale. Father Mazzetti had been trained in Rome as an exorcist, and had established a great reputation in Sicily as the best at his specialized craft. And so it was not unusual when he received a letter from the Duke of Palermo, requesting his services. It seemed that the duke, a religious old man, suspected that one of his son's mistresses was possessed by demons. The duke wished for Father Mazzetti to speak with the young woman to determine if it might not be true. The duke's son was a gifted artist and musician at the age of only nineteen, and the Palermitan ruler wished to spare his oldest offspring any unnecessary pain or possible danger.

Father Mazzetti had the young woman brought to him under the pretense of attending a family dinner in the small village of Scarpino. The diary mentioned several un-described "tests" which the priest claimed to have applied to the young woman. Because she displayed certain indications, Mazzetti planned to expel the demon that possessed her. But when he confronted her, employing the instruments and prayers of his special service, the demon took the form of a serpent, destroying the woman and threatening to kill the priest by biting his throat out. Employing the Eucharist, Father Mazzetti claimed to have imprisoned the serpent under the altar of his church, where it would remain powerless for all eternity.

"That is all there is," said Father Mancusio, appearing unable to look Matthew in the eye. He appeared embarrassed by the story he had told.

"Do you believe it?" asked Matthew.

"Do you?"

Matthew laughed. "Oh, no. I asked you first."

The priest fidgeted about in his chair for a moment. "Well, the workers did report a snake escaping from the altar stone, did they not? Could it be that we have unleashed a demon upon the world because no one read the diaries of an old priest?"

"Perhaps, but I don't think so," said Matthew.

"You don't believe the story?"

He smiled. "I didn't say that."

"Well then, Signoreee, what exactly did you say?" The young priest seemed offended, and in no mood to play verbal games.

"I'm not so sure that a 'demon' has been let loose on the lot of us, is what I meant to say," said Matthew.

Father Mancusio seemed profoundly surprised. "Signoreee! If not a demon, then what?"

Matthew looked calmly at the young priest. "Ah, now, Father, I am not certain yet. I would like to keep all my options open at the moment."

"You are a strange man, Signoreee Cavendish," said the priest. "I hope that you do not take offense at my telling you so."

Well, at least the fellow was candid, thought Matthew. He grinned as impishly as he could manage, and extended his hand to the young pastor.

"You're certainly not the first person to tell me that!" He laughed disarmingly, and the priest joined him in some nervous chuckling. "Well," said Matthew. "I've got to be off now, Father. I would like to thank you mightily for all your help and cooperation. Hard to get these days . . . cooperation. Cheerio!"

Matthew left quickly and raced to keep his appointment with the village constable. He smiled as he moved through the narrow streets. The pieces were starting to come together, and he was beginning to think that he might be on to something bigger than a mere mention in his next book.

Chapter 7

New York City

The Touché shoot went very well.

Even though Sophia had never done a TV commercial, she had been able to work her way through the session as though she were a veteran. All she needed was to watch the other two models, and to listen to every word that was spoken. Her naturally intuitive mind allowed her to make all the right assumptions. None of the crew had any doubts that she had worked many European TV gigs.

She laughed aloud as she rode in the taxi back to her apartment. Gigs. She was starting to even think in the clever idioms of this new country, and it amused her. I am like a chameleon, she thought. I am supremely adaptable.

The thought was a comforting one, but it was not enough to sustain her. Sophia knew what she really needed to survive. Even though she had only been in the city less than a fortnight, she felt her inner energy beginning to wane. The last time she had changed had required much effort, and she knew the new moon was approaching once more.

Her biggest problem, she admitted, was logistics. She had not been in enough of the right places at the right times. She needed to be out circulating among the people, meeting the guiding lights of the age, the free spirits and free thinkers, the wild ones and the doomed ones.

Perhaps she was being too harsh in her feelings about Rob Lester. The thought touched her with a delicacy that she had not expected, and she turned it over in her mind, giving it special treatment.

The cab had stopped on Fifth Avenue just below the park, and the door was opened by one of Trump's Beefeater doormen. Sophia paid and tipped, then stepped out to the sidewalk. Immediately she was aware of the attention she began to receive. The open gaze and heated stares of both men and women were like the rays of the sun upon her flesh. It was a wicked sensation, a sensual treat. Dressed in thigh-high boots, tight jeans, and a peasant blouse, she looked like the height of fashion, even in a place where haute couture was the norm.

Entering the lobby and moving past the swarms of tourists and shoppers, Sophia paused to compose herself. What had she been thinking about? Oh, yes . . . Lester. Rob, the super-agent. There was a string quartet playing Mozart at the base of the atrium escalators; the music both soothed her and massaged her memory, bringing a bittersweet smile to her face.

Yes, she thought, I must rethink everything. I'm running out of time, and there is no room for panic or disorganization. Sophia stepped upon the escalator and began the slow ascent next to the marbled waterfall, the hanging gardens of the atrium. Her initial plans to discard Lester had been rash, she could see that now. He would be far more useful as a passkey, an entree into the worlds of the creative, industrious minds of this vibrant city.

Of course, there might have to be some changes in their relationship. Lester was the kind of man who expected sexual favors from his clients for getting them the choice jobs. He had been very up-front about his policy when Sophia had questioned him about it. "It comes with the territory," he had said with a smile.

To this, Sophia had simply returned his smile. She had planned to give him what he wanted until it killed him—which would not have taken very long.

But perhaps she could deter him from that deadly course. It might be possible to "educate" him, to make him understand that while there was no possibility for a physical relationship between them, there might be room for a more platonic, symbiotic arrangement. Something by which they might both profit. Sophia smiled as the escalator deposited her at the top level of the boutiques. She moved to the bay of elevators, thinking that she would like a shower before dinner. And then she would have a long talk with Lester.

He took her to a well-known club on the Upper East Side called Starkers. It was a big place on two levels. Downstairs contained the usual bar, band, and meat rack, while the second level attempted to be more civilized—tables, candles, a small stage with a young guy playing classical guitar, and a spread of appetizers to go along with the drinks. Rob had attempted to start the evening in the downstairs bar, but when she made it clear that they needed to talk, he ushered her up to a table on the second tier.

The place was amazingly soundproofed, and the blare of the rock music seemed like a distant memory as they took seats at a comer table.

"I gotta tell ya, I don't like the sound of this," said Lester. "Whenever a woman says 'we have to talk,' it means trouble for me."

"Not necessarily," said Sophia. "This is important."

"All right, so what is it? You didn't like the job? You don't want me to represent you? Come on, let's have it, babe." Lester seemed more hyper than usual, and he puffed on his cigarette without really even taking the time to inhale.

"I will be frank with you, Rob. It is the best way. We will, as you say, 'cut the bullshit,' right?"

Lester laughed. "Yeah, let's do that."

"All right," said Sophia. "I would like you to know that while I think you are a very good agent, and I respect your professional skills and knowledge immensely, I must stress that I have no romantic interest in you whatsoever."

Lester seemed to relax visibly. He smiled and almost laughed. "Is that all!? Listen, sweetie, that's okay with me. Hey, are you kidding? I can dig it, no time for love and all that stuff, sure. Sure, I can play it that way. No strings attached."

What the hell was he talking about? She occasionally still had trouble with some of the American idioms, and Rob seemed to be suffused with a never-ending supply of "hip" expressions. Yet, she had the impression that he still did not fully comprehend what she was telling him.

"I'm not sure I understand what you're saying, Rob. What do you mean, 'no strings attached'?"

He smiled easily, then took a sip of his drink, a move planned to be dramatic and suave. "I mean, it's okay if you want to get it on and not worry about my falling in love with you. I can handle it, okay?"

"I didn't think you were comprehending me. No, Rob, what I'm saying is this: let's cut off the physical part of our relationship altogether."

Lester appeared to have been stabbed. He sat bolt upright and his eyes widened. "What! No sex? Is that what you're saying? No sex, at all? You mean it's a just-let's-be-friends kind of deal?"

Sophia nodded, pushed a strand of blond hair away from her full, liquid eyes. "Yes, that is exactly what I'm saying. Believe me, it will be for your own good."

"Yeah, I've heard that one before . . . ."

"This time it is true. You don't know everything about me. I would be very bad for you."

"C'mon, I thought we had an understanding. What was all that business the first coupla times, huh?"

"I would call it a *mistake*," said Sophia. "I misjudged you."

"What?" Lester seemed confused.

"Listen," she said. "To put it as bluntly as possible, I think we can do more for each other by being business associates than by merely fucking each other. Can you understand that?"

Lester laughed. "Hey, do I look like a schmendrick? Of course I can dig that, but why? Why can't we have a little of both?"

"Because you don't know me. You don't know how bad I could be for you."

There was something about the way Sophia spoke those words that stopped Lester in his tracks. His leering grin vanished and he seemed to be considering her words seriously for the first time. After a pause he spoke in a self-conscious whisper. "Hey, listen, what are we talking about, here? Let me be frank—you got AIDS, or what?"

Sophia smiled despite the serious nature of their conversation. "No, it's nothing like that. No diseases . . . or anything you could imagine."

"Then what is it? Jesus Christ!" Lester paused. "What is this 'bad for me' business? What're you . . . in love with some heavy-weight boxer, or something? Is there some other guy you're hung up on?"

"No. Now please don't keep asking me these silly questions. I told you: you wouldn't understand." Sophia paused and looked at him, regaining her composure. "At least not now. Maybe later on, though. Maybe later I will be able to tell you."

"Really? Hey you're a real princess, you know that?"

"Rob, don't be angry or hurt. It is not becoming on you." She could not believe the way he was reacting, and in doing so, he revealed a side of Rob Lester that few people ever saw.

"Ah, I'm not hurt . . . at least I don't think so. Pissed off a little, yeah, but not hurt."

"Nobody ever hurts you, right?"

He looked at her with a wounded expression, uncertain if she were joking or being serious. "I don't know. . . ." Lester looked away from her and across the room where other couples talked over drinks.

"It is very difficult to explain my position, Rob, but I need to be free, I need to . . . to see lots of different men, and women, too, actually."

He looked at her for an instant, his blue eyes widening a bit. "What're you trying to tell me: you a nympho or something?"

Sophia smiled. Maybe this would be the best way to leave it. "Yes, I guess you could say that's part of my . . . problem."

Lester's expression brightened. "Really? Wow, I've never known a real nymphomaniac!"

"That's only part of the whole story, and believe me, I am only telling you all this because I trust you. I can assure you that my . . . my condition in no way affects my ability to work."

"No, I'm not sure that it doesn't. In fact, I know plenty of jobs where it would definitely help things along!"

It was amazing how his attitude had changed, she thought. As soon as she explained things in terms that he could grasp, Rob Lester presented no more problems. He seemed fascinated by her explanation, excited that he was actually dealing with one of those mythical creatures: the nympho.

Sophia smiled. "So here is the deal," she said slowly, picking up her untouched glass of white wine, sipping it delicately. "I am going to be very successful in this business; therefore, I can make you a lot of money. In exchange for your earnings, I would expect your tacit understanding while I deal with my . . . my problem."

Lester smiled as he sipped his Campari and soda.

"You mean I should keep my mouth shut while you fuck everybody's brains out? Sure. I can do that. You make me rich, and you can take on the New York Jets for all I care!"

"Let's drink to it," said Sophia, holding up her glass in toast.

Lester touched his glass roughly to hers. "Why not?" He finished his glass in one long swallow, a wistful look on his face. "I'll tell you one thing, though . . . . . ."

"What is that?"

"I'm going to miss you. You were good, baby. I'm not bullshitting you when I say you were probably the best I ever had . . . and I've had my share, you know."

"Don't miss me," she said. "I was too much for you anyway."

Lester looked at her as she radiated her own brand of sensuality, her special beauty.

"You know," he said after a moment's reflection and appraisal, "I think maybe you're right."

Chapter 8

Vienna, 1791

One of his earliest memories was of his father, Papa Leopold, touching the keys of a harpsichord or a piano and demanding the instrument's pitch to within an eighth of a tone. Before he had learned to read German, he was reading music in his mind. Little Wolfgang's ears had been magically sensitive, his fingers lithe and almost supernaturally quick. Crystalline memories of being in the circle of astounded adults as he played, while his father beamed with pride.

But memories seemed to be all he had lately. If only he were not such a goddamnably bad businessman! If only his Konstanze were not so sickly all the time! If only there were ways to protect and warrant the music he'd created!

If only the world were fair . . . .

Mozart laughed at this crazy little wish as he sat on the outdoor table of his favorite *konditore*, a pastry shop on the Domgasse near his previous home. He had lived in the Figarohaus for three years, until it became too expensive for him and his fragile wife. How he had loved that woman, and now . . . how he sometimes despised her!

She was as devoted to him as a house pet, as helpless as a child, and less passionate than either. What with his home life being so miserable, his financial situation taking him to the edge of poverty itself, and a new emperor ascending to the throne, it was incredible, even to Mozart, that he could still continue to produce musical masterpieces with the precision and punctuality of a Swiss clock.

The war with the Turks had finally ended and the Viennese court was starting to pay more attention to frivolity and the arts again. The ten-year reign of Joseph II had just ended and Leopold II was now in the palace, but Wolfgang hated the man. He seemed to have no soul for music, and even less understanding of what it meant to *create* anything. Leopold II, despite being told by many esteemed men (even Haydn himself) that Mozart was a "national treasure," refused to issue him a royal stipend. Even though *Don Giovanni* proved to be the most popular opera in the history of the city, Mozart remained estranged from any of its profits—such had been the nature of his original agreement with the theater owners.

Almost destitute, Wolfgang had appealed to the Vienna magistrates, asking that he might be appointed as "humble assistant" to Kapellmeister Hoffman at Saint Stephen's Church. It was a grand ploy, except that the magistrates were so overwhelmed with such a modest petition, that Mozart was appointed to the post as an honorary employee without a salary.

Fuck them all! he thought viciously as he finished his pastry and coffee. It did not seem to matter anymore what happened to him. He had just nursed Konstanze back to a fair simulation of good health, and perhaps she would have to take in sewing or laundry to pick up a few extra ducats.

And I will continue to give music lessons to the few in this city who can afford me, he thought as he downed the last of his *linzertorte*. Picking up his coffee cup, he drank down the final swallow, the rim almost touching his forehead, obscuring his vision.

He didn't see her until he put the cup down.

Then, he could not stop looking.

Shining blond hair enveloped her head like spun gold, and her long, aquiline face seemed like a piece of Greek sculpture, so perfect were its lines. She had eyes of the most penetrating green he had ever seen, and their gaze had him fixed like a butterfly under a pin. If she'd told him her name was Helen of Troy, he would have only smiled.

Suddenly she was sitting at his small table, having somehow slipped down in front of him, during the instant that he sipped the last of his coffee.

Astonishing!

He cleared his throat and tried to speak. "Yes?" The word fell off his lips hoarsely.

The woman smirked, her mouth glistening with the sensuous moisture of youth. "You are Wolfgang Amadeus Mozart?"

He nodded. "There is none other."

"Oh, I know . . . your music aspires to Olympus. Surely the gods themselves have never heard such strains." Her voice was even and refined, suggesting a maturity that was unexpected in one so young.

Mozart laughed nervously. "Well, I've never heard anyone express it quite like that, but, yes, I agree with you: my music *is* special."

The woman smiled openly this time, prompting him to continue.

"My father keeps telling me to write more simple stuff, so that more of the people can understand what I am doing. 'What is slight can still be great,' my father said, but that is not my style. I would first jump into the Danube before writing less than *my* music!"

"Good for you, my Amadeus. It is said that you are the world's foremost musical genius, and upon even first meeting you, I am already inclined to agree."

She stroked his ego so skillfully he did not even think to ask her name or her purpose in sitting at his table. By the cut of her clothes, it was apparent she was an extremely wealthy woman—the wife of a great landowner, or perhaps a duchess, maybe even an emissary from the Court of Leopold II. It would be wise to not be too arrogant with this woman until he knew more about her.

"Uh, thank you, Madame . . ." he said more cautiously, as he watched her breasts heave and swell above her bodice. It seemed as though they had a life of their own, that they were straining to break free of the constraining cloth. Finally, coming out of his trance, he addressed her once again. "As much as I enjoy the praise of strangers, I am compelled to ask if there is anything I might do for you . . . ."

She reached out to touch his hands.

"These are the fingers which dance upon the piano keys with such magic, are they not?"

"So I've been told, yes."

She stroked his fingers lightly, stirring passion in him that he had not felt since his first times with Konstanze. "I would have you give me lessons, Mozart . . . ."

He was stunned! Surely she did not mean what she said. He had never had a female student, and indeed, it was rare to hear of any women studying under one of the masters in the city.

"What?" he asked politely, but not hiding his surprise. "You wish to study the piano?"

"In a sense. More precisely, I wish to study *you*, Amadeus."

"Me? You mean my music?"

She tilted her head slightly as though considering her answer carefully.

"Well, your music will make a good beginning . . . ."

And it did.

The woman introduced herself as the Countess Sophia Bellagio from the city of Como in northern Italy. She had a large house on Schullerstrasse complete with servants and maids on every floor. Although she was not Austrian by birth, she understood the Austrian concept of *gemdltliehkeit* very well: good living with charm and graciousness. On every visit to her home, Mozart was treated to the finest breads, cheeses, wines, and pastries.

And she took her music lessons very seriously for several weeks, until the roles of teacher and pupil became reversed.

Wolfgang had been seated with her at the piano when it happened. She had been practicing a little rondo he had written especially for her lessons, when he became aware of what could only be described as an overwhelming scent. It seemed to envelope him like the snakes of Laocoon tugging at his consciousness, squeezing off his powers of will and concentration.

It was a raw, pungent, animal smell. It was the aroma of rutting, the heat-musk of desire. It was the scent of mating and release. The music in his mind, in his ears, faded away like smoke. The only thing he could concentrate upon was the ripe body of the woman seated by him.

She stopped playing, turned to face him, and he could see an inferno boiling like a volcano beneath the Sargasso green sea of her eyes.

"Is there something wrong, maestro?" she asked with a coy upward turn of her lips.

"I, I don't know . . . ." was all that he could say.

She laughed with a suggestion of cruelty and stood up from the bench they shared. The rustle of her skirts seemed loud and exaggerated, almost like a melody in itself. He sat transfixed, as though under the influence of a powerful drug, and watched her unfasten her gown. With a smooth, graceful motion, she peeled off the pieces of clothing, which seemed to fall away from her like the layered dried husk of a butterfly's cocoon.

Golden light of early afternoon entered the conservatory window, bathing her flesh with a warm, vibrant light. She seemed to surge with an inner energy, a sexual power that was unstoppable.

Wolfgang became as rigid as a maypole, feeling as though he would burst from his britches, hurting himself from the wretched codpiece. He tore at his clothes with a feverish joy, laughing and smiling, on the edge of hysteria.

The countess joined him in his merriment as she climbed up on the bench, spreading her legs over him as she let the final piece of underwear slip away from her. He had never seen a woman so free in her nakedness, so bold and so proud. In the middle of the day, with no shame! It fired his passion to the point of confusing him as though made drunk. His fingers became clumsy imitations of themselves and he fumbled free of his clothes like an awkward child just learning the task.

Taking his head in her hands, she guided his face into the golden triangle of her pubic hair, which was fine and wispy and soft as the down on a newborn chick. Her lips seemed to part magically as he raised his tongue to her. When he touched her, a galvanized current passed through his body. She was like an electrolyte, the heedless fire of an animal in heat. Her body odor was sweet and heavy. He had never imagined a woman could be so *clean*.

Pulling her from the bench, he threw this madwoman, this sex-creature, across the top of the piano. She landed with such force that the strings and hammers gave forth a single discordant sound, but she responded with laughter that was most musical in itself.

And so she became the instrument of his pleasure, atop what had always been the instrument of his pleasure. It was a glorious, hedonistic coupling, the likes of which he had never known. Compared to this woman, his wife was a cold slab of stone.

When she was finally finished with him, there was a brief, silent rest, and suddenly they were at each other again. Wolfgang had never known himself to be so full of sexual energy but here he was, standing at attention, and ready to cavort once more . . .

. . . and it was after dark by the time he stumbled away from her house, feeling as though he had just run a race through the Alps. His head was surprisingly clear for such an experience, and upon introspection he found it odd that he had been able to draw upon such boundless sexual reservoirs. He never had known himself to be much of an animal when it came to lusty adventures, and yet this Countess Bellagio had totally enflamed him, torched his very soul.

If only he could write music that could have such an effect on people! Then his immortality would be guaranteed, he thought with a sad smile.

The lessons continued for the next month. And the things she taught him were wondrous and dark and full of magic. He often fancied that she might indeed be some kind of witch or sorceress, but in the final analysis, he didn't give a damn what she might be.

His life was in a curious state of flux, and he was not sure how to deal with the strange brew of emotions and ideas that filled his mind and his soul. The countess had made him feel more alive than ever with her bedroom spells, but his health in general seemed to be on the decline. He had contracted the ague, and now it threatened to overtake him completely. His breath whistled in his lungs and he coughed up great gobbets of catarrh each morning, sometimes mixed with blood.

On the economic side, his finances seemed like they might take a turn for the better. He was being paid a handsome fee from the countess for her "lessons," and of course there were the plans of Herr Schikaneder, the owner and manager of the Meisterhaus Theater.

Wolfgang did not care for Schikaneder as a person, even though he belonged to the order of the Freemasons. There was something oily about him, something which suggested a foulness, a despicable aspect. But the small, thin man had come to him with an offer that seemed attractive, an opportunity that would be hard to resist.

Herr Schikaneder had written the libretto to an opera called *The Magic Flute*, which showed surprising merit. Schickaneder wanted Wolfgang to compose the musical score for the opera, and they would share the profits. In spite of the man's horrible reputation, Wolfgang was attracted to the prospect of writing music for such a story: full of fairies and spirits and creatures of the night. It was a dark and magical tale that fitted his moods and his general outlook.

Even the countess encouraged him to embark upon *The Magic Flute*. She told him that it was a monumental project that would guarantee him a place in the pantheon of musical giants; she felt it would be a fitting use of his great mental energies.

Wolfgang was flattered by the words of Herr Schikaneder, but he was more inspired by the encouragement of Countess Bellagio. Before meeting her, he had been feeling so bereft of human feeling that he had been channeling all of his soul into his music. But now the woman was bringing him back to life! For the first time in many years, Mozart was beginning to feel happy again.

He accepted Schikaneder's offer and began work on the musical score of *The Magic Flute*. The oleaginous theater owner was so overjoyed at this decision that he had a small pavilion built on the grounds, where Mozart could work without distraction or pause. At first Wolfgang thought this gesture was a magnificent demonstration of the esteem and regard of Herr Schikaneder, but he soon realized that the pavilion was more like a prison.

His meals were brought to him there, and he was not allowed to leave the premises until his daily work had been inspected by the theater owner each evening. The pavilion was hastily constructed and was therefore full of drafts—on rain-filled afternoons, Wolfgang would sit in the small confines of his musical jail wracked by a terrible chill. His illness progressed unchecked, and the coughing spasms became worse. He complained to his wife and his employer that his strength seemed to be leaving him and he began to again revel in thoughts of death.

At one point he told Schikaneder that "death is the only worthwhile goal in life. It is our only real and devoted friend. "

Schikaneder smiled and agreed with him, saying only that he should stay away from his friends until the opera had been completed.

Mozart managed to do this only because he had become obsessed with finishing the musical score. Sophia would come to him in his tiny pavilion in early evening, and they would steal a few precious minutes of lovemaking from his work, and their encounters left him in a most curious state. During their bouts of love, he felt as vigorous and strong and full of life as he had ever in all his days . . . but when she had left him, he felt more drained and pale and weak than ever before.

The day finally arrived when the completion of the opera was in sight. Wolfgang had finished all but a few parts for a few instruments, and he could already hear the entire orchestra roaring in his mind. It was not good music, it was great music—even by his own high standards. He knew this in the depths of his soul, and he was pleased beyond measure.

He sat in the pavilion that evening, putting the finishing touches on the vellum sheets, when there was a soft knock on the door behind him. Turning and throwing up the latch, he watched a familiar figure enter. It was Sophia wearing a black gown that made her seem thin and waspish.

Moving to him, she straddled his legs where he sat on the tiny stool, and lifted her skirts. He could smell the essence of her loins rise up and intoxicate him, and he was instantly ready for her. Lowering herself, she seemed to draw him up into her more deeply than ever before. and he felt as though he could not bear the sensation. But just as he was about to explode into her, she grabbed him with her secret muscles and shut him down, preserving the pleasure and the moment of final release. As she rode him wildly, he felt that she could play him like that indefinitely, and the pleasure crashed over him in ever-heightening waves, until the pleasure became a pain, a torturous thing from which he cried out for release.

Afterward, as she kissed him and prepared to leave, she paused and looked deeply into his eyes. "I have a surprise for you," she said in a soft whisper.

"Any more surprises from you, I don't think I can bear," he said only half in jest.

Reaching into her cloak, Sophia produced a sealed envelope, which she handed to him. "Open it."

"What is it?"

"A commission."

His heart leaped wildly, and his hands began trembling. "What? From who?"

"Please, open it."

Breaking the wax seal, Wolfgang tore away the parchment paper and began to read the document. It was indeed a commission naming a handsome sum of money to write a *Requiem*, a mass for the dead.

But it was unsigned . . .

Mozart looked up from the parchment to Sophia. "Is this a joke?"

"No, of course not."

"But there is no signature. It is invalid."

Sophia tilted her head, and her lip curled up in a slight, impish grin. "No, it is valid. The person who commissioned this piece wishes to remain anonymous, that is all. The commission will be paid through me, as I have been named the executor of the transaction. Everything is perfectly legal, maestro."

"But . . . he wants to be anonymous? I've never heard of such nonsense! I thought the nobility wanted it to be known that they were patrons of the arts?"

Sophia smiled. "Some of the true nobility do not need such gratification."

Wolfgang sighed and slipped the commission and the promissory note into his blouse. "Very well, I shall begin it directly. The music for *The Magic Flute* will be completed on this very day, and I am already thinking of the dominant themes I might employ in this new Requiem."

"That is wonderful news, my Wolfgang." Sophia turned to leave the pavilion.

"One more thing . . ." said Wolfgang. "For *whom* is this *Requiem* being written? Do you not think I should know this?"

For an instant, she looked grim and serious, but she banished the expression with a sultry smile. "No. Your patron would like that to be also a secret . . . ."

Wolfgang grinned. "Oh, he does, does he? Well, you tell him that I shall most likely discover his secrets, despite his silly wishes!"

Again she appeared serious as she took her leave. "Perhaps you will, Wolfgang . . . perhaps you will."

The Magic Flute was an incredible success. The opera played to full houses for more than two hundred successive performances. It was a record unequaled in the history of Viennese theater. Unfortunately, because of the wording of their contract, Wolfgang received very little of the profits, and Herr Schikaneder became impossibly wealthy at his expense.

The oily bastard was having a statue of himself erected while Mozart struggled to pay the rent on his small dwelling!

But this injustice was slight compared to the other slaps of Fate he had received. Konstanze was again confined to her bed with the ague, and Wolfgang himself had been deteriorating badly, losing strength to the point that he could barely cut his meat at the table. His work on the great *Requiem* slowed because of his ebbing strength and spiritual energy. Despite his great musical achievements, he lived like a pauper, and he simply did not care any longer.

Even his noble wench, Sophia, had been giving signs of deserting him.

Not that he could blame her. She was so young and full of flame and breath! And he already seemed like such an old man. Their lovemaking was a pale and hollow shell of what it had once been, and he now felt so weak, so sickly, that he feared it would be impossible for him to perform.

As he lay in bed with a raging fever, his thoughts ripped about in his mind like sails in a storm. He shifted his concentration between the unfinished *Requiem* and his sweet Sophia. He could not remember at what point the realization struck him, but he suddenly knew he would never recover from the terrible fever that consumed him.

He knew at that moment he was going to die.

Goddamn it all! Fuck them all! Nothing matters now . . . .

But he knew that was not true. There was much that mattered to him. He became angry and frustrated because his power and his life were slipping away.

He drifted off into a hazy dreamlike state, opening his eyes to discover that he was standing at the conductor's post in a large concert hall, which was filled to capacity. It was dark beyond the proscenium, but he could sense the presence of the audience—a large, tenebrous mass behind him. With a flourish, he guided the orchestra through the *finale* of his final composition, and listened to the building thunder of applause at his back. But there was something about the sound of their clapping that was wrong—it was too harsh, too sharp. It was a ratcheting sound like sticks of wood being struck together. Slowly, Wolfgang turned to face his audience and he saw the sea of bone-white faces, the eyeless sockets, and eternal grins. They called out to him with ghostly whispers of "Bravo!" and "Encore," and he finally understood for whom he had been composing his mighty *Requiem* . . . .

Chapter 9

New York City

The telephone trilled its electronic birdcall, pulling her from the depths of a black and dreamless sleep. It was almost painful to be awakened so unnaturally.

"Hello. . ." Her voice was a throaty whisper.

"Hey, babe, I'm sorry to wake you, but I've got some great news! I mean great news!"

It was Rob, his effervescence and energy bubbling even higher than usual. Sometimes, all his hype was not very charming, and she was so exhausted from the previous night that she was in no mood for him.

"What do you want. Rob?"

"I just got a call from John Linton over at Ernst and Passmore. They've just seen the footage from the jeans commercial and they went through the roof!"

"What are you trying to tell me, Rob?" Sophia was coming to full consciousness slowly.

"I'm telling you that they loved you, baby! Can you dig it?"

"Yes, I think so. Would you like to be more specific?" She sat up in the bed, her mind suddenly clear, her senses alert. There was a stiffness in her joints, which signified a Change coming on, but she tried to ignore it as she listened to her hyperbolic agent.

". . . so Old Man Passmore was sittin' there watchin' the rushes, and all of a sudden, he signals the projectionist to stop, and he turns to me and he says: 'All right, who's the blondie?' . . . and he's talkin' about you, baby, right? So I smile and tell him you're a new chick from Europe, that you're big over there, and he says he wants you for as much work as you can handle—the expensive perfumes, the exotic vacation spots, all the elegant Continental stuff! I'm tellin' you, honey, the whole joint was buzzin' about you! You are a very hot item right now."

Sophia smiled as she listened to Rob's story. It never failed to please her to know that men and women were so wildly attracted to her when she desired it.

"That's nice. . ." she answered softly.

"Jeez, you know you're gonna get stuck-up on me if you don't watch it! I just get you some of the fattest TV deals in all of Oz-land, and all you can say is 'that's nice'?"

She giggled into the phone. "Don't be silly, Rob. You know I'm excited and pleased, but I was still sleeping before you called."

"Yeah, well, I hope this whole number woke you up! I'm tellin' you, Sophia-honey, we are going to make a killing in this business! A real killing!"

"I sincerely hope we do, Rob."

"Right, now listen, don't forget. . . you've got an audition with Stephen Sandler down in the Village this afternoon, right?"

"Yes, I've got it on my calendar."

"Just checking. . . but don't be late for it. Sandler doesn't crap around."

"I won't be late, Rob."

"Yeah, now listen, I have some new contracts that I'll need you to look over and sign. Howzabout if I come over tonight and we can go through this stuff over dinner?"

"You mean a strictly business dinner?" She laughed softly so he could pick up her playful tone.

"Aah, yeah. . . 'strickly bizness' . . . of course! I'll see you, tonight, baby. Be by around eight, okay?" He hung up the phone before she could answer him, and it bothered her that he wanted to see her tonight. Everything was happening so fast for her that she had almost lost track of the days, of the ancient cycles. Tonight would be cutting it close.

Checking the clock, she discovered the morning was quickly dying. She had the appointment to see the artistic director of the Circle Six Theater in Greenwich Village, and it would be best if she began getting ready.

A shower would be nice right about now, she decided, as she thought again about how far civilization had progressed since the end of the previous century. It was so easy to take all the wonderful gadgets and inventions for granted, even for someone like herself. Things such as cell phones, electric lights, automobiles, radios, and televisions were such intricate parts of everyone's lives now . . . it was hard to imagine how anyone ever got anything accomplished in previous centuries.

The story is often told that when you meet Stephen Sandler, he turns out to be everything you've heard about him: tall and handsome, gracious, urbane, witty, and extremely bright. He seems to have read every great book, seen every respected play, and spoken with every person of influence. And yet you learn of his great breadth and depth without a hint of braggadocio. He always speaks softly, with a studied humility that is invigorating. He slips shining facets of wisdom into his conversation with a natural grace, as easily as one might slip beads on a string.

Sandler was the one whom the New York drama critics had hailed as the most influential man in American theater. At the age of sixty-two, he barely looked fifty. He wore a head of thick, silvering hair like a lion's mane, and he dressed with the casual flamboyance of any person who knows he can do as he pleases and no one will dare object. His shoulders were broad and muscular, his waist still lean and youthful. From the platform of his famous theater the great names of contemporary film and stage had emerged. He was a godfather, a Pope, and a kingmaker all rolled into one. If Stephen Sandler liked you, honey, you were going places.

It was that simple.

And there was no question that Sandler liked her. Sophia breezed through the series of readings he had gathered for her, demonstrating her inherent talent for languages and dialect. She reminded him of a chameleon, so subtly could she ease from one role or character to another. He knew that her looks and her abilities were perfectly suited to the stage or the camera, and she was a natural for the phenomenon called "stardom."

And although he wasn't usually the kind of man who made decisions on a "casting couch," he had to admit to himself that this was one gorgeous woman, a lady he could really sink his teeth into. Despite his vigorous appearance and seemingly great health, Stephen Sandler hadn't been sexually active for years. His analyst told him that he was channeling too much of his energy into his work that there was no time for the simple stimulation of sex.

What the hell, thought Sandler, as he watched Sophia Rousseau light up the dim stage. . . I don't really care what was causing the problem. All I know is I couldn't get it up with a fucking crane till this lady came along. He hadn't had a hard-on like this since he was six-fucking-teen. He had two new plays to cast, and one musical, and he needed a new face, a fresh talent. Perhaps she would be the one. . . ?

Even if she wasn't the one, Sandler had made up his mind to spend some time with her.

There were footsteps behind him in the almost deserted theater. Someone was padding down the aisle and slipping into a seat directly behind him. He felt a hand touch his shoulder lightly.

"How's it going?" whispered the familiar voice of Richard Hammaker.

Sandler turned to look at his playwright in the half-light of the theater. Hammaker was a short, dark-haired man. His beard was a bit scraggly, his clothes always on the shabby. side, and he had the suggestion of a wild-eyed Rasputin-type. He often had the appearance of being just on the edge of some kind of emotional outburst. There were heavy lines engraved into his young face that bespoke some troubling problems he had weathered earlier in his life. He was not a particularly attractive man, and his personality was more than abrasive. He had many acquaintants and colleagues in the theater world, and few friends . . . . but he was one hell of a good playwright.

"Hey," said Hammaker. "I said how's it going?"

"Terrible. . . until this last one." said Sandler. He pointed up to the stage where Sophia still performed. "She's very good."

Hammaker chuckled once cynically. "Yeah. I can see that. She looks like she should be doing French jeans commercials."

"She does." Sandler smiled.

"You gotta be kidding!? What're you gonna do—cast my play with a bunch of refugees from MTV? With fucking air-heads like this one?" Hammaker's voice was getting louder with each syllable, and some of the others in the front seats were turning around to see who was causing the disturbance.

"Take it easy. Dick! And keep your goddamn voice down," Sandler whispered harshly. "She's no air-head, believe me. This lady's very hip, and very talented. Sit back and watch her for a while. Then talk to me."

Hammaker slumped back into his seat, and Sandler smiled. His playwright was probably one of the brightest new talents on the New York stage. He'd had two off-Broadway hits last year, was already widely acclaimed in Europe, and it looked like he might have two more hits this year. The British loved his biting satire and the French liked his subtle intellectualism. The American audiences liked his earthy vernacular style, and his original plots. It was just a matter of time before Time had his picture on the cover, thought Sandler. And if Hammaker wasn't such a miserable son-of-a-bitch most of the time, he'd be an all right fellow to be around.

Stephen Sandler signaled for Sophia to pause as she finished the reading from *The Three Sisters*. "Okay, Ms. Rousseau, that was very impressive."

"Thank you," she said, looking at him with an instant of sultry satisfaction. Just looking at this woman was making him hard! It was incredible, as if she had some: kind of power over him. "Is there anything else you want me to try?"

"Yes," said Sandler. "I'd like you to read from this. . . ." He held up a copy of *The Vindication* by Richard Hammaker.

Immediately, one of his gofers ran up the aisle, grabbed the script and ran down to hand it to Sophia Rousseau. She looked through the front matter of the script and looked out at him.

"What part?"

"Act One. Scene Two. Try the part of Eleanor." Sandler motioned to a group of actors who were sitting in folding chairs on right stage. Pointing to one young man, he said, "Alec, get up there and read the part of Ted."

The young actor jumped to attention, carrying his script up into the lights to face Sophia. They began reading the lines.

After a few minutes of listening to the dialogue, Sandler knew his instincts had been correct. Ms. Sophia Rousseau was perfect for the role of the complex, enigmatic Eleanor in Hammaker's new play. Leaning back, he turned and looked over his shoulder at the playwright everyone in the Village theater-crowd called "Richard the Turd."

Hammaker was listening to his lines with a look of intense angst. but Sandler knew he was impressed. "Well?" he asked.

Hammaker leaned forward and whispered respectfully. "She's not bad. Especially for a first reading. . . maybe you're right. . . ."

Sandler laughed. "Maybe? Come on now, Richard! Have you ever known me to be wrong about things like this?"

Hammaker grimaced. "Not often, no."

"Then trust me. I didn't get my reputation because of my good looks. you know. . . although I probably could have!"

"Steve, you're a fucking egomaniac."

Sandler looked at his playwright and grinned. "Yes, of course I am. But aren't we all?"

It had been one of those high-energy, high-octane days for Rob

Lester, and he was riding across town in a big, ancient Checker cab—maybe the last one in the city— with a grin that felt like lockjaw. If he' d still been into coke, he would be eight miles high right about now.

Christ, he felt good.

Patting his breast coat pocket, he felt the bulk of the folded contract from Ernst and Passmore pressing outward. To some goons it might feel like paper, he thought, but to me it's like gold bullion! What a great fucking business As the cab cut a hard right onto Fifth Avenue, just below the park, he looked down the brightly illuminated street, flanked by columns of light.

What a great fucking town!

The cab eased to the curb opposite the Trump Tower, and Rob paid the driver and climbed out. It was a cool evening, but not uncomfortable. There were crowds of people on the sidewalks, some shoppers, some tourists, some late-working office-types. Fifth Avenue, by the park, was very classy-looking, small boutiques, big "name" stores, and of course the Trump Tower itself.

Rob crossed at the light on 56th Street, passing close by the steaming breath of a horse in front of its hansom cab. He could see a young couple in the back, snuggled against each other under a Tartan blanket. It made him think of how he had never taken a ride in one of those cabs, or gone to see the Statue of Liberty, or even taken a ride on the Staten Island Ferry. Hell, he'd never even driven across the Brooklyn Bridge to see the skyline at night like they do in all the old movies. He was a typical New Yorker in that respect, but today he regretted it.

Maybe someday I'll have a little more time to do that kind of stuff, he thought as he headed for the glass entrance to the Trump Tower. Sure, said a little voice down in his heart. Sure, you'll do it when you're an old fart . . if you do it at all. You work so hard, you're going to kill yourself with ulcers or heart attacks or cancer, and you know it. You'll never live to be sixty, you asshole.

The thought sobered him up a bit, as he considered his brother, who had decided to live in a cabin in the Maine woods, chopping wood, eating the bark off of trees, and teaching school in some ridiculous little town where the big excitement for the evening is when they turn on the neon sign on the roof of the supermarket. But maybe his brother had the right idea . . . .

Who knows? Who ever knows?

Lester stepped up to the curb and approached the opulent entrance to the Trump Tower. The doormen were dressed like those guys on the gin bottles, and they looked very uncomfortable and more than a little cold as gusts of pre-winter air slapped at them. Entering the lobby, Rob noticed that it was immediately warmer, and surging with people—mostly tourists who wanted to see one of the most outrageous buildings in all of midtown. There was a string quartet playing Beethoven—at least it sounded like Beethoven—and the escalators zigzagging through the atrium were also filled with human traffic. What a crazy place to live, he thought. Nothing like being ostentatious or anything like that. He nodded with familiarity at the security station—all the guards knew him by now—and headed for the elevators.

When he stepped off at Sophia's floor, Rob had to admit he was impressed with the design of the condominium apartments. Even the connecting halls were decorated with impeccable taste. He knocked on the door and checked his watch: 8:00 P.M. sharp.

After a pause, a small hidden intercom speaker hummed with Sophia's lightly accented voice. "Yes?"

"Okay, honey, it's just me. Open up."

Another pause. "Rob, I've been trying to call you. Where have you been? I'm not feeling too well and I wanted to cancel our appointment."

He almost laughed. "Appointment? Hey, what're you talkin' about? I'm just dropping by so we can grab some dinner and do a little business."

He paused and heard nothing in response.

"Hey, baby, what're we gonna do—talk to each other through this speaker all night? You lettin' me in, or what?"

Another short pause, then: "I'm sorry, Rob. . . I'm not thinking clearly. . . I told you I'm not feeling very well." She paused and he stood staring at the featureless door, feeling like a jerk. "I don't know if I can see you tonight . . . I'm not hungry. . . ."

"Sophia, what's going on? You okay? You sound kinda funny."

"I am . . . I am all right. . . ."

"Well, you sure as hell don't sound like it. C'mon, open up. Now you got me worried."

A pause, although he could hear her ragged breathing near the speaker. "Oh, Rob, I don't know what to do. I feel so alone. . . ."

What the hell was going on? he thought. Man, it was tough to figure these women out. You never knew what the fuck they would be coming up with next. Here's a lady who's got the world by the ass, and she's cryin' about something. I should have such problems.

"Sophia, open the door. I've been standing out here for ten minutes. You're making me feel like a jerk. " "Rob. . . you're the only one I would even think of trusting. . . ." Now what was she talking about? "Sure, honey, of course you can trust me. I'm your agent, and I'm your friend. I'll be whatever you want me to be. . . . Are you gonna open the door?".

"I don't know. . . I don't know what to do. . . . Oh, Rob, you shouldn't have come! I lost track of the days, of the time. It's the wrong time of the month. . . ."

Lester was thinking that she must be having one hell of a period to be sounding this weird, but he tried to keep his tone light and unconcerned.

"Hey, baby, I can dig it . . . it's okay. Look, I'll just stop in for a minute. You sign these new papers and I'll be history, okay?"

Another pause. Longer this time. Then he heard the locks of the door clicking solidly. As the door swung open, he was not prepared for what he saw.

Sophia was dressed in a long burgundy robe, and her hair was pulled off her face, wrapped in a long ponytail. Her face was puffy and bloated in appearance, like the doughy, pinched features of an old, Asiatic peasant. Her complexion was pale and seemed to have a sickly greenish tinge in the dim light, and he immediately felt panic rising in his chest as his heart started a rhythmic pounding. She looked terrible.

"Jesus Christ, what's the matter with you?" He rushed in and took her into his arms. She seemed weak and unstable, and he had never seen her like this, never imagined that she could even be like this. She just wasn't the fragile, helpless type.

"I'll be all right," she said. "It's just a passing. . . condition. . . that I have. It's something I've learned to live with."

"I hate to tell you this, but you look like shit! You sure we shouldn't be getting you to a doctor?"

Sophia managed a smile as he guided her over to the couch in the center of the room. As she passed beneath the hot, clear beam of a track light, he could see that her skin was definitely taking on a greenish cast. It was scary just looking at her, but he didn't want her to realize that he was getting a little panicky. She needed a doctor, that was for sure.

"No, no, Rob. . . you don't understand. A doctor's the last thing I need. I've been through this before. . . . I'll be all right, believe me. Let me sign the papers and then you've got to go."

Instinctively he reached for the papers in his breast pocket, but then he realized what she was saying. "Hey, you got to be kidding.

I can't leave you like this, there's something wrong with you. You need some help. I—"

"No! No, you can't stay!" She jumped up and started pacing about the room, her hands feeling her face as though searching for something on its roughening surface. "Oh, goddamn it, I should've never let you in! Never let you see me like this!"

Rob walked over to her as she stood looking out the floor-to-ceiling window-wall. The towers of light beyond the park made the city look like a magic castle. "Hey, it's okay. I can help you, honey. I'm your friend, remember."

She would not look at him as she spoke. "I have not made many real friends. . . never. It was always so dangerous. . . and whenever I did, it always ended the same way. . . ."

"Listen, I don't know what's going on here, but we can handle it, okay?" He put his hand on her shoulder and gradually turned her about to face him. "If you've got some kind of medical problem, we can get the best doctors in the city to have a look at—"

He stopped as she looked up at him. Her skin was becoming cloudy and translucent. Tiny lines, like cracks in crystal, were appearing all over her face, as though invisible spiders were spinning fine-lined webs. The greenish tinge was more evident now. . . but it appeared to be a layer of flesh beneath the cloudy outer layer that seemed to be cracking and flaking, as though it were going to peel away.

"Sophia, baby. . . Jeezus, what's happening to you!" She stared at him, but said nothing. As he watched, he saw her eyes begin to sink deeper into her skull, changing color from their usual green to an orange-yellow. She was shrinking in her robe, becoming taller and thinner, and he thought for an instant that maybe he was having the biggest flashback hallucination of his life. It was like watching her through the distorted lens of the granddaddy of all the great mescaline-acid-peyote highs.

Sophia staggered away from him, across the room, almost tumbling over an ottoman, and moved toward the bathroom down the hall. Her movements were stiff and awkward, showing little coordination or purpose. She bumped into the wall and spun about drunkenly. She appeared to be trying to speak, but the words would not form in her throat; her jaws seemed to be locking.

Rob moved to her quickly and saw that her face was getting worse—all her skin, actually. Christ, it was starting to harden and crack. . . like it was going to fall off! What the hell was happening to her?

"Hey, look I gotta get you outta here! I'm gonna call an ambulance."

"No, Rob. . ." Her voice was hoarse and faint, a gross whisper. "Do not be alarmed. . . . I am all right. . . . I promise you."

"All right? You look like you got *leprosy*! Like you're dyin'!"

"No, it is okay, believe me. . . . Stay with me, and you will know my secret. I will have to trust you now, it is too late for anything else. . . ."

"*Secret?* Trust me?" What the hell was she talking about? "Yeah, okay, baby, I believe you. Just tell me what you want me to do."

"Help me into the bathroom. Then I want you to put some water into the tub. . . ."

Rob put his arm around her and he could feel the drastic effects of change in her body structure. Her shoulders seemed to be curling inward, her spine was becoming more pronounced, and she felt dangerously thin. She also was getting taller by the instant—already a head taller than he. What the hell kind of weird growth-disease problem was this?

Since there was no light in the hall and he couldn't find the switch, he was forced to move along in semi-darkness. He could feel her bones under the robe. She felt like a shriveled-up old woman, and it was scaring the shit out of him. He tried to keep all the weird thoughts out of his mind as he hefted her into his arms and moved down the hall to the bathroom. Laying her on the thick carpet, he fumbled for the light-switch panel on the wall.

Finding it, he flicked at all the switches and suddenly the room exploded with light and color—purple as the main motif, accented by white and yellow. Sophia had rolled over and was lying face down on the carpet, her body convulsing rhythmically. Quickly, he turned on both faucets at the deep oval-shaped bathtub, then turned her over.

All of her skin was falling off.

Not all of it, really. . . but the outer layer which had given her a human appearance slowly flaked away in large translucent chunks. Jesus, what the hell was happening here? The new flesh was a shining, scaled surface, shimmering greenly in the track lighting.

Man, you've got to get the fuck outta here! Sophia's body continued to shrink away, elongating more rapidly now. Despite the heart-wrenching terror that threatened to overtake him, Rob watched in mute, shocked fascination. He stared with the rigid revulsion of a kid watching a couple of piranhas feed in a pet-store aquarium. She was changing. . . .

More quickly, and with each stroboscopic blink of the eye she appeared to be growing longer, transforming into something beyond his most disturbing nightmares.

She's turning into a monster. . . . My hottest client is a fucking *monster!*

He backed away from the writhing thing on the bathroom floor, and fell over the doorsill out into the hall. Staggering, forcing himself to move, he still could not take his eyes off the creature that had only recently been a beautiful woman.

Having established a reasonable distance of safety between himself and the thing, he continued to watch it change until its form was wholly recognizable. . . . an enormous snake, a serpent with the shiniest scales he'd ever seen. Like polished metal, the serpent's body reflected the light in an explosive prismatic display of beautiful colors. He couldn't ever remember seeing such a fantastic combination of colors.

That damned snake was the most beautiful thing he'd ever seen. . . .

Time became a smear upon the edge of his mind, and he had no idea how long he'd been standing in the darkened hallway just to watch the undulating flow of colors across the creature's scaly flesh. It was moving and thrashing about, rearing up like a great Indian cobra, its great yellow-red eyes flashing at him for an instant. Then it slipped over the side of the tub and into the water, sending out the tapering tip of its tail to grasp the faucets with a prehensile surety, then cut off the excess current of water.

The serpent's movements were a precise, poetic thing to watch. It was a creature of such unparalleled grace and beauty, that even a brash, insensitive clown like Rob Lester could not avoid being affected by its presence. All thoughts of flight and terror were subsiding in him now. Just watching the thing's movements in the tub seemed to have a vaguely hypnotic, soothing effect on him.

Gradually, he felt drawn to the fascinating creature, and began edging back, closer to the bathroom, without being aware. Slowly, the serpent turreted its head until its gaze locked into Rob's. Its large, yellow-gold eyes looked like iridescent blisters on each side of its perfect head. A long, shining tongue lashed and snicked at the air as a sibilant sound gathered in the back of its throat.

Get outta here, man, he thought, just turn around, and get outta here! He drastically wanted to follow the shrieking warning of his forebrain, but he could not.

Slowly, he walked back to the threshold of the bathroom. Surrounded by the purple trappings, the serpent assumed a regal bearing, and Rob felt as though he were being granted an audience with a potent ruler. Staring into the creature's eyes was like looking down a well of golden light. He felt fixed by the thing's gaze, pinned like a bug on a piece of dry cork. Its head weaved slowly from side to side—the motion both deadly and sublime.

"What are you. . . ?" he said in a voice that was only a cut above the silence.

The serpent rose up higher until it resembled a thick green stalk, growing before his eyes. Higher the head came, until it was even with his own. Its eyes narrowed and focused sharply upon him and the hissing sound in the back of its throat gathered strength and force. . .

. . . and it spoke to him.

Chapter 10

Paris

Matthew Cavendish did not like spending time or money in France, especially the famed "City of Light." To him, Paris was an overrated sinkhole with a few silly tourist attractions, more whores than kippers at a fish market, and a giant, ugly rusting piece of Erector set. If you pushed him, he would probably tell you something about learning in early childhood to despise the French because his father had so loathed the folks across the Channel.

"They didn't call it the 'French' Channel, did they, son?" his father would say with sneering pride. Matthew could still hear his father saying those exact words.

He had grown up in a home where the French were constantly being compared unfavorably with the English. "Frogs" was the usual term his father had used when describing the people of France. They were berated for their lack of fighting ability, their tendency to bite the hands that fed them, and of course their irritatingly nasal way of talking. Matthew's father was fond of saying that a Frog always sounded as if he were about to vomit instead of talk to you.

And of course, there was the little ditty his father recited at a pub the night he took Matthew out to celebrate his graduation from the University:

The Frogs, they are a funny race,
They fight with their feet,
And fuck with their face!

It was quite an "educating" evening, as Matthew recalled it now with a smile.

Try as he might to overcome the anti-French prejudices that

had been drummed into him as a boy Matthew had capitulated years ago. Even though he found French cuisine shamelessly better than most bland English fare, and even though he admitted that the Normandy countryside was probably the most beautifully bucolic he had ever seen, he. still found France to be a prissy, snobbish, highly nationalistic place, which he visited only when necessary. Despite his feelings, his books, translated and published by Le Livre du Poche, were wildly successful in France. He was a well-known, popular writer in cities such as Marseilles and Paris and Cannes, and was often invited on tours and interviews and television appearances.

Frequently, Matthew turned down the offers but on the few occasions when he did travel to France, he had used the opportunities to establish good contacts for information. The English Consul in Paris, for instance, was a fan of his books, and had extended an open invitation to dine at the English Consulate whenever he visited Paris. Befriending such a man gave Matthew access to a variety of influential people in the city and the government infrastructure.

And so, he found himself seated at an alfresco table of a small cafe on, the Rue Rive, staring at a bespectacled, bearded man in the opposite chair. The man wore an out-of-fashion suit and a mismatched tie. His manners were proper and also out of fashion; he was a man displaced in time and would have been far more comfortable in an earlier age. His name was Francois Maillet, and he was an inspector with the Paris Metropolitan Police.

"If you're a. friend of the English Consul, you could not come with a higher recommendation," said Maillet.

Matthew smiled. "Thank you, Inspector. I have need only of a few minutes of your time."

"However I may be of service, please!"

Matthew leaned forward and tried to look stem and serious. "Very well. . . You are familiar with my books, Inspector Maillet?"

"*Mais oui!* Who is not?" Maillet smiled.

"I wouldn't know," said Matthew dryly. "However, the information I ask of you is needed to complete an important chapter in my next book."

"Monsieur Cavendish, it would be an honor for me to assist you. What is it that you need?"

"I have been following a young woman from Palermo, tracing her progress across Europe, and I have reason to believe that she arrived here." Matthew patiently retold his story of the strange blond woman in Palermo, the unexplained but seemingly natural death of the clothing salesman, and the various reports of an enigmatic woman making an appearance in Berne, Munich, Marseilles, and Nice. In each case, witnesses retold a similar story—a strikingly beautiful woman had taken up with a man of wealth and position, only to disappear without a trace, after the man had died of apparently "natural causes."

Matthew presented the evidence to the Inspector in the form of newspaper articles, depositions signed by witnesses, and even a few photocopied police reports.

". . . and while there is no evidence of foul play on the part of this mystery lady, there seems to be a very high case of coincidence going on."

"Incredible," said Inspector Maillet. "You would have made a wonderful policeman, Monsieur Cavendish."

"Well, you have to be a bit of a detective to do the kind of work I do," said Matthew, getting a bit impatient. He wasn't sitting about to get flattered by this silly copper! He needed information—as soon as possible. "Do you have anything in your recent files that sounds similar? I have reason to believe she came to Paris."

"I can have this checked out this afternoon," said Maillet. "Where can I reach you?"

Matthew sighed imperceptibly, giving the inspector the address and phone number of his hotel. "I shall be awaiting anything you can tell me," he said with a smile.

Chapter 11

Arles 1899

There is a small antiquarian shop in the center of this French town of 20,000 people. Situated close to the Rhone River, and Port-St.-Louis on the Mediterranean, Arles caters to a fair share of international tourists and vacationers from the surrounding provinces. The antiquarian shop has become, therefore, something of a souvenir shop, as well as a repository of things old, and most times forgotten.

Its owner, an old man in his eighties, died two summers ago, and since there were no known heirs, the place and all its contents were put up for public auction. The shop seemed like the perfect diversion for a widow in her early forties, who had inherited her husband's vast wealth after a boating accident. The sums from the insurance policies alone would allow her to live out her days in comfort, but she wished to have an idler's profession, and the purchase of the curiosity shop was just the ticket.

It was a small shop, but its interior seemed to defy the laws of physics, seemingly holding more than its numerous shelves and nooks and alcoves than would seem possible. The shop was truly a gestalt experience: a case of the sum of the parts being far greater than the whole. It was so jammed with junk and memorabilia of earlier times, that no one could accurately detail all that was contained in it.

The prior owner had long-ago stopped keeping track of his inventory, and the acquisition of old junk had merely become a natural part of his life as natural as eating and sleeping. The junk would come in, and some of it would go out. It was the natural order of things.

The new owner, the youngish widow, was not altogether interested in what might be found in her shop. She simply needed a profession, a place to go each day where she might have the chance to meet interesting people, to talk, and to generally enjoy herself with little pressure or insistence.

And so it was that she did not know of the thick leather-bound journal that rested in a far corner of the shop, buried halfway down a stack of old photograph albums and bound ledgers.

The book had been stolen by a housekeeper, after its owner had committed suicide. In the confusion and shock, which followed the man's death, no one missed the journal. The housekeeper had mistakenly thought it might be worth some money someday, but she died without making a franc. The journal was bound up with a stack of other old books, sold to a junk man, and it eventually reached the dusty confines of the shop.

If anyone might ever had it, they would be in possession of one of the great artifacts of the art world—an additional look into the disturbed mind of a man who signed his tormented paintings with only his first name: Vincent.

December 12, 1888—I have finally done it! I have left the drab cold landscapes of the north for the hot suns and bright days of the south of France. My friend, Paul Gauguin, has urged me to leave Paris and I have now believed him. He promises to meet me here and says we will share a studio together. That I will believe when it happens. Gauguin is such a bombastic, impulsive ass! And yet I admire him, as he admires me. We shall see if he is good to his word.

January 4, 1889—I have just received another letter from Theo, wrapped about notes totalling 150 francs. What a wonderful brother I have in Theo! No man could ever want a better sibling, that is for certain. His "allowance" to me keeps me alive. Is it not crazy to imagine that once I begged him to quit his lucrative position at Goupil's Gallerie to become an artist with me!

Then the family would have had two starving wretches to worry about! At least Theo makes my father proud . . . while I, at the age of thirty-five, am still a problem child, still a crazy dreamer.

Speaking of dreamers, I am still waiting for Paul, yet a letter says that he is on the way as I write these lines. Somehow, I must confess to believing him. He claims to have a great need to be in the south for the colder months. He claims it is good for the soul, and I believe him. Arles is truly a beautiful place, where even in the winter there are flower gardens of crocus and daffodil, and greenhouses where there are blooms and flowers all year through!

It is the color—the vibrant living color of this place—that will set me free, that will save me!

January 17, 1889—He is here at last! Paul arrived by coach with a brace of baggage the likes I have never seen. He claims that he sold a painting in Paris just before he left, and had to wait for payment—thus his delay in arriving. We will work well together, this I am sure. We will fight well together, of this I am also sure!

January 29, 1889—I have been in this village more than a month and I still have not had one of their women! The southern girls are easily more beautiful than any of the northern peasant stock. Their faces are so finely angled, their eyes so big! They sit on their porches and in their sunny parlors sipping absinthe, and smiling at all the men who pass by. And yet they avoid me like a disease, and I dream of finding the prostitutes of this town. Always the whores for Vincent! Why must it always be this way for me?

February 18, 1889—I had a terrible fight with Paul. We started drinking early in the day, and we ended up hurling insults, and finally our glasses, at each other. He is off at one of the cafes now, finding a woman, while I sit here with a pen in one hand, my prick in the other!

If I do not have a woman soon, I feel that I will explode like a cheap bomb. And yet I am painting like a madman already. To count up, I have painted ten gardens in ten days! It is nothing for me to spend fourteen hours a day at my easel. The colors are finally coming to life, and I can feel the energy of my body flood through my brush and alight the colors of my palette!

I feel that I am painting well, and the thought comes to me that perhaps fucking and painting are incompatible, that a man cannot do both well, and must make a choice.

For me, the choice is already made! The women won't have me . . . not yet anyway.

February 22, 1889—Paul is truly my friend. He has brought a young woman to meet me from the cafe where he drinks. She wanted to see my work, and she stayed to fuck me! What an experience! She was lean and young and full of energy. Such a rocking and a thumping—she, me, and my straw mattress! She has given me the inspiration and the element in my life that has been missing. Now I feel like I can paint forever. Just give me some tobacco, some drink, and an occasional woman, and I can be the artist of my dreams!

March 7, 1889—Spring comes early to this part of France! Already the gardens are blooming with color and my palette is aswirl with inspiration. I have been learning to express the passions of humanity by means of reds and greens! There is a relationship between my colors and life itself! I can feel it and I know it! I am painting sunflowers because there is a special essence in the sunshine that these plants have captured, and capturing the flowers on canvas, I will thus capture that special essence of the sun!

March 9, 1889—Paul and I share a studio where the light pours in like golden liquid. I am supremely happy here. I paint all day and spend my evenings in the cafes and brothels. The prostitutes are like sisters and friends to me. They do not reject me as an outcast because they are themselves outcasts. Yes, the whores give me my pleasure, but I long for a wife! I am filled with energy and the passion of all great art! Thank God for the wine which keeps me from becoming too crazy. When I take another drink, my concentration becomes more intense, my hand more sure, my colors more correct. Sometimes I believe that my painting can do nothing but improve because I have nothing left but my art. Sad? Yes. True? Unfortunately, yes.

April 14, 1889—Some days I am high as the birds which wheel and keen in the skies above my easel, and then suddenly I feel as though I belong with the white, eyeless worms beneath the flat rocks of the garden paths. My life is a jagged run of great joy and great pain. Sometimes I grow so tired of the starving conditions, the wretched life I choose to lead while I wait for the world to recognize me.

Am I truly crazy, as some say I am? Some of the village children have taken to waiting outside my studio window, only so that they might scream "madman!" when I come to the sill for a breath of air.

But my thoughts are this: I don't care if I am crazy—as long as I become that 'artist of the future' of whom I spoke to Theo.

April 23, 1889—Today is the most glorious day of my life!

My painting, "The Red Vine," has been sold! Instead of working today, I have begun drinking as soon as I received the news, and I will no doubt drink up the profits of the sale within the next sunrise. But I care not!

May 3, 1889—Today, Paul refused to eat at the same table as I because he claims I am a filthy pig and that he risks catching diseases by eating with me. Enraged, I threw my cup at his face and he struck me with his fist before storming off to the cafes. I fear we are incompatible, despite the wondrous atmosphere of this place, despite the stupendous number of canvases we have created here.

May 17, 1889—I have often felt that if I did not have a woman I might freeze and turn to stone. I may never need feel that way again—Her name is Sophia Rousseau and she entered my studio as though coming from a dream. To say that she is the most beautiful woman I have ever seen is such a silly cliché I am embarrassed to think in such terms. And yet it is true.

She was dressed like a woman to the manor born, a woman of social standing, education, and exquisite breeding. She told me she had come from Paris in search of artists, having heard that the truly talented have left the city for simpler climes. I smiled and told her that I was perhaps the finest artist in all of France, but no one yet knew that fact. I showed her my work and I am convinced that she was impressed with its vitality and utter newness. She even told me that she had seen nothing like it in all her days.

Pressing my good fortune (after all, one does not have an angel walk through his door every day!), I asked her where she would be going, and how long she planned to stay in Arles. To my surprise, she said that she lived by no man's schedule, and that she traveled freely in search of what she wanted. She said that it was possible she might be staying in Arles for a good while. I told her that there was only one good hotel in the village, and recommended that she stay there. She smiled at this, excused herself, and returned to her waiting carriage.

I walked to the door of the studio, watching her, trying to imagine what kind of perfect body might be hidden beneath the folds of her dress. I told her to visit me at her convenience, and to my shock and delight, she said that she would be doing so!

May 26, 1889—Sophia has come again! And again, she chose a time when she knew Gauguin would be out on one of his binges.

She offered to pose for me, but the painting was never begun. As her clothes dropped away, I became overwhelmed with desire and a hardness in my prick I hadn't known since being fourteen years old!

To say that we fucked would be a blasphemy, a miscarriage to describe what truly took place. Locked together like a single organism, we aspired to the place of the gods. This woman, this Sophia, is different, in an almost scary way. I had always thought that only men actually liked sex, and woman merely tolerated our affliction and our hunger for it. But here is a woman who seems to like the sport as much as I!

June 24, 1889—With Mademoiselle Rousseau as my inspiration, I am painting with a furious, soul-burning energy. When I paint I am not conscious of myself anymore. and the images come to me as if in a dream. When I am painting like that, I know that I am creating beautiful art. Until I met this woman, only when I was painting did I ever feel that totally unleashed, totally free feeling of wanton fulfillment. But now my fucking is like my painting and I soar to the heights of my soul with her. She is an angel, this woman, and she tells me that she knows in her heart that I am a gifted painter, a great artist, and that someday the world will recognize my potent talent, my "special vision." That is her phrase: my special vision. She says that I see the world differently, that I "feel" the world differently . . . and that is why she comes to see me.

August 15, 1889—My entries in this journal—what I have come to call my "secret" journal—have been more erratic lately. Still, I pour forth the letters to Theo as a way of resting and relaxing from the furious pace of my work, but there are things I do not tell him, that I can explain to no one, and those are the thoughts reserved for this separate ledger. Sophia has been coming to see me less frequently, and when I ask her why, she only smiles. When I ask her where she goes when she is away from Arles, she only smiles. She is the most mysterious woman I have ever known, and she is easily the most self-assured, the most confident. I commented upon this once, and she laughed very musically, saying that she had learned how to act from the best teachers—men. For some reason, this threw me into a wildly depressive state, and I drank myself into a disgusting stupor after she had left my studio that day. I think that I had been entertaining crazy fantasies of marrying this independent woman! I think that I had become terribly possessive about her little "honey-pot," and the thought of other men dallying about with her drove me into a frenzied state of mind. How silly of me to think that I could possess a woman so magnificent. I should consider myself fortunate to merely use her on the off occasion!

September 10, 1889—Sophia visited me today. She has begun the curious habit of inspecting my work, my output of canvasses, from one visit to the next. She seems overly concerned about the chronology of when they were completed, comparing the times to the times of her visits to me. She looked especially hard at a canvas of a row of green cypresses against a rose-colored sky and a crescent moon in pale lemon.

October 2, 1889—The energy to paint fourteen hours a day is no longer in me. I find that I grow tired so quickly and that the visions and dreamy images of my work are not as clear. This bothers me and when I tell Paul he simply laughs. When I mention it to Sophia, she only nods in silence, as though she understands perfectly.

October 27, 1889—I am alone more and more. Paul is so disgusted with me, so angry and passionate all the time, that we can no longer talk. This morning it occurred to me that he has never met my Sophia . . . it is uncanny how she has timed her visits to avoid him . . . and he has accused me of fantasizing the whole affair with this mystery woman. He claims that no one in the village has ever seen her come here, that no one knows of her, and that she probably exists only in my "demented" mind. How bizarre all this is becoming! Could it be that I have imagined such a woman? Could I have imagined such fucking? No, it is not possible—she is as real as I am! And yet the laughing jeers of Paul has set me to thinking that perhaps I am as crazy as everyone says.

November 23, 1889—This is the worst day of my life, and I am very drunk as I try to pen these words. Sophia has left me! A messenger delivered her note today: a terse, cold sentence which said that she must leave for Italy, and that she could see me no longer. I can't believe it! To neither see nor touch that incredible creature ever again! It is unthinkable, yet she states it so simply that there is a part of me that believes it totally. It is to laugh or cry. I don't know what to do. I know that I feel more sick and more troubled than I have ever felt. And if this is the pain of love then I have finally felt it!

November 30, 1889—She is truly gone. Of this I am certain. I have tried painting to soothe my pain and suffering, but there is something missing, and I know that I must struggle to regain it. I am tempted to tell Theo of this woman and her effect on me. I am tempted to hire men to investigate her past, to track her down. And perhaps I would do this if I had the funds to finance such a hunt. But alas, for me it is only a fantasy, a fairy tale in which I find her and bring her back to my studio forever. I find myself thinking of painting with very dark colors, with the bloodiest reds I have ever mixed, but I know not what to paint. And I am ill with a list of petty diseases. I cough up terrible gouts of mucous, and I shiver when there is bright sun on my skin. I have terrible fits at night when I lie in my bed in a sweat. I must start sleeping at longer stretches, must stop sitting up in my bed, staring at the moon while Paul grinds on through the night with nose-rattling snores.

December 19, 1889—A month has passed and I am truly mad for her touch and the lingering smell of her cunt in my beard. My health continues to slide as I do not eat regularly, and I do not take care of what Paul calls my "most basic needs." But worse, I know I am truly mad. None of the colors look right anymore! My palette is a place of confusion and the colors of the oleanders and the rose-colored twilights come no longer to me on canvas. I thought the absence of her would be good for my painting, but I have seen little to cheer me. It occurs to me again that painting and fucking are not compatible. This fucking weakens the brain. If we really want to be potent males in our work, we must sometimes resign ourselves to not fucking much! There are times when my thinking seems to clear, when I do not hear the flies buzzing in my ears, when I can think clear thoughts and plan beautiful canvases. It is at those times that I know she was bad for me, that her fucking was *killing* something in me. In ways that I can never explain. And then I think about this and I know that this also sounds crazy, and that I am probably so sick and so mad that it no longer matters what I think or what I feel.

January 15, 1890—I feel so embarrassed for what has happened, and yet there is no way to show these feelings. After the argument with the whore, I still do not recall cutting my ear, or the first days in the hospital. Only Theo's face bending over me do I really remember. Upon returning to the studio, I learned that Paul had left, heading for Brittany, says Theo. I am tempted to say that I am happy he is gone, but that would be untrue. More truthful is to tell how lonely it has become without him. Even his quarrelsome nature is preferred to the silence. I don't even want to think of how much I miss the woman.

April 13, 1890—The calendar says that it is April so I must believe it. I have lost track of the passing of the days and nights, and even the months. I have only recently broken my silence and written to Theo. I feel used up, like an old, ugly whore! I am mixing colors again, and I am seeing the colors of spring come back to this place with a wild and happy vengeance, but I am not painting good canvases.

May 16, 1890—The world seems more cheerful if, when we wake up in the morning, we find that we are no longer alone, and that there is another human being beside us in the half dark. That's more cheerful than shelves of edifying books and the whitewashed walls of a church, I'd swear! And that companionship is something that the Fates have denied me. Sophia is less than memory, like a half-remembered dream. I cannot imagine ever being happy in my life. Even the village is against me now, having the inspector jail me for being an incompetent. I have been in and out of the hospital so many times that I fear I am becoming a nuisance to everyone. It is only too true that heaps of painters go mad. I shall always be cracked, but it's all the same to me. When I become a nuisance to *me*, I will simply kill myself.

Chapter 12

New York City

Rob Lester awoke in his apartment; sprawled like a drunk on his living room couch, still in his clothes. Sunlight filtered through the sheer curtains and warmed the leather upholstery, touched his clammy cheek. He felt fuzzy-headed, as though he'd been drugged, and his mind was filled with bizarre images and pieces of a nightmarish dream.

What the hell am I doing here?

The thought edged slowly through his mind as he sat up and tried to start thinking straight. He had no memory of returning to his apartment, of falling asleep. And that bothered him. He was not a big drinker, and no longer a drug person, and he was not accustomed to having pieces of his life end up missing."

The last thing he remembered was getting up to Sophia's apartment.

There was a dull throbbing in the back of his head, at the base of the skull. It was just enough to keep him from getting up and walking around just yet. Just lay back and relax, he told himself. Take a coupla deep breaths, and you'll be fine.

He lay back for a minute, trying to relax, but the troubling images of his dreams kept returning to him: a darkened room, shadows running down a long hallway, the sounds of some kind of creature breathing . . . its air hissing in and out like a piece of pneumatic machinery. There was something about the dream, but he I could not make it come clear. He had the vague impression that in the dream, she had been in some kind of trouble. He thought he was saving her. . . then there was the half-remembered scene of stepping past a threshold and staring into the face of a monster. . . .

Shaking his head, Rob tried to get the image from his memory. He never had nightmares! He always slept like a little kid, and yet he knew that he was deeply troubled by the previous night's dream. For one thing, it had seemed so damned real.

And there were other things that bothered him. Why couldn't he remember coming home last night? And how come he fell asleep on the couch and didn't even take off his clothes. He never slept in his clothes. That was one of those things his mother had always told him to never do—it would "ruin" them, she had always claimed—and he had always tried to abide by that ironclad law of childhood.

No, he had to remember! He knew that something weird must have happened last night, and he wasn't going to let it go until he figured it out.

Slowly, he moved across the couch and picked up the phone. Dialing Sophia's number, he still tried to put the pieces together. As he listened to the ringing at the other end, he felt as though he were very close to getting the "whole picture"—the dream and the missing hours last night—as if there were only a small bit of the puzzle still not slipped into place. He let the phone ring about twenty times .as he continued to dwell on the events of the previous night. Sophia didn't answer, and it was a fifty-fifty shot that she was there, and just had the phone turned off. She did that sometimes when she didn't want to talk to anybody.

Hanging up the receiver, Rob forced himself to stand up, to ignore the insistent throbbing in his head. If this weren't a cheap champagne hangover, it sure as hell was a great imitation. And yet he knew that he hadn't had any champagne last night—cheap or otherwise. Even though he had obviously slept, he felt exhausted. He walked into his bedroom, slipped out of his "ruined" clothes, and lay down to sort things out.

And quickly fell asleep . . . .

. . . but this time the dream was sharper, more clear.

The creature was talking to him, and Rob Lester listened.

Its voice was like a whisper in his mind. He wasn't sure if he was actually hearing it, or maybe just thinking that he was hearing it. Or maybe its thoughts were simply entering his mind.

He didn't know, and didn't really give a damn. He listened to its message as though in a trance as he stared into the serpent's electric, neon-yellow eyes. It was such a beautiful creature! So big and sleek and smooth, and the most incredible eyes he had ever seen.

And it spoke softly, intimately, to him:

"Listen . . . you now share a secret as old as the world. I was here before the Great Temples at Luxor, the Pyramids of Giza, the Colossus of Rhodes. . . . I walked with Alexander at Philippi, with Aeneas at Carthage. . . . I saw the horror of the Black Death, the joy of Polo's return. I watched Michelangelo transform the Sistine Chapel; and I listened to the heresies of Galileo. Kingdoms have risen and fallen all around me, and yet I have persisted. I am the Geraldine to Coleridge's Cristobel, I am the Vlad of Desire. I am as old as the world. . . . You will know this of me now, but you will never speak of it . . . not even to me . . . ever. . . . It will be a simple fact of the world in which you live. . . . I am the power of lust and the promise of fulfillment. . . . You will be my holder of the keys, the keeper of the secret, and you would die before releasing what you know. . . . You will understand what I require. . . and you will never disapprove. . . . For this faithful service, I will grant you your life."

Suddenly the creature rose up higher on the stalk of its own body and leaned forward, caressing his face with its velvet scales, curling past him and then retreating with the suggestion of sexual flirtation. Every movement of the serpent was hypnotically perfect and undeniably attractive. There was a poetic rhythm to its motion that seemed to fascinate him. As it pulled away from him, he felt a coldness in the air about him, like a breath of winter. He shuddered once, and abruptly knew that he must leave the place.

There was an empty elevator, a silent taxi, a clinging darkness . . . .

. . . . replaced by a burning, white light.

Rob blinked open his eyes, fighting off the sunlight that had invaded the bedroom through a half-open shade. Sitting up, he tried to orient himself. Already the dream was fading from his mind. Within seconds of being fully awake, he could remember nothing—other than a numbing sensation that it had all been so real, so chillingly real.

He'd never had a feeling like that, never felt so . . . so disturbed by something that just wouldn't make itself clear in his mind. But perhaps that was the reason it was so disturbing: he could not get a handle on the damned thing.

Well, he thought resignedly, at least he was feeling better and he could get back to work. Maybe he'd been overcome, by one of those weird twenty-four-hour flu viruses he d heard about but never experienced firsthand. What he needed was a shower. His mother had been right about sleeping in your clothes—you felt like a real slime the next morning.

Just as he was heading for the bathroom, the phone rang. He checked his watch as he moved to answer it. "Yeah?" he said casually.

"Rob? Rob Lester?" said a vaguely familiar voice. "Yes, that's me. Who's calling, please?"

"This is Stephen Sandler."

A jolt of electricity shot through him. Holy Shit! Sandler! Calling me. "Well, hello, Mr. Sandler. . . how come you're calling me on my home number? This must be pretty important."

Sandler chuckled softly. "You weren't at the office so let's not play games, Mr. Lester. The actress you sent to the audition for *The Vindication*, Sophia Rousseau . . . I want her."

Rob laughed. "Yeah, you and every other guy still straight in this town. She was good, huh?"

"She was more than 'good,' Mr. Lester. She was stunning. Not only is she a beautiful woman, she is also a talent of the first mark. I want her to play the part of Eleanor in Hammaker's new play."

Rob smiled. This was too much—Sandler calling him at home! The guy must be desperate for Sophia. It was the same reaction everywhere he showcased her. She was going to make him a mill if she made him a dime. She was that property that every agent dreams about, and he hadn't even tried to find her—she'd walked right up to him, right out of nowhere.

He let Sandler wait in silence for a moment before replying. "Eleanor, eh? That *is* the lead, isn't it?"

"Have you read the play?" asked Sandler, sounding somewhat surprised.

Rob chuckled. "Me? No, of course not! Haven't you heard, agents can't read. It's just that I think you should know my client's not interested in parts that aren't leads. Can you dig it?"

There was a silence on the phone, and for an instant, Rob was afraid that he may have overstepped his bounds with Sandler. Then: "Yes, Mr. Lester, I'm offering your client the lead in my play. Would you like me to get down and beg for her services?"

"Oh no, that's not necessary. Why don't we take a lunch tomorrow and see if we can work out the details?"

Sandler cleared his throat. "All right, name the place and I'll be there."

"How about the Russian Tea Room? I haven't been there in years," Rob said.

"I'll bet," Sandler said. "That will be fine. Two o' clock?"

"You're on."

"There is one more thing," Sandler said. "Would it be possible for Ms. Rousseau to join us?"

Rob smiled. "I don't know. I'll have to check it out with her. I can let you know in the morning, how's that?"

"Fine. Just leave word with my office if I'm not there. I would like to talk to her a little bit . . .outside the pressure of the theater. . . just to get to know her. . . ."

"Sure," said Rob. "That makes sense. You'd like to make sure you're not signing on the next drug O.D. for the Daily News headline, right?"

Sandler cleared his throat. "Yes, Mr. Lester, something like that. . . ." The man sounded as if he might be losing patience with Rob's snide wordplay. "I will await word from you tomorrow morning, but we shall be meeting for lunch no matter what."

"I'm looking forward to it, Mr. Sandler. Thank you."

"Good-bye, Mr. Lester."

There was a click at the end of the line, which communicated more than an hour's continued conversation could do. But what the hell. . . he knew his flippant attitude couldn't snafu the deal when the Money Man was superhot for one of his clients. Producers and directors and boards had an understanding with agents and agencies in general—they knew that the artists' reps were a necessary evil, an obstacle that must be cleared before any deals could be forged.

And if they wanted your client bad enough, they would take any amount of shit from you—it was all part of the game.

Who really cared? Who really gave a damn about anything except nailing down that dollar? God, he was ecstatic! He'd finally hooked Sandler! He couldn't wait to tell Sophia how she'd affected the most successful, influential (and of course the most wealthy) producer in New York.

Dialing Sophia's number, he waited impatiently for the sound of her phone ringing. "Sophia Rousseau's residence. May I help you?" A young girl's voice melted through the phone. It was Sophia's service.

"I'm trying to reach Ms. Rousseau, but I guess she's not in, right?"

"Yes, sir. . . would you like to leave a message?"

"Do you know where Ms. Rousseau might be? Or when I can expect her to be back?"

"No, sir. . . would you like to leave a message?"

"How come you guys didn't answer this morning when I called?"

There was a short pause, then: "We were instructed to begin taking Ms. Rousseau's calls after 9:00 A.M. You must have called before that time, sir." There was another pause. "Would you like to leave a message?"

"Yeah, tell her to call Rob as soon as possible—either at the office or my apartment. It's extremely important that I'll talk to her as soon as I can. And tell her she's got a lunch date tomorrow at two o'clock with me and Stephen Sandler. You got all that?"

The answering service girl repeated the entire message flawlessly. Thanking her, Rob disconnected, and began to immediately worry about his client. Where the fuck was she? Every once in a while, she would pull a little vanishing act on him, and he wouldn't hear from her for a day or two. And now that he thought about it, it was always about the same time each . . . .

Maybe she was one of those chicks who turned into a real monster every time it was "that time of the month" . . .?

Chapter 13

After the waiter had served their selections and the usual comments of how good everything looked and tasted had been delivered, Sandler decided to get down to business. But it was going 'to be tough to keep thinking straight with a woman as stunningly beautiful as Sophia Rousseau seated across from him. She wore a simply designed satin dress of golds and yellows. It clung to her body like a living creature, showing nothing yet revealing all. Sandler had many years of experience in dealing with women, but in the presence of this incredible woman, he felt as if he were an adolescent boy all over again.

Sandler was the kind of person who always felt comfortable in a group of people because he always felt as if he were in control of things. His demeanor was always smooth and radiant, oozing self-confidence and savoir-faire.

But not this afternoon. Ever since Lester brought her into the Russian Team Room and seated her directly across from him, he was transformed into a different person—a person who felt overwhelmed by the stunning presence of this woman, who was left at a loss to make mundane conversation.

How could you be mundane around a goddess like Sophia?

She had a way of looking at you that was reminiscent of the way a hungry cat in the zoo will regard the silly gawkers beyond the bars of its cage. It was as though she could look inside your eyes, right through to the back of your skull where your thoughts were scrawled like graffiti on a dirty wall. You had the feeling that with a woman like her, there weren't going to be any secrets kept from her. She was going to know you, Jack, and that was the price you were going to pay. Take it, or leave it.

Well, here goes nothing, he thought recklessly. "Let's not continue with the small talk, Mr. Lester, he said as forcefully as he could manage. He accomplished this by purposely avoiding her gaze.

"Whatever you say, boss. But please, just call me Rob, okay? That 'mister' business is a little stiff, don't you think?"

Sandler smiled, thinking: that's not the only thing that's getting stiff. . . . A bad joke, but nonetheless true. A woman hadn't had such an effect on him in more years than he cared to remember.

"Very well, Rob. . ." A nervous look into her serpent-green eyes, and he saw the suggestion of a fantasy fulfilled. "And Sophia . . ."

He looked away as he continued.

"The terms are simple and to the point. You play Eleanor in the stage version, with an option to play the lead in the film as well. You'll get top scale for the stage run. The movie's negotiable, okay? I'll have the papers in your agent's office tomorrow."

"Is the film already budgeted?" asked Lester.

Sandler nodded. "The funds for the production have already been assembled, yes. The studio is of course waiting to see how well the play will be received, but I think it's just a formality."

"Listen, Mr. Sandler, I know how much it costs to make a movie so let's not talk about twenty mill as being a 'formality,' okay?" Lester smiled, and it was a good icebreaker. Sophia also smiled, and Stephen felt obliged to do the same.

"True. . . true . . ." he said. "But believe me: everybody in the industry thinks so highly of Hammaker's work that there's little question they're going to go ahead with the film."

"He is that good?" asked Sophia. Her voice was smooth and full of control. Stephen nodded, barely allowing himself to look at her.

The blond hair falling over her shoulders was like a cascade of golden light. Incredible.

"Oh, yes," he said finally. "Hammaker is one of those rarities in the industry. He is hot, but he is also good. He might even be in the genius class. We'll have to wait and see."

"That's interesting," said Sophia. "I've heard the same said about you, Mr. Sandler. . . ." She smiled as she spoke to him, and Stephen would have sworn that he felt the lightest of possible brushes against his pant leg by her foot.

Had it been an accident, or intentional?

He dared to stare into her eyes for an instant, and there seemed to be a furnace roaring behind her steady gaze. He could feel the heat of absolute desire smack him in the face for a moment, like standing in front of an oven when the door was pulled open for a second or two, then quickly closed.

"I was talking to you, Mr. Sandler. Are you all right?" Her voice intruded upon his thoughts and he was suddenly aware of staring off like a zombie, lost in his own crazy thoughts.

"I'm sorry, I was thinking of something else. . . . What were you saying?"

"I only said that some people have called you a 'genius,' too."

"Well," said Stephen, feeling suddenly giddy, "I'm afraid they're right!" Everyone laughed at his little joke, including himself, but under the table, he felt her unslippered foot touch him suddenly and stroke his leg. It was a bold, direct move and she stared at him openly, nakedly.

"We shall see about that, Mr. Sandler. . . we shall see. . . ."

He swallowed hard, and reached for his Campari and soda. This woman was spinning him around. What the hell was her game? She didn't need to coax a part out of him. Christ, he'd already promised her the moon! What'd she want to do? Thank him?

That would be a real twist.

Lester jumped back into the conversation and started ironing out some of the details of the deal. Stephen had to admit that for a young guy he was as sharp as they come. He didn't miss a trick, and yet he wasn't trying to pull any fast ones on him. He just wanted to make sure that his client was getting the best deal available and that the normal, expected protections were being included in the paperwork.

The conversation concentrated on the business end of things for the remainder of the meal. Sophia remained relatively quiet, and as much in the background as a woman of her stunning physical beauty could. Stephen found that he was able to concentrate on the conversation but that every once in while, she seemed to give off a wave of sexual heat that almost slapped him in the face. It was as though she were a queen bee sending out pheromones to drive her attendants and suitors wild with desire. It was as though she were sending him a little message—a message that said I'm still here. . . and I'm waiting for you. . . .

The notion that perhaps she could actually control her sexual power stunned him, and he passed the rest of the lunch conversation in a kind of auto-pilot mode: giving the appropriate responses and reactions, but having little recollection of what was actually taking place.

Finally when the three of them prepared to leave, he found himself asking Sophia to come down to the Circle Six that evening.

"We'll be having our read-through tomorrow night," he said facilely, "and I think it would be good for you to spend a little extra time getting familiar with the script. Is eight o'clock good for you?"

"Very well, Stephen," she said as she stood and accepted her coat from Lester. Her use of his first name seemed so natural that he didn't even realize she had done it until minutes later.

They walked to the sidewalk and it was apparent that Lester intended to accompany her somewhere. There was a burning desire in Stephen to suddenly reach out and pull her away from him, to proclaim to all the passersby on the crowded street that he wanted this woman for himself, and he didn't give a damn who knew about it. He didn't care if they did think he was going nuts.

And that made Sandler think about how much power this woman seemed to have over him—to make him feel so . . . so crazy. He knew that everybody had a few random, crazy fantasy-thoughts every day of their lives. We have all had flashing thoughts of killing this one, or running away from that one, or even raping this other one. Everybody harbored those kind of secret thoughts, but this time Stephen suspected that he was serious.

. . . and that's what scared him.

They said their good-byes and thank-yous and turned away from him, making their way down the sidewalk. Stephen watched them blend into the faceless crush of bodies. She seemed fairly close, quite comfortable with Lester, and Stephen found himself wondering if she was fucking him.

It was another one of those crazy, secret thoughts, only this time it was tinged with jealousy and the first touches of possessiveness. And that was bad. . . .

Yet, he could not take his eyes off her as they walked away from him. She had casually tossed her short fur jacket over her shoulders against the early autumn coolness of the day. Her ass moved freely beneath the satin dress and he was convinced that she wore nothing beneath it.'

Wow . . .

Finally forcing himself to turn away, he joined the ever-changing, always moving throng of Manhattan. When they had gotten a decent distance away from Sandler, Rob jumped out in front of Sophia and did a quick little parody of a Russian Cossack dance, then he yelled out exultantly, "Oh, man, we did it, baby! Can you believe it? A lead on Broadway and the option to do the flick!"

Sophia smiled. Several people paused to look at Rob as he capered about on the corner. But only a few really paid attention. The rule in New York was to ignore all.

"Does this mean I'm going to be a star?" she asked.

Rob grinned broadly as he took her arm and fell into step next to her. "You bet it does, honey! The way I see it, there ain't no stoppin' you now!"

They paused at the corner at the Avenue of the Americas, and the traffic boiled and streamed past. Sophia was suddenly conscious of all the noise and the smells and colors of this world and time. It was so loud, so harsh and garish, she found it surprising that she had adapted so quickly to it. She was still feeling a bit lightheaded from the Transformation of the night before, but she tried to ignore the usual after effects. Things were finally starting to happen for her, and she was feeling her blood run. Her need would soon be fulfilled.

The traffic eased and the crowd surged out across the intersection. Rob held out his arm and she took it lightly, following his lead.

"You going back to the apartment?" he asked. Sophia nodded. She could feel the stares of men who passed by them. She had been practicing, and it was definitely working. Thank the gods she could be selective about it, or she would be overwhelmed constantly.

"That's cool, babe," said Rob. "I gotta go back to the office and make some calls. I got some paperwork to do, too."

She smiled and nodded. "I'll keep busy. . . ." she said.

"Yeah, right." He paused as they reached the next intersection where the crowd collected and waited impatiently for a change in the traffic. "Hey, listen, are you going to see Sandler tomorrow night, like he asked?"

Sophia shrugged. "I might. . . Why? You don't approve?"

"No, it's not that. . . it's just that we probably won't have all the paperwork done till tomorrow. I want everything to be legit. I'm not sure I trust that guy."

Sophia giggled. "I thought Sandler was the best!"

Rob grinned. "That still don't mean you can trust him, honey. But don't worry, I can handle him. . . ."

"I'm sure you can, Rob."

He turned and took her hand in both of his. "Listen, Sophia, the way I see it, there ain't no way they can stop us from going straight to the top! Together, we make a hell of a team!"

She smiled. "More than you know, Rob. More than you know."

He looked at her quizzically, but decided to let her comment pass. Checking his watch, he seemed to grow more harried. "Jeez, gotta get outta here, babe. Talk to you later, okay?"

"Tomorrow morning, yes."

He turned to slip into the crosscurrent of another stream of pedestrians, then looked back at her. "You busy tonight?"

She rolled her eyes slightly. "Yes, I've got a date with Eddie."

"No shit? I didn't know you've been seeing him."

She shrugged. "Just a few times. It's . . . it's not working out." She was looking at him with a relaxed, casual air, when she noticed his expression had changed and Rob looked somehow different—suddenly distressed, uncomfortable. "Is there something wrong, Rob?"

He swallowed hard and looked at her with puppy-dog eyes. For an instant, in the crush and swirl of the crowd around him, he dropped his high-energy agent's mask, and he looked like a lost little boy. "I don't know," he said. "Something's bothering me, but I don't know what it is. I just had the feeling that maybe you should know about it."

She smiled at him and reached out to take his hand. "I understand. Maybe when things calm down a bit we can talk about it?"

Her response did not seem to offer much solace, but he forced a smile to his face. "Yeah, right, okay, I'll call you in the morning when I have all the papers ready."

Before she could reply, he had turned away and was carried off by the main current of moving bodies.

"Okay, hold it . . . that's it! Now turn! Quickly, that's it! That's what I want to see! More little-girl stuff. . . let's see you pout. . . that's it! . . ."

Eddie kept an almost continuous patter while he worked.

She had come to his loft apartment in SoHo for a sushi dinner he claimed to have prepared himself, and then they went around the block to his studio to take some "private stuff," as the photographer had phrased it.

Eddie Cherenko was one of the "primo" fashion and commercial photographers in the city. His work was on the covers of the biggest magazines in the country—he had evolved a very unique style, a recognizable "look," and that was what it took to make it big.

And now Eddie was flying on cocaine as he leaned into his

camera lens. He turned and twisted and backed in and out of the set—a surrealistic plain covered with counterfeit dollars and dominated by a single leafless tree—which he had created for a major bank advertisement. With a lot of leering and grinning, he directed Sophia through and about the set. She knew what he wanted and she knew what she needed. Unfortunately, she had discovered rather quickly that the two of them were not receiving an even exchange.

This was the third time she had seen him and already, she knew that he was wasting himself, a meteor blazing briefly across a single night's sky. It was a combination of good fortune, large sums of money, a trace of a talent, and kilos of drugs. Eddie was one of those lucky people who had been deemed to be talented by the folks with the money and now he could do no wrong. He was being shoved down the public's throat as one of the culture's latest geniuses, and no one would know the difference.

Well, almost no one . . . .

Sophia had her own special way of determining things, and Eddie Cherenko had not been passing the test.

As she snaked and sulked about the photographic set, she was quickly becoming bored with the whole scene. Of course, there was a certain amount of narcissistic pleasure to be gained from it all, but it was basically shallow and unfulfilling.

"Okay," said Eddie, pausing to take a vial from his pocket, a vial filled with white powder and specially designed to dispense just the right amount to be inhaled by a veteran. He didn't care that it was no longer in fashion to be a cokehead, he liked it too much. The vial flashed as Eddie Jerked his head back all in one smooth motion. Now he was looking at her again with red-rimmed eyes and a lopsided grin. "Okay. . . you can start taking it off, if you want. . . ."

She smiled into the camera and began to undress. She did it slowly, with a liquid simplicity that even she found sensual and diverting. Eddie's directions were punctuated by the clicking of the camera's shutter, and his labored breathing.

"Oh, that's beautiful, baby. . . beautiful. . . that's it, now turn this way. . . more. . . more!"

She turned and let the last of her dress slide away from her. It whispered down her legs and pooled around .her high-heeled shoes. That she wore no underwear excited him even more and he could hardly continue talking as he snapped off more frames. She whirled and spun and dipped and danced for him, and her long, golden hair open like a Japanese fan.

"You're incredible, baby!" said Eddie, moving closer, still pretending to shoot her with the 50mm lens.

"I've been told that before," she said with a teasing laugh. "Yeah, I'll bet you have. . . ." He moved closer to her eased the camera down to a nearby stool, and reached out to trace an index finger down her arm. Despite the cool air in the open studio, her flesh was hot and shiny.

Taking a step forward, she moved in closer to him. Her full breasts pointed up and out at him, and he could not stop looking at that kind of perfection.

"You want me, don't you?" she asked in a heavy whisper.

Eddie laughed. "What the hell do you think, bitch?" Roughly, he unbuckled his jeans. There was the quick sound of his zipper being jammed down. "It's time to let the monster out of his cage," he said with mock-threatening tones as he wriggled free of his clothes.

"The monster's been out of its cage for a long time now," she said.

"What?"

Eddie moved against her, and she could feel the hard heat of him against her thigh. He reached down and used it like a club to tap and probe at her inner thighs. "Right here," he said. "Right here on the floor. . . ."

"I wonder how many women have heard those exact words, in this exact place?" She asked as she descended to the floor covered with unrolled seamless background paper.

Eddie laughed. "What the hell do you care! You just want it . . . I know. I've seen your type before."

"I don't think so," said Sophia.

Ignoring her, Eddie slipped down on top of her. His actions were raw and tough, coarse and insensitive. He was selfish and obnoxious, and she was not going to regret what she must do this night at all.

As she lay back and opened her legs, he moved roughly into her. She knew he was the kind of man who really did not like women, and that he used sex as a means of striking back, as an outlet for his deepest feelings. He moved within her in a series of harsh, meant-to-be-punishing strikes, but she reciprocated and moved with him, and threatened to carry him away. She could feel the anger and the frustration draining from him as he became swept up in her symphony of movements, her calculated choreography. She brought him to orgasm three times during the night, and each time, he was weaker by tenfold. And it was not until the last time that he began to notice her, to begin to think that there might be something different about her, something wrong.

During their final entanglement, he peered down into her green eyes and saw the bottomless pit beneath them. It was the pit into which he was about to plunge, and for an instant he seemed to see it, to know it.

"What's happening to me?" he asked weakly. His voice was hoarse as it rasped out of his throat.

She threw back her head and laughed, then squeezed him more tightly with her thighs and her vaginal muscles. It was a rippling, peristaltic motion, and he could actually feel her drawing his juices out of him. It was an erotic moment, a painless, yet terrifying experience.

"Who are you?" asked Eddie, his voice now less than a whisper. He sounded like a throat-cancer patient. "What are you?"

"I am the one who pulls away the veils of hypocrisy," said Sophia. "I am the one to expose you for what you are."

She smiled as she thrashed him against the floor, holding him in a loving death-grip and milking the life from him.

He felt as though there were a funnel in his groin, a vortex spinning and churning like a great invisible whirlpool. Then the center of the spinning chaos fell away into eternity, into the oblivion of emptiness, of nothingness. And he could feel himself, the thin veneer of personality and human essence that defined Eddie Cherenko, slowly being whipped down into the maelstrom. He could feel himself being sucked away like dirty water at the bottom of a bathtub drain. And all the while there was the paradox of pleasure staring into his eyes with a living green fire. . . .

She relaxed her muscles and he fell away from her like the dry husk of unharvested cornstalks. There were many times when she truly regretted doing what her nature demanded, but there were other times when she derived a distinct pleasure from her work, and tonight was such a night. She moved away from Eddie, and slowly dressed in front of a full-length mirror. There was a slight suggestion of a glow to her warm flesh and she knew that she had received only the leanest of sustenance.

But she felt refreshed and boiled with excitement and anticipation. Finally she had made the proper connections, and would be admitted into a new inner circle. Not only would her career now be taking a dramatic turn for the better, but her access to the right kind of individuals would also be increased.

She looked about the studio and shook her head. This one had been like so many of the others. It never changed from one age to another in that respect. So many who showed potential and so very few who ever fulfilled the promise.

She turned away from the debris of the evening and disappeared into the night.

Chapter 14

Darien, Connecticut

Richard Hammaker pulled easily on the wheel of the rented Lexus, and its power-steering moved it majestically around the corner. He entered a tree-lined suburban street. Every tree was at least one hundred years old—oaks and poplars and elms that reached out and canopied the road like the ceiling of a great cathedral. The properties alongside the street were equally wooded and superbly landscaped with each sprawling home occupying a small vantage point atop a manufactured knoll. There ain't no slums in Darien, he thought with a silent, ironic chuckle.

As Hammaker looked about, he knew that these were the homes of the super-successful, the *very* well-off, and the plain old rich folks. He saw Stephen Sandler's manse off to the left, and Richard wheeled into the long driveway, which lost itself along a twisting row of evergreens. It was tough handling the big car because Richard hadn't owned one since moving to Manhattan, and this was the first time he'd ever thought to rent one to get to Sandler's place. Usually, he'd taken the train, but now that he was a successful playwright, making some real money for a change, he had decided to splurge on the car. You only went around once, and all that good existential crap, right? He parked it in front of a three-door garage beneath the first floor of the house, and then made his way up a series of flagstone steps, past a garden of boxwoods that smelled like old dog turds, and to a set of double oak doors. After ringing the bell and waiting for almost thirty seconds, he heard Stephen's voice through an unseen speaker.

"Yes? Who is it?"

"You know goddamn well who it is!" said Richard. "You can see on your overpriced TV monitor and your secret camera, now let me in, Stephen!"

Muffled laughter from the speaker, then: "Ah, that can be none other than my pleasant playwright from the Big Bad City. Entrez vous, mon ami!"

The door was opened by an electronic latch being slipped, and it sighed inward a few inches. Richard pushed it open, and let himself in. He walked past a foyer tiled with mosaic pieces from Mexico, and worked his way down a short hallway to the second level where Sandler awaited him in his study. The room was large and lined with oak bookcases and smoked-glass doors. There was the obligatory large executive desk facing the door, and a wall unit filled with state-of-the-art stereo and video gear. Another wall was crammed with posters, photographs, and awards—the memorabilia of a life devoted to theater and cinema. Anyone's attention could not help but be drawn to the incredible display of success and good fortune on Sandler's "trophy wall," as the producer referred to it and Richard was no different. You couldn't miss the Tonys and the Oscars, the Circles and the Gabriels, all mixed with other prestigious trinkets that the average mook on the street had never heard of. In addition, there were framed covers from Sandler's books and posters from his plays. He was a real Renaissance man, one of the last of his kind.

Yeah, this was the office of a guy who's made it big who had all the right moves, and who had parlayed them with the just right combination of talent and luck. "Hello, Richard, you're late," said Sandler who was seated behind the large desk, manipulating a console of electronic switches and touch panels.

"The traffic was pretty bad," he said, looking at his producer with undisguised shock. Jeez, the man looked terrible! Richard had barely seen him in the last two months, and the guy looked like he'd aged *twenty* years. As Richard stepped closer into the room and approached the desk, he could see that it was no optical illusion. Sandler looked like he was on Death's fucking door! His thick mane of hair was thinning into a white, wispy nimbus. Liver spots marred his forehead, and his eyes seemed to have shrunk to small, sparrow-like balls of dull lead.

"What's the matter, Richard?" asked Sandler, trying to smile. Even his teeth looked longer, more yellowed.

"That's what I was going to ask you," he said with his usual frankness. "I gotta tell you, Stephen, you're looking pretty rough around the edges. Is there something wrong? I mean, are you sick?" He said the final word as though it meant much more than its normal usage; he said it to mean cancer because Sandler's appearance all but screamed out the dreaded word.

The producer smiled and exhaled slowly. "No, there's nothing wrong with me . . . at least that's what my doctor tells me. He ran every test imaginable and all he can conclude is that I am 'run down,' but that's it. No degenerative diseases, no consumptive ones, either."

"I don't, want to sound like an alarmist, but I think you oughta get a second opinion."

Sandler laughed. "Good old Richard! I can always count on you for an honest answer! Everyone else has been lying through their teeth, falling all over themselves to tell me how damned good I look when I know I've been coming apart at the seams!"

Richard shrugged. "Maybe it's that profligate life of yours finally catching up with you."

"Maybe you're right," said Sandler, smiling but perhaps believing the notion to some extent.

Richard looked about expectantly. "Where's Miriam?"

"I sent her to Europe about six weeks ago. She's still over there somewhere."

Richard smiled. "It must be nice to have that kind of power."

Sandler shrugged. "It's not really power. It's just money."

"Okay, I'll settle for the money." Richard pulled up a chair next to the desk, still amazed at how downright awful Sandler looked.

"Money's not going to be a problem for you anymore, Richard. That's why I wanted to see you today—we've got some plans to discuss."

Richard felt a hot flush race through him. It was not the idea of the money that excited him as much as a sensation of relief, of instant realization that he might no longer have to struggle merely to survive. "Okay," he said after a pause. "I'm ready. . . ."

Sandler cleared his throat, picked up some papers off one corner of the large desk. "All right, let's keep things simple. After four weeks of sell-outs, *The Vindication* paid back its investors. After eight weeks of packed houses, great reviews, and plenty of media-play, we have a hit on our hands."

Richard sat forward in his chair, rubbed his hands together. "You're sure? It's no fluke, is it? Could it be?"

Sandler smiled. "No, it's not a fluke. No way. You don't see figures like these every day. I know a hit when I see one. This sort of thing happens once a year—when all the critics love you and the audiences love you too. No Richard, this is too solid. I hear everybody who knows anything saying that you're going to win all the awards this year."

"No shit . . ."

"So face it. It's a hit. And that's not even mentioning the film version. They've just about finished casting it, and they want to start shooting next month."

"I know, you told me that last week, remember?"

"Did I?" said Sandler, running his temples carefully. "I didn't realize my mind was beginning to fail me, too. Well, did I tell you why they're having such a hard time casting this thing?"

Richard shook his head.

"I'll tell you why: because all the heavyweights in Hollywood are beating each other over the head to be in this one, that's why."

"You're kidding?"

"Listen, kid, they all smell Oscars here, and they all want a chance to get one of those little bastards can you dig it?" Sandler laughed and dropped the papers to the desk.

Richard was truly amazed. He knew things were going well, and he knew he was going to make close to a million after all the smoke had cleared, but now it looked like it was just the beginning "You know what's funny?" he said.

"What's that?"

"I don't even think *The Vindication*'s my best play!"

Sandler nodded slowly. "No, I don't either, but I think that should tell you something about this whole thing."

"Yeah, it does: that the public doesn't know it's ass from a hole in the ground." Richard grinned and shook, his head.

"No," said Stephen. "That's not what I meant."

"I didn't think so. I was just being facetious. Sorry, Stephen. . . what were you trying to say?"

"I was just pointing out something you seem intent on ignoring: casting Sophia Rousseau in your play has helped make it the big hit that it is." Sandler's voice seemed to inch up the octave scale, as though he were emotionally involved in what he was saying.

Richard smiled. He was wondering when they would get around to talking about the incredible Ms. Rousseau. "Now, Stephen, why do you claim that I'm 'ignoring' Sophia's part in all this?"

"Because I think you are! I think you are ignoring her for God's sake! She tells me that you come down to the theater and you talk to everybody but her. She's getting a complex about it, Richard.

She thinks you don't like her!"

"No, it's nothing like that." He didn't want the conversation going in this direction. He didn't feel like explaining certain things about himself, even to someone like Sandler. "You wouldn't understand, Stephen. Maybe I can explain it someday. . . ."

Sandler cleared his throat. "Richard, you're not jealous of her, are you?" Jesus, what an asshole thing to say! He couldn't believe his producer would even think of something so ridiculous!

"Jealous? Stephen, what're you talking about?!"

"Look, we both know she's gotten a lot of attention from this play, Richard. You know how fast the media can make somebody a goddamned star! She's been interviewed on twenty different TV shows and her picture's been on every magazine cover except *Scientific American*."

"Yeah, I know that. . . but that doesn't mean shit to me."

Sandler chuckled. "She's had movie offers and a chance to do three different TV series, and she's even been offered a show in Vegas, and you're going to tell me that doesn't mean a thing to you? C'mon, who the hell are you, Saint Richard of SoHo?!"

Richard almost laughed. He wondered if Sandler realized how close he was to the truth? "I'm telling you honestly, Stephen: it's okay with me that Sophia's getting all the publicity. It's as you said—she deserves it. She is damned talented."

"And incredibly beautiful!"

Richard smiled and nodded. "Yes, of course. And she's very beautiful, too."

Sandler leaned back in his chair dramatically. "Well, thank you! I'm glad that you approve."

"You know," said Richard, "you sound like you've got a personal stake in all of this. . . ."

"You're damned right I do! I'm your fucking producer, aren't I?"

". . . and you're Sophia's lover," said Richard with a grin.

Sandler fell back into his padded chair as though pushed. "All right, so what? I haven't made any great secret of it? So what? I'm actually kind of . . . proud of it, actually."

"That's why you sent your wife off to Europe for the last two months?"

Sandler glared at him but said nothing.

Richard immediately regretted lashing out like that. He was always attacking people with his nasty tongue, and he knew that it must be tiresome as well as irritating.

"I'm sorry, Stephen. I shouldn't have said that. I can be a real jerk sometimes."

Sandler shook his head. "That's all right. Maybe I deserved it. . . . I'm just not used to getting what I deserve. Most people are afraid of me, afraid to tell me what they're really thinking, anyway."

"Yeah, well I guess I'll never be accused of that. . . ."

"Richard, as long as I have known you, you've always been an outspoken, miserable son-of-a-bitch. But as I'm thinking of it, maybe I was wrong, too."

"About what?"

"About your being jealous. You've never been the egotistical sort, really. When I think about it, it's not really your style to be doing the *Tonight Show* or smiling off the pages of *People* magazine."

"I don't like to smile in public," said Richard.

"So maybe I was wrong. I apologize, too, Richard."

"No need for that." Richard got up and walked around the room, pretending to scrutinize some of the memorabilia on the walls. "But I did find it kind of strange you and Sophia have been seeing so much of each other. Now, mind you—that's not the same as being jealous, okay?"

"What you mean is: what's a woman like her see in an old fart like me?" Sandler smiled softly. "I think that's a question that I ask myself, so it's more than fair for you to think it, too."

Richard held up a hand. "Really, Stephen, it's none of my business. I'm sorry I brought it up again."

Sandler held up a hand in a gesture of mild protest. "Please, as long as we're being honest, let's stop all the goddamn apologizing for it. It's getting kind of sappy and disgusting."

Both men laughed, and Richard returned to his chair opposite the desk. There was something odd about Sandler's mood, about his overall attitude. His humor and even his anger had a fatalistic tinge to it. He talked as though he were leaving off several telling phrases from the ends of his sentences, like "especially in my condition" or "and afterward it won't matter anyway. . . ."

Maybe it was just Richard's imagination overworking and filling in the blanks, because he was so affected by Stephen's appearance, which was admittedly ghastly. Something was wrong with him, and he kept thinking that he should try to find out what it might be.

"Now," said Sandler, "I hate to break up the party, but we've got to talk a little shop here."

Richard shrugged, wondering if his producer was artfully changing the subject. "All right, go on. . . ."

Sandler rose from his desk and walked to a small portable bar. His motions were slow and deliberate, almost feeble. He poured himself a Scotch and soda, and a dry white wine for Richard, then brought the glasses back to the desk. It had always been their custom to have a drink while business was discussed.

Sandler held up the glasses in a toast. "It's been quite a few years now, Richard. You're getting the success you've always deserved. Here's to it continuing!"

"Skoal," he said and sipped the wine.

"Cheers," said Sandler as he tossed back the Glenlivet in one hefty swallow. "Now, a few things to cover, and then a few things to think about. Sophia's agent has accepted the terms for the film version, and casting was wild about getting her for Eleanor. That's no problem. But we have one coming up if she decides to take the Vegas offer."

"Isn't she under contract for Christ's sake?"

Sandler nodded. "Only until New Year's. Then we have the option to negotiate a new one. We weren't as sure we were going to have a hit back when we drew up those papers, remember?"

"Hindsight is always twenty/twenty, right."

"Just so," said Sandler, forcing himself to smile. "Anyway, Lester, her agent, has let it slip to me that the Luxor is offering her three hundred grand per week to start."

"What? That's absurd!"

"No, it's called 'show business;' remember. Nobody ever said it was fair or realistic." Sandler grinned. "You should know how ephemeral it all is, how goddamned fickle the public is! That's why everybody jumps while things are hot. That's why we're having this conversation, for God's sake!"

Richard sighed, leaned back in his chair, and sipped from his wineglass. "All right, go ahead."

"Now, we know we can't match the Vegas offer, so we might have to face the possibility of continuing the run without her."

"She isn't the whole fucking show, Stephen."

"You know that, and I know that, but I'm not so sure about the Great Unwashed knowing it . . . and they're the ones buying the tickets."

Richard was getting pissed, not at Sandler, but only at the truth he spoke. "Melanie's been doing wonderful as her understudy."

"I agree. So does everyone else. But you still have to wonder if the show will fly with her in there."

"Well fuck it! I say let the chips fall. If we lose Sophia, then we give Melanie her chance. She's deserved it." Sandler nodded, then pushed away from the desk and walked slowly to the bar where he fixed another Scotch and soda. He tossed this one down immediately, then prepared a third for the trip back to the desk. Again, Richard was appalled at how bad the man really looked. He could not help going back to the same dark thought. His skin had become so ashen and drawn against the bones of his face. And with his sunken eyes, Sandler had taken on a skullish appearance. It was a scary presage of what was coming for him, and for all of us. . . .

"Okay," said the producer as he again settled in behind the desk. "We go with Melanie. . . all right, that's fine with me. That's what my instincts would have told me, but I wouldn't want to go against your own wishes on this I one."

Richard laughed. "It wouldn't be the first time!"

"No, but maybe I'm mellowing in my declining years. . . ." Sandler drained off more of the Scotch, then looked squarely at Richard. It was a chilling expression.

"What's the matter?" asked Richard.

"Now, listen," said Stephen. "This next thing is very important. Right now, you're the hottest thing on Broadway. The critics are impressed, and the best thing you can do right now to ensure your continuing good graces is to come back with a second show that's better than the first one."

"Yeah, I realize that. . . ."

"You bet your ass! You know how the drama snobs are: once can happen to anybody, there's a million flashes in the pan! But two in a row and you're suddenly 'legit' in their eyes. Give 'em two in a row, and they'll love you forever. . . even if you turn into another Kryhauski and serve 'em up garbage for the next twenty years."

Richard smiled. "I don't think it's all that simple, really."

"Oh, yes, it is! I've been in this business all my life, so don't tell me different. Listen, you give 'em another hit and they'll be afraid to ever trash anything you do. They'll be afraid they don't like it because they don't understand it! And no critic can bear to be accused of that!"

Richard laughed and so did Sandler, but it was a hollow, rattling kind of laugh, which was kind of frightening. Sandler looked at him expectantly. "Well, Richard, do you have a play ready we can follow up with?"

He could feel the urgency in his voice, and that sounded odd, but he tried to ignore it. "Yes, of course. I told you that *The Vindication* isn't my best. What about *Tea Time*?"

Sandler smiled. "Yes, that is a vicious little piece, isn't it?"

"It might not play in London very well, but what the hell?"

"Oh, don't count out the Brits! They take self-satire better than most."

"So you think we should go with that one?" asked Richard.

Sandler nodded. "Yes, I do. I think I should get started I on it Monday morning."

There it was again—that urgency in his voice. "Don't you think you're rushing things a little?" asked Richard. "We've got plenty of time."

Sandler smiled ironically. "I'm not so sure of that. . . ."

Richard felt his stomach turning. He knew what was coming. "Stephen, is there something you're keeping from me?"

"Not really. . . it's just a hunch, I guess you'd call it. It's hard to explain."

"Are you sick? Really sick?"

"You already asked me that," said Sandler. "No, it's nothing the doctor's can find. But. . ."

"But what?"

Sandler looked at him squarely and the man's small dark eyes seemed to bore into him. "But I have a feeling that I'm not going to live much longer, that it's just about over."

"Jesus, don't talk like that. We can check out other doctors, we can—"

"No, it's just a feeling I have. . . . I almost know it. That's why I want to get things rolling with the next show."

"Stephen, do you have any idea what's wrong? Is there anything I can do?"

Sandler looked as though a new thought just occurred to him. "If I tell you something, you must promise not to think I'm crazy, all right?"

"I think that's an easy promise to keep," said Richard. "What is it?"

Sandler drew a long breath, looked up at the ceiling for an instant, then slowly exhaled. "All right, listen. . . ."

Chapter 15

Scarpino, Sicily 1891

"This is the village of my ancestors!" Mauro Callagnia said proudly to her.

He was a tall, handsome boy of nineteen, who literally bristled with energy and invention. Everything he touched or attempted became a natural ability under his hand. He was an expert horseman, a deadly archer and swordsman, an accomplished musician, poet, and painter. He had so much to give, he was like an unending fountain.

"It is so small and unimposing," she said as they drew their horses to a stop before the old wall and gate that marked the entrance into the small mountain village of Scarpino. Miles below them, huddled in the hazy cloak of twilight, lay the city of Palermo, the current home of Mauro's family.

Mauro smiled. "It is from such humble beginnings that many great things may come," he said.

She nodded, and looked carefully down the narrow streets ahead, then started to direct her mount toward the central avenue.

"Wait," said the boy who was already a man. "We should wait for the rest of the caravan, don't you think?"

She did not really wish to wait for Mauro's family, especially his father. She did not feel comfortable in the presence of the Duke. "Very well, Mauro. You are right."

She looked back down the trail, which snaked back and forth across the hills, to see the remainder of their party slowly negotiating a narrow path. The line of horses carried men and women in gaily-colored dresses and suits. Even in the failing light, she could see the mark of breeding and royalty in their carriage. Her young

Mauro was the product of admirable bloodlines, and it was certainly no accident that he was so talented and gifted.

A minute passed in silence as Mauro's father, a Duke whose family title originated before the formation of the now defunct Kingdom of Two Sicilies, appeared over the nearby ridge. She noted that he was a hale man with great stamina and strength for his age. The Duke's face was creased from the years, but a fierce intellect raged behind his bright eyes. There lay a hard casting of determination in his features. The Duke carried a reputation as a man to be respected, and to be dealt with fairly.

Sophia was forced to admit that, although she feared few men, she could possibly fear the Duke of the House of Callagnia.

"What took you so long, father!" Mauro smiled after his greeting.

"A slower horse, and not my age, if that's what you imply, my son!" The Duke turned and signaled to the rest of the family party. "Follow me, it is not far now!"

Mauro assumed the lead, and led the procession down the central avenue of the village. It was a narrow street that leaned to the left, and ascended the hill toward the small village church, whose spire rose above the low-slung houses like an aspiring dream.

As they approached the rectory, a moderately large residence beyond the church, she felt a twinge of apprehension. She had come this far because she had always been cautious, always watchful of the fears and superstitions of the humans. It was easy to become overconfident, and she had always tried to be vigilant against that failing. Of Mauro, she had no fear or distrust—he was so in love, so infatuated with the joys of the flesh that he could never be a problem.

But there were others who were not so intoxicated. It was as though certain men—admittedly few through the ages—were immune to her powers of entrancement, and while she had only seen the man several times, she suspected that the Duke might be such a man.

And so, she thought with a sense of adventure and daring, perhaps it was a reckless thing to accompany this brilliant boy to his parents' anniversary dinner.

She would know soon.

The procession wound its way toward the rectory, and as the line of horses passed, many of the villagers appeared at windows and doors to have a look at the last of the village's *nobilia* in a time when nobility was a dying art form. She looked down at the people in their ragged clothes and their ragged faces, returning their stern expressions with looks of patronizing kindness and false friendliness. It was the haughty carriage that the peasants expected, and she gave it to them with little effort.

Finally they reached the rectory where they were greeted by two small boys, presumably acolytes who worked for the pastor. Everyone dismounted as the boys tended to the steeds, and faced a tall, wizened old priest who walked forward with open arms to greet the party.

"Welcome, my children," said the priest. "Come into my home. Dinner is almost prepared."

They entered the foyer to the stone and stucco rectory, and she was introduced to Pastor Mazzetti.

"Sophia," said the Duke's wife, Dulcima, "I would like you to meet my mother's brother, my uncle, the Pastor Francesco Mazzetti!"

The old priest reached out and took her smooth white hand in his. His palm felt like the bark of an olive tree. He smiled and his runneled face looked as though it might crack like old leather. She smiled back and curtsied, but she could not avoid the intensity of his gaze. This was a man of great confidence and faith . . . and, therefore, power.

"I am pleased to make your acquaintance, Signora," said Mazzetti. "You should feel privileged to attend what has become a grand family tradition . . .."

"She is my guest tonight, uncle!" said young Mauro with a burst of pride as he cut into the conversation. "Is she not beautiful!?"

The old priest smiled, nodding. "Yes, nephew . . . she is that, and more, I am certain."

An old woman appeared in the doorway, which led deeper into the house, and nodded silently, catching Father Mazzetti's attention. He looked about at the assembled guests and brought his hands together in a practiced gesture. "And now the dinner is served. This way, everyone . . . ."

The anniversary dinner was indeed a wonderful affair. Seated at a long table headed up by Father Mazzetti were the Duke and his wife, her brother and his wife, their daughter Carmina, and of course Mauro and herself. Mazzetti had arranged the chair assignments so that Sophia was seated at his right hand—presumably the place of honor, but she was beginning to wonder what might be the true motivations of the priest. He kept looking at her throughout the dinner with intense, probing eyes.

After having glossed over the usual family pleasantries and toasts to good health and long life, the conversation about the table had drifted, inevitably, into politics. Sophia knew this topic was not unusual among the noblemen of Italy because there were finally signs that the unending upheaval and unrest of the country might be nearing surcease. She listened to the banter with a halfhearted interest, while running her long fingernails up and down Mauro's thigh beneath the table.

". . . and I think the best thing that ever happened to us as Sicilians, was getting rid of Premier Depretis," said the Duke as he reached for more wine from a crystal decanter.

"Of course, brother-in-law!" laughed his wife's sibling. "You belabor the obvious, don't you think? Since our new prime minister is a Sicilian, it is to be expected that he would look out for the interests of the Island!"

The Duke nodded. "Perhaps, but he must do it with some tact, with diplomacy, yes?"

"Francesco Crespi is no fool," said Father Mazzetti. "Let's not forget he fought with Garibaldi many years ago. He has made the ascent to power up the rear face of the mountain—he knows how difficult and delicate and lonely it can be at the top."

Sophia watched the priest as he spoke. He seemed to be totally engaged in the conversation, and yet, she had the distinct impression that he was observing her, recording her every movement and reaction. Even though he appeared to be in his late sixties or early seventies, he appeared bright and strong. An interesting old man, she thought with a smile.

"Still," said the Duke. "I think Crespi's taking office is the most important thing to have happened to all of us since the beginning of the Risorgimento!"

The Duke's brother-in-law shook his head. "Some would say that Humbert the First's ascension to the throne is the real key to everything . . . ."

The Duke seemed to flush with a moment of anger. "That fool! Do you really think that the crown prince of Germany should be the King of Italy! It's time we throw out the house of Savoy once and for all!"

Father Mazzetti smiled. "Ah, me . . . the Duke will always be a headstrong man, a man of impulse and raw emotion."

Everyone laughed softly except the Duke.

"And what of it, uncle? My personality has served me well,

has it not?"

The priest shrugged. "Perhaps," he said, "but you're starting to sound like Antonio Labiola."

The Duke appeared perplexed. "And who is he?"

"A professor at the University of Rome who has been teaching Marxism to his students."

"Marxism!" The Duke exploded with laughter. "Do you actually think that a nobleman like myself could ever espouse the writing of such a crackpot as Marx?"

"Why not?" Father Mazzetti said sotto voce "You seemed to have embraced the socialism of Mazzini well enough."

"Oh, please!" said Dulcima, the Duke's wife. "Must we talk of politics endlessly?"

"I'll talk about what I please!" said the Duke.

Dulcima turned to the Pastor. "Uncle, I fear you agitate him. You do this for your own amusement!"

The priest smiled. "I am an old man . . . . I need something for my amusement!"

Everyone laughed as the priest used the opportunity to gaze sharply and quickly at Sophia. She could not escape the hard, cold aspect of his glance.

The moment was interrupted by the appearance of the pastor's cook, who began clearing away the main-course plates and dishes with a clattering efficiency. The conversation at the table fragmented as though on cue into smaller one-on-one exchanges. The Duke seemed to be upset with his wife, while Dulcima's brother was making amusing small talk with his niece Carmina.

"My family is rather outspoken," said Mauro, leaning close and whispering in her ear.

"Don't sound so apologetic" she said absently, trying to cast unnoticed glances at the priest. She was feeling more and more uncomfortable, and she was thinking of ways she could handle it.

"I'm not being apologetic," said the boy.

"Oh, yes, you are!" She smiled and kissed his cheek.

Even that small gesture seemed to excite him and she could sense his desire pulsing from his body.

The cook reappeared with a tray of Sicilian pastries and a small urn of espresso. She placed it in the center of the table and everyone oohed and ahed appropriately.

"And now the dessert!" said Father Mazzetti clapping his hands. Everyone smiled as he began to pass about the tray and the cook began pouring out small cups of the dark, sweet coffee.

The tray was passed to her, and she selected a cream and almond pasticerria. As she placed it on her plate, the cook offered her a small gold-rimmed porcelain cup of espresso. It was a delicate, exquisite piece of work, and she marveled at the relative opulence in which the priest lived when one considered the humble surroundings of the village.

Such were her idle thoughts as she sipped the thick dark liquid from the demitasse cup.

Drawing the porcelain away from her lips, she felt a stabbing pain in her stomach, and an almost instantaneous numbing sensation spreading outward from her head down into her limbs. It was a paralyzing effect, turning her to stone. Even her breathing seemed to be affected and she had the sensation of suffocating.

Poison!

The single thought pierced her like an arrow, and she glanced about the table as she began to straighten out like a plank and slide from her chair. She tried to cry out, but no sound would come. The power of the potion was strong indeed, obviously imbued with the priest's blessing to have any effect at all. She would need all of her cunning and strength to overcome it.

Everyone was talking at once at the table, and as she slipped into a semi-comatose state, she was only vaguely aware of the torrent of voices that swirled and eddied over her.

"My God! What's happened to her?" cried Mauro. She could feel his soft, gentle hands on her as he helped lower her to the floor.

"Let her be!" cried the priest in a sepulchral voice. "Stand back!"

Mauro turned to his father, who had left his chair, and was rushing to her side. "It's true, then? Is it true, Father?"

"Father," said Mauro, "what is happening here? Of what do you speak?"

The priest advanced and huddled over her. She could see him through a filmy, gauzy aspect , which had overtaken the light in the room. She was fighting off the effects of the poison, and her body was sending signals that she would be able to overcome it with time. She was thankful for that, but there was still a panic deep within the core of her being. A panic like a glowing coal that threatened to burst into flame in an instant.

"She failed the tests!" cried Father Mazzetti. "Stand back from the Demon! Stand back from the Possessed Creature that she is!"

"What!" cried Mauro. "Have you all gone mad?" He reached

out and pushed at the old priest, who was leaning over, peering into Sophia's glassine eyes.

Suddenly the Duke lashed out with his large hand and smacked Mauro in the face. The force of the blow knocked him back off his feet so that he went sprawling.

"Silence!" cried the Duke at his son. "You mewling pup! What do you know of this woman other than the fire of her loins!"

Mauro propped himself up on one elbow, stunned and confused. "Father, what you speak is madness! My mistress Sophia might beout of control, but she is no demon!"

"No, she is far worse!" cried Mazzetti, who now held a gold crucifix over her face. "Her food was laced with ground bitter-root. . . enough to choke a man, and she noticed it not! It is as the tales have told—a monster tastes not of man's food!"

The Duke moved to his son and held him in his arms. "My son, I am sorry for what I must do, but it is for the best."

"Oh, father!" The young boy sounded very panicked. "What are you going to do with her?!"

"We have suspected for a time that the young woman is possessed," said the Duke, as the rest of the dinner party gathered about to peer down at her in a ragged circle of faces. "And so we have brought her to the finest exorcist in Sicily—our own Father Mazzetti!"

"Bring her into the church!" commanded the old priest. "I must prepare myself . . . ."

Sophia could feel the effects of the poisons coursing through her supple body. Soon the effects would be lessened enough for her to affect a change. Soon but not yet. And so she was powerless to stop them from lifting her up from the cold stone floor and out into the night. The sky above the foothills was a brilliant, midnight blue, laced with stars and frosted by the wind. They crossed a small courtyard, past a fountain, and into the sacristy entrance of the church.

Her vision was blurred, but she could still determine that the tough old priest had already assumed the mantle of his office, his silk raiments of the priesthood. He stood like a man posing for a sculptor or a painter, striking a posture of defiant strength.

"Take her out to the altar," he said as calmly as his voice would allow. Even in her distressed state of mind, Sophia could detect the metallic scent of his fear. Fear was indeed the mind-killer, and if she could capitalize on Mazzetti's own fears and self-doubts, she still possessed a chance.

She was carried out of the sacristy and into the nave of the church, where the white marble altar lay surrounded by statues of the saints and several elaborate stained-glass windows. As she was placed before the altar, the priest moved down beside her and anointed her forehead with oil. Her muscles were beginning to contract involuntarily. Either the effects of the poison were wearing off, or they were getting worse.

Suddenly there was a stinging sensation in her face, and after being so totally numb and paralyzed, she was ecstatic to feel even the faintest pain in her cheeks. Mazzetti had sprinkled holy water on her, and the droplets burned like acid. It stung, but it was such a sweet stinging.

She could see Mazzetti standing over her, holding up a gold crucifix. In a booming, echoing voice, he began speaking in Latin: "In the name of the Father and the Son and the Holy Spirit, and by the power and authority granted to me by the Holy Mother Church and Pope Leo the Thirteenth, I invoke the rite of exorcism over this woman . . . ."

Mazzetti continued droning on as Sophia secretly smiled at him. His prayers were totally ineffectual; she wanted to cry out and laugh at him, and tell him what a fool he was. More feeling was returning to her cheeks, her limbs. Soon, she would show them that their silly poisons and potions had little real power over a being as great as she.

Yes, it was happening now . . . .

She could feel the power returning to her once-numbed body. In an instant, the juices of the changes were produced and shot through her soft tissues. She could feel her flesh hardening, flaking, and sloughing off, as she began the transformation to the True Form.

The Duke was the first to notice and he cried out in an uncharacteristic voice of alarm. "Father! Look! What does she become?"

"Oh, my God in heaven!" yelled Mauro. "What are you doing to her! She's dying! Can't you see that she's dying?"

Father Mazzetti paused, placed the crucifix upon the altar.

"Silence!" he said quickly. "It is all right! Behold the power of the Lord!"

Suddenly, the priest turned and opened the small tabernacle atop the altar, bringing forth a small golden chalice. Slowly, and with great reverence, as he continued to mumble through the endless Latin prayers, Father Mazzetti reached into the chalice and produced a large, paper-thin wafer of unleavened bread—she knew it was the host, the Eucharist. Holding it carefully between thumb and forefingers, the priest placed the host inside a magnificent gold benediction mantle. It was a chalice-like object that held the Eucharist face-outward in a circular, glass locket surrounded by delicate, radiant spires of gold.

The cast beams were intended to suggest a great irradiation of light from the central figure of the host, but in this case, it was not necessary.

As soon as the old priest turned to face his adversary, the Eucharist began to glow with white heat and light, a miniature sun in his hands. The shadows in the small village church were banished by the brilliant explosion of light. The golden benediction mantle became a torch so bright that no one dare look directly upon it.

Sophia had almost finished the transformation and it progressed rapidly now. In the short moments of the priest's preparations she had assumed the changeling shape of the magnificent green serpent. She reveled in the return to her natural form, and writhed in ecstasy as the Duke and Mauro reeled back from the horror they now perceived. She moved quickly, arching up in her spine and dislocating the hinge of her jaws, unfurling her great hollow fangs. Cobra-like, she reared up to face the foolish priest and his pyrotechnic show to impress the masses. Tightening her coils, she prepared to spring—

—and was stunned into immobility by the searing white wave of energy which hit her like the shock wave of a fiery explosion.

How foolish she had been! How wildly overconfident and arrogant! She had amused herself by walking proudly and defiantly into the lair of her natural enemy, and now he was proving to be her match . . . !

"Behold the beast!" cried Mazzetti. There was a collective, horrified gasp from the assembled dinner party, Carmina had swooned into the arms of her mother.

"My God!" cried out young Mauro, who fell to his knees, grasping the legs of his father in supplication for forgiveness and in thankfulness for seeing the true evil with which he had become involved.

Sophia could see everything taking place with a deadly clarity, but at the same time she felt totally blinded, totally overwhelmed by the power and light emanating from the Eucharist. It was the first time in her very long life that she had ever encountered such a force, and she was truly shocked by its fury and total domination.

Resisting with all her strength, she could do nothing, and as the priest approached her with the Eucharist, the blinding light felt as though it would sear the flesh from her bones. The pain became an intolerable wave, and she succumbed to its numbing paralysis, slipping into a terrible coma-like state in which she was stingingly aware of everything around her, but completely and irrevocably powerless to react.

The priest reached out and touched her dry, scaling flesh. She tottered for an instant, then fell to the stone floor. Her coils remained stiff and tight in the grip of a rigor mortis-like power.

Moving to the altar, Father Mazzetti spoke again. "Lift the altar stone! Quickly now!"

"Father, what are you doing?" asked the Duke, as he moved with his son to fulfill the priest's request.

"Just do as I ask!" said Mazzetti, almost delirious over the show of power at his command.

Quickly, silently, Mauro and his father grasped the corners of the marble altar and heaved upward and away from the massive base. Sophia lay frozen in constricted coils by their feet, watching and suddenly understanding what the priest intended. A shudder of abject horror rushed through her, and she wanted to scream, but no sound could ever come.

The two men eased the marble slab to the floor and looked up to face the priest.

"Take the beast and commend it herewith!" cried Mazzetti. He had a wild-eyed, prophet-in-the-desert look to his features. Mauro and the Duke moved rapidly, automatically. She could feel them as they hunched over, reaching out to wrap their fingers around her girth. The touch of their warm, soft flesh against her scaled coolness repulsed her, and a shudder passed through. Unable to fight back against the blinding heart-of-the-sun light of the Eucharist, she felt herself being lifted from the floor.

Up, over the edge of the altar she was roughly carried. The droning Latin prayers of Mazzetti accompanied this, and despite her terror, she felt a spasm of utter hate wash through her. She vowed her vengeance against this old man who deceived her. She would punish him! He would regret his actions of this day!

Now she was being dropped into the hollow center of the altar. Like a thick-walled casket vault, like a coffin, it accepted her with a dark, mute finality. She felt the cold stone against her flesh, colder even than the scales that protected her.

No! This could not be . . . ! She fought against the paralysis that gripped, railed against the force of the Host, but her power was for nothing compared to the awesome magic of the priest.

Looking up from her crypt, framed by its rectangular walls, she could see the streaming light of the Host still lacing her like a lethal radiation. She heard the grunting effort of the men as they lifted the capstone, an immense slab of white marble, and heaved it up to the edge of the altar.

"Enclose the beast called lamia!" cried out Mazzetti. "And the Lord shall entomb his Adversary forever!"

The sound of heavy stone, grinding, grating, sliding against heavier stone echoed through the hollow crypt of the altar. She cried out to them for mercy, but the sounds were only in her mind. She could do nothing but watch the rectangular slab slowly creep across the altar's topmost edges, sealing her within like a moldering corpse.

Except that there would be no moldering.

There would be no mindless, black oblivion here. No she realized with a rising panic, with a thick column of terror rising up in her mind. Instead, she would be alive in this total darkness, in this state of eternal paralysis. She would be conscious of the nothingness that entombed her.

Forever.

The thought shot through her being with a searing, exquisitely painful reality.

No! The single word reverberated through her mind as she watched the last edge of light being constricted and finally pinched off as the slab slid into place. Stone met stone with a final resonant thud, leaving her in a place of total darkness, of a silence so deep and so profound that she felt she might go immediately mad . . . .

Chapter 16

New York City

She was enclosed within a tiny box. Inside the box, there was a terrible darkness, an absence so total, so complete, that she felt as though it were something she could touch. And the box which held her, was contained by another box and that by another, ad infinitum, the intricate, endless combinations of an Oriental puzzle box: she could not see beyond the confines of her own, initial enclosure, but she simply knew that the boxes went on forever.

Forever.

The word echoed in her consciousness like a child's taunting song.

It was a stinging rush of sensation and pain so terrible that she could bear it no longer. Raising her long fingernails to her face, she felt the urge to tear through the flesh and cartilage, to savage her brain, to silence its maddening thoughts forever.

Forever.

She looked desperately through the palpable darkness, looking for a spark of light, either real or metaphysical, but there was nothing but the absolute and final knowledge of the boxes going on and on. . . .

Sophia opened her eyes and rolled over to see the red numbers. There was a moment of total disorientation, and another wave of abject terror crashed over her. She willed herself to full wakefulness and recognized the face of the digital clock giving substance and value to the dark bedroom. Four-thirteen in the morning. It had only been a dream. No, that was not right: a nightmare, a memory.

Placing a hand to her forehead, she was not surprised to feel the slippery patina of sweat there. Her breathing rasped in her breast, and she forced herself to sit up. The dream had been very real, unbelievably vivid. It was the first time since her escape she had actually relived the experience that had entombed her for almost a century.

Getting up slowly, reaching out for the switch that would fill the room with soft lamplight, Sophia stood for an instant and massaged her temples. It had been a most horrible dream, and she could not expel the images from her mind. She kept thinking that she would prefer death the final nothingness, to the false-death of the entombment, even if it was only to be for a single day, a single hour, a fraction of a minute . . .

Never again. The words cut through the fog in her brain with a crisp clarity. It was a vow she had made to herself and would never break.

Naked, she walked into the hall and worked her way to the study, where she kept an assortment of cordials and liqueurs behind a wet bar. She felt an overwhelming urge for a drink, and she would indulge herself despite the lateness of the night.

The dream had been a catalyst, she knew that now. It was forcing her, for the first time, actually, to remember and to think about what she had endured. She had lay in the darkness, twisted and crippled by the ever-presence of the Eucharist on the slab above, plotting her revenge upon the bones of Mazzetti.

Pouring out a double shot of Irish Mist into a snifter, Sophia brought it to her lips quickly. There were certain human amenities, which she had grown to appreciate, and actually become semi-dependent upon. The dark amber liquid slipped down her throat easily, scoring a warm path, which seemed to cry out for more.

She had never endured such dreams. Never. Why was it happening now? The thought plagued her, and she was convinced that there was some special significance, some meaning to the experience. She did not believe that things happened to her purely out of happenstance.

No, there was purpose and portent in all things. She had lived too long to not realize such things. Was that dream nothing more than a grim warning to always be vigilant, to always be wary of the possible fate awaiting her?

Or was it something more specific? She imagined that it might be a harbinger, a precognitive message that there was danger in the future, that she must be extremely careful.

But there was no way of knowing . . . and the images of the terror-dream had been so vivid, so real that she did not really want to dwell upon them.

But you must. You must face the reality of who you are and what could happen to you. . . again.

Never again.

She walked past the couch and stood in front of her window-wall. The curtains had been pulled back and the incredible, stone forest of the city rose up before her. Despite the hour, much of it still burned with light and a furious, internal energy. It was such a jubilant place, a city so alive and feeding off its own phoenix-like sparks that it would never die. It was an entity unto itself, and she believed that even if humankind destroyed this city, another would spring up from the ashes, perhaps of its own accord. There was something about the city which 1intrigued her endlessly.

The notion had been a diversion from her dream, but now her thoughts were returning to it. No longer out of loathing but in a more contemplative manner. She knew that she would never let something like that ever happen again.

Never again.

She would kill herself first. It was that simple.

Sitting on the edge of the couch, she watched the moonlight as it washed coolly over her nakedness. She sipped again from the liqueur, and took a soft, even breath. It was so lonely to be the creature she was, and yet there was a solace in it—a comfort that she would always be unique.

But in the world of humans, unique was often equated with evil, and this thought intrigued her.

She considered the idea that she was "evil" and almost immediately rejected it, using the natural world as her model. When the leopard brings down a wildebeest or an impala, it is a simple, single death. Is the leopard evil for hunting down her prey? No more so than the blue whale which strains in tons of microscopic plankton—a million deaths in one catastrophic feeding.

Numbers meant nothing. Nor did moralistic judgments. There were no morals to be discussed when considering survival in the natural world. One did what was necessary to survive, and this was true in the supernatural world as well.

The thought calmed her and she smiled into the moonlight, sipping again from the snifter. The liquid burned and soothed simultaneously as it coursed down her throat. The memory of the tomb was fading now, and she was feeling better. As she looked out upon the city, she gained a new appreciation for simply being alive to it all.

Being as old as she was, the tendency to become jaded with the world and its peasant-stock of inhabitants was always possible. Therefore, Sophia had always tried to be adventurous, to always explore new ways of seeing the world, new ways of living within it.

If you could maintain that level of dedication, the pure, simple sensation of being alive would always be fresh and new.

Finishing her drink, she placed the snifter absently upon a table at the end of the couch, and stared out at the last hour of night as it huddled around the city. The night was her best friend, and she had been living such a vital busy life during the day that she had lately forgotten how refreshing and curative its powers could be.

She needed to relax as completely as possible, to wash away the psychological dirt and feel renewed once again. As the moonlight transformed her warm, tanned flesh into a pale blue marble, she leaned back and spread her legs as wide as possible.

Slowly, letting her hands and fingers touch lightly across her breasts, encircling the aureolae, and then descend across the flat, firm expanse of her belly. Watching her hands, feeling the light touch of pleasure, she admired the perfect geometry of her flesh.

More slowly, her hands descended, increasing the anticipation and her natural desires. By the time her fingers touched the first downy blond wisps, she was already wet and hot. Her long fingernails traced a path over her mons, and she arched her back as though rising up to meet her own delicate touch.

As her fingers slipped into her, a ripple of pleasure radiated outward from her loins. Slowly at first, her fingertips massaged the hot, slippery area.

But soon her fingers moved more quickly, and the nightmare was briefly forgotten.

Chapter 17

In Flight

Even though he had felt the new "hypersonic" plane had been a colossal waste of money, Matthew Cavendish had decided to use it for Trans-Atlantic flights because it was simply faster than other planes. He loathed flying with a deep and sincere sense of dread, of abject fear. Therefore, the quicker he could get the flight over with, the better he felt.

But there were problems with the H-Liner. For starters, it felt too big—something carrying this many people shouldn't be able to stay aloft. Secondly, any joint venture with the French was most likely doomed from the start—they had a way of buggering up even the simplest of deals. And as soon at new hyper-liner by the Yanks was ready, he'd be switching allegiances

A flight attendant brought him a bloody mary as he opened up his briefcase and spread out some of his workpiles of papers and clippings and some of the photocopied material from the Paris Metropolitan Police files. French Inspector Maillet had been a very good contact, and very thorough. When the unassuming Inspector had turned over the file, he asked the same question everybody seemed to ask him: "Do you think it would be possible to get a mention in your next book?"

Matthew smiled and sipped his drink. He found it amusing that the average sod of a person wanted to be "on the telly" or "in a book." It was as though they were unconsciously grasping for a little immortality. People were impressed with TV and books in the modem age the way the common folk reversed religion and magic and superstition in previous ages. Books and television were part of a mystical, semi-mythic land where few of the peasants were ever permitted. It was a rare and special treat to be included among its practitioners.

The bloody fools, he thought with a wry twist of a smile.

He adjusted his glasses and began to take some notes on the material.

There were confirming reports from the Surete on parallel events in Nice and Marseilles. Apparently the woman in question had little fear of being known or discovered, and there were always a few witnesses to her modus operandi—albeit peripheral ones.

In Nice, she had taken up with a Spanish sculptor by the name of Ramon Velez. He was a young man of some European fame and was highly regarded as a blazing new figure in the inner world of art cognoscente.

After spending a month with Velez, the woman disappeared from his circle of friends. A week later, Velez checked into a hospital and died the next day of unknown causes. Friends of the sculptor reported that his last girl friend had been known only as Sophia.

Now, that had been an interesting name, thought Matthew. An odd and distinctive name. Since she had continued using such an odd moniker, it had been a bit easier to track her down to his present destination.

There had been a similar incident in Paris. Perhaps the most successful and talented photographer in the city—a dashing "Continental" playboy named Jacques St. Reynard, who also happened to be the best fashion photographer in Europe—was now among the deceased. The police investigated his death since he had been found dead in his bathtub with a goodly amount of cocaine in his bloodstream, and determined that it had not been caused by any kind of overdose. Cause of death was listed officially as "unknown." As an addendum to the report, interrogations with St. Reynard's closest friends and work associates reveal that his death was particularly sad in light of his latest discovery, his latest hot model, who had promised to be the most commercial "look" in many years. Again, the reports said the model's name was Sophia, but this time there was a last name: Rousseau.

Matthew flipped through the pages of the police reports, checking and double-checking the facts. It was a very thorough report, and the inspector had really outdone himself in the hopes of being included in Cavendish's next book. There were photos of Ms. Rousseau taken from St. Reynard's lab, copies of weekly magazines in which several of her fashion ads had already appeared, and there was even a copy of her passport application and a print-out of the airlines' reservation she had made two months ago.

Matthew was very proud of himself. He had picked up the smallest of clues, the slightest suggestion of something amiss and had doggedly tracked down his story. It had taken more than the week he had originally figured upon, and Mrs. Whittington had shipped him more than a few extra oxford shirts and pullovers, but he was excited now. He was on the hunt of what he believed was the real article, an entity which up until this time, he had figured was just another fanciful tale.

But as he had often discovered, most silly stories were based, somewhere along the line, in truth.

He kept careful notes of his methods and the dates and the information that he had slowly accrued. He would write the book of his career about this one. It would be a modem tale of detection and revelation. Matthew could imagine the lurid cover of the book already—stacked up in great numbers and gaudy displays at all the best bookshops. He could already see the crowds of his fans swarming over the book tables and gathering up his latest piece of sensationalism.

Only it wouldn't be sensationalism, he thought coolly. It would be a chronicle of perhaps the most incredible discovery of our century. Matthew was certain that his name and his place in literature would be secure if he could bring this one off.

His thoughts were invaded by the flight attendant, who asked if he wanted another bloody mary.

"No, thank you," he said. "But could you tell me if we're on schedule?"

The young woman smiled. "Oh, yes, sir. We'll be touching down at JFK in about forty-five minutes."

Chapter 18

New York City

As the taxi carried Rob down Broadway he rolled down the window, letting the fresh morning air wash over him. The streets and sidewalks of the city overflowed their banks with a steady current of frantic humans. The men moved without topcoats or quilted parkas, and the women swished and flounced along in full-cut skirts and the latest fashions.

It was that time of the year they called "Indian Summer," and it was always one of the best times to be in Manhattan—at least Rob had always thought so. It was a mixture of the cooler, less humid air of autumn and the crisp, bright sunshine of summer. It was one of the only times that you could wear a suit or a sport coat and be comfortable both in and out of doors.

He was wearing one of his three-piece worsted wools this morning, and it felt perfect for the weather and his mood. He had a lot of deals to work on today, the biggest of which was Sophia's showdown with Tantamount Studios. They had signed Eric Terranova for the lead, and Rob knew he didn't come cheap. So that meant that they were going to pay dearly for Sophia if they wanted her.

And he knew that they wanted her.

Hell, everybody wanted her! He was getting calls from all the studios, the TV producers, the photographers, and all the agencies all the way down to the guys doing the local car-dealer stuff. It was a real pleasure to say no to the deals with only six figures in them! Let the other guys eat their hearts out. . . Rob had finally entered the Big Leagues.

The cab pulled to the curb in front of his office's building, and he jumped out, giving the guy a nice tip. *What the hell, I can afford it, and besides, I'm feeling good!* He entered the lobby, waved to the security guards, who all knew his face but probably couldn't tell you his name, and caught an elevator just before it was closing.

When he entered his office, Justine had a stack of messages for him.

"Good morning, Mr. Lester. There's one here that's pretty important. . . ."

He smiled, taking the stack of small paper squares.

"They're all important, baby."

Justine did not smile. In fact, she looked rather grim. "Hey," said Rob. "What's the matter here?"

Justine reached out, pulled the top message from the stack in his hand, and held it up for him. "Richard Hammaker called this morning, first thing. He called to tell you that Stephen Sandler died last night. . . ."

The sentence smacked him like the back of a woman's hand. "What? Sandler's dead? How?"

Rob took back the message and read it quickly, but it revealed nothing more than what Justine had said.

He moved off toward his private office. "Put a call through to Hammaker for me, honey, right away."

The buzzer went off as he sat down at the big executive style desk, and he picked up the phone to hear it ringing on the other end. "Thanks, Justine."

His secretary clicked off the line and the call was answered at the other end. Hammaker's raspy voice was clearly recognizable.

"Richard, this is Lester . . . I got your message. Just got into the office. What's going on?"

"Not much," said Hammaker. He sounded as though he might have been crying. "He's just gone, that's all. Died in his sleep last night. His wife had just gotten back from Europe a couple of days ago, and she had called me a couple of times because she'd been so worried about him."

"Huh?" asked Rob, still trying to let the reality of Sandler's death sink in. He was wondering what this was going to do to the negotiations with Tantamount—if it was going to change anything.

"The guy's been looking terrible lately," said Hammaker, speaking rapidly. "I guess the change was even more drastic for his wife. She hadn't seen him in a while."

"Is she handling all the arrangements?" Rob didn't really care about that kind of shit, but it seemed like the appropriate thing to say.

"Yeah, the funeral's tomorrow." The playwright gave him all the details and he scribbled them on a pad. He wasn't sure if he would bother with the whole ritual, but Sophia might want the information. He knew she had been getting pretty close to Sandler. Rob often wondered what she saw in Sandler physically, and he wondered a lot if she was shtupping him on a regular basis. She was always talking about how brilliant the man was, how fucking talented he was.

Yeah, well all that talent and all that brilliance wasn't doing him much good right about now.

"Does anybody else know?" asked Rob.

"Hell yes! This is big news, didn't you know? The media will be swarming all over poor Miriam for the next day or two. Then, after that, it will be old news, they'll probably leave her alone." Hammaker sounded extremely contemptuous of journalists and their TV counterparts.

"I'd better tell Sophia," he said. "She liked Sandler a lot. She was pretty close to him."

"Yeah," said Hammaker. "I know . . . they were getting very close, the two of them."

Rob chuckled. "You noticed that, too, huh?"

"How could you goddamn miss it?" Hammaker sounded a bit snide in his response. "Neither one made any secret of the little fling they were having."

"Well," said Rob, trying to make light of the whole deal. "That's all part of what they call Show-Biz, ain't it, Mr. Hammaker?"

"I'm not sure if that's all there is to it." There was a pause on Hammaker's end. He sounded a bit disturbed to Rob, and he was wondering if the guy was okay.

"Richard? Are you there?"

"Yeah, I'm still here. . . ."

"Anything wrong?"

"I don't know. There's something that maybe I should talk to you about. It sounds pretty crazy, and maybe it is. Maybe Stephen was getting a little crazy. . . . I don't know. "

Rob wasn't exactly wild about the dramatics Hammaker was injecting into their conversation. "Richard, what're you talking about?"

Another pause. Then, finally: "I'm not sure. Sandler told me a few things a couple weeks ago that sounded pretty weird back then. Now that he's dead, I'm not so sure anymore."

"I still don't know what you're talking about. Was somebody after Sandler? Was he getting threats or blackmail or something? Maybe you should go to the police."

Hammaker laughed for an instant. "No, no . . . it's nothing like that. Nothing that 'theatrical' I assure you."

Rob shook his head silently. This guy was being theatrical enough for both of them but, then, what could you expect from a damned playwright?

"Well, ah, what is it, then? Do you think you might wanna tell me?"

"That's what I was thinking myself," said Hammaker. "Maybe you are the person to talk to first. . . ."

"You're making this all sound very mysterious," said Rob.

"I'm not sure what it is," said Hammaker. Another pause. An exhalation of breath. "How about meeting me for lunch? You free?"

"No, I've got to see the people from Tantamount, but maybe the best thing to do would be to postpone—in light of Sandler's dying and all. Make 'em sweat a few more days, and see what this new wrinkle is gonna do to everything."

"So you'll meet me?" Hammaker's tone of voice revealed neither disdain nor enthusiasm.

"I think so. Let me make a few calls and I'll get back to you within the hour, okay?"

Hammaker agreed and Rob hung up the phone. He had always thought the playwright was a weird guy, and through the last few months that he had gotten to know him, nothing Hammaker did had belied that notion. But now the guy sounded a little more than just weird. He sounded. . . disturbed.

Shrugging, he buzzed Justine and had her put through some calls.

They met at an out-of-the-way Thai restaurant down in the Village upon Hammaker's recommendation. Rob had never been there, although he had heard people talk about the place. It was one tiny dump of a place—no atmosphere, cheap fixtures, bad lighting, the works—except that its very un-fashionableness had helped make it become fashionable among the SoHo theater crowd. And the food was pretty good, too.

Hammaker was acting as strange as he had been on the telephone that morning. Of course, Hammaker was a pretty strange guy anyway.

He spent most of the meal talking about how Thai food was so totally different from any of the other Southeast Asian countries. To hear him discourse on the subject, you might think he'd taken a degree in the cuisine of Thailand, Rob thought, but he knew the guy was just being nervous and blowing some smoke to cover it all up.

Finally, when the waiter was bringing them their second coolers of iced coffee, Rob decided he'd had enough farting around.

"Okay," he said in a calm voice. "You and I don't make a habit of taking lunches together, so let's get down to business: what was it you wanted to see me about?"

Hammaker leaned forward on his elbows, stared at him with his dark Rasputin eyes, and exhaled slowly.

"All right," he said. "But just keep in mind that I'm just telling you what Sandler told me. I hope you don't think I'm crazy."

I already think you're crazy, thought Rob as he looked at Hammaker. With his unruly beard, large wildish eyes, and his Sunny's Surplus wardrobe, the playwright did not exactly cut the most awe-inspiring figure. But what the hell, weird though he may be, the dude could write.

"Go on," said Rob. "I'm listening."

Hammaker went on to tell the story of his visit to Sandler's Connecticut manse, and how the man had been drinking, and when the conversation finally touched upon his involvement with Sophia, the producer/artist had felt compelled to talk.

"And what did he say?" asked Rob, who had listened to the introductory paragraphs with growing impatience.

"He said that he was in love with Sophia. . . ."

Rob laughed. "Yeah, right, who the hell isn't? I mean, who in their right mind wouldn't fall for that chick if she gave you a roll or two?"

Hammaker nodded grimly, sipping from his iced-coffee as though not even tasting it. "Perhaps. . ." he said distantly. "But Sandler also told me that he was afraid of her."

"What? *Afraid* of her?" Rob felt a cold chill rise up from the core of his being and race through him instantly. "Did he say why?"

Hammaker shrugged. "Not really. . . I asked him the same question immediately. I mean, it's not normal for you to be terrified of the woman you love, is it? So I poked around and I pushed and prodded him, and I got him to keep talking about it. I got the feeling that he wanted me to do it. That way he wouldn't feel as foolish about talking about his feelings."

"Yeah, I know what you mean," said Rob. He was getting a weird, undefined feeling about what Hammaker was telling him. It was as though he knew on some unconscious level exactly what Sandler had been trying to say. There had always been a part of him that found Sophia to be just a bit further than one might call "exotic." Sometimes the woman was downright strange, and sometimes she was out-and-out weird. A faint, flash of a dream that somehow seemed like more than a dream passed through his mind. The image of Sophia's soft flesh cracking and peeling and falling away strobed across his mind's eye, and he felt another chill shudder across his shoulders.

"Are you all right?" asked Hammaker.

Rob nodded quickly, probably a little too quickly. "Yeah, sure, I'm fine. . . go on with the story."

Hammaker took a deep breath. "Anyway, when I pushed him about being scared of Sophia, he finally gave in and tried to explain what he meant. He said that he'd never had a woman sexually the way he had Sophia. He said she was a 'total sexual creature'—those were his exact words, and it scared him."

Rob remembered his own initial encounter with Sophia and how she so totally dominated him with her physical presence in the bed. She was the best fuck he had ever had, but it was a hell of a lot more than that, and that's what Sandler had been trying to tell his playwright.

"It scared him," Hammaker continued, "because he said that he started getting these crazy thoughts. . . you know the kind of crazy thoughts you get when you're lying in bed, just before you drift off to sleep, and they seem so rational and well thought out until you review them the next morning. . . ?"

"Sure," said Rob. "Yeah, I know what you mean. Go on."

"Okay," said Hammaker. "So Stephen tells me that he starts having these thoughts that Sophia's not human. . . ."

"What! What the hell're you talking about!" Rob's response was louder than he had intended, and people at the other table turned to stare at him. Embarrassed, he began to speak in a harsh whisper. "What the hell does that mean—not human'! Was Sandler going nuts?"

Hammaker seemed unaffected by Rob's outburst. It was as though he had expected it somehow. He shook his head slowly in answer to the question. "No, I don't think there was anything wrong with his min—-right up until the end. Stephen was always a brilliant, perceptive man. There was little that passed beneath his notice. He picked up on everything."

"Then what was he talking about? You just don't go around claiming that someone we all know isn't human!"

"He wasn't sure what he meant when he said it. He said it was more of a feeling than anything he could base on facts. He said that he'd never been in the presence of a woman like her before. She was definitely different— that he was certain."

Hammaker paused, sipped from his glass cooler, and pulled out a cigarette, then realized this was unlawful. In defiance, he put in his mouth unlit, hoping someone would tell him to not light it.Then he cleared his throat, and continued: "And he was convinced that she had something to do with his declining physical health."

"Explain," said Rob, experiencing a general sense of unease. He was not sure he wanted Hammaker to explain anything, but he felt compelled to listen.

"Stephen claimed that he had begun to deteriorate from the moment he first slept with Sophia. He felt that there was some kind of connection—as strange as it might sound. And he backed up his suspicions by pointing out some of the weird coincidences that surrounded her."

"Like what? What're you talking about?"

"Well, apparently, when Stephen got intrigued with the whole notion, he started investigating things a little more deeply than most of us would bother. He could be very, very thorough—that was one of the secrets of his success."

"Investigating things like what?" asked Rob.

"Like who else she had been seeing, and what had happened to them." Hammaker exhaled a thick nervous column of smoke.

"And? What had happened to them?"

"You might not believe this, but they'd all died."

"C'mon, what're you talking about? Who died?"

Hammaker leaned back in his chair and tried to create a small wry, grin. "Well, let's see . . . there was that photographer Cherenko . . . and before him there was Bruce Olds, the poet . . . and Gregor Krolczyk, the modem composer. They've all died within the last two months."

"And all of them had been seeing Sophia?" Rob was amazed not only that the three men had died, but that Sophia had been running with them. If it were true, she certainly had been living a bit of a secret life.

"Oh, yeah," said Hammaker "Stephen told me that he had been trying to track down her whereabouts in Europe, but so far, he hadn't heard anything. I guess he never did. . . he didn't live that much longer."

"This all sounds like a bunch of crazy coincidence," said Rob. "We're not talking about any real evidence. . . and evidence of what? You don't have any idea what Sandler was talking about, do you?"

"No, not really?"

"Then what're you trying to say here?" asked Rob harshly. "That Sophia actually killed these guys? C'mon! That's ridiculous!"

Hammaker shrugged. "Perhaps. .. I know it sounds impossible. For one thing, she has no motivation to do it."

"You're starting to sound like a cop."

The playwright smiled. He was an odd-looking little fellow. It was no wonder there were so many strange stories about him circulating through the theater crowd. That he was gay was one of the less mysterious stories traveling the circuit. Rob had even heard one rumor that told of Hammaker spending twelve years as a Trappist monk in upstate New York. Now that was one hell of a rumor.

"That brings me to one of my most important questions.Do you think I should go to the police?"

Now it was Rob's turn to grin. "Are you kiddin'? They'd laugh you right out of the precinct! Unless they decided you might need a short trip to Bellevue."

"Really that bad, eh?" Hammaker shook his head and stared off at the crowd at the other dining tables.

"Yeah, I'd say so." Rob paused. "Look, you've got zero evidence. That's the most important thing. And that part about her 'not being human' is the kicker. Ain't too many cops in this town waitin' to buy that explanation for anything."

"So what do we do?" Hammaker sounded serious and a bit desperate.

Rob was not certain how to respond. He shrugged. "What can you do? You can keep an eye on her, if you want. But beyond that, I don't think you can do anything. Really, man, what can I tell you?"

Hammaker pushed back from the table. "Nothing, I guess. . . but at least I feel better sharing this with somebody. .I mean, hearing all that stuff from Stephen was weird enough, but now that he's dead . . . it makes it even weirder, you know?"

"Yeah, I get the idea." Rob signaled for the check, and their waiter, probably a young actor hoping to be the next DeNiro, moved instantly to place the tab on a tiny silver tray by Rob's diamond-ringed hand.

"And besides," Hammaker continued. "You seem like the most natural person to talk with when Sophia is concerned. You've known her ever since she first came to America, haven't you?"

Rob nodded.

Hammaker's expression became a bit more wild-eyed as he stared at Rob. "Tell me something: did you ever fuck her?"

So stunned by the question, Rob had difficulty making the words come forth. "No, of course not," he stammered. "I make it a policy that you don't dip your pen in company ink. It's bad business, you know?"

Hammaker grinned and nodded, but Rob was getting the impression that the dark little playwright did not really believe him.

"Yeah, well, if you don't mind, I'm going to watch your client a little more closely for a while," he said softly. "Stephen Sandler was not just a brilliant producer to me, he was also a very good friend."

"I understand how you feel," said Rob, meaning it. "You do whatever you feel you have to do."

Rob pulled out his billfold and searched out the Diner's Club card, placing it on top of the check in the tray. Hammaker noticed this and waved him off.

"Please, this one is on me . . . for three good reasons: one, I asked you to meet me here; two, they don't take fancy cards in this dump; and three, I'm a wealthy man now—I can afford it." Hammaker managed a small smile after this attempt at some levity.

Rob nodded, and accepted the offer by merely putting away his credit card. Rob wasn't exactly looking toward the poorhouse himself, these days, but he would take a freebie anytime. "My father told me to never turn down something for free," he said. "Thank you."

Hammaker signaled for the waiter, who seemed to materialize from thin air to take the tray with check and money.

"Can I stay in touch with you?" asked the playwright. "Just in case I run into anything important?"

Rob shrugged. "Sure, it's fine with me. Do you expect to really find anything?"

"I don't know. I just feel like I owe it to Stephen. You know what I mean?"

Rob grinned. "Yeah, sure, but listen, I gotta tell you watch yourself around Sophia. She's a handful, and she definitely travels in the fast lane."

"I know all that," said Hammaker. "I just hope that's all there is to her!"

Chapter 19

Funeral services for Stephen Sandler were fittingly held at the old Revere Theatre on 48th Street, one block off Broadway. It was at the Revere, Sandler had once told her, that he had gotten his start forty years earlier as a stagehand.

The old building was filled to overflowing with friends, relatives, and just about every working professional in the business. More than seven hundred seats were filled, plus the balcony and the large SRO crowd. Like many of Stephen R. Sandler's legendary shows, it was a first-class production.

The entire stage was filled with hastily painted backdrops and flats from many of Sandler's most famous plays. Collected and arranged in front of these, forming a large semicircle about his polished ebony casket, were tiers of mementos and props from his musicals and movies. Posters, photos, and objects symbolizing some of the most famous titles in film and stage history. If you weren't familiar with the breadth and scope of Sandler's vision and work, you would be constantly recognizing a famous piece or another and thinking, "Jeez, did he do that, too?" And of course there were the floral arrangements, which flowed over the stage in a bright cascade of soft color. Everyone who couldn't fly in from the West Coast or Europe had sent flowers, plus the usual ritualized tokens of esteem from many of the attendees.

Sophia sat in the third row with her agent Rob and the rest of the cast of The Vindication. To her left sat Richard Hammaker, the dark and brooding playwright. As the services moved from one speaker to another, she was aware of Hammaker's gaze upon her.

Several times, she turned and glanced at him and he returned her look with a hard, cold stare. She could not be certain whether or not he was especially upset by Sandler's death or if there was some other thing wrong with him.

There was no doubt that he was an intriguing man, an out and out mysterious man. No one in the cast or around the theater knew that much about him (for she had discreetly asked). No one even knew where he lived, and that was strange. It appeared that he had no friends—other than Stephen Sandler. Only Sandler had indicated, however obliquely, that he knew much of Hammaker's real story. Only Sandler never revealed much of it—despite her seductive efforts.

Of his genius there was no doubt. Some humans announced the presence of their special talents, their boundless abilities as though they were shining a lamp into a dark room. Sophia was especially sensitive to the signals, and she was drawn to it as a moth to flame.

She felt drawn to Richard Hammaker.

It was undeniable, although upon reflection she suspected that perhaps she was denying it to herself.

But it was no wonder that she might feel that way. Look at him: short, dark, almost oily. He was like a twisted little gnome in a Grimm fairy tale. None of the women in the theater found him appealing or in any way attractive, and he made no effort to make himself more likable. Hammaker was often rude and arrogant, moody and irascible. He could be extremely abusive to those he perceived as beneath him, and he did not seem to care what anyone thought of him.

And another oddness about him was his total lack of sexual interes—-not just in her, but in anyone. She had heard it theorized that the libido could be sublimated and re-channeled into creative endeavors, and that, in fact, was where most humans derived their incredible creative energies.

Her dear, troubled, crazy Vincent had often spoke of such things—as though he knew it was true on some elemental level of his being. Apparently, Hammaker had lost his sexual urge in his work, using it to stir and enflame his imagination. There was no denying the passion of his plays and the driven nature of his characters. They were so very real, Sophia knew this.

And yet, there was a power, a strength that emanated from him, which she could not ignore. She knew that he was becoming a challenge to her. He represented an enigma that must be investigated, a puzzle to be solved.

For if there was anyone who might penetrate the defenses of Richard Hammaker, it would surely be Sophia.

Looking back to the stage, she saw that the final speaker of the service was drawing to a close. After he finished, there was a commencement of music, and ushers appeared at the aisles, leading out the family through the vast ocean of padded seats, allowing everyone else to follow.

Hammaker walked ahead of Sophia and Rob, his head down, apparently deep in thought.

As she watched him depart, ignoring the thousands of eyes watching her, whispering about her presence and her beauty, she heard Rob whispering in her ear.

"Jeez, I'm glad this thing's over. I hate funerals!"

She half smiled. "I'm sure there aren't too many who actually like them. . . ."

"Hey, you know what I mean."

"Yes, I suppose I do."

They walked in silence until they reached the huge, grandly decorated lobby of the Revere. They were surrounded by burgundy brocaded wallpaper lined in gold, marble steps and gilled handrails rising up from both sides of the reception area. The place was a dinosaur. Never again would theaters be built like this.

"Well, back to the real world," said Rob. "Back to work for the living, right?"

"Yes, you're right about that."

She answered him absently as she searched out Hammaker's unmistakable figure in the crowd. There he was, standing off by the glass doors to the street, nodding solemnly at many of the luminaries who had come today. He did not appear to be in a hurry to leave.

"Oh, listen," said Rob. "While I've got you right here, I should tell you that I'm supposed to hear from the people at the Sands in Vegas today. What should I tell them?"

She shrugged. "Tell them I haven't made up my mind yet. When I get the schedule from Hollywood, I'll know what kind of time frame we're looking at."

Rob shook his head. "You know, you can't keep jerking off those people forever. . . ."

"That's not what I'm doing."

"Yeah, well, don't forget one thing: I'm sure they can find some other broad to work their club for a lousy hundred grand a week, you know?"

"And that is precisely who she would be, too—some other broad.' She would not be Sophia Rousseau, and they want Sophia Rousseau, don't they?"

" You bet they do."

"Then I think they will wait. . . . You tell them I said that. I think they will be cooperative."

Rob grinned. "I gotta hand it to you, Sophia baby, you've got a lotta style. Okay, I'll handle it." He turned toward the door, and paused to look back at her. "Want to stop for brunch on the way back?"

She smiled as she shook her head. "No, thank you. I think I'll wait here for a while. There is someone with whom I would like to speak."

Rob smiled. "Whatever you say, baby. Talk to you later."

He slipped out past the glass doors where the press and the television reporters had been asked to remain behind. She knew that they would like to speak with any celebrities who might venture out into the massive crowd on the sidewalk, and that was one of the major reasons that so many of the attendees remained in the huge lobby, smoking and talking, making new acquaintances or renewing old.

She smiled as she thought of her sweet Rob. He was so helpful, so eager to please her all the time. He was a wonderful agent, but he was an even better companion. She was so happy to have allowed him to get so close to her. Even though he did not know it, he was closer to her than he would ever imagine. She hoped the time would never come when she might need him, but it was comforting to know that he was available.

Turning in the crowd, coolly ignoring many of the celebrities who openly stared at her as the hot new kid on the block, she sought out Richard Hammaker.

He was still standing by the front doors and he was looking directly at her.

"Hello, Richard," she said as she walked up to him.

"You don't seem to be too broken up by all of this," he said with a touch of accusation.

"At the risk of sounding prosaic, you force me to remind you that 'death is a part of life'."

"Yes, I've heard that somewhere, I think." He looked at her with his dark, sunken eyes. They were the eyes of a madman, of a genius. His dark beard sprouted from his face in slick, curly strands. He looked oddly out of place in the tailored black suit, and yet the absence of color on him seemed totally appropriate, too.

"Are you waiting for someone?" she asked, staring into his eyes. He returned the stare without effort, and she admired his strength.

"No," he said, softening, shifting his gaze toward the crowd of journalists and onlookers beyond the glass. "I don't know what I'm doing right now."

"How about joining me for brunch? I know a very nice place close by."

Hammaker appeared stunned by her invitation. He rubbed his beard nervously, apparently not expecting any such tactic from her. "What? Are you serious?"

"Yes," she said. "You and I have been . . . let's say 'at odds' for far too long now. I think it's time we had a talk."

"Really?" Hammaker was slowly getting back his chutzpah. He grinned lopsidedly at her through his beard.

"Yes, Richard. What with Stephen dying, I think we should clear the air before things become intolerable."

He considered this for a moment and then nodded his head. "All right. Where to?"

"Follow me," said Sophia, pushing open the glass doors to be consumed by the anxious crowd.

Chapter 20

The huge plane touched down with a scritch of its tires and minimum of vibration. As the runway ripped past the window, Matthew Cavendish stretched out his long legs and tried to relax. Thank God the damned flight was finally over! he thought. He was feeling terribly claustrophobic, and he never felt that way except when he flew on that bloody French plane!

As the plane taxied to a halt by its terminal, Matthew unfastened his safety belt and gathered up his carry-on luggage. He ignored the farewell instructions of the flight attendants being piped over the intercom in English and French—the hell with them and their silly, nasal language! For the next hour he was herded and prodded through a variety of lines where authorities satisfied themselves that he was not a terrorist or someone scheming to break any United States Customs laws. Finally, when he was allowed to be on his way, he felt vaguely disoriented and terribly fatigued. He made his way to the International Air terminal, which was aswarm with people from all over the world. It was like standing in the lobby of the U.N. Building at lunchtime. Not that he'd want to ever enter that lair of criminals.

Making his way to the streets, he found a skycap willing to hail him a cab, and the inchworm journey from JFK to the Belt Parkway through Queens and Brooklyn began.

It was the first time he had been to New York City in more than two years, and Matthew had to admit that he did miss the vibrant town more than he had realized. Unlike Paris, he found New York to be everything it claimed itself to be. There was always something to do in the city, always something happening. It reminded him of London m many ways, although there were many people who would tell you the cities were in no way alike.

Well, there was no accounting for taste, he thought. Some people even like Paris!

The cab moved along steadily along the Belt Parkway heading west toward Manhattan. The three narrow lanes of the outdated expressway were jammed with native motorists, all pushing the posted speed limits, and all driving like Grand Prix veterans. Only in Germany were the drivers worse than here, he mused.

As the cab passed near the Verrazano Narrows Bridge, Matthew could not resist admiring the towering structure. There was a magnificence in great architecture that could not be ignored. Smiling, he settled back into his seat. It felt good to be able to appreciate the finer things in life and he truly felt sorry for all the dull slobs of the labor class who shambled through their entire lives with never a nod toward the Arts. The poor fools, he thought sadly.

"Hey, pal, this yer first time?" The cabbie's voice invaded his thoughts, banishing them.

"I beg your pardon?" said Matthew.

"I seen youse lookin' at the Verrazano," said the driver. And I was wondrin' if youse every been to the City before."

"I visit occasionally," said Matthew.

"Well yer lucky today. . . it's real clear. When we get around this next bend you might be able to see the Statue a Liberty! Looks better'n ever."

"Yes, I've heard rumors to that effect," he said, not wishing to get into a lengthy conversation.

The cabbie looked back to the roadway and carefully negotiated a few slower cars, working his way out to the leftmost lane, closer to the water where Gravesend Bay gave way to Upper New York Bay. As the cabbie swung onto the Brooklyn-Queens Expressway, heading north through Red Hook, he gestured out the window with a crooked thumb.

"Hey! There she is! Look at that, ain' she bee-u-tee-ful? Whadayasay, mister!?"

"She is very beautiful, indeed, sir," said Matthew, smiling in spite of himself. Looking beyond the marine terminals and the docks, Matthew could see the enormous statue on Liberty Island, and he was forced to admit that it was indeed a heartwarming sight. He realized this simple cab driver, who probably pulled this same routine on every foreign passenger he carried, did indeed have something to be proud of. This was without a doubt the most unique country in the world.

And it was no surprise that the object of his search has also been drawn here.

The thought of Sophia filled his mind like a dark, consuming presence. As he was reminded of his reason for coming to the city, he felt his mood change to something more grim and resolute. His cab had moved off the expressway and entered the line for the Battery Tunnel. Soon they would be entering the mouth of the tunnel, which yawned before him like the maw of a great beast.

The image lingered In his mind, disturbing him. He wondered, for the first time since beginning his epic quest, if he were doing the right thing. He wondered If some things were better off left alone. . . like the old wives tales warned?

The cabbie paid the toll and rolled forward into the tunnel entrance. Well, thought Matthew, it's too late to worry about it now.

Matthew selected the Warwick Hotel for his Manhattan sojourn. (Matthew pronounced its name "War-rick" in the fashion of his mother-country.) Whenever he came to New York he always stayed at the Warwick for several very good reasons. Firstly, he liked the location at the corner of 54th Street and the Avenue of the Americas (he was close enough to walk up to the southern exposure of Central Park, and yet not far from Broadway and the theater district, or his agent's office). Secondly, the Warwick was an old hotel—not in the shabby or rundown sense of the word—but in the way they conducted business. And thirdly, because there was a distinctly English feel about the Warwick which began with the polished dark walnut fixtures and ended with the courteous treatment by the staff.

After he had stowed away his wardrobe and familiarized himself with his room and its location (his window looked across the street at the innocuously modem New York Hilton), he took the elevator down to the lobby. He wanted nothing more than to sit in one of the hotel's overstuffed chairs and have a bowl of privately blended pipe tobacco, but now he'd have to take the simple pleasure outside. The New York do-gooders had been passing laws to keep him from doing it just about everywhere.

Puffing easily, trying to savor the experience, his mind kept running on, pushing things, imagining possible endings to his story, denouements to his investigation. It occurred to him he had not thought to call his literary agent and let him know he was coming to New York. Morris always liked to know in advance so that he could arrange some of the usual nonsense for writers to do while in town: lunches with editors, autograph sessions at some of the bigger, more conspicuous bookshops, strategy meetings with your agent.

Not that Morris was any different from any other literary agent in Manhattan, thought Matthew, as he grinned around the stem of his pipe. No, no . . . Morris Howard was simply dancing the dance to a tune that had been playing in this town for a long, long time. And who could blame the young chap? The old rituals remained in vogue because they still worked—it was that simple!

Getting up, he walked to the row of phones off the lobby and dialed up his agent's number. It rang several times and a female voice greeted him.

"Hello, Morris Howard Agency. May I help you?"

"I should think so, Esther!" he said brightly. "Might I talk to your boss, if he's about?"

"Is that you, Matthew?" asked Esther.

"Do you have any other Englishman in the stable who sound like me?" He chuckled good-naturedly. "How are you my dear?"

"Busy, but that's the way we like it. Just fine, Matthew. Everything's fine. How are things over there in Merry Old?"

"I wouldn't know, dearie. I'm not over there. I'm over here, you see!"

"What? You're in New York, and you didn't tell us you were coming? Why not?"

"Kind of short notice, and I really didn't want to trouble anyone. I'm working on a new book, and I'm on the track of something hot at this very moment"

"Oh, well, Morris isn't here right now anyway. He's out to lunch with one of his science fiction clients. But he's going to be so glad to hear you're in town. Where shall I have him reach you—the usual spot?"

Matthew smiled and puffed on his pipe. Yes, the Warwick. Tell him, I shall be stopping by to explain everything to him during the next day or so . . . as soon as I get my schedule worked out. I shall be seeing you soon, sweet lady. Cheerio!"

Hanging up the phone, Matthew decided to take a walk. It had been several years since being in the city, and he always found a walk through Manhattan's streets to be invigorating.

He stepped outside into a brisk. autumn wind, and he found that his sweater and corduroy jacket were just enough to keep him comfortable as he strode south on what had once been called Sixth Avenue. It was mid-afternoon, the sun was bright, but not hot, and the sidewalks were teeming with people of all ages, sizes, and types. It was a palette of color and movement, and Matthew loved it. He loved this city, and whenever he was here, he wondered why he didn't come over more often.

As he passed Radio City Music Hall, he resisted the urge to gawk upward at the tall buildings across the street. Even though he was technically a tourist, he felt the urge to not act like one. It was as if there were some inner desire to be considered a native of this crazy, kinetic city. There was a mustachioed street-corner vendor at the next intersection selling wind-up toys. They were cheap and tacky-looking, obviously made in a place like Taiwan or Malaysia, where the labor costs were absurdly low, and yet a crowd had gathered about the vendor. In New York, Matthew thought, you can get attention for any bloody thing! No matter what it is you've got, you can always find someone who will be interested in it.

He continued walking, eventually entering the Diamond District—a block or so of shops filled with gold, silver, and gems. Most of them were owned and operated by Orthodox Jews, and Matthew wondered about the etiology of such an economic phenomenon. As he walked along, he could hear snippets of dialogue: bargains, deals, hagglings.

It reminded him of the kinds of talk you would hear at a Turkish bazaar.

Bloody incredible, it was.

He turned right at 46th Street and headed west toward the theater district. Spotting a newsstand, he thought he might purchase a copy of the *New York Times*—a paper he had always respected for their traditional journalistic values. As he reached for a paper, his gaze absently scanned across the riotous display of magazine covers, and he was shocked to see the face of Sophia Rousseau adorning the lurid front page of *People*. Picking up the flimsy periodical, he read the blurb in the left corner.

Learn Why Sophia Rousseau,
Broadway's Hot New Star,
is Looking to Hollywood!

Learn, indeed! thought Matthew as he nervously fished about in his trouser pockets for some cash. Here he was, thinking that he would be conducting a downright Holmesian investigation to find her, and her fucking picture was plastered all over *People* magazine!

He paid for the magazine hastily and began paging through its sheets (mostly black-and-white photos, and very few words) until he found the cover story. There he found a layout of photos of Sophia in scenes from a play entitled The Vindication. Captions and a very brief text informed him that the play had been a smash hit and was being prepared to be shot as a film within the next few months. . . and that Sophia Rousseau had been selected to reprise her stage role before Hollywood's cameras.

Anxiously, he looked across the display of magazines, and was not as surprised this time to see Sophia's distinctive honey-blond hair and perfectly featured face gazing into his soul from the cover of a high-fashion magazine entitled *Beau Monde*. It was a typically slick, mod, artsy-fashion pose and shot, but the face was unmistakably that of his prey.

Well, he thought, she has nothing if she doesn't have nerve!

"I say, sir!" he asked the newsstand vendor. "Do you have Variety?"

"Yeah, right on the bottom by yer foot! See it?"

Looking down to the corner of the plywood stall, Matthew spied several large tabloid-style newspapers, and among them lay a thick edition of the American Entertainment weekly. He purchased it, along with that day's Times. He walked to the end of the next block and found a place to sit by a small fountain-cum-sculpture that graced the entrance plaza to a new office building at the intersection of 46th and Seventh Avenue. There was a rather seedy-looking chap sharing the space with him, but neither man took notice of the other's presence.

Anxiously, Matthew searched through the index of the Times and located the theater pages. Rifling through the proper section, he soon found the information he needed.

The Vindication was playing at the Circle Six Theater in Greenwich Village. It was written by some sod named Richard Hammaker, and it was produced and directed by the world-renowned Stephen Sandler.

Matthew took down the phone number and address of the theater, plus the times of the performances. He then began paging through the paper more leisurely, until he noticed the lead article in the Entertainment Section. In his haste, he had overlooked a large spread that had a great bearing on his own activities.

He stared in disbelief at the headline:

NO MORE ENCORES FOR STEPHEN SANDLER

and a sub-header:
World Famous Director and Producer
Dead at Sixty-four. Huge Funeral at the Old Revere Theater

then quickly scanned several photographs arranged through-out the page-filling article. He was not surprised to see a picture of the woman who called herself Sophia Rousseau being escorted by a short, bearded man through a huge sidewalk crowd.

Despite his telling himself that he was no longer surprised, that he was no longer shocked, his heart was jackhammering in his chest, and his palms had become moist despite the late afternoon coolness in the air. Good grief, it was getting barmy, wasn't it?

The weather, or this whole story you're on, old sport? He asked himself the question as a means of loosening up, of calm-ing down, but nothing was going to ease the tension that he was suddenly feeling. He had the craziest sensation of urgency. He kept thinking that if he didn't do something fast, it was going to be too late . . . .

It was a singular thought, dark and manic, which kept running through his head.

All right, he thought. First things first. Get all the information you can. Write it up proper, and then come forth with a plan. Reach-ing into the breast pocket of his corduroy jacket, he pulled out a pad of paper and a pen. Calming himself by drawing a breath and looking up at the stream of passing pedestrians, he prepared to logically note down all the new information.

He did so in a methodical fashion, fighting the urge to be quick and crazy. One by one, he noted all the new facts, then branched off various paths of action. Within fifteen minutes, he had mapped out not just one, but several plans of attack. He smiled as he scanned over what he had written. It was a credit to his analytical mind and to his classical education and training. Never panic, he told him-self steadily. Always be prepared for the worst (even when you're hoping for the best).

One of the first things noted on the map of action alternatives was an overriding necessity: talk to his agent, and let the man know what the hell is going on. Very well, time to get moving, he thought. Morris' office was not far, and he could use the time spent strolling to order his thoughts and decide exactly how much of the story he would tell his literary representative. If Matthew divulged every-thing—down to his most dark and crazy suspicions, his agent might think he was losing his grip on things.

Matthew turned over the catalog of ideas and plans in his mind until he reached the corner of Fifth Avenue and 42nd Street, where the main branch of the New York Public Library loomed like a national monument. It was nearly 5:00 P.M., and the crowds were incredibly heavy, shoulder-to-shoulder, cheek to jowl from the curbside up to the storefronts. A solid pack of moving flesh. ,

He pushed his way through the current-like motion of the crowd and crossed Fifth at the light. Morris Howard s office was several doors down on Fifth Avenue—a very prestigious address for a very prestigious agent. Entering the building, Matthew ascended to the third floor, and stepped out of the elevator into a reception area.

"Matthew Cavendish here to see Mr. Howard," he said brightly to the young man at the desk. He looked tired and bored, especially since quitting time was so close, but he announced Matthew's presence without incident.

Nodding into his headphones, he spoke to Matthew.

"Mr. Howard will be right out. Take a seat, please. He had barely reached the couch, when he heard his name being called in a cool, professional tone: It was a familiar voice and he looked up to see Morris Howard coming toward him with his right hand extended, a genuinely warm smile on his face.

"Matthew! Good to see you! Esther told me you'd be calling, but I didn't expect you so soon! You look great."

Matthew smiled and shook his agent s hand. The man was in his mid-thirties and sported fashionable but conservative banker's clothing. Morris had dark hair in a stylish cut, and a softly angled, handsome face. The agent's most singular feature was his eyes—bright and penetrating, full of mischief and perceptivity. Along Publisher's Row, Morris Howard was considered to be one of the Hot Young Agents, and Matthew was proud to have his representation.

"Well, to tell you the truth, Morris, I was going to wait until tomorrow, until after I had gotten settled in, you see . . . but something came up, and I thought I might tell you about it today. . . ."

Morris Howard smiled and guided Matthew back through a hall of mirrors toward his luxurious suite of offices. "That's fine, Matthew. Come on back and tell me all about it."

They entered Morris's private office, and Howard turned to face him with a serious expression. "All right, Matthew, what's wrong?"

"Good grief! You can tell so readily?"

Howard grinned and shook his head. "We've known each other for quite a few years now," he said. "I think I can tell when Matthew Cavendish is disturbed. Do you want to talk about it?"

"Oh, yes, of course, but I certainly could go for a glass of something. You wouldn't have any port, would you?"

Howard shook his head. "It would go bad between your visits and you're the only client I have who would even think of the stuff, much less drink it."

Matthew laughed in spite of his present state of mind.

Howard moved to the small bar in a wall-unit which also held many of his clients' books, a small plasma screen with the latest media electronic. "How about some single malt? You drink that, don't you?"

"Under duress," said Matthew. "Ice and soda water. And some lime, if you've got it."

"No lime," said Howard as he reached for glasses and tongs for the ice bucket. He poured the drinks in silence, then: "All right, here you are . . . now, what's going on? Anything to do with your next book?"

"Indirectly, yes. And directly, yes."

Howard nodded. "Sounds interesting so far." Matthew drew off a long swallow. The whiskey burned its usual path down his throat and he felt instantly better. Inhaling deeply, he relaxed the breath and stared at his agent.

"All right," he said. "Let me start at the beginning. But promise me two things. . . ."

"What's that?" asked Morris Howard

". . . that you won't interrupt, and you won't think I'm mad as a fucking hatter!"

Chapter 21

She looked at Hammaker through the distorted glass of her brandy snifter, and the image was that of a twisted, hairy beast. It was an absurd idea. The playwright was no more of a bestial creature than she herself. Appearances could be quite deceiving. Besides, she thought with a touch of ironic humor, no beast would ever get himself as drunk as Hammaker had allowed himself this afternoon.

"I fear I am a true melancholy spirit, Ms. Rousseau," he said through slurring lips. A dramatic pause as he took another substantial quaff of his brandy. "Yes, a true case of Melancholia Artistica."

Now he laughed bitterly and stared at her with what might be called a sudden viciousness.

Sophia was truly amazed at Hammaker's behavior. In fact, her interest in him bordered upon true obsession. No man had ever displayed such total sexual disinterest in her. No man in all her memory.

In addition, he seemed to have re-channeled any sexual urges into pure aggression. They had been sitting in the stylish restaurant at the New York Hyatt Regency for several hours, having finished a leisurely brunch that had been well-lubricated with bottles of wine, and now cognac. During the course of the meal and the interstitial conversation, she had watched Hammaker's mood swings like a crazy and erratic pendulum.

At the beginning of their afternoon together, she would have described his demeanor as guarded or wary. He kept eyeing her with suspicion and naked curiosity. She wondered if he had much experience with women, but as the afternoon wore on, she didn't think it mattered. She began to realize that Richard Hammaker was one of the few people who treated both men and women absolutely the same. He showed no special recognition of gender, and the more she observed him, the more aware of the trait she became.

And it made him no less fascinating to her.

But he was doing his best to keep the conversation away from either of them, as people who might be interested in each other would—for whatever the reason. He seemed to be genuinely upset about the death of Sandler, confessing that Stephen had been one of his only friends. He went on in this moribund mood for more than an hour, continuing to drink heavily. She had never seen him behave like this, and she was surprised to see how much wine he had been able to consume and still remain at all coherent.

After listening to the entire mawkish tale of how he had met Sandler, she had switched from Montrachet Poulligny to Courvoisier, hoping that the change might begin to transform the playwright into something more bearable.

But it only made him more drunk.

"You know," he said, slumping back in his chair. "For the last hour I've been wondering why you asked me out."

She smiled, broadcasting her charm like a radio beacon.

"Have you now?"

"Yes, and even more so, I've been wondering why I said yes!"

Now we were finally getting somewhere, she thought with supreme confidence. "And why is that, Richard? Don't you like me?"

He tried to sit up in his seat, and did so with some difficulty. Staring at her with the glazed-over mask of someone who might pass out at any moment, he tried to make himself look formidable.

"What was that?"

She smiled again. "I just asked you if you liked me."

"Oh, yeah. . . well, that's a tough question."

"And why must it be so tough? I like you."

He shrugged, took another deep swallow of the cognac.

"So what? That's no reason why I should like you. Besides, I thought you liked Stephen. . . and he's dead now!"

What? Why would he say such a thing! His words had startled her for an instant, and she hoped that she had been able to mask her surprise. What the hell had he meant by that? Was he merely trying to be his usual abrasive, insulting self?

. . . Or had he intended to imply a deeper understanding of her relationship with Sandler?

There was nothing to do but be direct. "Richard, what are you talking about? You make me sound like some monster."

He laughed at her, almost mockingly. "Well. . . aren't you?"

She felt as though she'd been pierced by an arrow. Forcing herself to remain calm, she enacted a smile and reached out and touched his hand, stroking the soft flesh of his palm. "Now, Richard, does that feel like the touch of a 'monster'?"

He looked at her and his expression suddenly changed. The chemistry of her touch had transformed him as he smiled with a bit of warmth. "Actually. . . no . . . it doesn't?"

"Well, thank you."

He looked away, like a little boy who was suddenly ashamed of himself. "I'm sorry, Sophia, if I've been acting like an asshole. But you should know that Stephen's death has affected me very badly, and I guess in some ways I've been blaming you. I'm sorry."

"Me? How could you possibly blame me?" She could feel her pulse jumping and her blood cooling down. What was this little wretch of a man getting at?

But Hammaker just shrugged. "I don't know. I was getting a little crazy, I guess. I'm always a little crazy, so maybe this whole thing just pushed me a little further. Sorry, Sophia . . . I didn't mean anything by it. You shouldn't pay any attention to a miserable little turd like me anyway."

For some reason, she believed him. There was a sincerity about him and his words that could not have been fabricated from the alcohol haze in which he now operated.

"All right, Richard, thank you," was all that she said.

He forced himself to stand up, holding the table to steady himself. "Let's get out of here. I want to go home."

She left more than enough in cash for their afternoon revel, and followed him as he tottered toward the exit. She was the object of whispers and stares as she glided after the little man in the black suit, and for once, she did not appreciate the attention.

She caught up with him at the escalator, which moved them down past the cantilevered tiers of the atrium lobby to the street level. It was very late in the afternoon, and the lobby was getting crowded with a happy hour crowd at the nearby bar. There was a jazz quintet playing in tuxedos and the atmosphere was very much of a New York afternoon.

"Richard, are you going to be all right?"

"Yeah, sure. Just get me out to the bricks and get me a cab. I'll be fine."

Hooking her arm through the crook of his elbow, she walked him out to the street where a doorman in a typical epauletted uniform and white gloves nodded, then turned to hail a yellow Checker. Richard weaved back and forth, shifting his weight from one foot to the other while they waited. She held him firmly in her grasp, noticing his small, almost delicately boned frame, until a cab arrived.

The doorman helped her pile him into the backseat and then she followed. After she tipped the man, Hammaker gave the cabbie his address in SoHo, and leaned back in the seat placing his head on her breast. He was quite drunk, but his mind and body refused to give up. He remained awake, trying to sit upright, but failing.

"You'll be feeling better soon. We're almost home." "You coming with me?"

She smiled and blew in his ear warmly. "If you want me to."

"I don't really give a shit. . . ."

The cabbie, overhearing the conversation, giggled at this point, and Sophia shot him a caustic glance in the rearview mirror. Returning to Hammaker, she stroked the inside of his thigh, and he instantly closed his legs. "What's the matter, Richard?"

"Nothin' . . ." came a couched, slurred reply. "You wouldn't understand. . . ."

The conversation died until the cab reached his address downtown, and the driver announced his fare.

"I think I'd better help you in," she said as she pulled him out of the backseat. He seemed, if anything, even more drunk than the previous half hour.

"You're insistent, aren't you?"

"If you say so."

Sophia paid the cabbie, then held Hammaker firmly as they entered the building. A rather shabby-looking Latin concierge sat behind a wire-caged office by the elevator and stared out at them.

"Mr. Hammaker's apartment," she said casually to the tan-complected man.

He nodded sleepily and pushed a button which opened the elevator doors. Stepping inside with her cargo, Sophia shook her head. Why would Hammaker choose to live in such a dump when he was obviously making good money from his play? Especially since a movie deal had been arranged. He should be worth at least several million.

The elevator moved grindingly upward as the interior light bulb flickered ominously. Hammaker leaned against the back of the tiny cab, trying to focus his eyes on her. To say that he was a mysterious man was an understatement, but she would have him! She would conquer him, as she had all the others. His enigmatic ways only enflamed her appetite for him.

There had been many weird ones, eccentric ones in the past, although she was forced to admit, she had met no one exactly like Hammaker. By this point in her pattern of seduction, all the others had been pawing all over her, leering and panting like dogs.

Hammaker acted as though he could care less. . . and that bothered her. *Something is wrong, and I must find out what it is.* The thought repeated itself in her mind.

Finally the doors opened and she let him lead her down a narrow hall to his entrance: a plain metal slab that peeled maroon paint.

Very elegant.

Hammaker fished out his keys and diddled with all the locks, finally pushing the door inward. Surprisingly, the interior decorating was in great contrast to the building itself.

"Come in, my temptress," he said with a drunken, overly dramatic flourish. "You're the first woman I have had in here alone since I moved in!"

That statement seemed to be funny to him, and he threw back his head and laughed. It was a very evil-sounding laugh, and she felt an odd emotion for her—a touch of fear.

As Hammaker flopped down on a leather couch, Sophia looked quickly about the room, taking in its fixtures and decorations. She had long ago learned that you can discover much about a person by the way they live, by the way they adorn their quarters.

The living room was small but literally jammed with furniture. It was filled with what was now called antiques.

Lovely old pieces of oak and mahogany, all carved and edged and finished with a craftsman's touch, atop a thick, maroon and gold Persian rug. There were marble-topped tables with exquisite Oriental urns, gilt-framed oils in the classical style. The room could have easily belonged to a pair of elderly sisters, except for the almost incongruous collection of framed playbills and posters from Hammaker's years in the theater.

"I think I need a drink," said Hammaker, an impish, almost giggling sound forming behind his words. "What about you?"

"No, I think I've had enough, Richard."

"Well get me one, would you? The kitchen's back that way and everything's in the upper cabinets. The roaches own the lower realms." He laughed again and stared at her with his dark, maddening eyes.

"I think you've had enough, too," she said calmly.

"Who do you think you are, my mother?" Hammaker laughed again. "Well, fuck you, too! I'll get it myself."

He shambled into the kitchen and rattled about in the cabinet of glasses and bottles. While he struggled, she moved quickly through the rest of the small apartment. There was a small room with a laptop and desk—his office, and beyond it another small room with a large brass bed and fin-de-siecle furniture. There were no photographs of any people, no mirrors other than the one in the bathroom, and no sign that Richard Hammaker had any close human associations with anyone.

As Sophia stood there, taking in all the clues, all the evidence of his life, she was touched by a wildly crazy thought: suppose he was not human? What if he were a . . . different entity. . . not wholly unlike herself. Similar, but still different?

How bizarre! How crazy!

No, she thought, more rationally, that is impossible. But why is she having practically no effect on him? The question was plaguing her and she was obsessed with knowing the answer.

And suddenly another, more terrifying, thought touched her: suppose she was losing her power. . . ?

No. That could not be. . . .

Then suppose he was taking it away from her. . . ?

Hammaker entered the room, holding a tumbler full of dark liquid. Unconsciously she stepped back from him as he made his way to the couch.

This is ridiculous! She thought. I have no reason to fear anything—especially an ugly little man like Hammaker.

"Sure you don't want something else?" he asked.

"No, thank you, I don't think so."

"Well, aren't you going to take off your coat and stay a while, or will you be leaving so soon?"

He spoke the words as if he were delivering the lines of a bad play, and he laughed as he finished them.

Turning to face him, Sophia decided what she must do. She slipped out of her coat and let it fall to the floor, then moved to sit by him on the couch.

"Richard, I must ask you something. . . ."

He sipped from the glass, then giggled. "If you want to know if I'm gay, the answer is no!" He laughed, and then began to sob. "Especially no!"

How had he known what she was thinking? What she was going to say?

"Surprised?" said Hammaker, trying to control the heaving in his chest. "Don't be . . ."

"What do you mean?"

"Do you actually think you're the first woman who's thought that I might be a not-so-flaming faggot!?"

"Well, no, it's just that—"

"It's just that you were wondering why I'm not sitting here with a big hard-on for you! Right, bitch!?"

Hammaker's voice had jumped a full octave, and as . loud as a bull horn. He stood up and loomed over her. His eyes had become wide and white and bulging, and his breath was coming in ragged pieces.

"You don't have to get so—"

"Don't tell me what I have to do! You don't know me! You don't know anything about me!"

Reaching out to him, she concentrated, focusing her phero-mone-like energies and bathed him in its warm, sexual glow. She could feel the anger and the loathing emanating from him in thick black sheets, and she sought to penetrate his defenses. It was a metaphysical confrontation, and she was ready for it. .

But Hammaker was not having any of it. He was glaring at her like a madman as he ripped at his suit coat, pulling it off. Then he pulled down his tie and yanked it free of the shirt collar. Suddenly she was helping him undress, thinking: yes! yes! I finally got you, you crazy bastard! She pulled his shirt from him and started undoing his belt. He threw back his head and laughed a howling, plaintive laugh. It was like the lonely, painful cry of a solitary animal.

Stepping back from her, he slowly unfastened his pants, letting them peel back away from his groin. "Is this what you want?" he asked hysterically. "Is this what you think you want?"

He paused to laugh again, and she feared that he was going to hyperventilate as his breath became tom and jagged. It was not until he pulled down his shorts that she understood his near lunacy.

Staring in disbelief, she saw the ravaged flesh of his abdomen and his left thigh. It was a rippled, swirled and pulpy mass of tu-morous-looking flesh. There was no penis, no testicles. . . just a great expanse of scar tissue, and a small prosthetic valve-device attached to a tube.

She only saw it for an instant before Hammaker pulled up his clothes, and collapsed on the couch in a fetal position. He cried wildly and hysterically for a moment as Sophia backed away from him. He was the monster, she knew now, and not in the physical sense that he might feel, but on a far more dangerous level. . . .

She knew instantly that he was a man who could not be controlled by her, and he was therefore, by definition, a threat to her.

Standing up, she backed away, and reached for her coat. Hammaker continued to sob into the leather of the couch—suffering from a combination of emotions. Shame, loathing, anger, and frustration all seethed and bubbled out of him like bile.

"When I was sixteen, I was working in a paper mill in upstate New York, near Buffalo," he said slowly, forcing the words in between his sobbing breaths. "A catwalk collapsed and almost dumped me all the way into a vat of nitric acid. It ate up my left leg and . . . everything else. . . ."

"You don't have to explain," said Sophia.

"You're only the third person, other than my family, to know about. . . this, about the truth."

"Please. . ." said Sophia.

"I don't know why I told you!"

"I think I'd better leave," she said, moving toward the door.

He looked at her and scowled, as though he found her suddenly repulsive.

"Yeah, you do that. . . now that you know you won't be getting any beef from the little weirdo!" Hammaker laughed crazily, and she felt herself shudder.

Sophia pulled her coat closer around her shoulders and neck. Now that she knew his horrible secret, she could feel the essential terror of Richard Hammaker. He was an alien creature. He was a monster who had the power to destroy her. It was a power he did not know he possessed, but she did not want to be near him when he discovered it. She moved closer to the door.

"You'd be weird, too, if you were like me!" he shouted at her as he rose from the couch and stepped toward her. He sucked in his breath in great ragged gasps. "Those rumors about being a monk for ten years—they're true! Talk about weird! Try being a fucking monk for ten years!"

"Richard. . ." Sophia attempted to speak, but her throat had tightened up, as though there were a great tumor growing there.

"I know!" he shouted as he drew closer to her. "I know: you're sorry. Well, fuck you, lady! There ain't nobody sorrier than me! So take your flouncy sweet ass outta here and find somebody else to play with!"

His breath was hot and foul as he yelled into her face, and she

felt an overpowering need to escape. She could sense the fear waft-
ing off of her in fetid waves, and she hoped that he could not smell it.

Backing up, she reached out and touched the door, the latch.
She held her breath until her hand freed the bolt, and the door swung
open.

"Good-bye, Richard. . . I don't know what else to say, really. . . ."

He looked at her with his wild Rasputin eyes, and a smile suddenly broke over his twisted, tormented features.

"That's good . . . that's very good," he said. "Now get the fuck
outta here."

He almost pushed her across the threshold, and slammed the
door. Relief and calm washed over her as she felt herself alone in
the cold, harshly lit hallway. To be away from him was such a
feeling of safety. It was a sensation that she had barely felt. . . but it
felt so good.

Quickly she walked to the elevator, stepped inside the small
cab, and descended to the lobby and the street. The concierge ignored her as she stepped out into the cool autumn evening, looking
for a cab. It would be difficult to find one on the narrow sidestreet,
and she walked up to the comer.

Richard Hammaker was a dangerous man.

The thought echoed through her head almost continuously. She
could not get the idea out of her mind. What should she do next?
There were so many options, and she knew she must make some
decisions quickly.

Reaching the comer, she signaled for a cab as several approached from the next light. The lead vehicle cut out of the pack
and veered straight for her, screeching to a stop only inches from
the curb.

"The Trump Tower, please."

When the cab had slipped back into the stream of traffic, she
settled back in the roomy seat and considered her options. As much
as she loved the city, she knew that she must leave it for a while.
When she arrived at her apartment she would call Rob and tell him
of her plans.

Chapter 22

The phone rang with a shrill insistence.

Reaching out toward the bedstand, Rob Lester fumbled about in the darkness for the phone. He had been lost in a deep sleep, and for a few seconds of total disorientation, he was reacting solely on automatic pilot.

Gradually, his bearing came back to him. As he placed the phone to his ear and mumbled a greeting, he reached down and adjusted the track lighting above his bed so that the darkness blended into soft amber.

"Hello. . ." he said a second time, hearing no reply. Looking down beside him, the young, naked brunette did not stir. Cocaine and champagne had put her down for the count for the rest of the night.

"Good evening, Rob," said the voice. "You will listen to me now. . . ."

Instantly, he felt totally relaxed. There was something about the voice that filled him with a warm familiarity, with a security that was beyond all description. Like the indefinable closeness of an infant and its mother, Rob felt a closeness to this voice. It was a compulsion to listen. . . and to obey.

Yes. . . the thought lingered on the flat plain of his mind. "Yes," he said aloud. "I am listening."

"The time has come, my Rob," said Sophia. "We must leave this city for a while, and I must have you accompany me. I am going to need your assistance, and possibly your protection. Do you understand?"

"Yes . . ."

"I have been thinking that you have reached the point in your life to make a change—a significant change. Tomorrow you will awaken with several new ideas firmly in mind: several key decisions which will be to our mutual benefit. Do you understand?"

"Yes . . ."

"You will decide to leave the Morris Agency. You no longer need them, and you know this. Your dream of becoming independent has come to fruition. You are now big enough to open your own agency, and tomorrow you will do so."

"Yes . . ."

"In addition, you will decide that you must expand your horizons. You will go quickly to Los Angeles to establish a West Coast branch of your new agency. Your plan will be to spend fifteen days each month in L.A., the other half in New York. This will occur to you over breakfast, and it will fill you with joy. You will spend every available moment cleaning up the details. Getting to L.A. will become the most important thing in your life. And, of course, you will want me to come along with you. You will encourage me to take the Vegas gig, and you will go ahead and prepare my way in L.A. with the film studios. Do you understand?"

"Yes. . . ."

"That is fine, Rob. You will remember nothing of this conversation. This will be less than a dream, but you will be driven to do everything I have ordered for you. Do you understand?"

"Yes, I understand."

"Very good, Rob. I will leave you now. When I say 'good night, sweet Rob,you will hang up the receiver and go to sleep immediately, is that clear?"

"Yes, it's clear. . . ."

"Very well. Good night, sweet Rob."

Slowly, he moved the receiver away from his ear and replaced it to the bedstand. Turning over, the memory of the call and the voice receded from mind.

It would be so good to fall asleep. He was so exhausted..

More sleepy than he could ever remember.

Chapter 23

Like many Englishmen, Matthew Cavendish possessed a distinct fondness for Indian cuisine. And so, it was no accident that he dined at an authentic Indian restaurant on 45th Street called Tandoor. Their beef kheema steamed and spiced his palate, their vegetable pakora was crisped to perfection, and their chutney sauces were delicate and cool. Matthew nodded silently to himself and smiled every time he sampled a new morsel.

He was extremely pleased with his decision to dine there. Taking the time to savor such finely prepared food represented a welcome respite from the pressure of his research. After a grueling discussion with his literary agent, Matthew freely admitted to himself that he needed a break from his crusade.

Morris Howard had been, to state things mildly, quite skeptical of Matthew's contentions and the validity of his quest of Sophia Rousseau. Matthew did not appreciate being told that he was chasing a fairy tale, and he had considered (even if it was just for an instant in the heat of the argument) just simply packing up and walking out, and finding himself a new American literary agent. It had been at that point that Matthew calmed himself and accepted the realization that most people, once they reached adulthood, suffered from a severe calcification of the imagination. It was a sad observation—the majority of the world refused to see beyond their silly little noses!

But it did not matter, thought Matthew, as he calmly finished his meal. It was only necessary for a solitary person to retain his imagination, his curiosity, and his respect for the awesome power of reality. Just one chap, that's all you needed.

And it appeared that Matthew Cavendish was that single person.

He accepted his fate with a smug little grin, and signaled for his waiter. Checking his watch, he could see how late the evening had become. Tomorrow, it would be time for serious research once again.

"You don't know me, Mr. Hammaker, but my name is Matthew Cavendish," he said into the telephone. "I have been referred to you by your stage manager at the Circle Six Theater—a Mr. Kane Witlowe. . . ."

"Yeah, what can I do for you?" said the voice flavored with a regional New York accent. Matthew could detect a touch of arrogance, a suggestion of not wanting to be bothered.

"I am a writer, and—"

"Hey listen, I'm not interested in giving any more interviews. Especially about Stephen Sandler. So why don't you just forget about it, okay?"

"No, no, Mr. Hammaker. I am not a journalist. I write books."

"Oh, yeah? Like what?"

"Well, I've done several best-selling books on what's usually called 'strange phenomena.' One called *The Dark Path* was quite well-known. . . ."

"Oh, yeah," said Hammaker. "I remember that one! Kind of like Frank Edwards stuff, yeah. You wrote that, huh?" Now Hammaker's voice inflected a bit of respect.

"Yes, that's correct. I—"

"Well, what do you want with me?" He was back to being flippant.

Matthew decided to use the direct approach: "I want to talk to you about Sophia Rousseau."

There was no immediate reply, but he could hear Hammaker's breathing through the other end of the phone line.

"Mr. Hammaker. . . ? Are you there? Hello?"

"Yeah, yeah. . . I'm still here. What do you want to talk about?"

"I'm afraid it would be quite impossible to discuss anything over the telephone, you think we might be able to speak over dinner this evening?"

"Jeez, I don't know. . ."

"I assure you that this is extremely important," said Matthew, playing what he hoped would be his best card. . . I think she has a connection in the death of Stephen Sandler."

There was another long silence on the phone line, and Matthew presumed that he had touched upon a sensitive nerve. From the articles and the quick research he had done, he knew that Richard Hammaker was very close to the late Sandler, and that the great man's death had been very upsetting to the playwright.

"Mr. Hammaker. . . ?" A little prodding never hurt, thought Matthew.

"Yeah, yeah. . . I'm thinking, okay?"

"Then tonight will be acceptable?" Matthew could be very forceful when he wanted to be, although he had always felt he would make a very bad salesman.

Hammaker sighed audibly into the phone. "Yes, all right. I can meet you around seven, I guess."

"That will be splendid! Do you have any particular establishment in mind?"

"Well, let's see . . ." said Hammaker. "Do you eat Chinese?"

"What? That sounds terribly cannibalistic!"

Hammaker chuckled. "Do you like Chinese food, Mr. Cavendish?"

"Oh, yes! Oriental cooking is just fine. Just give me an address, and I shall be there."

"Go to the Hunan Village on 41st Street, just off Second Avenue. Ask for my table, and I'll see you around seven, okay?"

"Very good," said Matthew as he quickly scribbled the data into his notebook. "I assure you, Mr. Hammaker, that you will not regret seeing me."

"Yeah? Well we'll see about that."

All the same, thank you very much. I shall look forward to meeting you. Good-bye, Mr. Hammaker."

Hammaker mumbled something into the phone and hung up, leaving Matthew holding the dead receiver. Well, the young man certainly wasn't the most mannerly, but of course, most young people who came to success early rarely were! He thought of the many rock groups who were as arrogant and churlish as they come. Nothing like a little aging to wise them up, eh what?

Checking his watch, Matthew saw that he had just enough time to take a good hot bath and arrange his notes for his meeting with Hammaker.

. . . and one more thing.

He walked to his valise, and from it removed a small, leather pouch in which he usually carried a few bowls of tobacco.

But there was no tobacco in the pouch now.

Matthew opened the thin leather flap and peered inside the container. It was a small gift from the Parisian Inspector Maillet—

a small sample of something his people had found in Sophia Rousseau's last known European residence.

Reaching into the pouch, Matthew pulled out a thin slice of the substance and held it up to the light. It was translucent, delicate like an insect's wing.

Maybe it's time I found out what this might be, thought Matthew as a slight chill touched down between his shoulder blades.

Chapter 24

"And you're sure you don't mind?" asked Rob Lester as he stared at her over his desk.

Sophia smiled and shook her head. "No, of course not. I think it's the best thing for both of us. Like you said: both of our careers are at a crossroads, and it's time to move on."

Rob smiled. She knew that he would be feeling sky-high this morning. Today, he had just announced, he was heading up his own agency—starting ASAP.

"All right, baby, I'm going to be tied up with lawyers and accountants for a few days. I hope you can dig it."

"Certainly, Rob. I understand. Don't worry about me. Everything will be fine."

"You sure you want to fly out to Vegas all by yourself, though?"

She shrugged sexily. "I would rather have you along . . . but all the arrangements have been taken care of. Manny Gold said I can start rehearsals the day after I get there."

"Yeah, you can trust Manny to take care of things. He puts on the best show on the Strip." Rob lighted a cigarette, puffed automatically on the Nat Sherman ultralight. "Now what about the play? You got that taken care of?"

Sophia shook her head. "No, not really. What with Sandler's funeral just happening, I did not get a chance to tell anyone."

"Jeez, honey, they're gonna flip out when you tell them you're going to Vegas tomorrow!"

"No, they won't. Stephen knew I had an open offer, and he knew that I had the option to leave the play after the first sixty-five performances. I'm just exercising the option, that's all."

"Yeah, but you know what I mean."

Sophia imagined that he sensed a hassle coming on, and didn't want any hassles when he was trying to get a lot of legal business wrapped up. She also knew that he was feeling an almost crazy urgency to get things taken care of so that he might get to Los Angeles as quickly as possible.

"Well, let me put it to you this way, Rob. I'm going to Vegas tomorrow. You're my agent, so you can handle the details at the theater. Besides, I have a feeling that Richard Hammaker will be happy to see me go."

"Yeah, you two never did seem to get along. . . although I did see you take off with him after the funeral. What was that ail about?"

"Oh, we had a long talk, that is all."

"You had a long talk, and you didn't tell him you were leaving the cast? What the hell did you tell him?"

"Rob, I don't think it's necessary that you get so excited."

His face flushed and he glared at her. "Excited? Look, I gotta lotta work to do and you're just makin' more for me! I wanna know why you didn't tell Hammaker what you're doin', that's all."

Standing up she faced him squarely across the desk and let her gaze link up with his. She used the "voice" as she spoke, and within an instant, he had entered a hypnotic trance.

"Rob, you will please remain calm when dealing with me. You will contact Kane Witlowe, informing him of my plans. If you must speak with Mr. Hammaker, you will tell him that you know very little of my future plans. Do you understand?"

Rob nodded slowly. "Yes. . . yes, I do."

"I wish to have no contact with Richard Hammaker ever again. Do you understand?"

"No contact. Yes."

"Very well, when I speak again, you will wake up with no memory of this trance. Do you understand?"

"Yes . . . "

"Awaken!"

Rob blinked his eyes, looked out the office window for a moment then back at Sophia with a smile. "So. . . :It. looks like we got no problems, baby! You get your tail out to Vegas and I'll catch up with you as soon as I can."

"That sounds wonderful, Rob."

"When're you leaving?" he asked absently, as though thinking about something else.

"I have a late flight tonight. . .;"

He clapped his hands together like a child. "Man, this is beautiful! I've wanted to do this for a long time! I have a feelin' we're going to have one hell of a great time out there!"

"I hope you are right," said Sophia.

Sixteen hours later, she languished in the wide-body jetliner seat as it slipped through the darkness over Arizona. She had been listening to music through headphones, and the selection had been written by an old friend of hers. Despite his maddening vision, Wolfgang would have never imagined his music might someday be heard by people traveling near the speed of sound while thousands of feet above the earth.

Sophia smiled. When you thought about it like that, it *did* sound utterly ridiculous.

And yet it was fact.

What an incredible race of beings were these simple mortals! She felt so many emotions for them: a subtle blend of pity, loathing, some love, and certainly respect.

They lived for so short a time, and yet some of them accomplished so much. At least that small percentage of them demanded to be admired.

She looked across the aisle and saw that the middle-aged man with a potbelly and an expensive suit was staring at her again. She had him pegged for an obnoxious business executive anticipating a binge in the casinos. For the last several hours, he had been making an issue out of looking at her, and talking to her. Thus the wearing of the stereophones.

But now she was feeling playful.

Removing the phones, she looked out into the rushing blackness of the night. Sailing along with the plane, above the wispy layer of clouds, lay a swollen moon, three-quarters full. Within a week there would be a New Moon, and she longed for the freedom that time would bring to her.

To be free again!

The thought tantalized her like a kiss upon her inner thigh, and she smiled as she stretched slowly and sensuously.

"Does it feel good?" asked the potbellied man. He chuckled basely. "It certainly looks good!"

Turning, she stared at him with her fire-emerald eyes.

For an instant he was transfixed like a bug under a pin. "Would you like to fuck me?" she asked softly.

"What!" he whispered harshly.

He looked as though he were choking for a moment. Then he

quickly looked about the other rows of seats to see if anyone had been watching them, had heard her words. But everyone was either dozing or reading.

He swallowed hard, tried to continue looking into her eyes. "What did you say just now?"

"You heard me. . . ." said Sophia.

This was going to be fun, she thought calmly. She could almost hear the man's heart beating in his fatty chest. He gave off great waves of desire, and its hot pungeance both repelled and intrigued her.

He tugged at his collar, adjusted his tie, and again looked up and down the aisles. "Where? I mean, how?"

"Follow me," she said, and left her seat, walking slowly toward the back of the plane.

As she reached the rest room, opening the door, the business executive was halfway down the aisle, his heart jumping in his chest, his breathing already getting labored.

"We'll never fit," he said as she entered the small enclosure and sat on the sink.

"Oh, yes, we will. Come in and close the door."

The large man squeezed into the cabin and forced the door shut. The air was suddenly oppressive, thick with his musky excretions.

Like a gymnast, she effortlessly raised her legs almost perpendicular to the ceiling, pulling up her dress to her waist. She wore no underwear and the man, upon seeing this, almost lost control of his muscular functions.

"Jesus. . . I don't believe this!" he whispered again as he fumbled with his trousers.

She pulled him into her and grabbed him with her muscles just to hear him gasp. He was a large man, but he was a weak man, and as she drew him into her, she could feel the almost total lack of essence in him.

He would be like a dry husk in an instant, and she only smiled at the notion.

"Oh jeez! So fast! My god!" He cried out as he began to climax, aided and abetted by her rhythmic contractions. In the close confines of the cabin, she could almost hear, as well as feel, the ratcheting of his heart. She could almost see the fat-encrusted muscle laboring and straining, beginning to burst.

Suddenly he went rigid; his eyes rolled back into his skull. As he slipped into orgasm, his heart recoiled against the strain and the pressure and the ecstasy. Releasing him, she watched him fall away from her, thudding onto the toilet with his pants puddled about his ankles. His eyes opened into oblivion, his chest now silent.

The fool! she thought with disgust, as she slipped down from the sink and opened the door.

The aisle was empty and the cabin was filled with a subsonic thrumming from the engines. None of the passengers stirred. There was not a flight attendant in sight.

Sophia glided back to her seat, sank into its cushions, and waited for the excitement to begin . . . .

Chapter 25

"She's a what?" asked Richard Hammaker.

Matthew Cavendish cleared his throat. "She is a *lamia*," he said, placing the accent on the second syllable.

"I've never heard of such a thing," said Hammaker. "What the hell is it?"

"A creature who has probably been with us since the beginning," said Matthew. "An incarnate, evil entity, a thing! . . . Good grief, man, you're asking me what it *is!?* I don't really know! All I know it that it/she *exists*."

"It's just too crazy. . . so hard to believe. . ." Hammaker rubbed his temples and shook his head as though clearing it. Matthew was not certain how he felt about the man. That he was intelligent and perceptive there was no doubt, but his personality seemed a bit unstable. Matthew was always careful around characters like Hammaker.

"How can you not believe!" said Matthew in a low, but harshly inflected voice—he certainly didn't want other patrons in the Chinese restaurant overhearing the more bizarre aspects of their conversation.

"Well, you haven't exactly told me the most believable story, Mr. Cavendish."

"It's no story, man!" said Matthew. He gestured at the stack of papers and clippings and photographs. "This is a bunch of bloody facts, not fairy tales. This woman, this creature, exists. She leaves a trail of dead men in her wake, and your friend Stephen Sandler was one of them. Why can't you see that? There's nothing to believe! It's right in front of you. Facts!"

Hammaker tugged at his beard. "I know . . . but it's still hard to imagine that now, in the twentieth century, there would be people still hunting down monsters. I mean, it sounds so ridiculous, doesn't it?"

This chap's rationality was getting to be downright boorish! "Please don't start on that round of claptrap, Mr. Hammaker. "

"Huh?"

"About how damnable modern we all are!" Matthew was getting irritated with this smug fool. "It is simply insane to presume that after a few thousand years of written language and a few hundred years of the scientific method that we know most of what there is to know about the universe."

"Well. . ." Hammaker began, but Matthew gestured him to silence.

"To put it in your succinct American terms, Mr. Hammaker: when it comes to the universe, we don't know shit!"

Hammaker smiled as he steepled his hands over the dinner plate. "You know, I think you're right. I'm just being a smug Westerner, aren't I?"

"You're being a smug something, but I'd rather not say exactly what."

Hammaker laughed again and sipped his tea. "All right, Mr. Cavendish, I'm sorry. I'm afraid I do believe your astute deductions. Now, what can you tell me about a lamia?"

Well, finally! thought Matthew. Finally this American was going to get down to tacks! "Very well," said Matthew. "It's like this. There is very little written or remembered about the lamia, and this had probably been to a creature like your Ms. Rousseau's benefit.

"Originally, there is a mention of a minor figure in the Greco-Roman mythological framework of an actual character made Lamia . . . but the references are obscure, and often contradictory.

"More frequent, and actually codified mentions of the lamia as a generic entity begin to appear in the thirteenth century in various European legends. But the prevalence of the lamia is most firmly seated in the medieval period, the Dark Ages."

Hammaker nodded, sipped his tea. "Makes sense. They were a superstitious lot in general, weren't they?"

"Yes, but this is not a superstition we're dealing with now, is it?"

"No, I suppose it isn't," said Hammaker. "Sorry. . . go on, please."

aste of that wretched green
: "And so, there are various
out the medieval landscape.
like Thomas Chatterton's
'To Miss C,' and of course
Samuel Coleridge, in which
ght be one of these lamiae
creatures. But pretty own occurrence is the poem
actually entitled 'Lamia' by John Keats. I've found some third-party
journal references who claim that the poem was written by Keats
after he met one of the last women to be involved with Percy Shelley.
There are other obscure references and even some actual accounts
of experiences with lamiae. It was almost always a female entity,
and it operated along the lines of a succubus."

"A what?"

"The succubus was a demon-type thing that would visit you in
your sleep and have sexual congress with you. It was greatly feared
by both men and women. Only the lamia was a bit different, and
more fearful."

"How's that?"

"The lamia was a seductive creature, and there was the element of sexuality, of course, but it was more vampiric in nature.
By that, I mean that the lamia, during sexual congress, was actually drawing off the soul, the essence of a victim. What I mean is
the victim's basic life-energy—a combination of the items which
comprise the transcendent human condition: creativity, imagination, ambition, passion, vision, and the other indefinable aspects
of what we call 'genius.' Do you follow me?"

Hammaker nodded. "So far. Is there more?"

"Quite. Listen: the lamia needs this energy-essence, this vital
soul-stuff, to survive. It is their life-blood, just as real blood is the
stuff that vampires need. In fact, the sexual connotations of the
vampire myths are probably bastardizations of the earlier lamia
legends.

"Anyway, it seems as if the most aspiring, the most talented
among the human race are the most desired by the lamiae. The true
genius among us is a very special person.He or she is in tune with
the universe in a way that the rest of us can never be. The energy at
their creative disposal must be awesome—it is the driving force of
all that exists, and to the lamia, this soul-stuff, this genius-energy,
must be the sweetest of nectars!"

"Incredible!" said Hammaker. "What great stuff for a play."

"Fuck your play, man!" said Matthew, hardly believing the moonful waxings of his companion. "We're talking about survival, not bloody plays!"

"I know, but this is all sounding so rich, so full of wonderful resonances. You can't blame me for responding to it, can you?"

Matthew shook his head. Artists were all alike! "No, Hammaker, I suppose I cannot. Now let me continue . . . ."

"Sure. Go ahead, I'm listening."

"All right, now where was I? Oh yes, now this next part is important: the actual physical shape, the body, of the lamia is not human—"

Hammaker interrupted him. "What was that?" A grave expression clouded his features.

"What's the matter?" asked Matthew.

"I don't remember if I told you. . . the whole conversation with Sandler. . . one of the things he said which really upset me, got me wondering if he was all right in the head. . ."

"What was that? What did he tell you?"

Hammaker looked at him and swallowed dryly. "He said that he didn't think Sophia Rousseau was human. . . ."

Matthew smiled ironically. "So. . . your friend was more perceptive than most. He must have known what was destroying him, and yet he had no real power to combat it—like a drug addict. And yet he tried to warn you and lacked the words to articulate things any better."

"He never mentioned a lamia, if that's what you mean," said Hammaker.

"No, no, he wouldn't have known about them, most likely." He paused and finished the cup of tea. The Hunan Village had served up passable fare, but the tea had been an atrocity to the palate. Wincing as he allowed the final cold swallow to slip downward, he continued: "And so, let me go on. . . . As I said, the human form is not the lamia's actual shape. Legend says that the actual shape is that of a serpent."

"What?" Hammaker's expression was now one of revulsion.

"Yes, that's right. A giant snake with golden eyes and scales of every color of the spectrum. If seen in its 'True Form,' as it's called, the effect of light shimmering off its flesh is supposed to be hypnotic."

"This. is amazing. . . simply incredible." Hammaker was shaking his head slowly, trying to accept everything that Matthew was telling him.

"Yes, it is . . . but there's more. Listen: the lamia is a change-ling, and can assume the shape of a female human. But, like many other transformational beings of fact and legend, there is a bit of small print in the contract. "

"Meaning?"

Matthew cleared his throat and ran his index finger down the edge of his neatly trimmed beard. He smiled and held up his index to emphasize the point he was about to make.

"Meaning that once a month the lamia must return to her True Form—the serpent body—and remain in that form for at least twenty-four hours."

"You know this all sounds ridiculous, don't you?" Hammaker almost allowed himself to grin.

"Bloody hell!" said Matthew. "I don't care what it 'sounds' like! It's true, dammit! We're on the trail of something inhuman . . . something evil. . . and it's about time you accepted that fact."

Hammaker leaned back in his chair. "Hey look, I'm not trying to piss you off. I'm sorry, Mr. Cavendish, all right?"

"If that is truly the case, then there are two things you will do for me. . . ."

"And what's that?"

"You will stop grinning like a Cheshire cat at the serious things I'm telling you, and you will begin calling me Matthew. Mr. Cavendish is so Victorian, don't you think?"

Hammaker smiled. "Whatever you say, Matthew. . ."

"Now, where was I?"

"Twenty-four hours. You said the lamia must stay a snake for twenty-four hours."

"Oh, yes! I didn't say it—the legends do. But I suspect that the folk tales are true enough on this. The actual transformation is linked to the appearance of the New Moon—that's when there is no moon visible in the sky."

"So it's a cycle," said Hammaker. "Like the werewolf legends."

"Precisely. Or any of the many other were-beast legends throughout the world. Apparently, from what I've been able to dis-cover, a lamia needs this period of time in her true body to replen-ish her powers, to recharge the batteries, so to speak."

"Does she have any control over the . . . the, uh . . . transforma-tion?" ask Hammaker. "Or does it just happen, right on time."

"I'm not certain of this, but I would think that the lunar-cyclic change occurs automatically, like clockwork, without possibility of interruption, or control. I don't think she can do anything about it."

"Is that good, or bad, do you think?"

Matthew shrugged. "I don't know. Legend says the lamia is immortal in either her True Form or the body of the female human, but that seems unlikely."

"Sounds hard to believe. Seems like a flame thrower would do a pretty good number on her." Hammaker grinned.

"That might be true, but I've only come across two ways to kill a lamia; one, deprive her human form of her needed soul-energy, or whatever you want to call it; or two, behead her serpent body with a silver-bladed sword. "

"Hmm," said Hammaker. "Not exactly your average household item, is it?"

"No, but one could be acquired without a terrible amount of difficulty."

Matthew rubbed his hands together as an image of himself welding a heavy silver-bladed sword flashed through his mind. It was a serio-comic impression: tall, lean Matthew Cavendish, arms akimbo, trying to swing about a huge Excalibur-type weapon. He had never been a very athletic man, and the thought of accurately striking something with the blade of a sword seemed only remotely possible to him.

"Yeah, right," said Hammaker. "I'm sure Tiffany's could whip one up for you in a few days."

"Enough sarcasm, please. You keep interrupting me, and I forget where I was in my narrative. . . one of the plagues of old age-you'll soon see for yourself!"

"You just mentioned the two ways to kill a lamia."Hammaker was grinning in spite of himself.

"Oh, yes! But of course, the lamia may be imprisoned if she is kept within a stone crypt or altar as long as either is within a church."

"A church! Does it matter what denomination?"

"How should I know? Are you trying to be funny again?"

Hammaker shrugged. "Actually, no. Not at all. I think I'm trying to make light of this shit because otherwise I'd be scared to death. All this stuff makes my skin kind of crawly, if you wanna know the truth. I mean, that business about entombing them in a church. . . it kind of disrupts my atheistic tendencies, you know? I mean, it kind of implies some kind of possible truth in the Judaeo-Christian tradition, doesn't it?"

"Good grief! Who gives a bloody tinker's damn about the Judaeo-Christian tradition? I'm just telling you what I know about the lamia legends. None of them might mean a fucking thing!"

"Then what the hell are you telling me for!?"

"Because it's all I know, for Christ's sake!" Matthew paused to compose himself. It wasn't good to keep getting excited like he was. He drew a breath and continued. "Besides, it's better than knowing nothing at all when we go after her."

Hammaker looked at him oddly for a moment. The color seemed to be draining away from the man's face. "We're going after her?" he asked.

"Yes, I thought we might, yes."

"Why? She sounds like a pretty damned formidable, dangerous. . . thing to be messing around with." Hammaker was drumming his fingers on the table nervously.

"And that is precisely why we must destroy her!"

"Why me?" asked Hammaker. "Why am I the lucky guy to get picked to go off on a monster hunt with you? What makes you think I want to help you?"

Matthew shrugged. Hammaker was making sense, and laid clear his presumptuousness. He would have to take his best shot.

"Because she killed the best friend you ever had. . . ." he said slowly.

Hammaker looked away, pretending to be studying the collection of tables and other diners scattered throughout the Hunan Village. He inhaled, exhaled, wiped a single drop of moisture from the corner of his eye. He was a strange chap, but Matthew found he liked him quite a bit. There was an honesty about Hammaker, a sincerity that could be sensed almost immediately. Matthew imagined he was a man with few friends, because most people usually do not want to hear the truth so often and in such bold terms as Hammaker often told it. Hammaker was the kind of fellow who would always let you know where he stood on any issue. Admirable trait, that.

Finally the playwright turned back to stare at Matthew.

"How do you know he was my best friend?"

Ah . . . he'd struck the correct raw nerve, it seemed.

"I could discern that from the way you talked about him during dinner. Only someone who felt a great deal for another would have been so concerned about him. When you saw him wasting away and felt so helpless, your feelings for the man were quite obvious."

"I see," said Hammaker.

"So. . . am I correct? Do you wish to help me track down this creature?"

"I think I'm crazy, but yes! I'll help you."

"Good show, old sport! I knew that I could count on you the moment I met you." Matthew extended his hand and they shook on the arrangement. He felt immediately better and more confident now knowing that he had an ally, a confidant in the entire affair. He had been so angry and hurt when his agent gave him the impression that he was off chasing a silly fairy tale. . . and now he felt vindicated.

Matthew signaled for the check, and looked at his watch.

"Good grief! It's getting late. I have to make a phone call."

"What's the matter?" asked Hammaker.

Matthew quickly told him about the filmy, translucent material the Parisian police had found in Sophia's last Continental residence, and how the good Inspector had smuggled him a sample.

". . . And so," he continued. "On the way over here, I made a stop at your marvelous Museum of Natural History. I have a good friend who works there—Jack Carrington. Taxidermist, he is. He promised me he would have some of his colleagues in the lab check out the sample. Tell me what I've got, you see."

"And. . . did they tell you?" Hammaker sounded intrigued.

"No, not yet. But I must call him back this evening. Jack said they might have something for me quite soon."

"There's a phone out by the front desk," said Hammaker. "Why don't you give him a call from here?"

"Good idea! Won't you excuse then? Be back in a bob . . . ."

"Sure. Go ahead."

Matthew pushed back from the table and walked to the reception area where two phone stations (one could hardly call them "booths" anymore) awaited him. After checking the number in his ever-present notebook and finding the proper coins, he dialed directly to Jack's office.

"Carrington, hello?" The man's British accent was immediately apparent, and Matthew found it comfortable to hear the language pronounced correctly once again. "Hello, Jack. . . it's Matthew."

"Ah, yes, I've been expecting you. Getting ready to go for the night, I was. Glad you rang up!"

"Then I'll get right to the point, old boy: did the lab get a chance to look at the sample?"

"Oh, right-o . . . it was no problem. What you have there is the shedded skin of a snake."

Matthew did not speak for a moment. He felt as though his heart and all his organs had contracted for an instant. He could feel his adrenaline shocking through him, and at that moment he knew that everything he'd suspected was true. It was an instant of cosmic recognition and acceptance, it was like a zen *satori:* the lamia was real.

Matthew coughed self-consciously. "A snake, did you say, Jack?"

"Yes, that's right. Must have been a rather big fellow, too!"

"Really? You can tell that from the sample?"

"Somewhat," said Carrington, "Can't give you exact dimensions, of course, but I can rightly tell you this is no bleeding garden snake!"

"Quite. . ." said Matthew. "Now just one more thing, Jack: can you tell me what species it might be?"

Carrington paused for a breath. "I was hoping you might not ask me that, old man. Totally new DNA pattern. I'm afraid it's got us all a bit stymied, you know?"

"Species unknown?" asked Matthew quietly, thinking that he would be very surprised indeed if the skin had been identifiable.

"Absolutely unknown!" said Carrington. "None of us have seen anything even remotely similar. You might have something very valuable there—where did you get this specimen, anyway?"

"Sorry, but I'm not at liberty to say right now, but I would like to thank you for the quick work, Jack."

Carrington chuckled. "Matthew, you'll never change! Always a bit of the mysterious with you, isn't it?"

"Yes, I suppose there is. Got to keep up the image, you know."

"All right, I'm going to ring off and go home, if you don't mind. Do call me if you need any further assistance, won't you, Matthew?"

"I certainly shall, Jack. And thank you once again. . . good night."

As he replaced the receiver to its rack, Matthew began thinking of what he had just learned. It was the first real concrete and physical proof that his prey actually existed.

But his feelings. were still unclear to him. Something was wrong, something which needed sorting out.

When he approached the table, Richard Hammaker was studying his expression. Matthew sat down without speaking.

"It was a snake skin, wasn't it?" said Hammaker.

"Why, yes. . . of course it was."

"Don't you feel vindicated? You were right all along, it seems."

Matthew looked at the playwright, who was grinning in a small, admiring way. At that moment, his thoughts and his feelings on the whole issue began to crystallize.

"Yes, appears that I was right," he said. "But instead of feeling anything like elation, or even excitement, I think that I am mostly just scared. . . ."

Chapter 26

Las Vegas

Arriving in Las Vegas at night is the preferred way to see the Strip for the first time. Her chauffeur from the Sands told her that as soon as the big Silver Cloud pulled away from the terminal. Sophia agreed with him as soon as she saw the famous street filled with light and motion. It was a magically impossible scene, and she wondered how Vincent might have tried to paint such a vision.

After a quick tour, she met Manny Gold, the famous entertainment director at the Sands. Mr. Gold was a short, balding, round-bodied little man who smoked big cigars and wore lots of gold jewelry. The gold was his trademark, presumably after his name, although some people said that Gold wasn't even his real name, that it was something that ended in berg or stein, but that Manny had had it legally changed many years ago. Besides, the word, Gold, suggested money, and *that* was what Vegas was all about.

He personally escorted her to her suite—an incredible batch of rooms near the top of the hotel. The decor was French Provincial and there was white wood and gold trim everywhere. It was a rococo dream, a garish display of opulence and surplus, but she loved it.

Next she was assigned a bodyguard, and introduced to Brenda Rowley, the stage manager at the hotel. Brenda informed her she would be meeting with the choreographer and the bandleader in the morning so that they could begin to plan out her act. They would want to start rehearsals as soon as possible.

"Is there anything I can do for you, Ms. Rousseau?" asked Manny, as he leeringly ogled her perfect breasts, which threatened to burst forth from the silk blouse she wore.

"No, I don't think so. I'm going to take a bath and change. Then I might go down to the casino, and walk around a bit."

Manny smiled, nodded, blew out a large blue cloud of smoke. "Yeah, that's fine. You just yell if you need anything. I'll have Tony stay right outside the door. Ain't nobody going to bother you here, Ms. Rousseau."

"Thank you, Manny." She escorted him to the door where he paused for one last ogle. "Good night."

Closing the door, she began shedding her clothes as she entered the bathroom, which was twice as large as most apartment living rooms. There was a sunken tub of pink marble with solid gold fixtures. A rack of perfumed soaps, oils, and bath lotions awaited her choice on the edge of the tub. She turned on the water, adjusted the temperature, and added some soothing bubble solution.

While the tub filled, she examined her body in the wall-to-ceiling mirrors and smiled contentedly. A perfect female body. There was no human form, which could match hers, and yet it was a pale carriage compared to her True Form. She longed for the New Moon when she would be free of her human prison, when she could languish for a day unfettered and naked to the air.

She could, if she truly wanted, transform at that moment, but unless she was in extreme danger, the change was a slow, exacting process, taking hours, which she could not spare. If she were in a life-threatening emergency, her autonomic nervous system would take charge, transforming her into the serpentine shape far more quickly. But that was a painful, punishing experience, commenced only under the greatest danger possible.

Slipping into the bath, she relaxed as the warm, perfumed water caressed her smooth, firm flesh. It was a good time to review recent events. The nightmare of Scarpino had recurred several more times, and she had been concerned about that. It was as though her subconscious mind had been trying to warn her of impending danger—that was her interpretation of the recurrence. She had no special precognitive powers, other than the usual intuitive feelings, but she believed that the nightmares represented a distinct warning, and that she should remain vigilant. There was nothing wrong with taking precautions. And, of course, there had been the almost disastrous scene with Richard Hammaker.

It would be best if she never saw the man again.

Such thoughts repeated themselves as she tried to examine every possibility until she had finished with the bath. The thought also touched her that she needed some special nourishment. She was going to have to begin using Rob more directly. He would have to begin searching and procuring prospective partners. There had been nothing spectacular since Sandler, and before him, only a few momentary flashes of the gift. It was occurring to her, although she might not wish to face it— the modern world was less conducive to producing a genius than at any time in history.

Especially in America, she thought with a burst of insight.

There was something about the American culture which she had noticed in the relatively short time she had been in New York: this country was not kind to its artists and thinkers .

Throughout history, there had been times when the gifted were abused, but in general, the genius-types had been revered and respected. In America, Sophia detected an anti-intellectual sub-current, which coursed through the society at large. Artists and scientists were always depicted to be eccentric, odd, and in some way strange. She saw it on television dramas and sit-coms, in cartoons, in radio and TV commercials, everywhere. One of her lovers had off-handedly mentioned that the country's attitude toward its artists and thinkers was a by-product of the Protestant work ethic that dominated this country's beliefs for hundreds of years. The basic premise of which was hard work—that is, work in which your hands grew dirty, and your back sore—was the only ennobling kind of work to be done, the only real work.

Sad, thought Sophia. Sad and strange. . .

She dressed in a long diaphanous gown with no underwear. The fabric clung to her like a thin coating of oil, and she looked magnificent. Her hair surrounded her face, falling across her shoulders in a careless fall of waves and curls. She looked casual, yet stunning; elegant, yet sensual.

As she glided through the casino, the heads of the patrons, both male and female, turned to watch her passing. She stirred up so much desire that she could feel it like waves of summer heat rolling up in steamy, convective currents.

Pausing at a craps table, she studied the game for a few moments. She had seen variations of the dice-throwing game over the ages, and. despite the seemingly chaotic nature of the play, she gradually picked up the basic rules of play. Pass. No Pass. Come. No Come. Hardways and Easy. She bought into the game with several thousand dollars, and made her plays, not really caring whether she won or lost.

After several minutes, she noticed a slight commotion in the aisle to her left. Looking over, she could see that many of the people at the tables were pointing farther down the aisle, and murmuring in concert. Apparently someone of notoriety was approaching.

Even the play at her own table stalled as the distraction grew closer, and as everyone looked up, she could hear murmurs of surprise and the mention of a man's name on the whispering lips of the players.

Tommy Adestra.

That was the name that fell from their lips. It was spoken with hushed, almost magical awe. It was a name of legend, a name known all over the world. A name that meant power and wealth and talent.

Looking up from the lush green table, Sophia watched a small procession advancing like a Roman column between the rows of casino tables. In front, like two flanking centurions, marched a pair of large, menacing figures—young, overly muscular, cinder-block men. The bodyguards continually scanned the crowd in front of them, as though looking for trouble in an instant. In their midst walked Tommy Adestra with several sycophants in tow. Tommy walked with a casual grace, his head held high, his back straight, an easy smile on his aging face. His hair was getting gray and thin, and there were too many wrinkles on his familiar face, but his bright blue eyes were still full of spark and shine, and his deeply tanned flesh still had a vibrant glow. Even for a man in his sixties, he had the look of vitality and energy. He was like a magnet, drawing the attention and the admiration of the crowds to him.

Even Sophia had to admit there was a magic about him. There was an aura of power that radiated from him; it was special and intoxicating. Adestra gave the impression of a famous ruler, a popular monarch, who had decided to go out slumming amid his subjects. There was that air of diffidence, of casual power, which she found so suddenly appealing.

As the small entourage approached her table, she continued to stare at the world-famous singer, film star, and entertainer. He was walking and talking with his small group of hangers-on, his head easily turreting back and forth, catching glimpses of the admiring crowd, when he abruptly caught sight of Sophia.

Immediately their gazes locked and there was an electrical charge building in the air like the imminent arrival of a thunderstorm. Everyone else must have sensed it, too, because the murmuring and the laughter seemed to die, and as a silence settled down over the crowd, everyone seemed to be watching Tommy Adestra as he moved quickly to Sophia, taking her hand and kissing it before giving her that famous smile.

"Hi, baby . . . I don't think we've met," he said calmly. "But I think it's time we did."

"Do you?"

"Hey, I know who you are, and you know me, too."

"That's right," she said as she turned on her special attractions, although she sensed that she didn't even need them in this instance.

Tommy looked approvingly up and down her body.

"Nice dress," he said.

"You don't mean that," she said.

"You're right. What I really meant was 'nice bod'."

"You should always say what you mean," said Sophia, picking up her chips from a little wooden rack on the edge of the table. She stepped closer to him. He was wearing a strong, masculine cologne.

"I usually do." Tommy smiled. "I don't know what came over me."

"I do. . . ." Sophia smiled.

"Yeah, I'll bet you do."

He paused, looked back at his entourage, and then gestured that they all get lost. One of the cinder blocks nodded and gave everybody a meaningful glance that they should scatter, and suddenly the procession was breaking up amid mixed murmurings. One of the other centurions hung off at a polite distance.

"They sound disappointed," said Sophia.

Tommy shrugged. "Fuck 'em if they can't take a joke."

"All right. . ."

"Why don't you come with me and have a drink," said Tommy, his blue eyes radiating naked desire.

"I don't like bars," she said.

"Who said anything about bars? I've got a permanent suite up on the penthouse level."

"And?"

Tommy grabbed her arm above the elbow. He held her with a confidence and a strength that she could only admire.

"And I think we should go up there and have a drink and get to know each other a little better."

The Power of this man excited her the way few men could ever hope to do. Just standing by him, she could sense the aura of his Essence radiating outward, warming her like rays of the sun. She wanted him. There was a tingling in her cunt and she could feel her own hot juices leaking down the insides of her thighs. She wanted him and the Essence of him that would give her life. It was going to be fun playing with this special man.

Sophia smiled.

"Don't you really mean we should go up to your penthouse to have a drink and then get laid?"

Tommy Adestra grinned and nodded.
"Yeah, I guess you're right. Let's go."

For a man in his sixties, Tommy was an incredible specimen. His body, although beginning to show signs of wear and stress, sagged very little. He had remained hard and firm and well conditioned. Physically, he mirrored the power and determination of mind and talent that had kept him on top for so long.

It was nearing sunrise and he was not yet showing signs of stopping a sex-a-thon which had begun on the balcony, gradually moving to the audio-video studio, and finally to the bathroom with its sauna, Jacuzzi, and sunken tub. Sophia was sprawled across the edge of the tub on her elbows, her ass higher than her head and shoulders. Tommy moved with a deliberate rhythm, like a steam-driven piston. With each new move, she would grab him with her inner muscles and slow his withdrawal, and each time he would cry out with pleasure, but he would not succumb to the final release.

He moved with grace and confidence of a man half his age and she now understood why there was such a legend about this man. His gifts and his talents were immense, and she was happy to have chosen him for this special night. Ever since her arrival in this century she had been needing a man like Tommy Adestra, and she had decided that she would take everything from, him this night, that she would fill herself to bursting with the magic stuff of life. She had been waiting so long for a moment like this that she would not let it escape her.

At last, he slipped over the edge and climaxed for the third time that evening, and she knew it was a testament more to her power than his. As he collapsed into her with a final thrust, she grabbed him with her inner muscles and he made a sound as though stabbed through the heart. She released him and he slipped into the tub limply. Turning over to face him, she glided into the water like an eel and moved to him, kissing him and caressing him.

"Baby, you're incredible," he said between gasps for breath.

"So I've been told," she said, stretching out and relishing the sensation of such fullness, such a feeling of brimming over with the Essence. She had sensed the stuff of genius in Tommy, and she had taken hungrily, greedily, from him. She had wanted everything he possessed in one furious session of sexual symbiosis.

Tommy leaned back in the tub and sank down so that only his head was above the water. She looked at him and saw immediately that his complexion had lost its color and vital glow. The ashen pallor of the face that now stared dully at her was like a death mask.

Indeed, she thought. It was a death mask.

"Man, I feel like shit all of a sudden," said Tommy.

His head lolled over to one side and his bloodshot eyes tried to focus on her. "What the hell's the matter with me?"

She looked at him and saw the confusion, and the pain, and the lack of all the things that made Tommy Adestra the man he'd always been. It would not be fair to let him die like that, to not know what had happened to him. She had let that happen too many times in her long past, and sometimes the memories still haunted her. Her lovers had deserved better than that. Perhaps that was why she had not denied the suspicions of Stephen Sandler during his final days.

"Oh, jeez," said Tommy Adestra. "What the hell is *happening* to me?"

He had asked it merely in rhetorical fashion, but she answered him: "You're dying, Tommy."

With a great effort, he turned his head, looked at her and seemed to reflect the glow of her beauty.

"What?"

"You heard me."

"What *are* you, you bitch!?" His pale features twisted into angry indignation. Such fight, even to the end. "My guardian angel?"

"No," she said. "But I think you deserve to know. Listen, Tommy. . ."

Chapter 27

New York City

Matthew Cavendish sat at breakfast in the Warwick dining room, staring at the headline of the sensationalist tabloid:

TOMMY DEAD IN VEGAS

There was a sub-header which read:

Heart Attack Fells World-famous Entertainer

And then a long article that detailed the events leading up to the discovery of the body by one of Adestra's bodyguards when he checked the bathtub of his boss's hotel penthouse.

Matthew found the article to be very coarse and written to include a host of lurid details about Tommy Adestra's life and habits that should not be public knowledge. But there was one tidbit, which Matthew found extremely interesting—the paragraph which mentioned that Adestra had picked up a young actress in the hotel casino the night before and had spent the evening with her. When she departed early in the morning, Adestra's bodyguard testified to police that the famous entertainer was taking a shower. In fact, the bodyguard had stated, he could hear the man singing in the shower, and there was no mistaking his boss's singing.

"Got here as fast as I could. Everything's pretty jammed up this early in the morning!"

Looking up, Matthew saw Richard Hammaker standing before his breakfast table. The playwright was wearing his customary blue jeans, oxford shirt, and a leather flier's jacket. His dark hair was curly and formed a black nimbus about his pale face.

"Good morning, Richard. Sorry to call you at such an hour, but this is getting crucial."

"I know, I heard on the radio while I was getting dressed, and it's in all the papers. Pretty big splash for a bum like Adestra."

Matthew gestured for Hammaker to take a chair. "So you didn't like the man?"

Hammaker shrugged as he slipped into the leatherback seat. "I don't know. . . he was one of those guys like Elvis to me . . . I could never understand why everybody thought he was so hot. I mean, he had a few classic songs, he did a few good movies, and what else?"

Matthew grimaced and speared another piece of bacon with his fork. "Don't ask me! I never understood the lionizing mania you Americans have for your pop stars. "

Hammaker smiled. "Yeah, right. You Brits don't do that sort of thing, right."

Matthew shrugged. "I admit there've been a few lapses, but by and large, I'd say that's correct."

A waiter appeared at Hammaker's shoulder with a pad and pencil.

"I'll have the eggs benedict, grapefruit juice, and coffee," said the playwright.

Matthew waited for the waiter to stride off before speaking. "All right, enough of the small talk. We've got a few decisions to make."

"She killed him, didn't she?" asked Hammaker. "It was her, wasn't it?"

"Bloody well right it was her!" said Matthew.

"What're we going to do? We can't prove anything."

"Prove anything to whom? We know it's true, and that's all that counts!"

Hammaker nodded grimly. "Yeah, I guess you're right. But what are you getting at?"

"Can you make the trip with me to Las Vegas?"

Hammaker looked off toward the other diners. "I was afraid you would ask me that."

"Spare me the dramatics. You know what I'm saying: I've got to go out there after her and I want your help. Are you game?"

The waiter reappeared with the glass of juice and a cup of coffee. Hammaker thanked him and watched him depart before replying.

"Yes," he said softly. "I'm game . . . but you've got to explain something to me."

"Name it," said Matthew.

"What are we going to do when we get there?"

Good grief, this fellow could be thick when he wanted to be!

"Hammaker, my good lad, we are going to kill her!"

Regrettably, almost two weeks' waiting time elapsed while Matthew gathered up the materials and supplies he would be needing for their assault upon Las Vegas. Finally, the last item was ready, and after receiving confirmation, Matthew had arranged to meet with Hammaker and make the pickup together.

After meeting the playwright at the subway station on Houston Street, Matthew guided him along the un-crowded street to a small storefront just off Broadway.

Roland Krugh, Armorer said the sign across the grimy glass window, which was protected by a lattice of steel bars.

Entering the shop, Matthew thought it smelled like a leather tannery. Beyond the slapdash counter and a flimsy-looking partition, he could hear the clanging sounds of a small foundry. He and Hammaker stood in the barren, dirty anteroom for a moment before a youngish man with hair and beard like Christ, and wearing Ben Franklin eyeglasses, came out to the counter. He looked like a hippie from another era, and he wore a leather apron over regular khaki work-togs.

"Can I help you?" asked the shopkeeper.

"Yes. My name is Matthew Cavendish. I believe you have an order ready for me."

The longhaired man adjusted the red bandanna around his head. "Oh, yeah, I remember you, man. Yeah, it's ready. Just hang on; and I'll be right back."

As the shopkeeper returned to the back of the shop, Hammaker looked about the practically empty room. "How in hell does an armorer stay in business in the twentieth century?"

"I don't know. . . why don't you ask him?" said Matthew.

"I mean, it seems absurd, doesn't it?"

Matthew shrugged and looked at his unlikely partner.

"Oh, I don't know. I think that if there's a possibility of anyone running a strange business, you should expect to find it in New York, don't you think?"

Hammaker smiled and nodded. "Yeah, I guess you're right."

The shopkeeper abruptly arrived carrying a long object wrapped in oilcloth. He placed it carefully upon the table and began unwrapping it.

"Here you go. . . take a look at this and tell me what you think."

Matthew watched as the thick brown cloth fell away from the object. It fell slowly, almost seductively, finally revealing an ancient weapon encased in a heavy leather scabbard. The shopkeeper slowly, dramatically slid the weapon from its case. Forged from a single piece of metal, its handle was wrapped in leather and laced with a braided leather thong. The thick but graceful hilt gave way to the long thin blade, which grabbed even the feeble light of the shop and hurled it back with a shining vengeance.

It was a beautiful sword.

Excalibur, thought Matthew, could not have been more perfect.

"Wow. . ." said Hammaker.

"That blade is sterling silver, man," said the shopkeeper. "Took me forever to get it right, but it was worth it, right?"

"Oh, yes," said Matthew. "It is quite beautiful. And you are quite certain that it is silver? It's very important that it be silver."

"Oh, yeah, man, it's silver all right. I couldn't fake something like that if I wanted to. Besides, after you ordered it, I was really curious to see what it would look like, you know?"

"It is a stunning piece of work," said Matthew, unable to take his eyes off the shining blade.

"Thanks." The shopkeeper paused. "Oh, and dig this. . . ."

He reached under the counter and pulled out a piece of paper. Lifting the silver-bladed sword he passed it through the paper, neatly slicing it.

"I don't hafta tell you guys: that blade is sharp, right?"

Matthew was impressed. "Quite sharp enough, yes."

"That's incredible," said Hammaker. "You made it right here?"

"Oh, yeah, we make everything right on the premises." He reached under the counter and checked an old, worn ledger book, glanced up at Matthew. "Let's see . . . you paid in advance, so all I need is your signature that you received it. Sign right here."

Matthew signed the book and returned it to the longhaired smithy. "Thank you very much," he said as he slipped the sword back into its scabbard and began wrapping it in the oilcloth.

"Hey, it was a pleasure, man. We don't get many orders like that one."

"That reminds me," said Hammaker. "I was wondering exactly how much call there is for a business like this?"

The shopkeeper smiled. "Yeah, I can dig it. Everybody asks me that, but you'd be surprised how many people want suits of armor, re-creations of ancient weapons, stuff like that."

"Really? Like who?" Hammaker was apparently still not convinced.

"Well, there's lots of medievalist societies and clubs, costumers for various kinds of conventions, interior decorators, stage managers, collectors, and of course your usual batch of nuts."

"Yeah," said Hammaker with a smile. "And in what category would you put us?"

The shopkeeper adjusted his bandanna and his glasses. "Hard to say. . . you guys might just be a whole new category of your own."

You have know idea how bloody right you are, thought Matthew.

Chapter 28

Las Vegas

She had been dreaming again.

But this time it was just a dream, and not a nightmare. Sitting up in her satin-sheeted bed, Sophia let the images and the memories of the dream slowly fade away.

She had been fucking John Keats in a meadow outside of Downshire Hill. It had been a bright spring day. She had told him her name was Fanny Brawne, and he was totally in love with her. John had been writing with a furious, maddening passion and he was at the top of his form when she met him. Even in the dream, his rendering of "To a Nightingale" and "Ode on a Grecian Urn" were fresh and beautiful to her. John had been such a burning star! He would have died young without her involvement because of the way he lived, and in fact, he had been taken by tuberculosis before she actually killed him.

Getting up, Sophia walked to the shower and stepped in.

For some reason, she could not get the memory of Keats from her mind, and as the warm water cascaded over her, she remembered the day he showed her the poem so simply entitled "Lamia."

"You know. . ." was all she had said to him after reading it. And John had merely smiled. By then he knew that he was dying and he did not care. She followed him to Rome under a new identity and stayed with him until his lungs would no longer work for him.

Turning off the water, she stepped out and toweled herself dry. She would have to hurry if she would make the auditorium in an hour. After three weeks of intensive rehearsal, she was finally ready to begin her show. Everyone had worked hard and, as the run continued, Sophia would improve and the show would only get better. She had enjoyed working with the crew, and Brenda Rowley had been a dedicated stage manager—setting up the show with all the hype and publicity that would ensure a great opening.

In fact her entire sojourn in Vegas had been excellent.

She had learned so much about jazz dancing from her choreographer, Nelson Williams, and she had taken great delight in seducing the avowed-homosexual black man. Manny Gold had been like a father to her, even though he was constantly angling for "a little trim" as he often phrased it. Sophia would have gladly given him his request, but she knew the effort would have probably killed him.

And she needed Manny, at least for a while longer. Just as she was slipping into her Danskin, the phone rang.

"Hello?"

"Hey, babe! How're you doing?"

"Rob! Are you here, in town?"

"Yeah," said Lester. "Just got off the plane. Can you come out and get me?"

She told him about her final rehearsal within the hour, and then promised to send the hotel limo. "Why don't you come right down to the auditorium and watch the show?"

"Yeah, I guess I should, huh?"

"You don't sound very enthusiastic," she said.

"Hey listen, I'm beat! I've been flying back and forth between the City and L.A. for almost a month now, and it's starting to knock me out. Sorry I haven't been able to see you till now. . . . I tried to call whenever I could."

"I understand, Rob. You've been a very good agent, don't you worry."

"Yeah, right," said Lester. "Well, listen, I'm going to go out to the front of the terminal and watch for the hotel limo, okay? See you soon . . . bye."

Sophia hung up the phone, then quickly called Manny Gold.

The final production number had been inspired by Sophia's ideas and input. It was a lavish song and dance routine, detailing her incendiary career symbolically, and it ended with a spectacular striptease routine, which Nelson Williams had choreographed. Even though there had been few audience members during the rehearsals, Sophia knew it was a hot ending, and it would bring down the house.

After the finale, she jumped down from the stage and ran out to where Rob was sitting.

"Well, what do you think?"

"Fantastic, babe. . . I didn't know you could dance that well!"

"I can do anything I want, Rob. You should know that by now."

He shrugged. "Yeah, I guess you're right. You ready for some lunch?"

"Yes, I'm starving, but I'll have to change first."

"No, you won't. I'll get something from room service. I gotta talk to you."

"Is it that important?" She looked at him seriously to see if he was getting ready to make some silly joke, but his expression revealed nothing of the kind.

"Yeah, I think it is," said Rob.

"All right. Let's go upstairs."

They left the auditorium and passed through the lobby to the elevators. Rob did not speak as they walked along and that was her signal that something was definitely wrong.

"All right, tell me," she said when they entered an elevator alone.

"Some guy's been asking around about you."

"What? Who?"

"Matthew Cavendish, a writer who had called for me a few times while I was out of the New York office. When he finally caught up with me, he asked me a lot of questions about your career."

"So what's so terrible about that?" Sophia looked at him carefully. It would be best for her to appear unconcerned. There was no sense in getting Rob alarmed. She could handle whatever was happening by just being careful.

"I don't know," said Rob. "The guy was a little weird, I thought. After he hung up, I checked him out because I thought the name sounded familiar."

"And?"

"And he writes books about strange phenomena—you know, the real weird shit—and then I heard he's had a couple of best sellers." Rob appeared worried, perplexed.

"So?" Sophia tried to seem nonplussed, but she was wondering why such a writer would be asking about her. There could be no reason unless he suspected something. But how? It did not seem possible. . . and yet, she recalled Stephen Sandler becoming suspicious near the end. In fact, hadn't Rob told her about Sandler confiding in that monstrous freak, Hammaker, that he feared she wasn't human? Hadn't Hammaker foolishly spilled this to Rob? She realized she couldn't ignore Rob's latest news. She must prepare for any and all contingencies. . . .

"What do you mean: 'so'?"

"I don't see why this should worry you, Rob."

"C'mon, honey," he said. "What're you playing dumb with me or what? Now why would a guy who writes about rocks falling out of the sky and the people bursting into flames suddenly be interested in you? It don't make sense."

Sophia smiled. "Maybe he considers me a strange phenomenon . . . I know some of the drama critics do!"

The elevator came to a halt and the doors opened on a lavishly carpeted and decorated floor. There was no one waiting for the car, but the conversation abruptly halted until she and Rob reached the door to her suite.

"I had a bodyguard for the first few weeks," said Sophia.

"Really?"

She nodded, unlocking the door.

"When I was here, he would stand outside the room like a statue. And whenever I went out, he would follow me, always at a discreet distance. It was driving me crazy so I had him dismissed."

"You sure that was a good idea?" asked Rob as they entered the garish parlor.

She smiled patronizingly. "I can take care of myself. With your help, of course."

"Hey ,babe, I'm no bodyguard."

She looked at him with a penetrating gaze and spoke in the special voice. He was instantly attentive under her subtle influence.

"You will not be concerned with the clumsy investigations of Matthew Cavendish," she said. "You will go to Los Angeles and prepare a way for me."

"All right. . ."

"I will need a house with some privacy—something in one of the canyons will be appropriate. I want you to set things up for me so if I must leave here quickly, I will have a place to go. You will do this as though it were something discussed long ago, and you will not question my plans. Understood?"

"Of course. . ."

She smiled. Poor Rob, he had no idea he was being manipulated so totally. She wished that she could trust him implicitly, that she need not resort to this kind of control, but he had allowed her to gain control by gazing into her serpent eyes that night, and now she would take advantage of that fact. Besides, she thought easily, she had not survived for this long by trusting people.

"You will awaken when I clap my hands," she said.

Rob blinked at the sound that followed and looked around the suite. "Nice place. They're treating you right, kid."

Sophia moved to the phone. "I'm ordering lunch. What are you going to have?" .

"I don't care. The filet mignon's always good. That'll do it for me."

She ordered for both of them and hung up the phone.

Rob was sitting in a straight-backed chair looking about the room.

"You know," he said, "for the life of me, I can't remember why I came up here. I know there was some thing I wanted to tell you."

Sophia chuckled as she moved to the bar to make a white wine cooler. "Well, then, it couldn't have been very important, could it?"

Opening Night.

Surprising even herself, Sophia felt nervous. The huge hall at the hotel was filled with patrons, and the warm-up act had put them in the right frame of mind. They were primed and ready for a big show, and as the orchestra kicked in with the first number, she took a deep breath and waited for the mechanical platform to lift her up from behind the set.

Suddenly she could hear the applause from the audience and feel the heat of the lights on her flesh. The other dancers were suddenly surrounding her and everyone was moving in concert.

Sophia danced, gliding about the stage with effortless grace, letting all the practice and the training take over. It went just as Nelson had said it would, and as she basked in the wildly enthusiastic applause, she could barely wait to. get on with the show.

Each number seemed to go better than the preceding one. As Sophia grew more comfortable with herself and with her audience, she began looking out among the sea of faces, trying to establish contact, that personal rapport that Nelson Williams had said was important, and which set apart the great stage entertainers from all the rest.

And that's when it happened.

As the orchestra cranked up for the finale, Sophia was idly scanning the huge crowd, staring momentarily into the eyes of the throng. For an instant, her gaze passed over the lean, bearded face with the large, Rasputin eyes, the curly cloud of black hair. . . .

No! It *can't* be!

And then her musical cue arrived and she was forced to break contact, spinning off to begin her dance. She lost all spatial orientation with the audience for an instant, and could not locate the exact spot where she had seen Hammaker's face.

And it *was* Hammaker! Of that she had been certain. He had been grinning at her like a simpleton! The shock of seeing him out there had disrupted her so thoroughly for a moment that she feared she might fallout of synch with the orchestra. But her training had paid off and she picked up her cues perfectly, moving to the music through the intricate routine.

Each time she faced the audience, she attempted to catch sight of his absurdly grinning face, but her movements were too quick, too full of spins, turns, and abrupt changes in direction. She would have to wait until the number ended before she could see him again.

But what was he doing here?

The thought echoed through her mind as she worked through the erotic dance routine, which ended with her totally nude for an instant, masked by a dazzling display of laser lights and spots. As she stopped, frozen in that final pose, there was a very brief moment in between the flashes of the laser lights, when she could see the audience. And in that frame of an eye-flash of time, she found him once again.

Hammaker.

Still grinning. Staring at her with his oddly buggish eyes. And there had been time for her to notice one final thing. There had been a man seated to Hammaker's right—a man with medium-length sandy hair, a carefully trimmed beard, and wire-rimmed glasses.

Even in so brief an instant, the tableau had been imprinted on her mind like an image from a photographic plate. As the hall was suddenly immersed in darkness and a stagehand rushed out to wrap her in a robe, Sophia could still see the intense stare of the man next to Hammaker, and she knew in that single terrible moment that he was the hunter and that she was, for once, the prey.

Chapter 29

Well now, that was quite a show, thought Matthew as he squinted from the rising glare of the house lights. Now I can see why she's caused such a stir—she's absolutely stunning!

Looking around the audience, Matthew could see that Sophia had produced a similar effect on the assembled crowd. She was an incredibly erotic creature, which made her all the more dangerous, to be sure. Matthew inhaled slowly, held it, then let it out to calm himself. Surprisingly, he had found himself becoming sexually excited. . . . Imagine!

"She saw me. . . I know she saw me!" said Hammaker, still smiling like a madman. "I'll bet we scared the piss out of her!"

"Really," said Matthew. "Do you think any of us are actually capable of scaring a . . . a creature like her?"

Some of the people around them began to shuffle out, and Matthew allowed himself to be carried along with the rest. Hammaker followed, talking in too loud a voice.

"Of course we scared her," he said. "That night she tried to seduce me, remember. . . ? I told you how upset she got when she found out about me! She was freaked out then, and she's freaked out now!"

Matthew nodded as they moved toward the exit, which emptied into a large reception hall and lounge. He was not a big drinker, but by God, he needed one right now. He had only been half listening to Hammaker's ravings, but the mention of the disastrous seduction attempt focused his thoughts more clearly. He recalled Hammaker's confiding in him the story of his accident and his affliction—Matthew still found it ghastly every time he thought about the man walking about without a pecker—and how the knowledge had so disturbed the lamia.

Hell, it had disturbed me, thought Matthew.

"Hey, are you listening to me?" Hammaker tapped his arm forcefully.

"What? Oh, yes, of course. . . I agree with you completely."

"Well, what're we going to do about it? How are we going to handle this?"

Matthew steered them toward one of the many bars in the reception hall. The barman looked at him, awaiting his order. "A vodka gimlet for me—make it a double—and what's it for you, Richard, a bloody Mary?"

"Yeah, that's fine. On the hot side."

The barman went straight to work, and Hammaker looked at him expectantly. There was a more than usual wildness in his eyes, and Matthew surmised that he had gotten the scent of the prey and was getting crazy for the kill. He suspected that Hammaker was getting caught up in the unreality of what was happening, and was not conscious of the physical dangers possible.

The barman slapped the glasses down and Matthew passed the currency to him. He sipped the gimlet quickly, feeling its cool warmth scald his throat.

"I'm not sure how to handle this," said Matthew, stepping away from the bar. "We must be extremely careful. I don't think you realize that."

"Sure I do. But I think we've got to act fast. If we don't, she'll either figure out a way to get rid of us, or just split."

Matthew sipped again. "Yes, you're probably right, but our best chance is to catch her in her True Form. The new moon is still a week away. And besides, we can't go walking about the streets brandishing a bloody silver sword!"

Hammaker chuckled. "I say we should go after her now. As soon as possible."

Matthew gulped down the remainder of his drink. As he looked out into the buzzing crowd, he felt the sudden urge to just cry out, to simply scream unintelligibly, to release the insane tension he felt building up inside. Every now and then, the plain naked truth of what he was planning would come clear in his mind, and his more rational side attempted to reject it.

It was mad! It was impossible!

And yet here he was, standing with a silly cocktail, discussing the destruction of a mythological entity with a half-crazed playwright.

But of course there was nothing mythic about Sophia Rousseau. She was as real as the tiger in the jungle, the shark in the deep; she was as real as any other predatory beast—and twice as dangerous.

"Matthew, is there something wrong?" Hammaker sounded suddenly more solicitous, less brash.

"No," he said, still gazing off into the faceless mix of the crowd. "I'm just feeling scared, that's all. Nothing actually wrong with feeling like that, is there? I mean, only a fool wouldn't be scared of a monster like her."

"I must be a fool, then," said Hammaker. "Cuz I'm not."

Matthew shook his head and produced a handkerchief to mop his perspired brow. "Look, Richard, I was just sitting in there, and I felt the power of that bitch! She's a sexual creature, she is! I haven't the foggiest idea how I shall react in the face of such preternatural force. . . and that's what scares me!"

"I can dig it. That's perfectly understandable. She excites you, doesn't she? Isn't that what you're saying to me?"

"What? What are you ever getting at?"

Hammaker grinned. "She turns you on! She gives you a hard-on like the handle of a fucking hatchet—that's what I'm talkin' about! Now, am I right? Isn't that what you mean with all this talk about 'power' and 'force' and all that shit?"

Hammaker certainly had a way of putting things. "You don't mince your words, do you, lad?"

"Well, am I right, or am I right?"

Matthew nodded, wiped his brow again. "Yes! You're bloody well right! And it scares the hell out of me."

"Well, that's my point: this bitch doesn't do that to me, re-member? I know it, and she knows it . . . and that's why she's afraid: because of me."

Hammaker was correct, Matthew knew that. But he was still very apprehensive about what to do next. Looking at Hammaker squarely, he knew that he would have to stop all this foolishness and get down to tacks.

"You're right, Richard," he said in a steady, even voice. "Let's go back to the room and see what we can work up in terms of a strategy."

"Now you're talking! And forget the strategy, I already have an idea. . . ."

Chapter 30

Slipping into the robe, Sophia found herself surrounded by smiling people—the chorus of showgirls, the dancers, the stage-hands, Nelson Williams, and Brenda Rowley. Everyone was grinning and exclaiming at once as the praise and excitement and congratulations cascaded over her. In that instant, Sophia knew what she must do.

"Oh, Sophia, you were fantastic!" Brenda pushed through the crowd and hugged her.

"Thank you, thank you," she kept saying, slowly allowing an expression of discomfort, and finally outright pain color her features. She was hopeful that someone would be perceptive enough to notice she was obviously suffering from something.

But nothing happened until the crowd of well-wishers thinned out and she began to walk toward her dressing room. With an exaggerated limp she winced from the imaginary pain.

"My God, Sophia! What's the matter with you?" said Nelson, who had been standing alongside Brenda. "Did you hurt yourself?"

"I don't know. I think I pulled a muscle."

"Oh, no!" said Nelson. "Don't say such a thing, honey!" Sophia winced, attempted to take another step, and grabbed onto Williams's shoulder for support.

"Oh, Nelson. . . I'm sorry, but it feels very bad. I can hardly take a step."

"Jeezuz, honey, this doesn't sound good at all." He slipped his arm around her waist and helped her down the corridor to her dressing room.

"How'd you do it?" asked Brenda excitedly. "When'd it happen? Is it getting any better?"

"I don't know. . . right near the end, I felt something go ping down the back of my thigh."

"Did you do your stretching exercises before you went on?" asked Nelson as they approached her door.

"Of course."

Williams turned to Brenda. "You'd better call a doctor," he said. "Sounds like it might be a hamstring."

"Is that bad?" asked Sophia, trying to appear pained and apprehensive.

Nelson shrugged. "Well, honey, let's just say it ain't good, okay?"

"It's a pulled hamstring, all right," said the hotel physician, Dr. Gorsuch. "Although, I can't feel the damage."

"What do you mean?" asked Sophia.

"Well, it's a common enough injury among dancers and football players," said Dr. Gorsuch. He was a thin, wiry old man who reminded her of a spindly-legged bird. "But they're usually on such well-muscled types that it's tough to find the point of the tear by palpation—with your hands, that is."

"How long will she be out?" asked Brenda, who had been standing in the corner of the dressing room wringing her hands and smoking almost continuously since Dr. Gorsuch had arrived.

The old man shook his head and rubbed his pointy chin with his long, bony fingers. "Hard to say. Depends on how she responds to treatment. Three to four weeks at least."

"Oh, my god! Manny's going to die! He's going to absolutely die! Are you sure, Doc?"

"Nope. No doctor's ever 'sure,' but I just gave you a pretty good opinion. If this lady's in as much pain as she's indicated from my examination, then she got a pretty bad tear, and it's going to take at least that long to heal properly."

Sophia reclined on the couch trying to look appropriately upset. She wished it weren't necessary to go through all the silly rituals to affect her plan; she felt as though she were wasting time.

"Do you think we should take her to the hospital?" Brenda was asking. "Isn't there anything they could do there to speed things up?"

"No," said Sophia forcefully. "No hospitals."

"Honey, you'd better read the fine print in your contract," said Nelson.

"What are you talking about?" She suddenly felt very defensive.

"He means," said Brenda, "that the hotel, in agreement and by arrangement with our insurance companies, has the contractual right to demand medical care and attention for any of its performers."

"What!" Sophia was shocked that Rob would allow such a thing! "Well, you can forget about your contract I'm not going into any hospital."

"It's a standard clause," Dr. Gorsuch said to her. "But don't worry about it. There's no need to send you to the hospital. Nothing you can do for a hamstring except wait."

"If I were you, dearie, I'd just go home and let people wait on me for a while." He looked at Nelson and Brenda, shaking his head. "I wouldn't waste the hospital's time with her. All this woman needs is to forget about dancing or jogging for a few weeks."

Gorsuch used that line as his exit cue and quickly departed, obviously not interested in getting into a debate. "I would like to be taken to my room," said Sophia.

Brenda sighed and rolled her eyes. "I don't blame you, honey. Just hang on and I'll get somebody to send down a wheelchair. But I'll tell you—Manny's going to absolutely flip."

Sophia nodded, trying to appear distressed.

Once within the safety of her room, Sophia began packing. Thankfully, she had possessed the foresight to plan alternative living quarters. She called Rob's Century City Suite, leaving a message on his answering service that she would be contacting him tomorrow afternoon, and that she hoped he had arranged for living quarters.

Things were happening quickly, but she sensed that there was a reason for everything and she knew she must be prepared. She had not survived this long without being resourceful and extremely careful.

Suddenly the phone began ringing and she debated answering it. It was probably Manny Gold, and she did not really wish to talk with him.

The hell with him, with *all* of them.

Chapter 31

"Are you sure this is a good idea?" asked Matthew as he followed Hammaker up the fire stairs.

Both men were dressed in corduroy jeans, pullover sweaters, thin leather driving gloves, and jogging shoes. Matthew carried the silver-bladed sword, which he had come to think of as Excalibur. In one hand Hammaker carried a small knapsack with a can of white gasoline and some emergency roadside flares; in the other, he toted a long-handled fire ax stolen from one of the racks on a floor below.

"Be quiet, we're almost there," said Hammaker. "What are we going to tell them if we are apprehended?"

This whole thing was mad. Completely mad! Of course, thought Matthew, he himself was probably slipping into a special, calm kind of madness himself. . . . His agent had said that he would have to be mad to pursue such a story as if it were real. Well, fuck it. What did it matter anymore?

"We're not telling them anything because we *won't* be getting caught. It's four in the morning, so there's not many people out now, anyway." Hammaker signaled that Matthew should follow him to the fire door, which led into the corridor of suites.

"No. . . just the cops and the criminals, isn't that the way its goes?"

Hammaker smiled. "Yeah, and who are we—the good guys, or the bad guys, right?"

Matthew was about to attempt something humorous, but Hammaker had already pushed through the door and was stepping out into the hallway.

It was deserted and the ceiling lights were dimmed, although not enough to diminish the glitter of the brocaded wallpaper. They walked quietly down the hall toward the central core of the building where the elevators and service storage rooms were located. Hammaker walked briskly toward a room marked HOUSEKEEPING.

"Okay," he said, standing in front of it. "Keep an eye out for anybody. . . . Here goes."

Swinging the ax up over his head with a practiced circular motion, Hammaker brought the blade down just above the knob and the lock assembly. Surprisingly, the cheap brass and steel assembly gave way after the first blow, emitting little more than a soft crunch. Matthew was quite amazed to realize how little noise had been made, and how flimsily the door had been constructed.

"All right, let's move it!" Hammaker whispered as they slipped inside the supply room, which was cluttered with maids' carts and shelves full of cleaning liquids, plastic trash-can liners, brushes, paper products, and other bottles and boxes.

Hammaker spattered some of the camper's lantern gasoline over the tile floor, and produced a pack of matches.

"Okay, just a little bit to get it started. We don't want a conflagration. Besides, I have a feeling the automatic sprinkler's going to kick in and douse it anyway."

Tossing the lighted matches to the floor, he danced back from the burst of intense flame.

"All right, we're outta here!" he whispered.

Pulling shut the supply room, Hammaker moved down to the elevator doors and the fire alarm box on the nearby wall.

"Happy New Year," he said, and activated the alarm.

Instantly the serene, quiet softness of the hallway was invaded by the klaxon sound. It was a shrill, insistent clamor that wanted to panic him, and Matthew had to struggle to keep from losing control. This whole thing was crazy! They were going to be caught and punished!

"Okay, let's move it!"

Doors began flying open amid the worried cries and voices of the patrons. Suddenly Matthew was moving down a hall filling up with frantic people in gowns and robes.

"Please take the fire stairs at the end of the corridor!" yelled Hammaker as he wielded the ax like a fireman. His booming authoritative stage voice sounded remarkably authentic. "Walk, don't run! There is *no* danger!"

Incredibly, the people began following his instructions! In potential panic-situations, people look for an authority figure, a savior, and will generally accede to whoever steps forward or appears to fill that role. Hammaker was playing it beautifully.

"All right, this way! Quick!" said the wild-eyed, bearded playwright.

He led Matthew down another intersecting corridor toward Sophia's room—the location of which had been gleaned from a bellhop for a hundred dollar bill. In addition to the other surprising aspects of Richard Hammaker, Matthew was amazed at the manner in which Hammaker threw about his nouveau wealth. The kid would have probably tipped them off for a twenty.

Other people were appearing at the doors to their rooms and Hammaker charged past them, fire ax in hand, yelling evacuation instructions. Every one of them accepted him as a vanguard fireman; no one questioned their presence in the hallway.

When he reached the creature's suite, Hammaker paused and raised the ax. He was breathing hard, but he was obviously ready for anything. Incredible, thought Matthew. The man is a fucking lunatic! *He* wants this woman more than *I* do!

"Get back! Here goes!" Hammaker raised the ax and slammed it into the door. The wood and steel surrendered with an almost soundless chunk under the wail of the klaxon. He raised the tool for a second swing.

People passed them in the hall, running, not walking, but still not in a panic. Soon, thought Matthew, the firemen would be swarming the halls, and by that time, he hoped they were finished with their grim business.

The ax crashed down a second and a third time, and the doorlock assembly gave way, the door almost flying off its hinges as it flew inward.

"Hurry up! Get in! Quick!" Hammaker ducked into the suite and Matthew followed, unwrapping Excalibur and holding it out in front of him like a torch. We're going to die, he thought calmly to himself. Oddly, there was no panic in his inner voice, no dread, or maddening terror—just a quiet simple recognition of a fact.

Hammaker kicked the door closed behind them, and they stood cautiously at the entrance to the unlit room. Where *was* the bitch? She couldn't have left the suite—they would have seen her coming up the hall. No. She was in there, waiting for them. . . . .

Fumbling for a wall switch, Matthew found one and threw it up. The recessed lighting filled the room with an orange glow revealing the room to be deserted. Hammaker reached out and took the sword from Matthew, handing him the ax—which was just fine with him. I don't think I could use it anyway, he thought in that weirdly calm inner voice.

Hammaker led him across the room, down a short hall that led to the bath and bedrooms. With each step down the narrow strip, Matthew kept expecting them to be jumped upon from some unseen place. Despite the wail of the alarm in the hallway, there was a general impression of silence in the room. His footsteps on the carpet sounded obscenely loud. Hammaker's breathing was a rasping, asthmatic sigh—a sonic beacon to signal their advance and do them in.

The end of the hallway was marked by an open door, a black rectangle like the entrance to an abyss. Matthew imagined the scaled creature waiting, coiled and weaving, ready to spring at them. Each step closer to the entrance to the room boomed his pulse another notch until it was like a drum pounding out a rapid rhythm behind his ears. He watched Hammaker's short, stocky figure pass the threshold and dissolve into the shadows.

It's going to *get* him, he thought wildly. The panic rose upward in him like a molten volcanic column, and he realized that he would be helpless before the thing's power, that he would not be able to help poor Hammaker when it struck them.

"Jesus Christ!" said Hammaker, and Matthew felt an icy brace of adrenaline-shock.

He moved forward, entering the room automatically, not knowing by what force or energy he moved. His mind had gone instantly and momentarily numb, and in that single piece of time he knew that, terrified as he might be, he was at least *not* a coward. He moved into the darkness expecting to face his death, but knowing that he owed whatever help possible to Hammaker.

The lights suddenly blazed, and he blinked away the blinding white glare.

"She's *gone,* man," said Hammaker, standing by the door to a bathroom off the bedroom, his hand on a light switch panel.

"What?" asked Matthew. He barely recognized his own voice.

Looking about the room, he could see that it had been vacated. The closet door, hanging open, revealed a barren enclosure, naked wire hangers upon a solitary pole. There was not a single trace of habitation.

"We missed her," said Hammaker. "She's on to us, and she split."

"But *where?*" asked Matthew.

"We'll find her."

Matthew leaned against the wall, breathing deeply. To feel the relief and sense of safety wash over him was almost intoxicating.

He grinned at his odd partner. "You know," he said, "for someone who was reluctant to join the witch hunt, you've become quite the zealot."

Hammaker smiled. "Yeah, I *have,* haven't I?"

"You really hate it, don't you?"

"It?" Hammaker looked at him squarely. *"Her.* Yes, I hate *her.* I'm sorry, but I can't think of her as an 'it,' at least not yet. There's something slimy, something evil and shitty about her, but most of all she killed the best friend I've ever had."

"Revenge will be sweet, eh?"

Hammaker nodded. "You're fuckin-A right it will."

"But we've got to find her first."

"We'll find her. She's got too high a profile to stay hidden too long."

"It is less than a week till the next new moon. She'll change then, and that's when we should strike." Matthew listened to the words he was speaking, and wondered instantly how and why he had become so involved in the entire affair.

Because she is a corruption, said a soft inner voice. An abject parasite. She is *evil.*

True enough, but why must I become her executioner? Adversary thoughts ricocheted about his mind like bullets. He felt confused, but worse, he felt very scared.

"Hey," said Hammaker. "Are you all right? You look like you're hypnotized."

"What? Oh, no," said Matthew. "just wool-gathering . . . just thinking about all this fine mess! Sometimes I wonder where it's going to end. If we'll ever catch up with her."

"We will. But we've got to do some quick detective work." Hammaker cocked his head as though hearing the fire alarm for the first time. "We'd better get out of here before we get arrested for arson."

Chapter 32

Los Angeles

"We finally struck pay dirt, babe!" said Rob Lester, as he hung up the phone. "I *told* you Uncle Robby would take care of everything."

"Rob, it's been almost a *week*." Sophia was seated across a large, oak desk. Her agent was ensconced behind its massive bulk buoyed up by a high-backed, deeply padded chair. The office was papered in woven grasscloth, decorated with original poster-art, and lots of pottery, sculpture, and shelves of books Rob had never read. Vertical blinds, which doubled as a panel of mirrors when closed, slatted the late afternoon sunlight. It was a very chic office, and Rob was making every effort to blend in with the California style.

Rob stood up and walked around the desk to take her hand. He was wearing a tennis outfit, which looked ludicrous on him, since she knew that he had never played tennis in his life. .

"Hey, babe, let's not dwell on the past! It's a bitch to find decent housing in this town," he said with a smile. "You heard what I said on the phone—we got the perfect place up off Malibu Canyon. C'mon, we'll take a ride over and check it out."

Sophia stood, smoothing her silk dress. Although she was acting distressed, a wave of relief had washed over her from the moment she heard that a possible residence had been found. While staying with Rob had not been difficult, especially since he was within her sphere of hypnogogic control, she still longed for her own private fortress. She would do it right this time—a full-fledged security system, and maybe even a full-time security staff. If she had learned anything about this new century, it was the *ease* with which information was disseminated, and how, once you achieved the status of a 'known' person or a 'celebrity,' it was practically impossible to gain real privacy.

Following Rob from the office, she walked down the lushly carpeted hall to the elevators leading to the parking garage. Once inside the elevator, she looked at her young minion in his designer clothes, his styled dark hair, and the naive sparkle in his eyes. In that moment she felt a sharp hatred for all the hypocrisy and sham that comprised human civilization. She wished she.could divorce herself from the whole ugly scenario, feeling that she would truly enjoy having as little to do with the human race as possible.

The doors opened upon a grim concrete cavern. She followed him to a row of Mercedes automobiles, then waited until he unlocked the passenger door to a sleek silvery one. Climbing in, she felt the softness of the upholstery caress her.

"Okay, let's roll 'em," said Rob.

He motored out of the parking garage beneath Century Park and headed for La Cienega. The traffic brawled and snarled with its usual contained fury as the afternoon rush approached. Rob cursed and tapped nervously on the steering wheel as they inched along toward Pico Boulevard. He muttered some small talk but she did not respond. When he saw that she wasn't paying attention, he popped a CD of one of Van Morrison's classic into the player. Instantly the interior was awash with brilliant sound, and she sank deeper into her silent cocoon.

For the week she had been living in Los Angeles, she had not allowed herself the freedom to fully explore it, to begin to know it; and so far, she had been forced to deal only with impressions. And her initial impressions of the city were *bad.*

So many shallow people. So many concerns with image and style. All color and flash and glitter, but so little substance in anyone. Even Rob seemed to have been caught up in the cultural shuffle. Despite staying in his new quarters for almost a week, she had barely seen him.

It occurred to her that she should have taken the time to brief him more thoroughly on her intentions, on her fears, and needs. She longed to be stimulated and challenged, to find mates that filled her ever-present need. Was it possible in a city such as this? Perhaps, but she had her fears .

The Mercedes caught the light at Pico, and Rob ripped a sharp left. As they headed southeast toward Santa Monica, Sophia looked about the car's exterior. Ever since arriving in the city, she had been almost pre-cognizantly aware of someone watching her, almost always. And yet, when she tried to catch them, to actually *see* whomever it might be, there was never anyone there.

Frustrating. So very frustrating. And yet she *knew* that she was being watched. For the last two nights she had even dreamed of her pursuer, and the oily, bloated visage of Hammaker still lingered in her mind's eye like an ugly stain.

The bastard.

The ugly, freakish, deformed bastard! What did he want with her. Why was he doing this? Didn't he understand the rules of the game?

Was there a car out there following them? Were they being watched at that moment?

The sounds of Van Morrison switching to a new track punctuated the gliding silent motion of the Mercedes as Rob hung a right on Highway One, heading west towards Malibu. She glanced out at the Pacific, actually the Santa Monica Bay at that point, and watched the surf cresting and curling in toward the sandy white beach. The geography along the highway was an endless stretch of modern architecture crammed and jammed and stilted as close to the beaches and the water as possible. The roads were filled with Corvettes, Porsches, Lotuses, and countless other small, fast, open-air cars.

Was one of them filled with watchers. Or pursuers?

She did not know, but the question burned in the pit of her being like a miniature sun, a birthing star. Looking across the blue water, she could see a fiery sunset approaching. Many evenings, the pollutants in the sky formed an interesting refractory like prism and produced some of the most spectacularly colored sunsets she had ever seen.

That something so beautiful could be born out of atmospheric filth served as a meaningful and ironic metaphor for her and her existence with the humans. The thought touched her and made her smile in spite of the building tensions within her.

Reaching out, she turned down the jazzy, R & B phrasings of the singer. "How much longer?"

"I told you—it's out off Malibu Canyon Road. Not much farther."

Rob listened to the album in silence, tapping his fingers on the steering wheel in time to the music. Sophia had no choice. Although she had been acquiring a taste for modem music, she still preferred the stately thematic material from the previous century. So much of what passed as music was little more than noise.

When they entered Malibu, she found it interesting to note how much the *same* everything seemed to be. All the women were blond, the cars were all white, the houses were all slant-roofed and slatted wood. She did not really want to live in Malibu, but its very sameness, its anonymity in its slavish imitation of itself, may be the best place to hide, to blend in.

"Okay, here we go," said Rob. They had reached Malibu Canyon Road, and he turned right at the traffic light. Almost instantly the car was hanging close to the edge of a road chiseled out of the sheer face of a chasm. She looked out her window in shock as the car clung to the wildly curving road. No guardrails, no fences, nothing to stop a car from plummeting off into the depths of the canyon.

Cars and vans and sports cars all whipped along the canyon road in both directions at high speed. Rob struggled to keep pace with the insane drivers, but still they blew their horns and ripped past him at every chance.

"Can you believe these assholes?" he cried. "It's a wonder they aren't going over the edge like lemmings!"

"Be careful, Rob," was all that she could say. Despite her "immortal" status, a car which fell into the canyon might ignite and bum. She did not wish to think of what the fire could do to her. . . either it would kill her, or entomb her in a charred carcass of a living death. . . she did not know, and had no desire to ever know.

The crazy road snaked and twisted through the canyon interminably. The farther along they traveled, the more panicked she was getting. She wanted to ask him to turn back, but she knew it was impossible, and she knew it would sound ridiculous.

Just get it over with, she kept thinking. This road would take some getting used to. After all, thousands of people negotiated it every day without a problem. It was just a silly fear she would have to overcome.

Rob approached an intersection that seemed to leap out from behind the cliff face to surprise them. He stopped behind several other cars and turned to her with a smile.

"Hell of a view, huh?"

"It's scary."

"Only at first. You get used to it." He laughed as though just thinking of something. "Wait till you see your house!"

"What do you mean?"

"You'll see. We're almost there."

The traffic blinked green, and Rob tapped the accelerator, turning left on Las Virgenes Road. The terrain was still treacherous and unrestricted. They rode for perhaps a mile before taking a right turn down a small, unmarked road.

"The road's got a name—Brujos Lane—but only for those who live on it. Kind of a privacy thing," said Rob.

The entrance had been almost totally obscured by shrubbery. It was indeed quite private. Lots of trees and shade and curves. Rob moved slowly, reading the numbers on the mailboxes until he saw the right one.

"Dis is da place!" he said with a grin. "You're gonna love it, babe."

She followed him out of the car and down a set of wooden steps. The house, barely visible through the trees and extensive landscaping, appeared to be a combination of stone and wood, built on several levels and decks.

Rob produced a key from his tennis shorts, unlocked the front door, and led her inside. In the fading light of the day, the interior was dark and cool. Large rooms, lots of windows, skylights, and clerestories. She liked it, but there was something about any house when it was devoid of furnishings that made it appear cold and harsh and uninviting. This house was no different.

There was a gloomy aspect to the place that bothered her. Perhaps it was the sense of foreboding, of being watched that continued to plague her? Or maybe it was the upcoming Change, which she sensed throughout the cells of her being?

"Hey," said Rob. "Don't you like it?"

"Yes, I do. I really do. This will be wonderful."

He smiled. "Yeah, great! Now let me show you the best part!"

Rob turned and led her down a wide hallway, down a quarter-flight of stairs into a sunken living room. He opened the sliding glass doors and stepped out onto a deck.

"Check it out!" he said, imitating a Chicano punk.

Looking past his outstretched hand, she could see that the deck hung suspended over the edge of a vast canyon. Like the edge of the roadway, the effect was at first dizzying. By some cantilevered magic, the entire side of the house clung to the side of a precipice. Below them yawned a steadily narrowing crevasse, a thousand-foot crease in the earth.

She stepped back from the deck, holding one hand upon the railing for support. "This is more than I expected," she said foolishly.

"Hey. . . only the *best* for my best client!" said Rob.

"I have all the papers ready to be signed. We can stop off at the realtor's office right now if you dig it. There's an option to buy if you really find that you like it—exercisable at any time."

Rob continued to ramble on about the house and terms, but she found that she was no longer listening. As the twilight gathered itself about the dwelling like a cloak, she thought she heard sounds coming from within the house.

Breathing.

Footsteps.

Chapter 33

Malibu

It was time.

Everything had come down to this final moment, and he wondered if he were ready.

Bloody hell, he was scared! But it was too late to think about it. Time to put up, as the Americans would say, or *shut* up. . . .

Once they had tracked her to Los Angeles, it had been a simple thing to hire private investigators to maintain round-the-clock surveillance on both Lester and the creature. (He had come to think of her simply as "the creature," since it was easier to plan the destruction of a beast than a thinking, sentient being, or worse, a real person.) Matthew had been glad to have Hammaker involved, especially for shouldering a share of the expenses.

Not that he was cheap, of course, but he had long ago learned to respect the value of a pound or a dollar. In fact, he probably had more capital than Hammaker, but the crazy playwright spent it like he was an Irishman, like there was no tomorrow.

Perhaps there wasn't, thought Matthew, as he climbed from the van and followed Hammaker toward the shrub-encrusted entrance to the house.

Dressed in black corduroys and a black pullover, he felt like a commando. A newly-purchased .44 Magnum hand gun with hollow-point slugs nestled in its holster at his belt. It was a formidable weapon, but the chalice of the Eucharist that he carried gingerly in both hands might prove to be the superior of the two.

Several nights ago, Hammaker had slipped into the sacristy of a Catholic church in Sherman Oaks to "appropriate" the items they might need. Having been a reluctant monk, and having all but lost his faith, he had felt no compunctions about the theft. Indeed, he had believed it totally necessary: no priest in his right mind would have willingly handed over a Host and a chalice for a monster killing.

I must be very crazy by now, thought Matthew. Or very smart .

Looking up into the quickly darkening sky, the moon was conspicuous in its absence. It was going to be a cool, dank night, the kind that wrapped around you like a heavy slab of wet canvas.

"Come on," whispered Hammaker, who was standing by the mailbox and the steps leading down to the creature's house. The playwright held Excalibur, which gleamed and shined even in the meager starlight.

What a beautiful weapon, he thought oddly. He was starting to get a bit barmy, he knew. The heady, giddy excitement of the kill was making him that way. Too late he was discovering that perhaps he was not cut out for any of this high-adventure stuff.

Joining Hammaker, Matthew crept with him down the wood steps and approached the front door, which the agent had left ajar. As they entered the foyer, they could hear voices echoing through the empty room. They're almost right *next* to us, thought Matthew.

But Hammaker was gesturing that they move again, and they passed a large room with skylights, and moved down a wide hall toward the source of the voices.

"Hey, whatsamatter, babe?"

"I thought I heard something. . . ." She *did* have a lovely voice, thought Matthew as he froze in mid-stride.

Hammaker dared to look at him, motioning him to rest, and both men stood stock-still in the shadows of the house, listening.

"*Heard* something? Yeah? Like what?" The agent's voice was cavalier, lighthearted.

"I don't know. A footfall, I think."

There was a silence. Matthew could feel the tension building, like an electrical charge.

"What?" The agent's voice was sharper now. "You mean like somebody's *in* there?"

"I think so. Yes, I really think so."

Matthew was suddenly afraid to draw a breath for fear he would be discovered. He and Hammaker stood in the hall, not ten feet from the sliding glass door that exited onto the deck.

"Damn, it's *dark* in there. I should've turned on some lights."

Another pause as Matthew eased air into his lungs, exhaled

with equal slowness.

"Where are you going?" The creature's voice again. "To turn on some lights. See what's going on."

Damn! The jig was about to be *up!* Instinctively, Matthew's hand touched the gun in the holster, his fingers slipping around the grip. A light breeze entered the hallway, and he could smell freshly mown grass, the scent of lemon blossoms.

As the agent stepped in from off the deck, Hammaker moved quickly, slamming Lester against the opposite wall like a rugby player taking out the interference on a pitch-out. Everything happened very quickly for a few moments. The agent went sprawling down the hall, stunned, and Hammaker whirled to face the creature on the deck.

Coolly, she regarded him as she leaned against the railing. Hammaker stood in the threshold holding Excalibur out in front of him like a samurai warrior. His hair was flying everywhere, his eyes wide and white. He was breathing in sharp, jagged pieces of air.

Matthew stepped in behind him, his hand still on the handgun's grip. The creature stood less than ten feet away from him and he could feel the heat radiating from her. She was looking into his eyes and they seemed to glow like coals. Just a trick of the light— not really happening, he thought quickly.

"We've come to welcome you to the neighborhood," said Hammaker.

"I've been expecting you," said the creature, her voice sounding hoarse, raspy. "This was all inevitable, I fear."

Hammaker grinned. "I think you fear right, lady." There was a stirring sound behind Matthew as Lester sat up and started to get to his feet.

"Watch him!" shouted Hammaker, keeping his eyes on the creature as she began edging along the length of the deck, putting some distance between herself and the sword blade.

Turning, Matthew faced the agent and pulled the gun from its holster. The Magnum was heavy in his hand. It was a large ugly weapon.

"Hey man! Take it easy! I'm not makin' a move, okay!" Lester stayed huddled on the floor. "What the hell's goin' on, anyway?"

Matthew continued to point the gun at him, wondering if he could possibly shoot a defenseless man wearing tennis whites. It all seemed so crazy.

There was a long instant of silence where everybody just looked at one another. Matthew could hear his blood pumping in his skull.

"Rob. . ." said the creature. Her voice invaded the silence with a cruel insistence. The voice had changed even more now: low, guttural, hypnotic. "These men wish to destroy me . . . and you must help me stop them."

Matthew watched as the words and the voice seemed to have an effect on the agent. All at once, he stopped trembling, cowering like a bloody hound, and looked off at the creature. He's her servant, her damnable Igor! She could control him like a fucking puppet!

Slowly, Lester began to stand.

On the deck, the creature emitted a long, moaning sound, which gathered in intensity until it became a banshee-like wailing.

The sound cut through him like a blade, slicing across the nerve endings like fingers on a chalkboard.

"What do we do!" cried Matthew, ashamed and terrified all in the same instant.

"Just keep 'im away from us, that's all!" Hammaker was still breathing hard, waving the sword at the creature. "Get the chalice ready, too!"

He and Hammaker stood at the entrance to the deck, back to back, like the final two soldiers being surrounded by an invincible hoard. The creature's wailing slowly tailed off, and it was replaced by another, more horrible sound. . . .

The sound of bones cracking, of tissue ripping, and splitting. Matthew stole a quick glance at the creature, and even in the star-light, in that single photographic instant, the image of the Change would be forever imprinted upon his mind.

The creature had leaned back against the railing, her back arched, neck back, mouth open wide. Her skin had become ashen and laced with spidery cracks like fractured china or porcelain. Even in that instant, the cracks grew larger, deeper and became deep bloodless wounds, gashes that lacerated the flesh to the bone and beyond.

Lester was standing now. He lurched forward, heedless of the weapon. In that single moment, the hapless agent had become transformed, changing into a looming figure of menace, a hollow-cheeked, slack-eyed zombie.

Matthew acted without thinking as he raised the gun and pulled the trigger.

There was a ripping sound which echoed off the face of the canyon and Lester abruptly spun around as though performing a dancer's pirouette. The slug had entered his right shoulder with such force that it had ripped him off his feet and turned him full circle. He caromed off the wall and began to slide back down to the floor. The wound in his back was a gaping, black stain in the twilight.

Turning, Matthew looked back to the creature, and was shocked at how quickly the Change was happening.

Hammaker was transfixed by the scene, shocked into stone-like paralysis.

The creature had become taller, thinner, sinking into the dress she had been wearing. Her eyes were *definitely* glowing now, burning with a fierce inner heat. Gone was the seductive green, replaced by orange-yellow teardrops of light. Her flesh was hard and gray and totally segmented into slabs of dead meat, flaking and falling away from an alien form beneath the skin.

"Oh, Jesus. . ." whispered Hammaker.

The chalice! thought Matthew. Got to *do* something! Go for it!.

Stepping forward, past Hammaker by several.feet, Matthew holstered the gun and held the chalice in both hands.

It was almost impossible to take his eyes off the miracle of the creature's transformation, although he knew that he must. Ringing the gold lid from the chalice, he reached inside and pulled out a large white disk. It was wafer thin and fragile to the touch, but as soon as he raised it from the lip of its gold container, he could feel it begin to radiate, to give off heat and power. It began to glow, surrounding itself with an aura of halo-like light.

There was a *Force* in the universe, Matthew knew at that instant, and that Force was being tapped, diverted, and channeled through the fragile Host. He could feel its immense power surging and coursing through the object; it was like holding the current of a raging river or a high-voltage line in your hands. Just being that close to the conflux of such power made him dizzy, weak, confused. . . .

The creature wailed again at the sight of the Host, and arched its back, pressing against the railing, backing away from its gathering light. She writhed and convulsed as though undergoing a seizure as she struggled through the final stages of the Change.

Bloody hell! he thought as he held the Host out at arms' length toward the creature. She screamed again, and began to dance the dance of one possessed or afflicted. It was a hideous, epileptic shaking, and as she moved, pieces of her flesh were thrown off in large, ashen chunks.

Hammaker remained transfixed, useless. Hadn't figured him to be the type to freeze up like that, Matthew thought as he jabbed him in the ribs with his elbow, breaking the spell.

"All right now!" he screamed. "Let's do it! Use that bloody

sword for Christ's sake!"

Hammaker looked at him and nodded. He was still shaken by what he had seen—it was obvious—but at least he was moving. He stepped forward, taking a place next to Matthew and raised the sword high above his head at a forty-five-degree angle. From this point he would bring the blade down and cut off the creature's head while Matthew kept it pinioned by the aura of the Host.

The glow from the Host was growing brighter, stronger, and just holding it caused Matthew's arms to tingle and vibrate. He didn't want to think about what forces he was playing with, but the thoughts jimmied their way into his mind. Clearly there were basic forces in the cosmos—the ground rules for every play that had ever been made that ever would be—and he had tapped into one of them.

Antipodal. Tidal. Cataclysmic.

The creature represented one of the opposite forces, and the joined presence of her and the Host was like the focal point of a great cosmic lens, the nexus of conflicting energies.

The pale lemony light of the Host illuminated the changing creature with a cruel honesty. She was ugly and evil and corrupt. .
.

. . . and she was beautiful and good.

For an instant, as the great vortex of power swirled around him, Matthew felt as though he were standing at the doorway to the wheelhouse of the universe, the place where all things came and went, where all meanings were accepted and rejected, where all that ever was, and ever will be, danced and capered like demons and angels in a mad, medieval tapestry.

Matthew blinked and forced himself to concentrate. The creature's wailing had become a vile hissing sound, like escaping steam of a great valve, but louder than a scream.

Matthew stepped forward, raising the chalice high like a beacon of paralyzing light, triumphant and full of self-righteous pride. When the weight hit him from behind, he went sprawling forward to his knees and then his face was impacting upon the slatted boards of the deck. With a dull ringing sound, the chalice was knocked from his grasp.

In a single eyeblink, he saw the reflective gold of the cup flash once and then disappear over the edge of the deck. The beacon-like brilliance of the Host extinguished in that terrible instant.

The hissing sound increased, tried to laugh perhaps.

The tiny bones of Matthew's face fireworked into exquisite patterns of pain, and the center of his spine felt as though it had been severed by a terrible blow. A dead weight pressed him down into the boards, and he fought against it to roll over.

Looking up, he saw the bloody, mangled torso of Lester sagging over him and Hammaker reaching down to pull the struggling man away. Suddenly Lester whirled and sprang on Hammaker like a cat. The playwright brought the sword down quickly, catching his attacker in the ribs, but it hardly slowed him down. Lester reached for Hammaker's throat with both hands, finding its soft center with both thumbs.

Hammaker dropped the sword to the deck as he attempted to pry the agent's hand from his neck. His eyes were bulging out of his head.

Matthew watched all this as though through a foggy lens, and he fought off the sensation to collapse, to simply drift *away*. He had been stunned, but the pain had kept him from simply passing out.

Got to *move.* . . got to get that fucking *sword!*

And he was suddenly reaching out, fumbling for the handle of the weapon, trying to grab it before it too was knocked over the edge, and into the dark narrow bottom of the canyon.

He forced himself to his knees as Hammaker and Lester danced beside him in a deadly two-step. The sword lay beyond their plodding feet and Matthew lunged forward, grabbing it firmly with both hands.

The hard metal handle felt cold and hard in his hands. He pulled it closer to him, backing away from the damned edge. He had to get the agent off Hammaker, he knew, but it had been most important to get the silver blade. His mind was still thick and slow as he tried to get his thoughts together. Acting without thinking was not his forte.

At that moment, Hammaker fell back against the railing with Lester still tearing at his throat. The two men were struggling as though in slow motion, and it hardly appeared that they were fighting.

But they were. . . .

Lester was emitting a low growl as Hammaker clawed at the agent's hands and then his face. His fingers groped below the brow line and suddenly there was an explosion of blood in Lester's face. The man squealed like a hamstrung pig as his eyeball was gouged from its socket by the frantic, choking Hammaker. As Lester staggered back, Hammaker lunged forward.

The two men collided, arms wrapped around each other, and slammed against the wood railing. Their combined weight fractured the pressure-treated two-by-fours, and the night was punctuated by the sharp *crack* of splintering wood.

Matthew stood helpless as the two bodies fell outward and away from him. Again, he watched the action as though everything had been slowed down. He could see Hammaker reaching out at the last moment, his fingers grazing the intact portion of the rail, his eyes wide with the ultimate horror, the final knowledge.

And then, just like that, they were gone. Neither man screamed on the way down. It was as if they had been swallowed up by a great beast.

They were simply *gone*.

Poor Hammaker, he thought. The poor, crazy bastard! Stunned. Shocked. Dazed by all that had happened, Matthew turned slowly to face the creature.

Almost forgotten in the flurry of events of the last few moments, she had used the respite to complete her incredible transformation. Even as Matthew stared at her, the last remnants of her human form were falling away from the shining scaly flesh beneath. The light of the stars danced on the long, thick column, which rose up from the husk that had been Sophia Rousseau. At the tip of the column bobbed the magnificent serpent head.

It was an enormous snake.

The biggest Matthew had ever seen. Even in the darkness its scales seemed to shine like polished coins—green and gold and blue. Yellow eyes flashed and blinked. Its tongue slipped out and tasted the night air. There was a hazy, burning sensation behind its eyes, and Matthew *wanted* to stare into that spot, that place right behind the creature's lens, where something threatened to move without warning.

It kept rising up, uncoiling up out of the shed quasi-human flesh, until it towered over him. He stepped back, looked up at the beast. Its flesh rippled as it moved. Smooth and graceful. Slippery and obscene. The colors danced across its polished scales, and it was so *beautiful*. Even its movements were like a simple, natural poetry. The creature was a kinetic artform.

"Come on, you bitch!" screamed Matthew, finally breaking away from the full vision of the monster in her True Form.

The perfectly shaped head tilted downward, regarded him with a single bottomless eye of gold. The tongue lapped the air again, and a sibilant sound became his answer.

Stepping forward, Matthew slashed out with the heavy blade, far below the head because he could not reach it. He was so weary, and the blade seemed damnable heavy!

He missed the curling bulk of its body by more than a foot, and the blade almost fell from his hand as he let its point touch the deck.

The gun!

He had forgotten about the gun, and although there was no mention in the legends about such things, he hoped that perhaps it was for good reason: no guns back then. A damned sight easier than a bloody silver sword, that was for certain!

Pulling out the Magnum, he aimed at the beast's beautifully formed head and pulled the trigger. Again the crisp barking report of the gun pierced the twilight. It was an odd sound, not at all like what a gun should sound like, thought Matthew.

The bullet passed through the thing's skull with a vengeance, the impact whipping its jaw back like the end of a cracking whip.

But the effect was only momentary.

Almost immediately, the slug's entry point began to draw up and close. There was no blood, no sign of the wound. The snake peered down at Matthew and hissed out a sibilant chord of laughter.

The bitch! The damned bloody bitch was going to *get* him.

The thought crystallized and held fast. Suddenly he *knew* that it was over, that she was too smart, too powerful. . . .

But for what it was worth, he emptied the handgun's clip into its body and head, and the creature merely bobbed and weaved under the impact, but *refused* to bleed.

And it was so fucking beautiful!

The red-gold blisters of its eyes peered down at him with a cool air of detachment. The beast seemed to know that Matthew hadn't the strength to raise the heavy silver blade, and it seemed content to observe her prey, to play with him a bit before the final strike.

Staggering back, Matthew had one final ploy, and he hoped that the great serpent-thing would go for it. He moved along the railing, past the break where Hammaker had taken his leave, then stood fast, picking up Excalibur with all his remaining strength.

What the hell. . . I'm going to die anyway. . . maybe I can take this thing with me? His thoughts spiked and jangled in his mind. Random, disconnected, but forming a coherent meaning. The base of the canyon was stone. It already contained the Host. If he could grab the serpent. Somehow plunge to the bottom with her. Entomb her in the stone crevasse with the Host . . .

It might work. It was worth the try.

"Come now, you big bitch! Come and get me!" he cried as he stood ridiculously close to the edge of the deck.

The serpent moved forward slowly, warily. It remained outside the range of the sword, but most likely well within striking range if it uncoiled its wonderfully muscled body. Its head hung in the air ten feet above him, looking down with a cold, reptilian silence.

It knows, thought Matthew.

It knew what he had planned, and was having none of it. Even though the more he looked at the sheer size of the creature, he doubted if he would even have the strength to heave it and himself over the edge.

As that last thought trailed off, he decided to merely fling himself at the thing, wade in with the sword flying and do whatever he could. Existentially, he was at the end of his tether.

Nothing left to do: except die.

Raising the sword, he took a step forward . . .

. . . and the serpent spoke to him.

But it was *not* speech in the physical sense. He felt a voice in his mind, a telepathic intrusion, which felt both vile and beautiful at the same time.

Matthew Cavendish. . . why do you hunt me like an animal?

"What?"

You do not hunt the lions in the jungles, the hawks in the sky . . . I am no different. Can you condemn me for only doing what my nature commands of me?

"You are *evil!* You are . . . anti-human! A fucking parasite!"

No more than you are parasites to cattle, to the plants and vegetables. Be reasonable. Matthew. You know *these things. They are basic analogies. No, you are hung up in foolish philosophical and "religious" grounds.*

"No!" The very idea was disgusting to him. Being caught up in some silly religious claptrap? Absurd!

Still, you cannot deny this: it is the nature of all creatures to follow their nature. I am only doing that which I must.

"You seek out and destroy the very *best* of us!" He spoke with as much conviction as his waning strength would allow. . . It was important that he keep her talking then maybe look for the chance, the smallest opening for an attack. But as he looked at the graceful serpent, stared into the golden depths of its eyes, he *knew* that it was a beautiful creature. The most beautiful thing he'd ever seen. . . .

"No!" he cried, trying to break the "spell" it was weaving about him. "You are a *disease!* You must be destroyed!"

You don't believe that, Matthew. . . .

Even the sound of its internal voice was seductive, and he listened without wanting to listen. What had it said? He shuddered as it used his name, paused in his attack as a part of his mind considered the truth in what it spoke to him. In an instant, he recalled the blur of events, the months of detective work and pursuit, and it seemed to stretch endlessly backward in time.

Why *had* he been so relentless in his search for this creature ?

How could the thing *know* what he believed and what he did not believe?

All this passed through his mind in an eye blink and he was aware of the thing staring down at him. It swayed almost imperceptibly as though it moved to unheard music. It *was* a starkly beautiful creature, he could never deny that truth. And for the first time, his conscious mind, that fortress of rational thought, admitted a possibility he would have never dreamed might have existed.

"No!" he cried out. "No! It can't be!"

Oh, yes. . . oh, yes . . . .

Its voice was clear and musical in his mind. So clean and beautiful. It penetrated his thoughts like a bright shaft of light.

Was it possible? How could it know his innermost thoughts, his innermost desires? Especially when he might not know them himself? And yet he was now faced with the need to answer the question. Time seemed to elongate, the moments stretching out like pieces of fresh taffy, giving him an instant's pause, a time to reflect upon her words, his doubts. Looking into the compelling beauty of the creature's eyes, he saw the image of his destiny glowing goldly.

It was true. . . .

The pursuit. The relentless, maddening pursuit, the need for vindication and recognition now seemed to be the palest of shams. He had *wanted* her, needed her—this terrible, magical beast.

"No! It can't *be!*" There was a pathetic edge in his voice as he tried to battle off its aura of influence. True or not true, he felt shame and anger at having his fantasies stripped bare, his innermost thoughts writhing like larvae under the harsh light of the truth. He may so desire the beast that swayed before him, but he loathed it also. The agony of love/hate boiled in him like a seething caldron. He must move *now,* or never.

"Now *die!*" he yelled as he lunged forward with the sword raised high.

For an instant the serpent's eyes seemed to pulse, to grow

brighter. Then the great head snicked quickly to the left, dodging the downward slash of the blade. Matthew fell forward, almost falling over the hollow, already dried-out husk of its shed female body. He grazed the smooth cool skin of the creature and whirled quickly to see its flat, perfect head turning to regard him with icy indifference.

As the head descended, its mouth opening slowly, he sensed his final chance, and jammed the sword upward.

But as he did this, a great tentacle-like thing had encircled him. The creature's tail had slipped up behind and around him, pinning his arms to his side, and constricting his chest with an effortless sliding motion. His silver sword fell from his grasp and clunked dully upon the boards of the deck. It was an impotent, hollow sound.

The great head lowered toward him, tilting to regard him flatly in the golden glow of a single blistered eye. Its coils tightened around him, and his last breath was squeezed out.

Looking up, the eye became impossibly huge and black; the pupil in its center grew larger to resemble the final darkness.

Chapter 34

She was naked.

Not merely nude, but *naked.* And he appreciated the wonderful difference between the two words. Moonlight streamed into the room, rimming her skin with a magic glow, dancing upon the sweaty patina of her flesh. She moved to him where he lay on the bed waiting. There was an aura of heat that surrounded her, radiated from her. Her scent instilled a madness of unfulfilled desire.

She reached down to touch herself and smiled. After running her finger up between the slit of her labia, she reached out and touched his lips. He could taste the hot wetness, the sweet musky scent of her, and he felt as though he might explode without ever touching her, without ever entering her.

But she smiled and straddled him quickly, lowering upon him and grasping him, actually pulling him up into her.

She was a monster. A beast. A creature.

But Matthew didn't care. He was smart enough to have avoided all this, and dumb enough to die. He recalled the final moment of their clash at the canyon's edge, and he knew that as he lay helpless in the coil of her body, she could have flung him into the darkness with a careless flip of her serpent's tail.

But she had not killed him.

And he had thrown himself upon her web of desire, willingly trapped while he feasted upon her sex, and she feasted upon his soul. It would go on till the empty husk of him went finally dry.

A terrifying thought, perhaps. . . .

But Matthew smiled as she rushed him to climax. There were far *worse* ways to die . . . .

Epilogue

Sophia had become very attached to Matthew as a person—as well as a source of nourishment.

The first hours after he'd died, she'd moved about the condo as though drugged. She hadn't anticipated trouble dealing with his death, and how she might work out the emotional geometry.

Despite his dry, scholarly mannerisms, the man had been a wonderful companion. Witty, perceptive, keenly intelligent, handsome in an understated, elegant way. Although he'd always known what it meant to be her mate, he'd retained an ironic sense of humor about the world. When Matthew Cavendish finally expired, she was experiencing a true sense of loss—a feeling totally unknown to her in all the centuries of her life.

Sophia sat naked by the window of her penthouse, which overlooked Sydney harbor and its famous opera house. She smiled wistfully as the rising sun hammered out coppery dents in the bay. Standing up, she reluctantly entered the bedroom where all that remained of Matthew still lay on the platform bed.

It was time to move on, but she wasn't sure where she would next go.

She paused to survey her Human Form in a full-length mirror before getting dressed. A habit born of centuries, even though she never showed signs of aging, she had fallen prey to the exigencies of female vanity. Her blonde hair framed her face in a nimbus of curls and waves—carefully arranged to appear *un*-arranged. High, full breasts; flat, delicately muscled stomach; flaring hips and long legs. She could change this body whenever she wanted, her skin melting into brown chocolate, her hair dark and kinky, or any other combination of colors and textures, if she merely desired it to be.

Dressing quickly in jeans and a loose silk blouse, she moved to her office and checked her online investment portfolio. The laptop's LCD winked at her like some guy across the bar, friendly and familiar. She typed in the passwords and command keys which accessed her accounts and other balance sheets in banks on three continents. When you live for more than two thousand years, you become outrageously wealthy and wise without even trying.

An hour at the keyboard accomplished everything necessary—accounts closed, funds and investments transferred to one of her other identities, and all traces of her presence in Sydney neatly disguised and forever lost in endless baffles of programming loops and nested routines. One of her lovers had been a software genius and he'd gladly traded his secrets for some time between her legs. She turned off the computer, and returned to the bedroom.

On his dying bed, Matthew had told her about a special "gift" he'd prepared for her—taped to the bottom of the top left drawer of her dressing table. Sophia now retrieved it—a manila envelope with her name written on the outside. Opening it with a sharply manicured nail, she began reading the first page of many sheets of paper:

> *Sophia:*
>
> *Several times you expressed veiled melancholy at being the only one of your kind. Your musings at whether you might be happier among a culture of your sisters started me thinking (a sometimes dangerous activity, that) and I threw myself into a private research project. The pages which follow are the fruit of that labor. Use the knowledge therein as you must. It is my last gift to you, my mistress of death and passion.*
>
> *Your Matthew*
>
> *Nota Bene: Always be on the watch for Hammaker. He won't stop until he finds you.*

After spending the next hour with his detailed notes, she finally knew where she would be going. She gave him a parting kiss, called for reservations to Thailand, and left the room forever.

As the sapphire surface of the Pacific passed beneath her at

38,000 feet, Sophia wondered what the police would think when someone finally decided to inspect her silent condominium. Its owner mysteriously vanished without a clue and the remnants of her companion looking more like an old cornhusk than a corpse. Poor, poor Matthew . . . .

She felt herself actually missing him. He was the only lover she'd ever had who understood her nature *beforehand*, and still chose to be with her. Hired by the mad Hammaker, Matthew had been hunting her down like she was a wild animal to be slain, but something changed when he finally trapped her and could have killed her. Instead, he joined her, knowing full well it signaled his death.

Such is the power of love. She smiled softly to herself, and returned to Matthew's thick sheaf of notes.

In a long, Burmese religious poem from the sixteenth century, he'd found reference to a serpent cult that worshipped a pride of lamiae. Matthew's margin notes to himself asked if this poem may have been Coleridge's inspiration for his mystical and erotic poem, *Christabel*. There were also cross-referencing notes to other numbered and paper-clipped sheets. A temple in Kawkareik with carvings on the walls of serpent-women; the obelisk of *Lang Suan* on the Malay Peninsula with its inscription describing a lair of giant green snakes which could change into beautiful women; a fragment from Rustichello's biography of Marco Polo which mentions his recounting of an encounter with a *succubi* of incredible beauty and the eyes of a serpent—this paper had extensive margin-notes in which Matthew had speculated that Polo may have been the originator of the popular medieval myth of the lamioe or lamia; excerpts from Philostratus' *De Vita Apollonii* which cites the homeland of a race of human serpents in the wetland delta valley south of the ancient city of Krung Thep—which Matthew had identified as Bangkok, Thailand. There were also many pages of maps, photographs, drawings, and other pieces of arcana that formed a *gestalten* mosaic, a picture of her possible past and perhaps a pathway home.

Although jaded by the erosions of time, the idea of finding her own kind, of living with her own flesh, excited her. Beyond that single notion, she wouldn't allow herself to think or anticipate. She would take her fate as she found it—or as it found her.

The city's humidity attacked her as soon as she departed Don Muang International Airport. Cabs were scarce and even a woman as striking as she had trouble getting a driver's attention. But once an old Chevrolet sedan had been commandeered, Sophia was being hurtled down narrow streets of color and noise.

"Can you take me to 'the Temple of the Emerald Serpents'?" she asked the cabby.

He was a small-boned, leather-skinned old man. He smiled and shook his head.

"What is wrong?" she asked.

"Never heard of that *wat*," he said. "Don't you know—there are over four hundred temples in city!"

"Well how might I find it? Who would know?"

The driver shrugged. "Not sure, lady. You want to go to good hotel?"

For the moment defeated, she nodded.

After a refreshing bath at the Hyatt International, she inquired at Chulalongkorn University of a Professor Song Damsat who might help her locate the temple she sought. The middle-aged, scholarly man had been transfixed as soon as he saw her and searched fervently for answers to please her. He seemed truly disappointed to tell her that *Tham Phraya Wat*, the temple mentioned in Matthew's notes, was on the dreaded "index" of banished shrines, which meant it was off-limits to tourists and Thais alike.

"I don't understand," she said, letting her gaze burn into him with unspoken promises of sexual interest.

"In the late eighteenth century, Chao Chakkri, the great Rama the First, banned all religious sects which were not following the strictures of Buddhism. He created an index which, despite many changes in the government, is still in force today."

"Seems rather silly," she said.

"Nevertheless, Madame, it is the law."

"Could you at least tell where it is so that I might see it?"

Professor Damsat tensed. "It is forbidden."

Sophia smiled and nodded. Without a word she moved around his desk, and dropped between his legs. His penis, even when it quickly stiffened was like a little brown root. His essence was so dilute, she knew she would gain nothing but information.

But it was all she needed at the moment.

After Damsat had wheezed out the location, she sank swiftly into the humid evening. The Temple of the Emerald Serpents lay south of Bangkok off the canal road to Port Klongtoi. She hired a cab to take her as close as possible—the electric signs which marked the location of a soap and detergent factory on the edge of a government land preserve.

Cruel moonlight filtered through tall trees as she moved off the road. Moist fronds reached out to touch her as she slipped through the first barriers to the jungle. Following the precise directions of the professor, she found the remnants of a road, its stones cracked and separated by the port-plant growth.

Guided by the cold glow of the moon, she walked through green darkness until the first edges and spires of the wat took substance from the shadows. With each step, she could sense the *oldness* of the place, the inescapable perception of time rotting away like the loam at her feet. Her breath quickened and she realized she grew anxious, almost excited. Had Matthew been correct? The possibilities flowed through her like lava.

Then, out of the darkness, something new materialized—the hard, bright lines of a security fence.

Before she had time to react, a beam of hard, white light pinned her like a bug on a piece of cork. Blinded for the instant, stumbled back, momentarily stunned into helplessness.

A staccato rush of Khmer, while not understood, still told her she was in the wrong place at the wrong time. Summoning up her will, she stared past the source of the beam.

"Get that light out of my eyes!" she commanded in French.

Almost instantly the electric torch attached to an AK-47 dropped and she could see a single man in the tan military fatigues of the military police. His childlike features were typical of men from the region; she estimated his age to be mid-twenties. Although he'd spoken harshly, his eyes belied suspicion and perhaps even fear. She smiled at him and this seemed to confuse him.

"Parlez-vous francais?"

The MP nodded. "Oui, Madame . . ."

"What do you want with me?" she asked as she moved closer to him. She knew by this time he was being bathed in her pheromones, swept away by her chemical messengers of desire.

"This is a restricted area. You cannot go any closer."

Sophia smiled at him again. "But I must go to the Temple. I simply *must* see it!"

"Madame, I cannot . . . ." His voice was weak, indecisive. He would be easy.

"Oh, I think you can," she said, moving a hand to the first button of her blouse. As her long fingernails worked, his eyes followed their movements, watching as the silky fabric parted to reveal the swollen quarters of her breasts. The MP licked his lips.

In a half-hearted gesture, he raised his weapon to hip level. "No," he managed to say.

"Open the gate," she said.

"I cannot!"

"You have the key," she said, loosing a second button. "I can see it on your belt."

"This is forbidden . . . !"

"Yes, I know," said Sophia, ripping away the final buttons, her breasts aimed at him like weapons. She moved so close, he had to drop the automatic rifle to let her hard nipples touch his chest. Like pointing fingers they scored the starch of his uniform. She grasped him through his pants and he actually whimpered.

"In there," she whispered huskily in his ear. "On the steps of the Temple . . . I want to fuck you!"

The man was trembling now; he fumbled with the keys to the security gate. His crisp uniform stained rapidly with his sweat as he threw back the hasp and pushed inward. "This way!" he said hoarsely.

She followed his lead to the entrance of the temple. The musty smell of ancient stone, a palpable sense of age and decay reached out to them. It mixed with the redolence of his sweat and the sweet juice of her steaming slit to create essence of all the forbidden. He danced and hopped out of his pants as she peeled away her designer suit.

Naked in the moonlight and shining with sweat, she leaned back against the rough stone, against the tiny carvings of twisted figurines, and took him into her. She was taller than he, forcing him to push up on his toes. Her lips almost grabbed at him, almost sucked him upwards. He gasped as she enveloped him, pulsing and squeezing to the rhythm of his effort. He grunted and sighed as she stared off into the unfocused distance.

She had no time for this. There was no pleasure in it; she did it by the numbers, as Matthew would have said. Waiting for the MP required little patience, and with the experience of centuries, her timing remained flawless. As he shattered into short bursts of elation, she drew his life from him as efficiently as a syringe might drain off a life's blood. His eyes collapsed into his skull as he fell away and out of her. The utter silence of his dying calmed her; the absorption of his essence briefly warmed her like a shot of bad whiskey.

That, and the night-heat and blanketing humidity left her covered with oily sweat. Abandoning her clothes by the entrance Sophia entered the temple carrying only the electric lamp from the AK-47. As its light played over the worn intaglios, she located the central altar where in more traditional *wats* a sitting, or perhaps a reclining Buddha, would be found. But here, in this place, no smiling fat man resided.

Instead, a sculpture of five snakes, coiled and tangled among themselves in Laocoonian ecstasy, and inlaid with shining green gems, dominated the altar. Beneath the main slab, if Matthew's information was accurate, she would find her entombed sisters. Reaching out with her free hand, she touched the edge of the heavy stone, then tried to move it. No, its weight was massive. Sweat ran down between her breasts, cut a salty ravine across her belly. She looked about the central chamber for something to provide leverage, but the place had been picked clean of all ornament and fixture. The gun barrel was too thin, too short.

A *Change.*

The only way she might move the slab—achieve her True Form. She exhaled softly. A Change was not something easily accomplished when forced, when attempted beyond the rhythms of its natural cycle. In fact, it was fraught with stress and terrible pain. Unless brought on by an acute fight-or-flight panic situation, it was very hard to effect by simple power of her will. Despite her sexual encounter, she felt weary, depleted. She missed Matthew's endless energy, his genius-essence. She would have to come back with the right tools. It would have to be tonight, before signs of her presence would be noticed by the zealots of the country's current regime. She would—

"I knew you'd be here sooner or later," said a voice from the shadows beyond the outer entrance to the temple.

A *familiar* voice.

Turning slowly, she felt her endocrine system go on red-alert. Her flesh began tightening, itching, tingling.

"Richard," she whispered.

A baritone chuckle. "The one and only, Madame. Your Friendly Neighborhood Accidental Eunuch and Fearless Vampire Killer." Richard Hammaker limped from the shadows wearing a set of industrial coveralls with the logo of a Japanese chemical firm over the left breast pocket. His stocky body appeared a bit bent—his usual posture. His black hair an explosion of wild curls, when combined with his wide-eyed expression, made him appear quite the madman. Something she'd always believed he was.

"I am no 'vampire'," she said haughtily. Her heart beat accelerated, her eyes blinked crazily. She actually feared this man, this ugly nemesis, who vowed to kill her.

She cursed herself for leaving the MP's weapon at the entrance. Hammaker might be immune to her power, but a clip of explosive slugs would end her problems with him.

"Yeah, right," he said satirically as he stepped wholly from the shadows. He hefted a heavy sword in his right hand, its silvery blade glowing fiercely in ambient moonlight. "Well, whatever you are, sweetheart, I've got you're fucking number. Can you dig it?"

She could indeed "dig it." A memory capered across her mind like a taunting harlequin. Of Richard Hammaker, genius-playwright and darling of the Manhattan Theatre World; of Richard Hammaker, the twisted freak showing her what was left of his sex organs and gibbering like a mad fool.

It had been the first time she'd ever made the mistake of trying to seduce a man who lived outside the carnal world.

She needed time. If she could summon up the strength to achieve the Change, she would need *time*.

Her heart ratcheted and her flesh grew taut, stretched as something struggled within for escape.

"Matthew never believed you were dead . . ." she said.

"He was right, wasn't he?"

"How did you find me?"

He chuckled darkly again. "Did you think you were the only one with access to Matthew's files? Before we caught up with you in L.A., I'd started scanning all his papers. Every night, I scanned stuff I thought might be useful if anything ever happened tohim. Locked them on CDs."

"And you've waited for me here?"

Hammaker shrugged. "It seemed the most logical. The soap factory's subsidized by the local government, but run by the Japs. I've got friends on Wall Street who've been bed with Tokyo investors for years. They pulled me a few strings and here I am as a consultant for the Rising Sun Boys. I don't do shit, 'cept sit around and wait to hear from one of the MPs. And tonight I did."

"I see," she nodded. "But why?"

"Why what?" said Hammaker, his fingers white-knuckling the hilt of the sword—Matthew's sword, she noticed.

"Why have you hunted me like this?"

He shook his head, smirked at her. "Oh, no reason, I guess—other than you killing my best friend, the man who believed in me when no one else did, whose belief made me a success! Other than you trying to kill *me*! Other than you being a fucking *monster*!" He threw back his head and laughed like a maniac. ". . . Oh, Christ, no! No reason at all!"

"You would deny me my nature?"

"Fuck you!" he screamed.

She needed only another moment. It was getting difficult to speak, her tongue beginning to thicken, but she forced out the words. "Are you obsessed with the hawk in the sky? The shark in the sea? Do they not only do what they need to survive?"

"Fuck them! It's *you* I want, honey . . . !"

Spittle flecked from his lips as he bit off his words. His eyes had bulged; madness lurched behind his whitened gaze. She had no choice. He blocked her only escape, and he was raising the deadly blade of silver. No!

He wouldn't take her like this. He could *not!*

The thought catalyzed her in an instant and the Change commenced in full. Holding up her hands she could see her skin becoming cloudy, translucent. Tiny lines, like cracks in fine crystal, grew wide and dark as the outer layer of her flesh began to flake and fall away. She could feel her eyes sinking deeper into her skull, and she knew they were changing from their usual green to an orange-yellow. As though from a great distance, she heard the growl of engines, the cries of other humans. Her bones were shrinking, crunching in upon themselves, as she grew thinner, taller. Despite his resolve and his madness, Hammaker had paused in mid-lurch to witness the Change. Her flesh continued to harden and die, cracking, splitting, falling away in hideous chunks. She leaned against the altar as her shoulders curved in to touch each other and dissolve beneath her roiling flesh. Her spine curved up and away, becoming more pronounced. Her arms withered and fell away like dead twigs; her legs melted into a single, shrinking column. As the last of her white, dead skin husked away to reveal new flesh—a scaled, shining surface that pulsed with an inner green fire. Her skull had widened, flattened to the sound of gristle and calcium grinding, shifting; her teeth shattered to powder as they fell from her mouth to impact on the stone floor. Pain symphonied within her as the panic. Change ravaged her energy reserves, but she kept her attention on Hammaker, who seemed staggered by the vision before him.

Almost complete now, Sophia rejoiced at the raw feeling of *power* that suddenly surged through her supple body. Writhing and balancing like a giant cobra, she weaved before her attacker, pinning him with her dead-yellow gaze. She moved with ultimate grace as great muscles rippled and flexed beneath her skin. The prisms of her scales caught the feeble moonlight and flashed it back like a spectrum of polished coins. Her body wove from side to side, a steady, biologic rhythm. The effect on Hammaker was hypnotic. He stood limp and helpless, the sword forgotten at his side.

She disengaged her great jaws, coiled back to strike him down as the vibrations of *sounds* growing more forceful reached her. Vehicles braking and boot heels scuffing stone. Oh, how she wanted to launch herself, to collapse her fangs into him and feel the plumpness of his body explode in redness . . . . !

No.

Moving with power and grace unknown in her Human Form, she ascended the great altar and entwined herself amidst the tangles of the Emerald Serpents sculpture, losing her shape in the infinite coils, the ultimate camouflage.

Closing her yellow eyes to slits, she watched men in tan uniforms storm the temple steps and surround him. Old Soviet-era surplus weapons bristled as their squad leader barked out orders in angry Khmer. Hammaker was helpless as they grabbed him and dragged him out. He would be lucky to escape with his life.

A single soldier lagged behind to pick up the electric torch, the sword, and the AK-47. When he reached the door, he paused, turned back to play the torch's beam over the *wat's* interior. It was cursory gesture, done more out of obligation than any belief he would find anything. As the beam passed over her, she knew she was safe.

When the growl of their vehicle's exhaust was less than a memory, she released herself from the statue and slithered down to the floor. Using her sinewy body as a natural lever, she lifted the edge of the altar's headstone easily. Elation swelled in her.

Soon, she would never be alone again . . .

With a final surge, she heaved the slab upward. As the angle increased, the intricate serpent sculpture broke loose and crashed to the floor in an explosion of stone.

A small price to pay, my Sisters. Come to me.

From the shadows of the prison-tomb there rose up the essence not of eternal life but of *death*. No emerald coils; only the smell of decay. The stench burned her nostrils and she drew back instinctively. Then leaning forward, letting the moonlight spill over the edge of the altar's interior, she saw them.

Dry and brittle, the five serpentine bodies lay untangled and distinct. Separated and arranged in a neat pile, like pieces of primitive sculpture, were the five severed heads of her *sisters*. Next to their half-rotted skulls, a piece of gilt-edged stationery mocked her. Even in the dim light, she could read Hammaker's elegant cursive lettering:

> *Surprise, O Lady of the Scaly Skin!*
>
> *This is just in case you ever get your ugly snout in here. You didn't really think I'd leave these little lovelies alive, did you?*
>
> *All my love,*
>
> *Richard*

She could feel power leaking away from her like dirty oil from an overworked engine. Curling up into a ball at the base of the ravaged altar, she let the Change overtake her.

After the trauma of the forced transformation and the stress it had placed on her body, the reforming process would be slow and painful. But not as sharp or hurtful as the loss which burned at the core of her being like a dying star.

How cruel the Fates, she thought as consciousness fell away like breakers on a lonely beach. As she slipped into a narcoleptic trance, Sophia welcomed the return to Human Form.

At least when she awakened, she would get the chance to cry.